COWBOY JUSTICE

MELISSA CUTLER

ZEBRA BOOKS
KENSINGTON PUBLISHING CORP.
http://www.kensingtonbooks.com

ZEBRA BOOKS are published by

Kensington Publishing Corp.
119 West 40th Street
New York, NY 10018

Copyright © 2013 by Melissa Cutler

All Kensington titles, imprints, and distributed lines are available at special quantity discounts for bulk purchases for sales promotion, premiums, fund-raising, educational, or institutional use.

Special book excerpts or customized printings can also be created to fit specific needs. For details, write or phone the office of the Kensington Special Sales Manager: Attn. Special Sales Department. Kensington Publishing Corp., 119 West 40th Street, New York, NY 10018. Phone: 1-800-221-2647.

Zebra and the Z logo Reg. U.S. Pat. & TM Off.

ISBN-13: 978-1-4201-3006-5
ISBN-10: 1-4201-3006-4
First Printing: October 2013

eISBN-13: 978-1-4201-3007-2
eISBN-10: 1-4201-3007-2
First Electronic Edition: October 2013

10 9 8 7 6 5 4 3 2 1

Printed in the United States of America

THE SECRET TO LOVING A LAWMAN

From the corner, Rachel let out a ragged breath that left the air in the room crackling with tension so brittle he could've snapped it like a stick of toffee.

Don't look at her. Do the task at hand and keep your mind out of the gutter.

He picked up his hoof knife and took to cleaning the hoof, prepping it for the shoe. Ignoring Rachel.

He was doing fine with that until he asked her to bring him the shoe. Because then she came too close and said in a husky voice, "You might not be a rancher by profession, but your heart is pure cowboy."

Don't look at her. "Cowboy lawman, according to your sister."

She let out a throaty laugh and strolled toward her perch in the corner. And then, as if he weren't having enough trouble keeping his thoughts virtuous, he watched the sway of her ass until she resumed her seat. Their eyes met, and the look she gave him singed him where he stood.

Forcing his focus to shoeing, he tested the smoothness of Growly's hoof with the pad of his thumb, filed down a couple rough spots, then fitted the shoe on. Before he had enough sense to restrain himself, he blurted, "Unlike Jenna, you dig my cowboy lawman vibe, don't you?"

"What do you think?"

Actually, he wasn't sure what the hell he'd been thinking, asking her that. He selected a No. 5 nail and a hammer, then tapped the first nail in place. Hoping to defuse the tension with humor, he painted on his best self-deprecating smile and said in an exaggerated Texas drawl, "Darlin', how about I show you my six-shooter?"

Rachel snickered. "I bet that's the line you use on all the ladies."

"Hey, a guy's got to work hard to earn the title Most Eligible Bachelor. My pretty face alone don't cut it."

Books by Melissa Cutler

The Trouble With Cowboys

Cowboy Justice

How to Rope a Real Man
(coming in May 2014)

Published by Kensington Publishing Corporation

Chapter One

The vandals brought beer. A bold move for trespassers. Then again, it was one in the afternoon, so either these punks carried the delusion they were above the law, or they set a new standard of stupidity from the other idiots who'd felt the call of duty to send a message to Rachel Sorentino.

Rachel watched through the zoom lens of her camera from the narrow canyon floor, hidden from view by a smoke tree, as one of four young men shook a can of spray paint. Not too difficult to imagine what he'd write on the boulder he and his buddies were grouped around. Catcher Creek's small, but zealous, group protesting her family's new business weren't all that creative, she'd discovered. Probably involved the word *bitch* and maybe the classic LEAVE TOWN OR ELSE. She wondered if these guys were better spellers than the rest.

Lincoln, her horse, sidestepped restlessly. She understood his discomfort. Even in the shade as she and Lincoln were, there was no escape from the weather. The surrounding walls of soil radiated the kind of dry, baking heat that pricked at the skin like needles and dried noses to the point of bleeding. Didn't help that this particular May was setting heat records all across New Mexico.

Not for the first time, she considered calling the sheriff's department, but that presented its own mess of trouble. Besides, this far off the beaten path there was no way a deputy would arrive in time to do any good. And she refused to consider the ramifications of Vaughn answering the dispatch call. Heaven help her if it came to that.

Like always, Rachel had no one to rely on but herself. Well, not exactly. She had Lincoln, her closest companion for over a decade. And she could always rely on the interminability of the ranch's problems, which hadn't given her a day of peace in all her thirty-two years of life. Yeah, she could definitely count on the presence of problems pulling at her—livestock problems, sister problems, money problems. The list went on forever.

She wiggled her hand into her jeans pocket and grabbed an antacid from the roll. As it dissolved on her tongue, she lifted the camera from where it hung around her neck and snapped a string of photographs, zooming in on the face of the vandal holding the paint. He'd written the *B* and the *I* in straight block letters on the boulder's flat face. She swung the camera right and snapped pictures of the truck. It was angled so she didn't have a clear visual of the license plate, but she could wait to capture that image while they were fleeing the sound of her gunshot.

The revolver in her saddlebag took .38s. She flipped the cylinder open and loaded ammo into two chambers.

Lincoln's restless sidestep grew anxious. He wasn't a fan of the gun, not the noise or the recoil or the bitter odor of gunpowder. But he was getting more accustomed to it since the grand opening of Heritage Farm, with its influx of tourists and media attention, had unleashed Catcher Creek residents' underlying hostility toward her family and turned the farm into a vandal magnet.

Rachel's first tip-off about the controversy was a low-key grumbling and grousing overheard in the shops and churches on Main Street, as reported by her youngest sister, Jenna, whose number-one hobby in life was keeping her finger on the pulse of the town's rampant gossip. The low grumblings evolved into a petition to add "anti dude-ranch legislation," as the petition authors dubbed it, to the next county ballot. It wasn't long after the petition took to circulating that the first graffiti appeared on the ranch, scrawled on the side of one of Heritage Farm's brand-new oil derricks.

Four months later, the protestors were still at it, and Rachel and her sisters were as determined as ever to make Heritage Farm a success.

She snapped the cylinder of her revolver in place, then spent a few minutes stroking Lincoln's neck and whispering words of reassurance into his ear. She offered him a Fig Newton, his favorite treat. He snatched it from her hand, his tension easing as he chewed.

After a few more words of praise and affection into Lincoln's ear, she straightened in the saddle and winced. The ulcer was bad today. She could actually feel it blazing a hole through her gut. She took the time to land another antacid on her tongue before raising the gun toward the sky, careful to aim to the left of the mesa so there'd be no chance of the vandals being hit by a stray bullet. She was a good shot, and the men probably stood at too great a distance for her to hit, but she respected the firearm enough to understand its inherent unpredictability.

The word BITCH had been neatly scrawled on the boulder, spelled right and everything. Impressive. She squeezed the trigger and braced for the deafening echo through the canyon.

Boom.

Her ears throbbed. The world went mute. All she could hear was the thud of her pulse in her ears and a high-pitched ringing. One of these times, she'd have to remember ear plugs. She kept her gaze on the vandals, who'd stopped painting and joking to scan the valley, searching for the source. They were too far away for her to gauge their facial expressions, but they weren't running scared, that was for sure.

She fired again.

This time, she kept her eyes closed for a beat as the recoil swept through her system. The violence in the sound and energy of the gun hurt her whole body, from her teeth to her toes. Lincoln reared. She tugged the reins, asserting her control, and lowered the revolver. The vandals were running to the truck now. Excellent.

Setting the gun in her lap, she lifted the camera. Time for the money shot.

But as fast as they leapt into the truck cab and bed, they were out again, their hands filled with rifles.

"Oh, shit." Damaged as her hearing was, her words were muffled and far away.

She dropped the camera to swing around her neck and took up the revolver again. The sweat on her palms interfered with her grip. She held it tight against her thigh as she dug for more rounds.

The turn of events had her reeling. Why was she loading rounds instead of watching the criminals' truck haul ass off her property in a cloud of smoke, like the other trespassers she'd caught had done? Who the hell were these guys?

She had no idea, but whoever they were, they weren't scared of her. Shooing them away with two wide shots hadn't worked. Grazing one in the leg might, but she'd have to inch closer to stand a chance of making a hit. The revolver wasn't designed for distance shots, nor did she have much practice with target shooting. Anyhow, inching closer would leave Lincoln vulnerable and alone. He might get scared and hurt himself trying to flee, even if she tied him up.

So she stayed put as the men lined up along the edge of the mesa, scanning the valley below. Bits of red earth crumbled at their feet, rolling down the steep slope like a mini-avalanche.

Rachel held her breath.

With a *whoop*, the lanky man with the short, dark hair fired in her general direction.

The sound rattled her to the bone. Lincoln tried to spin around. He wanted to run away. That made two of them. But if they turned and made a break for it, she'd give the shooters a clear shot once they'd climbed out of the canyon. Shrouded by shade and the smoke tree, her best bet was to stay still and convince Lincoln to do the same.

She tucked the revolver under her arm and offered him another Fig Newton. He refused to be pacified. She tossed the treat on the ground, grabbed her camera, and took a quick series of photographs of the men. She watched through the lens as one of them shouted something she couldn't hear over the ringing in her ears. Whatever he said, all four rifles swung toward the canyon she hid in.

She dropped the camera and grabbed the revolver, for all the good that would do. If she fired a round now, they'd know exactly where she was.

All she could think was that this couldn't be happening. She was on her own property, for shit's sake. Right now, though, she wondered if she'd make it out of the valley alive.

One of the men let out a whooping cry.

Gunfire rained over her. Shot after shot. Puffs of dirt exploded off the canyon walls. She ducked, holding her torso flush against Lincoln's mane. Time to take the chance and run. The idea scared her out of her mind, but she had to get Lincoln out of the line of fire. She had to save them both.

She stuffed the revolver in her waistband and gripped the reins with both hands. A bullet whizzed into the smoke tree, cracking a limb and sending splinters flying at Lincoln and Rachel.

Lincoln reared all the way up, his hooves clawing the air. Even over her muffled hearing, she registered his shriek of pain. Another shot sounded, too fast for Rachel to react, and Lincoln fell sideways. She vaulted from the saddle and face-planted in the sand.

The gunfire stopped.

A searing pain spread from her upper arm into her shoulder, but she didn't have time to wonder about it. She scrambled to her knees, spitting sand, and scanned the mesa for the shooters. They'd left the edge and were standing at their truck, leaning against the side of the bed, cool as could be. Two of them were laughing. Another was reloading his rifle's clip. The lanky, dark-haired man took a match to the glass pipe hanging from his lips. He took a couple puffs and passed it on.

Assured that she wasn't in immediate danger, she dropped to her knees. Lincoln lay on his side, his front legs pawing the ground. His breath came in shallow gasps. A bullet had pierced his chest. His hair was stained a slick, shiny red.

"No, no, no," she breathed, smoothing her hands over his neck and cheek. Her mind whirred so loud it felt like a silent scream on the inside of her skull. "Oh, Lincoln, what have they done to you?"

His saucer eyes watched her check his limbs for other injuries. His left hind leg jutted from under his body at an odd angle. Broken. The moment was too unreal to process. Her horse, her best friend, lay before her, dying.

A dry, angry sob broke free from her throat.

She'd put animals down before—it came with the job—but never her own steed. Never a friend. But she couldn't let him suffer, and no matter how the next few minutes unfolded, Lincoln had no hope for survival. Not here, tucked into a deep canyon, miles away from anything, bleeding from the chest, and with a broken leg.

She pressed her forehead to Lincoln's cheek and cried. Wails of longing and pain. Sounds so tortured, they shocked even her. Then Lincoln made a noise that reminded her that whatever misery she felt, his pain was worse by far.

Sniffing, she rose to her knees. Her spine was weak, barely able to hold her body upright. A glance at the mesa told her the men hadn't left. They were all taking hits of the pipe now. Even so, they kept their rifles close at hand, either slung across their shoulders or tucked under their arms.

Her focus returned to Lincoln. At the sight of his prone body and pained expression, her face crumpled into another silent sob as she prepared to do the unthinkable. The men on the mesa would hear her shot. Odds were they'd open fire at her again, but it was a risk she'd willingly assume. Lincoln had suffered too much already.

With her hands shaking so hard the cylinder rattled against the gun frame, she brought the revolver to Lincoln's ear. Bile rose in her throat. She pushed her tongue to the back of her mouth like a cork and locked her jaw closed. Then she pulled the trigger and let the recoil push her. The gun fell away as she heaved the contents of her stomach into the sand.

Another explosion of gunfire sounded from the mesa, but the only sound in Rachel's head was a howl of unconditional rage. It burned in her chest worse than the ulcer, worse than grief. How dare some group of young punks trespass on her property, defile her land, and shoot her horse? How dare they laugh and smoke dope like they weren't the cause of one of the worst moments of Rachel's life? Standing on a mesa in plain view like they were above retribution. They didn't care that somewhere in the valley, someone with a gun was seeing red. Maybe they planned to kill her too. Maybe they'd go after her sisters next.

The edges of her vision dimmed as a spike of adrenaline sent her up to her knees.

She pushed against the ground with her hands. A slice of pain rocketed from her left arm, straight to her spine, but she was hard-pressed to care. Whatever the damage, her arm was still functional, which was all that mattered.

With her gaze averted from Lincoln's face, she reached for her saddlebag. Into her pocket, she stuffed a handful of rounds. Next out of the bag was her cell phone. She got service in this valley, but it was sketchy at best. Nevertheless, she got a dial tone this time, and punched Vaughn's number from memory, having deleted it from the phone's address book more than a year ago. He picked up on the second ring.

"Rachel?"

She flinched at the sound of her name on his lips. That was a whole other kind of pain she didn't have time for now.

"I'm about to kill some men, Vaughn. You better get to Parillas Valley fast, and bring an ambulance."

Vaughn's heart had dropped to his knees when he saw the number of the incoming call. Rachel. This marked the first time he'd seen her number on his phone in sixteen months and twelve days. They'd crashed into each other's worlds since then, but it was never planned, and never involved much talking.

He answered with his eyes closed, his mind racing to come up with a possible reason for her call, but he couldn't think of a single one.

The sound of her voice stripped him raw. Hell, everything about Rachel stripped him raw, but this was different. Something was seriously wrong, and it wasn't only her gravely spoken words that told the story. He heard the agony and fury in her tone, but despite all that, he refused to believe she'd kill anyone. She wasn't made like that.

Still, he radioed for an ambulance and called Wesley Stratis off his patrol to follow him over the twisted dirt road that dipped near the now-dry Catcher Creek before disappearing into the rolling hills and canyons of Sorentino Farm.

He knew these roads better than he'd ever admit aloud. Parillas Valley in particular was scarred into his consciousness. So much so that the land came to him in dreams, the canyons sculpted by flash floods in the spring, the sheer vertical face of the mesa exploding from the valley, the single shade tree at the base of the mesa.

His eyes flashed to his glove compartment, but instead of reaching for the cigarettes he craved, he wrung the steering wheel and shoved the gas pedal to the floor.

Behind him, Stratis's patrol car and the ambulance worked to stay close, kicking up enough dust to block the sky from sight in his rearview mirror.

Rachel hadn't ended the call, so Vaughn set his phone on speaker and tossed it on the passenger seat, but he heard nothing except faint rumbles that could've been anything from a car starting to a low-flying airplane. Then, for the last twenty minutes it took to make the drive deep into the heart of the desert, miles from any vestiges of civilization, the phone was completely silent.

The first thing he saw when he made a left turn around a foothill that opened into Parillas Valley was the body of a man laying facedown in the dirt. He muttered a curse and scanned the desolate countryside for Rachel. He didn't see her, but identified a second man sitting against the mesa, using the wall of dirt as a backrest.

"Where are you, Rachel?" He ducked his head, squinting into the glare of the sun on his windshield.

At last he spotted her under the shade tree, approximately ten yards from the body in the dirt. She was upright, which most likely meant she was alive, but he couldn't tell if she was injured. All he knew was, she didn't rise or move in any obvious way, despite his convoy's dusty, noisy approach. That alone would've been enough to scare him shitless if he hadn't been at that breaking point already.

He picked up his radio and requested a second ambulance, then called Deputy Reyes to meet them at the scene.

What he needed to do was lapse into cop mode, to get into that zone of calm detachment that allowed him to do his job right and keep himself, his deputy, and the paramedics safe. He needed to unplug the wire that connected his brain to his heart. But this was Rachel he was dealing with, and he'd already proven over and over that with her, such a disconnect was impossible.

Still, the cop inside him never completely turned off. The minute he hit the brakes, he drew his firearm. He stood behind his open car door, assessing, as the odor of gunpowder smacked him in the face. Whatever happened here hadn't been fast or clean. Whatever happened had been warfare.

He scanned the surroundings for danger—the glint of metal from a concealed firearm, a lurking perpetrator, any reason he or his crew shouldn't rush forward to aid the victims. Today, though, the only firearm at the scene that he could see besides his and his deputy's belonged to Rachel.

She stared straight ahead without acknowledging him, her arms wrapped around her knees, her right hand curled around a revolver. Her hair was a disheveled mess, her face a smear of browns. Tears snaked a path down her cheeks through the grime. Blood soaked her left shirt sleeve and chest.

It was her blood that got Vaughn's legs working.

"Damn it, your arm! Were you shot?" He dropped to his knees at her side. When he eased the gun from her fingers, she turned her bloodshot, dirt-rimmed eyes on him. He flipped the revolver's cylinder open and found six empty casings. A rush of acid pooled in his mouth. *Dear God, what has she done?*

"They hurt Lincoln." Her voice was weak, hoarse as though from screaming.

Looking at the dull hopelessness on her face, he was overcome by the impulse to snatch her up in his arms and run away to some hidden place where he could lose his cool like he wanted to, without anyone witnessing the spectacle.

Biting his lip, he looked over his shoulder. The man

in the dirt lay unmoving as the paramedics worked on him, his shirt crusted with drying blood. Stratis stood over the man leaning against the mesa, who looked to be in his early twenties. He whimpered, and Vaughn couldn't fault him for it—his right thigh was a bloody mess.

Vaughn wrapped Rachel's revolver in the handkerchief he kept in his pocket for such a use and set it on the ground. "These men, they shot Lincoln?"

His fingers flew to her injured arm. She started to answer, but when he pushed her sleeve up, it stuck to the drying blood and she hissed through her teeth. Despite her obvious pain, she held still and allowed him to evaluate the damage. A bullet had grazed her arm near her shoulder, cutting an angry path through her skin and muscle. Dirt and pebbles compromised the area. She needed the wound cleaned and her shock symptoms and dehydration addressed immediately.

Another look over his shoulder told him the paramedics were too busy to see to her relatively minor injuries. They had the man on the ground rolled over and fitted with an oxygen mask, and were in the process of transferring him to a stretcher. The second ambulance probably wouldn't arrive for another half hour. Time Rachel couldn't afford, if there was any alternative.

Vaughn could have her to the hospital in Tucumcari in forty-five minutes if they left right now. But he was the sheriff, the boss; this was his game. He should direct Stratis to take her. Any other case, he would've had no uncertainty over his need to stay on the scene. But there was a huge part of him that still burned with the need to be Rachel's protector, and he knew it would kill him to stuff her in another man's car and watch them drive away.

Then again, if Rachel shot those men, there would be an investigation. Legally, ethically, he'd need to recuse himself should it come to that. In that case, he should probably appoint Stratis to run lead on the case right off the bat.

Fuck.

Take a breath, Vaughn.

What was happening now, his hesitation, that was the crux of his problem—Rachel short-circuited his intuition. Every time he got inside her orbit, he started second-guessing himself. More than anything, he hated that about their relationship. Or lack of relationship, as it was.

He peeled a sticky strand of hair from her wound. "Where's Lincoln now?"

She shuddered. "In the canyon. Dead."

His heart constricted. She loved that horse. "They killed him?"

Her tongue moved over the roof of her open mouth. "I'm thirsty."

Damn, she needed medical attention in a bad way. "I know. I'm going to get you water in a sec. Did those two men kill Lincoln?"

"Four men."

Vaughn reeled. *Four?*

Rachel continued. "But it wasn't them who killed Lincoln. It was me."

Vaughn got his face near hers, set his eyes right in front of her, and took her shoulders in his hands, careful to steer clear of her injury. "Rachel, listen to me. We only found two men. Where are the other two?"

Her gaze drifted past him. "They left. In the truck."

He followed her line of sight to the top of the mesa. When he saw what she was looking at, he rose to his feet, his jaw so tight his teeth ached.

Fourteen years in law enforcement had trained him not to rush forward, but to listen and watch, to pause and take in a crime scene all at once. Like a photograph that captured body positions and facial expressions, evidence scattered around the scene, the nuances a civilian's eye would miss. Today, though, he'd missed the writing on the boulder. Another testament to how Rachel messed with his self-control.

In block letters was a message that left him stone-cold. BITCH WE WARNED YOU——NOW YOU DIE.

So much for his job as sheriff. The need to protect Rachel blazed inside him, hot and dangerous, leaving no room for logic. "I'm getting you out of here." He squatted and draped her right arm across his shoulders. "Hold tight."

Her fingers squeezed him, but her grip was negligible at best. Not a good sign. He straightened his legs gradually, giving her body time to adjust to the movement. As soon as they were both standing, he shifted his hold and lifted her into his arms. She buried her face in his neck as he walked, and it should've felt perfect, being so close to her, but he was too disturbed by the message on the boulder to think past his wild, illogical need to flee with her. Whoever shot her and hurt her horse, they were going to pay. Every last one of them.

When they reached his car, he set her on her feet, opened the door, and helped her in. He unscrewed the lid from a fresh bottle of water and handed it to her. It slipped through her fingers. Gnashing his teeth, he held the bottle to her lips and dribbled water onto her tongue. He stroked her hair away from her face as she drank, then set the bottle in her lap and jogged toward the mesa to touch base with Stratis.

"Talk to me," he prompted his undersheriff of three years.

Stratis pushed the brim of his hat up with his finger. "We got a problem."

"Got that right. What's the status of the injured men?"

"Nonfatal gunshot wounds, both of them. But that's not what I'm talking about."

Vaughn scanned the ground. "Did you locate their firearms?"

"No, not yet, but—"

"Rachel said there were four men, and two of them took off in a truck. Probably took the firearms with them. I radioed Reyes. He should be here soon, along with another ambulance for the second man. Have you gotten names out of them yet?"

Stratis leveled his gaze at Vaughn. "That's the problem I'm talking about. Man with the leg wound is Jimmy de Luca."

Name didn't ring a bell. "And the other?"

Stratis swallowed. "He's still unconscious, but I recognized him. Pulled his wallet to confirm. Looks like Rachel shot Wallace Meyer Jr."

All Vaughn could do was blink. The tingling in his throat kicked up, making him jones for a cigarette. He looked past Stratis to the stretcher being loaded into the ambulance and swabbed his forehead with his hand. The tingling grew unbearable. Wallace Fucking Meyer.

"Don't talk to anybody, understand?"

Stratis's jaw rippled. "Understood."

"Not until we get the details," Vaughn amended. "If he's stable, stall the ambulance. We don't want Junior expiring on us—Jesus, I can only imagine the shit storm we'd be in if he died—but if we can wait until Reyes gets here, he can keep an eye on the scene and this de Luca guy while you ride in the ambulance. If Wallace Jr. comes to, press him for everything he's worth, because once he gets to the hospital, we'll lose access to him."

"Got it."

"Tell Reyes to look in the canyon. He'll find Rachel's

dead horse. Her camera won't be far away either. I'll call Kirby, Molina, and Binderman. Their day off just got cancelled."

He swung by the tree, grabbed the revolver, and locked it in the evidence bin in his trunk. He snagged his first-aid kit and got into the car. Rachel didn't turn to regard him. She was staring at the message on the boulder. Her wound gaped at him, a stew of blood, flesh, and dirt. He ripped open a pack of pre-medicated gauze and pressed it to her arm, securing it with a length of medical tape. She didn't seem to notice.

He turned the engine over and cranked the wheel, anxious to remove the graffiti from her line of sight. Once they were on the road toward the highway, he set his hand on her knee. "Do you know who those men were?"

She rubbed the elbow of her injured arm. "No."

Good. Because when she found out, she'd understand how screwed they both were.

"I'm sorry," she added in a whisper.

He squeezed her knee, hoping she didn't sense his agitation. "Don't say that. We're going to get you patched up, and then we'll talk. For now, rest. I've got to make some calls."

She closed her eyes. "Amy," she breathed.

"Yeah, I'm calling your sisters. They'll meet us at the hospital."

First things first, though. Time to alert his deputies that the Quay County Sheriff's Department just went into crisis mode. He dialed Torin Kirby's number, but his mind was on Wallace Meyer Jr.

The younger Meyer's delinquency was a sore topic in his department, muttered about for years. But under the protective watch of his father, the boy was exempt from the arm of the law—or, at least, that was what the good ole boy club believed. Still, what was the son of a bitch thinking, trespassing in the middle of the day to scrawl threatening messages on the property of a family already steeped in controversy? Did he ever consider he might get caught?

Then again, Wallace Meyer Jr. had the luxury not to think of consequences at all. It was a fact of life Vaughn became aware of as a teenager—thanks in large part to the Meyer family—that the people with the power called the shots. Wallace Meyer Sr., Tucumcari's police chief for the past twenty-eight years, had more power and political influence than any other law-enforcement authority in eastern New Mexico.

He glanced at Rachel. She'd opened her eyes and was staring out the window, unaware that no matter how justifiable her reasons for shooting the police chief's son, if Vaughn didn't do some fast thinking, her life as she knew it was over for good.

Chapter Two

Intense, the way Vaughn looked at her. Like she might conjure a gun and shoot someone if he let his guard down. He'd stayed by Rachel's side while nurses fussed over her and a doctor cleaned her wound, walked in step with the hospital bed as they rolled her to radiology for X-rays, and claimed the only chair in the room when they'd settled her into a private suite for her overnight observation stay.

The nurses called it a suite, but the room felt more like a prison cell to Rachel, with Vaughn as her jailer. He was too close, his stare too penetrating. Thank goodness for the drugs the nurses had given her, because otherwise she might have crumbled under his scrutiny.

He was dressed in his uniform, but had unbuttoned the collar and loosened his black tie. She was partial to the tie. Not too long ago, he'd done unspeakable things to her with that tie. Or maybe, he burned the ones he'd used on her and purchased replacements. She wouldn't fault him for destroying the evidence of their time together. Every single day she prayed to forget him too.

The room's fluorescent lights glinted off the sheriff badge on his chest. The reflection shimmered on her skin as she lifted her hand to touch his tie. The material was coarse, utilitarian, against the pad of her thumb. A zing of lust rippled through her belly.

Vaughn shot to his feet with a sharp inhale and prowled to the closed door to look out the narrow window. She fisted her hands in the blanket. Why had she done such a stupid thing as touch him?

When he returned to her bedside, he was careful to drag his chair out of reach, she noticed with an equal measure of gratitude and irritation. "Your sisters are waiting outside, and they're worried." His voice was strained, and he clutched the arms of the chair with a white-knuckled grip. "I know you want to see them, to show them you're okay, so please try, Rachel. Try to concentrate on my last few questions so I can let your sisters in the room."

She couldn't remember any questions. "Ask me again."

"After you called me from the canyon, what did you do next?"

"I reloaded my gun and climbed around the west side of the mesa."

"What were the four men doing at that point?"

It had been over a year since she'd looked at Vaughn long enough to really see him. Their mistakes in the interim had taken place in the dark of night, and were over too soon for her to notice anything but the way he made her feel. His thick, dark hair was a smidge longer than she remembered, combed and held in place with a touch of gel. A new scar, an inch-long jagged line that still glowed pink, ran along his jaw near his right ear, and time had etched new laugh lines into the corners of his blue eyes.

Yet so much about him hadn't changed. His face still disarmed her, with its high cheekbones, straight, squared nose and full lips that were the window to his emotions. Whatever he felt at any given time, she could always see it in his lips. His shoulders were as stiff as ever. That she remembered with perfect clarity. The way his shoulders began each morning relaxed, then crept ever closer to his ears as the day wore on.

"Rachel, please. What were the four men doing while you climbed the mesa?"

She rubbed her eyes and turned away from him. "Smoking dope, reloading their rifles, joking around."

"They didn't know you were coming to confront them?"

She huffed. "I wasn't coming to confront them. I was coming to shoot them."

"Jesus, Rachel, you can't tell me stuff like that." He flexed his hand and glanced at the closed door. His lips grew twitchy, and she knew he was deliberating some important choice. "Let's stop talking about what happened today."

She didn't understand his worry, but felt too weak to question him about it. "Okay."

"Has anything like this ever occurred on your ranch before? The graffiti or the people trespassing?"

She shrugged, then grunted when it sent a stab of pain through her injured arm. "A dozen or so times in the past four months. I kept photographic records on my camera and computer. I'll hand the pictures over to you."

He stared at her for a heartbeat, then vaulted from his seat and yanked the privacy curtain around her bed. "A dozen times? And this is the first I'm hearing about it?"

"It was no big deal."

In a flash, he was leaning over her, his fists punching the pillow on either side of her head, his expression livid. She flinched. Not that she was one to cower, but it was unbearable, having him close enough for her to catch the scent of his aftershave and feel his breath on her face. She wanted to look at his eyes—his eyes alone broke her heart—but she held herself in check, and instead stared down her body, to the place where his tie brushed her chest.

"I have my reasons," she whispered.

"Is it because of you and me?" His voice was even lower than hers, a note on the wind. With his hand on her jaw, he held her face until she met his eyes. "Is that it? You didn't want me anywhere near you? Is that why you risked your life, because you were too proud to ask me for help?"

If only. But pride had nothing to do with it.

She held his gaze, wondering if he could see the truth in her eyes.

The hand that held her jaw relaxed. "You're so damn proud." He slid his fingers behind her ear into her hair. "But you're going to have to trust me from here on out. What happened in Parillas Valley has put you in a situation. A real bad one. I'm going to do everything I can to get you out of this mess, but I've got to follow the letter of the law."

She stared at him, confused and—for the first time since Vaughn's patrol car barreled into Parillas Valley with its sirens blaring—afraid. "What?"

His eyes bore into hers, serious and sad. "Your and my every move is going to be scrutinized like nothing you've known before." His hand cupped her head; his thumb curled over her ear. "I need to know. Have you ever told anyone about us?"

The question stung worse than a slap. If she'd had the strength, she would have shoved him away, shoved him out the door and out of her life for good. She screwed her mouth into a sneer as bitter acid crawled up her throat. How could she want someone so badly who took every opportunity to remind her that their relationship was nothing more than a filthy secret?

Rachel had never confessed her affair with Vaughn to anyone, including Jenna and Amy, because she was a coward, through and through. To this day, her sisters had no idea Rachel was to blame for their mom's purposeful overdose on vodka and pills the year before. No idea that four weeks into her grief over losing their dad, she'd left their bipolar mom—who'd tipped over the mental deep end when her husband died—alone at night in the house so she could run off and get laid by the sheriff investigating Dad's death. Jenna and Amy, along with the rest of the town, had assumed she'd been home that night, and neither she nor Vaughn had corrected their thinking.

Not only was she too cowardly to face their wrath, but confessing the truth would've landed Vaughn in trouble with his job. He should never have been sleeping with a person connected to a possible murder investigation. She supposed he had his own reasons for going ahead with the affair, as she had hers, and the car crash that killed her dad was eventually deemed a freak accident, but it didn't change the facts. They had each done something horribly wrong, and Rachel's mom had paid the price.

"Rachel, I need to know who you told."

The fear in his voice dragged her to the present. Whatever he made her feel, the agony and the bliss, none of it mattered at the moment. She shook her head. "No one. You know that. But . . . I don't understand. Why am I in so much trouble? I was defending myself today."

She could see the outline of his tongue pushing around the inside of his lips. He stared past her, to the wall behind her bed, and took a deep, slow breath. Then he lowered his forehead to hers. The hand that had been holding her head dipped lower to clutch her upper back beneath the open hospital gown. The feel of his hand spanning her shoulder blades was the most marvelous and painful sensation she'd experienced since the last time he held her.

Of its own volition, her good arm hooked around his neck, clinging to him like he was the anchor she'd always needed him to be but he never had been.

His breath was ragged, his eyes closed. "Rachel, you shot a man in the back with an unregistered .38. You had every right to defend yourself on your property, but this man's name is Wallace Meyer Jr. He's the Tucumcari police chief's only child."

She swallowed, speechless. The revolver had been her father's, locked in a safe with a handful of hunting rifles, and she'd never given using the gun a second thought.

Wallace Meyer had been cop numero uno in Quay County since Rachel was young. She remembered seeing him on the local news, giving official statements on various crimes and drug busts. Tucumcari, the county seat, was thirty miles east of Catcher Creek, but the two towns were inextricably linked. Actually, every small town in Quay County depended on Tucumcari like a lifeline. Within its city limits were the county's only community college, library, and jail. Of the county's twelve thousand residents, over half lived there.

Vaughn and his deputies were responsible for policing the entire county, save for Tucumcari, which was the only town for a hundred miles that boasted a city-level police force. Meyer had spoken out against Vaughn during his campaign for sheriff three years ago. Apparently, Meyer and the old guard weren't Vaughn's biggest fans, though Rachel couldn't remember why. Vaughn had eked out enough votes to win, but there was no denying Meyer's sweeping influence.

And she'd shot his only child. Holy shit.

Vaughn's other arm wrapped around her waist. His hold on her intensified, lifting her torso from the bed. His badge dug into the vulnerable flesh of her breast, but all she could do was breathe and blink.

Let this be a dream. Then Lincoln would be alive and Vaughn wouldn't be holding her. She wouldn't be lying in a hospital bed on observation for wound infection, with her sisters worrying in the hallway. Acid, vicious and unrelenting, ate at her stomach, but she'd take the localized pain of an ulcer any day. She'd take the ranch problems. She'd bargain with the universe any way she could if she could wake up and realize the past five hours had been a nightmare.

His fingers stroked her back. "Whatever happens, whatever Meyer threatens to do to you, you stay calm. Don't talk to anyone, got it? Especially not the Tucumcari police. Any of them come sniffing around, you call me right away. This is my case, my jurisdiction. Don't let them bully you."

She wouldn't. As soon as she stopped freaking out, she'd locate her backbone. She was going to protect herself and her family, no matter who tried to push them around. "I need to see Amy and Jenna."

He brushed his closed lips across her forehead, then eased her to the bed. "Kellan's out there too."

Kellan Reed was Amy's fiancé. Rachel hadn't been real crazy about him when he and Amy embarked on their whirlwind romance last December, but now she was on board with his place in her family. Best part about Kellan was he took a lot of pressure off Rachel on the ranch. Over the past several months they'd eased into a comfortable partnership, dividing chores and making plans as they prepared to merge their adjoining properties after his and Amy's July wedding.

As good a guy as Kellan was, though, he did have one flaw that got Rachel's dander up. He was Vaughn's best friend.

"Do they know what happened?" she asked.

"Not yet."

"Were my sisters crying, last you looked?"

He smiled, his eyes crinkling with tenderness. "You bet."

"Good grief." She matched his grin. It was a relief to suspend her fear and smile at a joke like her world hadn't collapsed in on her. "This is the perfect opportunity for them to take their drama to a whole new level of annoying."

Quirking his eyebrow, he swiped a box of tissues from the counter in the corner and set it on her stomach. "There. At least they won't get snot and tears on your covers."

She almost laughed, he knew her so well. Then his question returned to haunt her—*Have you ever told anyone about us?*—along with the pain it evoked. Her gaze slid away.

Clearing his throat, he shook out his arms, as if he were shaking the memory of her body off his limbs. He did that most every time and she hated it. He buttoned his collar, tightened his tie, and adjusted the utility belt strapped to his trim waist. With a flick of his fingers, his radio came to life in a flurry of static and garbled words. Last on was his black Stetson. He smoothed his fingers around the brim until he got the angle just so.

He placed a hand on the privacy curtain. "Ready for them?"

At her nod of assent, he pushed the curtain to the wall and opened the door.

Rachel's sisters burst into the room as dramatically as she'd expected, but quieter. There were no shrieking hysterics, but plenty of wringing hands and hugs and tears. God, how those two women could weep. Rachel was eternally grateful that the drama gene her younger sisters inherited from their mother had skipped over her.

Hovering over Rachel's bed, Amy drew a deep breath and hiccupped. "We've been so worried. Vaughn was in here interviewing you for hours and the nurses wouldn't tell us anything except that you were shot and in stable condition."

"That's all they said? Geez. They might've mentioned I was only grazed by a stray bullet, not shot point-blank. I feel fine. You can stop worrying."

Jenna perched on the edge of the bed and took Rachel's hand in hers. "You're not fine. You're in a hospital." She let out a particularly melodramatic sniffle.

"Calm down, Jenna. Amy, you too. I'm not on my deathbed. I would've been cleared to go home tonight if the doctor wasn't so worried about infection."

Vaughn cleared his throat to catch their attention. "I need to get to work on the investigation, but I wanted to fill you all in on a few points first." He was all business now, hands clasped behind his back, his expression polite and distant.

Amy and Jenna wiped their eyes and made use of the tissue box on her stomach.

Kellan said, "Whoever shot Rachel, has he been arrested?"

Vaughn's gaze touched on Jenna and Amy, but skipped Rachel entirely. "Two of the four suspects are still at large. My deputies are running them down as we speak. As far as the two suspects Ms. Sorentino shot, their situation is complicated, being that one of them is police chief Wallace Meyer's son."

That got Kellan's back up. "Hell, no. That no-count

druggie, Junior, was on Sorentino Farm? I would've shot him too, only I wouldn't have aimed to wound."

Rachel huffed. "You think I was aiming to wound?"

Kellan sniffed. "Guess we got to work on your gun handling skills as soon as your arm is better."

Vaughn held up a hand. "Whoa, there. I know you don't really mean that, but—"

"Like hell I don't," Kellan said.

"—but you can't spout off about wanting to kill people around me. This goes for all of you. Keep your mouths shut about this, and stay clear of the Meyer family and the Tucumcari police. Don't even cross into the Tucumcari city limits until this is resolved. You need to let my department handle it. Charging the child of a law-enforcement officer with a violent felony is dicey."

"You're not going to let Junior walk, are you?" Kellan said.

"Trust me, K. Every last one of those men are going to pay for their crimes against Ms. Sorentino and her horse—including Junior. But there's an order to things, and I've got to play it perfectly to make the charges stick."

Kellan rubbed his temple. "I'm assuming, due to the personal nature of your relationship with the Sorentinos, you're assigning the case to one of your deputies or your undersheriff?"

Vaughn turned and faced Kellan square-on. "No. I'm handling it."

They exchanged a long, stony-faced look. For best friends, they sure didn't look friendly.

"Wouldn't that be a problem for making the charges stick?" Kellan asked in a quiet tone that was thick with meaning, like he knew all about Rachel and Vaughn's history.

Could it be that Vaughn was talking out of both sides

of his mouth, as insistent as he was that Rachel stay quiet about their affair? But whether Kellan knew or not, he made a valid point, one Rachel hadn't considered.

Amy walked to Kellan and slid her arm around his waist. "I, for one, feel better knowing you're taking charge of this, Vaughn. You and Rachel aren't friendly, and you're not on good terms with the Meyers, so there's no conflict of interest, right?"

Rachel ground her teeth together and pushed a fist into her stomach. The ulcer was killing her. Literally eating a hole through her flesh. "Sheriff Cooper has a lot to do. We should let him get to work."

Jenna patted Rachel's forearm. "I think we're missing the bigger picture here. All I want to know is, with two suspects on the loose, are we safe on our farm? We've got two families staying at the inn, paid up through the end of the week. Should we send them home early?"

Jenna's question cracked the tension in the room. Rachel took a calming breath and chanced a look at Kellan and Vaughn. They'd pulled in their horns and directed their attention toward Jenna, but on further inspection, she noticed Vaughn's shoulders had inched up another notch and Kellan's neck had gone splotchy red.

"That valley is miles from our homestead," Amy said. "How likely is it that Junior and his friends didn't know whose property they were on?"

Bitch we warned you flashed through Rachel's memory. Meyer Jr. and his friends knew exactly where they were.

"I'm not at liberty to divulge the details yet, but I have reason to believe they were targeting your farm specifically," Vaughn said.

"Why?" Kellan, Amy, and Jenna said in unison.

Vaughn tightened his tie. "That's what I aim to find out. For now, sit tight. I see no reason to send your guests home early."

"I'll stay at their place tonight, watch over everyone. But you keep us posted on any developments," Kellan said.

"Will do. I'm going to get on with the investigation, but I'll be close by." He fished a business card from his shirt pocket and brushed past Kellan and Amy to set it near the hospital's clunky phone at Rachel's bedside without once meeting her eyes. The business card was pointless. She knew his every phone number by heart.

"One of my deputies will be on watch outside your door tonight," he said on his way out.

She balked. "I can't see how that's necessary. Wouldn't it be safer for everyone involved if your deputies were all out looking for the suspects instead of holding one back to babysit me?"

For the first time since Kellan, Amy, and Jenna entered the room, he looked directly at her. "We're doing this my way, Ms. Sorentino. You're getting the guard. I'll be in touch."

Turning on his heel, he pushed out the door.

"I think a guard's a good idea," Jenna said.

Rachel chortled. "If that quack of a doctor had cleared me to go home, we wouldn't even be discussing it."

Amy stood at the foot of her bed, her arms on her hips, grinning sagely at her. "Not all doctors are quacks."

"Glorified mechanics, every last one of them," she countered. "They listen to the rattle in your engine, make assumptions about the diagnosis, replace a screw or a belt, and overcharge you for the honor of their service."

Jenna frowned and tightened her grip on Rachel's forearm. "You're not thinking of escaping while the guard's looking the other way, are you?"

Right. Like Rachel was entertaining the notion of

pulling her IV out and sneaking off in the dead of night in nothing but her hospital gown.

"Tempting as that idea is, I think I'll concede the point to the sheriff." She couldn't bring herself to call him Vaughn in front of her family, afraid a hint of their intimacy would seep into her tone.

Jenna blew her nose. "What happened out there in the Parillas Valley? How did you end up in a shootout against four men?"

Rachel rubbed her face. What could she say to make her sisters understand? Vaughn hadn't mentioned the graffiti, so Rachel wasn't sure if she was at liberty to. To complicate it further, her sisters didn't know about the other graffiti she found around the ranch, or the other vandals she'd successfully scared off with warning shots. They'd probably find out soon enough, and when they did, they'd probably give her hell for not telling them. But she was too bone-weary to get into a dust-up over it now.

"Vau—" She bit her lip and started again. "Sheriff Cooper told me not to talk to anyone about the details of the shootout. I don't know if he suggested that for our protection or for the good of the investigation. Let's just say, when I shot those men, they had it coming."

"Why? What did they do? You're scaring me," Amy said.

Geez, Rachel needed to stop flapping her lips. All this talking in obscurities and half-truths was making her head spin. "Nothing to be scared about. I'm sure the sheriff deputies will find the other suspects soon. Everything's going to be fine."

A nurse bustled past Jenna and Amy, a pink tray balanced on her hand with three paper cups. Meds, Rachel hoped. She sat up as much as she could. Her sisters scooted out of the way. As if she were a waitress, the nurse held the tray out and described the pills in each cup like they were dessert options at a restaurant. Rachel downed the ulcer med first, followed by the horse-pill-sized antibiotic.

She tried to turn down the pain med—she'd had enough of feeling like an idiot for one afternoon—but Jenna and Amy's protestations were loud and impassioned. When Amy threatened to hold vigil at her bedside until she took the pill, Rachel caved. She loved her sisters, but she was ready for some peace and quiet.

The nurse left after checking Rachel's IV.

"What happened to Lincoln?" Jenna asked. "Did he bolt when the men shot you? Should we send the farmhands out looking for him tonight?"

She couldn't shield her sisters from the painful truth of Lincoln's fate forever, or herself for that matter. She picked at a corner of the tissue box. "He was hit by a bullet." Her throat tightened up. No way in hell was she going to cry in front of her sisters, but it hurt so badly, the knowledge that she'd lost her closest friend. "I had to . . ." Her eyes pricked with moisture. She shoved her tongue against her cheek and held her breath, fighting the grief.

"You had to put him down," Amy finished quietly.

"Yeah."

Jenna leaned over and gathered Rachel in a gentle hug. "I'm so sorry."

Rachel patted her back and felt Amy on her other side, her arms around them both.

Rachel hugged them as much as her waning strength allowed. She wasn't real good at expressing it in words, but her family meant more to her than anything in the world. More than the farm, more than her own happiness.

She'd dedicated her life to sheltering her sisters from

one calamity after another, worked her fingers to the bone to keep the ranch running from the time she could get herself onto a horse, and filled the role of their parent when their mom and dad fell short. Even when all she wanted to do was retreat into herself, she stuck it out for them.

There was little she could do to shelter them from the mess she'd caused today.

A sudden pang of suffocation coursed through her. "I need time alone."

Jenna and Amy pulled away, looking hurt. Shit. She never could seem to say the right thing to them. Sometimes their feelings were as fragile as tissue paper. "I'm sorry," she amended. "I just—my arm hurts, and I'm tired."

"Come on, Amy, Jenna. Let her get some rest," Kellan said.

Jenna and Amy nodded. They flittered around the room, smoothing her blanket, refilling her water glass, and asking her a zillion questions about whether or not she wanted the television on or the blinds closed or extra pillows. Rachel worked hard to be patient, but the feeling of suffocation wouldn't abate.

Kellan must've sensed her growing agitation because he spread his arms wide and herded her sisters toward the door.

"We'll see you tomorrow morning," Amy called over her shoulder as Kellan shuffled her into the hallway.

"Can't wait," Rachel called with a wave.

As soon as she was alone, she took a breath, then swung her legs over the side of the bed. Her whole body ached, but she pushed through it, knowing she had only a small window of time before the pain med kicked in and she lost her ability to form a coherent thought.

Dragging her IV, she padded into the bathroom and

flipped on the light. The mirror was cruel. She looked like she'd spent the past year living in a forest. Dirt was everywhere, in the creases of her earlobes, coating her scalp, stuck in her teeth, and lodged in wrinkles on her face she didn't even know she had.

With a groan, she rinsed her mouth out, then grabbed a handful of paper towels for a quick wash that turned into a long wash. She kept scrubbing until she felt halfway human again. Once done, she braced her hands against the sink and stared at her reflection.

Time to face up to the possibility that she'd lost more in the Parillas Valley than her beloved horse. She'd always prided herself on her ability to circumvent gossip, being neither the fodder nor the circulator. She kept to herself, which was exactly how she wanted to live. But Wallace Meyer Jr. had stripped her of her solitary peace. He and his reckless friends. She wasn't sure she could survive the exposure the shootout would bring.

Lincoln was dead, her peace had been compromised, and for what? For Wallace Jr. and his buddies to send a message that she and her sisters weren't wanted in town? She'd assumed the vandalism had been Catcher Creek protesters of their dude ranch, but the Meyer family lived in Tucumcari, not Catcher Creek. What did Wallace Jr. care if she opened a dude ranch?

A spinning started in her head. The drug kicking in. Squinting at her reflection, she was struck with the panicky feeling there was something she knew but couldn't remember, some answer beyond her grasp. She reached into her head for the thought, but it danced out of range.

Succumbing to the pull of the medication, she shuffled from the bathroom, tugged the privacy curtain closed, and sank into bed with a grunt. At the table near her head was the phone. She reached over with her bad arm, sucking in a tight breath, working to ignore the pain. *Get used to it,* she warned herself. *Tomorrow, no more meds.* She needed a clear mind if she was going to solve her problems.

She lifted Vaughn's business card and read his name. With her fingertip, she traced the outline of his badge on the paper until the image blurred in her vision. She'd made a lot of mistakes in her life, but it was just her horrible luck that the two worst ones had collided right before her eyes and she'd been helpless to prevent it. She'd shot the son of a powerful person, and now, to salvage her future, she'd have to rely on the man who'd ripped her heart to shreds and kept coming back to poke at the wound.

She dropped the card on her chest and closed her eyes, praying for a dreamless sleep. But the only image she saw was Vaughn.

Chapter Three

With his gourd-shaped figure, bald head, and whiskers, Wallace Meyer reminded Vaughn of the walruses at the San Antonio Sea World he'd seen while on vacation as a kid with his parents and younger sisters. As disarming as Meyer's appearance was, Vaughn had run charity half marathons with Meyer over the years and knew the secret strength of his lumpy body. He'd waged political battles against the man, and therefore knew the intellect behind the whiskers and bulge of chew in his cheek. He knew the smug superiority hidden behind the genial eyes and ruddy complexion.

Meyer's shiny scalp was immediately obvious in the hospital waiting room. Next to him sat the tightly permed blond curls of his wife's head. Vaughn stood in the elevator hallway, his eyes on Meyer, as he reconstructed the armor of ego Rachel had punched a hole through. He smoothed a hand over his tie and swallowed repeatedly until the tingling craving for cigarettes dissipated from his throat.

He'd given up smoking cold turkey the day Rachel broke it off with him a year ago last February, to punish himself for ruining everything. It had seemed like a fit plan at the time, but as it stood now, he only craved a smoke when he had Rachel on the brain—a testament to how his dual addictions had become fused in his psyche. Pathetic, how a four-week affair a year and a half ago had screwed him up so royally.

He shook his arms and fingers out. *Get a grip, man. That's you making yourself miserable, not her. She has no control over your choices.* Ha. Right.

The futile self-affirmation brought a sarcastic uptwitch to the corners of his lips. Excellent. Exactly the face he wanted to present to Meyer. When he played the role of the smart-ass punk with no respect for the county's established guard, Meyer lost his cool. Vaughn loved it when the visage of paternal condescension evaporated from Meyer's face to reveal the disdain he usually kept in careful check. Didn't happen often, but enough to make Vaughn hungry for it.

He ducked into the gift shop for a pack of gum, dialing Stratis as he paid the cashier. "Where are you?"

"Outside the post-surgical recovery room, waiting for the all-clear to interview Junior."

"Any lawyers buzzing around?"

"Not yet."

Interesting. Vaughn had been so certain Meyer would've gone on the defense straight out of the gate that he hadn't given much consideration to the alternative, that Meyer had reached the decision that his son hadn't done anything criminal, or at least criminal enough to bring a lawyer into the situation.

"Did you get blood samples?" he asked Stratis. "If Junior's on drugs again, that could answer a lot of my questions."

"I sent Binderman to the lab with samples. He put a rush on it, so we should have the tox results by the end of the week."

The end of the week was four days away. Maddening, how slow the system worked.

That was the rub of enforcing the law in a rural county. Just about every forensic service the job required had to be outsourced to Albuquerque or Santa Fe. Every so often, they utilized the Tucumcari hospital's lab, but not when a crime had occurred, and definitely not when that crime involved a high-ranking Tucumcari official's family.

The hospital was little more than a sprawling complex of doctors' offices, an out-patient surgery wing, and an emergency room. At three stories tall, it was one of the larger buildings in town, but wasn't ideal for treating medical problems greater than broken bones or kidney stones. Or gunshot wounds, for that matter. Hell, broken bones and gunshot wounds were an integral component of life in the wild west of New Mexico's high desert.

Outsourcing everything from fingerprinting to tox screens was impossibly slow, which was why Vaughn had come to rely on his ability to get people to talk, perps and witnesses alike. Over the years on the job, he'd become a criminal psychology expert out of sheer desperation to deliver justice to those who deserved it, despite the staggering odds stacked against such an outcome.

He cracked his knuckles, took a slow breath, and lowered the volume on his radio. Then he sauntered across the lobby, whistling. Showtime.

When he dropped into the chair next to Kathryn Meyer, Wallace let his hatred for Vaughn shine through for a split second before his eyes shuttered into cool benevolence.

"Cooper. I was wondering when you'd find your way to me."

Vaughn flickered a glance at him before extending

his hand to Kathryn. "Mrs. Meyer, it's been a long time. I'm so sorry we're meeting again under such unfortunate circumstances."

She shook his hand with a strained, dewy-eyed expression. "Thank you."

"My deputy informed me Junior's out of the woods," Vaughn continued in his most consoling tone. "Sounds like the bullet was successfully removed without complication. You must be relieved."

"The Lord has blessed us with His mercy once again."

He patted Mrs. Meyer's hand. "I'm sure that's true."

Wallace stood and hitched his slacks up around his bloated belly. "Kathy, Sheriff Cooper and I are going to step away, talk business."

Vaughn stood, following Meyer's lead. "Would you like a cup of coffee from the cart out front, Mrs. Meyer?"

"That would be lovely. Thank you," she said.

He smiled with his kindest eyes, then followed Meyer through the sliding double doors and around the corner, out of sight from the glass-enclosed lobby. They positioned themselves in the sliver of shade on the side of the building.

It was seven o'clock, a half hour before sundown, but the heat was still oppressive and Vaughn's long-sleeve uniform and tie weren't helping matters. When he'd won the sheriff election three years earlier, he'd toyed with the idea of wearing a short-sleeve dress shirt, as he had while a deputy. But with the tie and the pens in his chest pocket, he'd looked like one of those Geek Squad workers who fixed computers, not a high-ranking law-enforcement officer. So instead, he suffered in silence through New Mexico's months of debilitating heat.

He jammed his hands in his pants pockets and rocked on his heels. "Chief, I just thought of something funny."

"I'm sure you're going to tell me about it."

"Yeah, well, it occurs to me that you have a press conference on the books for this Friday. One of those grandstanding affairs to publicly congratulate yourself about the drop in illegal drug activity in Tucumcari this year."

"What's so funny about that? I'm damn proud of those numbers."

Vaughn fished the pack of gum from his shirt pocket and popped a stick in his mouth. He'd purchased it exclusively for Meyer, because it drove him ape-shit. "You should be. Sure. But it's ironic timing, don't you think? I mean, if Junior's tox results show drugs in his system, which you and I both know will be the case, that could put quite the damper on your media party."

"Are you daring to insult my son while he's recovering from a near-fatal gunshot wound? Classy, Sheriff. Real classy."

Vaughn smacked his lips, enjoying the sound of squishing saliva as he bit down on the gum. "Classy's my middle name, haven't you heard?"

Swabbing a hand over his whiskers, Meyer said, "Tell me what happened in the Parillas Valley today."

"I don't think so."

"Son, you are not the first sheriff I've worked with in my lifetime, and you won't be the last. I understand you're dense when it comes to professional courtesy, being as young as you are, but there are unwritten rules in our profession that you would do well to follow."

"Uh-huh," Vaughn said stupidly.

Meyer's eyes flared with anger. His ears turned pink. Oh, yeah. The dumb punk act was crawling under his skin real good. Wouldn't be long before he blew his top.

"I'm going to ask you one more time," Meyer said with a forced grin. "What happened to my son?"

"Junior can tell you himself."

Meyer puckered his mouth and spit a nasty bit of juice from his chew into the potted shrub to his right. "Is the Sorentino property fenced?"

Guess he already knew some details of the crime scene after all. Didn't surprise Vaughn that Meyer did his research. He probably had a team of officers scouring Rachel's personal information, trying to dig up dirt on her. Vaughn had looked her up in the system himself as a matter of due process after her father died. At the time, she hadn't a single blemish to her name. Not even a speeding ticket.

"No, it's not fenced," he answered.

"Signed?"

Vaughn smacked his lips again, chewing the gum openmouthed for maximum effect. "Are you trying to tell me your biggest concern is whether or not I'm going to bring Junior up on criminal trespassing charges? That's cute. And really"—Stupid? Pompous?—"short-sighted of you."

"I'm not worried about you charging my boy with anything. I feel safe in assuming you'll show the same understanding toward my son as you've so graciously done in the past."

"True, true. My deputies and I have done our share of ignoring Junior's *growing pains* over the years. But what happened today, I think you already realize, was a lot more than boys being boys or whatever bullshit logic we've used to excuse his delinquent behavior." He blew a bubble and popped it with his teeth.

Sweat broke out on Meyer's neck as he watched Vaughn's mouth work the gum. Good. The fucker deserved to sweat it out. With any luck, Meyer would lose his cool right there in front of the Tucumcari hospital's main entrance, with half his adoring public as witnesses.

Meyer glanced side to side and leaned in toward

Vaughn. "It's a give and take, Cooper. My officers and I have held up our end of the bargain by looking the other way with regard to your sister. If you pursue criminal charges against my son, I can no longer protect Gwen from the"—he ran the chew along the inside of his lower lip—"consequences of her criminal proclivities. Her sticky fingers are going to catch up with her one of these days."

Here we go. Vaughn smiled his broadest smile, but his stomach took a dive. He hadn't considered what this latest development would mean for Gwen. But he'd always known he couldn't protect her forever. Especially now, with Rachel hurt. Not to mention that this case was the chance he'd been waiting twenty years for, the reason he'd first thought about a career in law enforcement as a bright-eyed sixteen-year-old—to crush Wallace Meyer Sr. and his entitled, arrogant family with the hammer of justice. Gwen would have to find a way to control herself, because it was time for Vaughn to play hardball.

He blew another bubble, then matched Meyer's lean-in—just two dudes sharing a secret. "I am profoundly grateful to you and your officers for the associative privileges you've afforded my sister." He gave an exaggerated wink. Meyer sneered. Vaughn allowed his expression to turn taunting. "But there comes a time when we each must face up to the crimes we've committed, and there's a big difference between shoplifting a candy bar and aggravated assault with a deadly weapon."

Meyer pulled back, nodding. Yeah, he recognized the fight in Vaughn's words. He knew Vaughn had dropped his gloves, prepared for a bare-knuckled battle. "Funny you should mention aggravated assault," he said in an oily voice. It was his turn to grin maliciously. "In my estimation, that's what Rachel Sorentino is going to be charged with."

Damn, he hated hearing her name out of the bastard's mouth, hated even more that she was on Meyer's radar now. Even though she was justified in shooting Junior, there was no doubt in Vaughn's mind her actions had marked her and her family for a lifetime of police harassment in Tucumcari. "Tut, tut, Chief. There you go, trying to do my job again. When are you going to get it into your huge melon that events outside your city's limits are none of your business?"

The pink of Meyer's ears flooded the rest of his face. When he spoke, his voice was thick with anger. "This is my damn business because it involves my damn son."

Vaughn chewed, fake-contemplating Meyer's words, and blew another bubble. It was a big one that popped with a *crack*. "I understand, Chief. Believe me, I do. And what I'd tell any concerned parent this early in an investigation is to go home and take care of your family, and let me do my job."

He patted Meyer on the shoulder consolingly, then reached into his pocket. "Would you like a stick of gum? It's spearmint."

Meyer eyed the gum with a rabid look. Vaughn halfway thought he'd start foaming at the mouth. Tamping his giddiness, Vaughn held the gum aloft and kept smiling.

"You may think kicking me while my only child's life hangs in the balance is something you can get away with, but you're wrong," Meyer hissed. "Seems you've forgotten who holds the power in this county. Don't think it's escaped my attention that you're up for reelection this year. If you're not careful, you'll find yourself back to picking shit out of horse hooves like your parents."

There it was, the look Vaughn had been waiting for.

The real Wallace Meyer. The bastard Vaughn was going to nail to the wall. He cocked his head to the side, eyebrows raised. "Not exactly the insult you intend it to be, Chief." If he could live his life with half as much happiness and love as his parents did, he'd consider his time on Earth a success. Of course, Meyer only saw their jobs and their economic standing, not the good, honest people they were.

"It's good to know you feel that way, because after the November election, your time of power is over."

"Yeesh. So dramatic. Guess I'd better make the most of my few remaining months in office." He flipped open his wallet and withdrew three dollar bills, which he stuffed in Meyer's shirt pocket. "Don't forget to buy your wife that coffee. My treat."

With a two-finger salute to his temple, Vaughn strode across the driveway to the parking lot. While he waited to question Junior, he'd use the laptop in his patrol car to look through the crime scene photos Binderman had found on Rachel's camera.

Given the scope of Meyer's influence, he could easily cost Vaughn his reelection. But he couldn't let fear of the future weigh his choices. He'd waited his entire career for a chance to show the world the true nature of Meyer and his son. Call it a personal quest, but he saw it as his life's work to strip rich, powerful bullies of their authority. If he lost November's election bid, he'd start over on his quest somewhere else, and this final challenge to Meyer's policy of corruption would stand as Vaughn's local legacy.

He could only hope.

As soon as Meyer and the hospital coffee cart disappeared from view around the corner, Vaughn spit the wad of gum into a trash can and dialed Nathan Binderman, his buddy Chris's younger brother and the latest member of Vaughn's team. He could've radioed, which was their usual protocol, but it was impossible to know if one of Meyer's lackeys were listening in.

"Binderman here."

"You at the scene still?"

"Logging shell casings, sir. The number's pushing forty. Looks like it was a hell of a gun battle."

"What caliber are the casings?"

"Mostly 2-2-3s, with a half dozen .38s in the mix. The 2-2-3 casings line up with the images from the victim's camera of the suspects and their firearms. Looks like they were packing AR-15s."

Vaughn froze midstride. "AR-15s? What are a bunch of young, country hicks doing with assault rifles?" Damn, he was glad he didn't know that sooner. He would've lost his composure for sure in front of Meyer. Rachel had been lucky to escape with her life with that many high-powered rifle bullets flying around. "Have you uploaded the camera's photographs to my e-mail?"

"Yes, sir."

"Has animal control been called about the horse's body yet?"

"They've come and gone," Binderman said. "I uploaded photographs I took of the horse and the canyon the body was found in."

"Nice work. I'm on my way to take a look at the photos. You're out of daylight. That going to be a problem for processing the scene?"

"No, sir. Kirby brought lights in before she and Molina took off. I'm set for the duration."

"I'll send Stratis to help you as soon as Meyer Jr.'s out of post-surgery observation."

From the photographs on Rachel's camera, Kirby had recognized one of the two men who fled the scene as Elias Baltierra, whom she'd arrested a couple years back for drug possession with intent to sell. She'd called Vaughn to get the green light to pursue the lead. With them chasing down suspects, Binderman processing the scene, and Reyes standing guard duty over de Luca's hospital room, his department was spread as thin as it could go. And he hadn't yet figured out who he could spare to stand watch outside Rachel's door.

Vaughn opened his patrol car door and stood aside while the day's hot air poured out. There was still no breeze to speak of, but at least the sun was setting. Maybe the temperature would drop below a hundred by the time the stars came out.

"Hey." He turned to see Kellan striding his way, a murderous look in his eyes, the posture of his two hundred ripped pounds of six-foot-four body tense with fury. Kellan was about the only man Vaughn knew who could make his respectably muscled, six-foot-one frame feel puny.

Vaughn straightened to his full height. "Something tells me you're not here to discuss the meal plan for Sunday's barbecue."

Scoffing, Kellan braced his hand on the roof of Vaughn's car. "We've known each other a long time, and I've never seen you do anything this stupid."

That got right to the point. The two of them had been inseparable friends since their early twenties after Kellan, a newly minted rancher in the area, hired Vaughn's dad as a farrier. The day Vaughn stopped by his folks' house to announce he'd been hired as a sheriff deputy, Kellan happened to be there, picking up some horseshoes. They went out for celebratory beers and the rest was history. He loved the guy like the brother he'd never had, and it looked like they were about to have a rare brotherly disagreement. "Not even that time we challenged those bikers to a game of pool and I called one of them Nancy?"

"Cut the act, Vaughn. You can't play this one off with a joke."

"I'm not playing anything off with a joke. Don't insult me like I don't fully grasp the stakes in this investigation."

"If you're so clear on the stakes, then why aren't you recusing yourself?"

Vaughn propped a boot on the edge of the door opening, scowling. "It would be impossible for me to convey how deeply I regret confiding in you about my history with Rachel, because now you won't let it go."

"You need to make things right with her, and this is not the way to go about it."

Vaughn scrubbed a hand over his chin. "Don't start with me, K. I've already told you, there's no way to make things right with her. We're over. Done. There's nothing keeping me from doing my job with this case. And that job is sticking it to the Meyer family like no one else has had the balls to do."

"I admit that your vendetta against Wallace Meyer is justified, but it's still not worth giving up on Rachel."

"Oh, my God, you're dense. There's nothing to give up on. Back in December, when Amy and Rachel's mom was dying, I let you talk me into *being there* for Rachel. I stood in that hospital hallway with you for hours, waiting to be there for her. When she came out of her mom's room and saw me, do you remember what she said? She said, 'Go away, Vaughn.'" It still made his insides reel to remember the way she'd looked while saying that to him. Like he was nothing but dirt on her shoes. "Giving it any more of a try would be pathetic."

"Fighting for the person you love is never pathetic."

"Who ever said I loved her?"

Kellan let out an incredulous snicker. "Please. It's written all over your face every time her name comes up."

"There's a huge difference between lusting after a woman and being in love with her."

"Trust me, I know."

The sun was broiling Vaughn where he stood. The shade from the brim of his hat wasn't doing him a lick of good. He unbuttoned his cuffs. "I am not in love with Rachel Sorentino, and I don't need you to help me get in touch with my feelings or some pansy crap like that." He rolled the sleeves to his elbows. "A year ago, you would've never butted into my personal life like this. Now that you're getting married, you think you're some kind of relationship god."

"Look, I don't pretend to understand what you and Rachel see in each other, but I do know that you should not be working her case. Let your deputies take care of it." He pointed toward the hospital. "Go back up to her room. Sit by her side and take care of her like I know you want to."

"I'm going to build a case against the men who shot her and make them pay for what they did. That's how I'm going to take care of her."

"Like I said, you've done some stupid things, but this takes the cake."

Vaughn shook his head. "That's really nice of you. Thanks for being such a great friend, asshole."

Grinning, Kellan clapped him on the back. "Think of how much easier it'll be for you both at my wedding if you two work things out, with you both being in the wedding party."

Man alive. He hadn't thought that far ahead. He bent forward and rested his forehead on the top of his car, cursing under his breath. How was he supposed to be in the same room with Rachel that long? It was liable to kill him. And that wasn't even taking into account the inevitable rehearsal dinner and other wedding-related festivities. He cursed again, louder.

"Yeah, you're over her, all right. Any fool could see that," Kellan said. "I'd better get going. Amy and Jenna are waiting in my truck for me to take them home."

After Kellan left, Vaughn glanced at the hospital's third-floor windows. Rachel was behind one of them. He was doing the right thing, staying on the case. Their relationship had been poisoned from the get-go, and nothing he could do or say could fix it. He tossed his hat on the passenger seat and slid behind the wheel.

He fired up his laptop and scrolled through the photographs backward, beginning with the last one Rachel took. In it, four men were in motion, either walking or running away from a rusty red pick-up truck. Each one's expression of malice had been permanently captured by the camera. He made notes of his observations and jotted questions the picture brought to mind on the pad of paper he kept on the passenger seat.

Twenty photographs and three pages of notes later, he hit the SCROLL button and a stunning image of a mesa at either sunrise or sunset filled the scene. The image awed him, soothing his stress from the day. To get the shot, she must've stood at the base of the mesa and photographed upward, capturing only the silhouette of its steep edge, which extended like a dancer's leg toward the ground. Half of a crimson sun crested above what would've been the dancer's upper thigh.

Vaughn stared for a long time, his breath gradually slowing, his peripheral vision fading. He felt himself drifting into the world of the image, just as the crimson sun lost itself in the swell of the ridge. The photograph was sensual, worshipful of nature's beauty. Perfection.

Man, she was a gifted artist. He knew she enjoyed

photography as a hobby, but he'd had no idea what that actually meant, having never seen her pictures before.

One click brought forth the next photograph. This one was of a coyote and its two babies, peeking their heads out of a darkened den carved into the red earth. He couldn't help but smile at the hope the image evoked. With each click, a new wonder was revealed to him. Images both small and expansive, every one of them taken on Sorentino land, he guessed. But the real treasure wasn't the discovery of the land's beauty, but the glimpse it afforded him into Rachel—the self she'd never revealed to him. The side of her he'd regret forever not getting to know when he'd had the chance so many months ago.

Suppressing the longing and frustration that realization brought with it, he clicked again. When the picture loaded, he let loose a volley of curses. He was looking at himself.

In the image, he was standing in front of Rachel's house, leaning against his off-duty truck, looking at something or someone off-camera and smiling as though he'd heard a joke.

He'd only been on her property a couple times in the last year, the most recent being when he'd stopped by to have a word with Kellan about the annual start-up of their fantasy baseball league. Kellan spent a lot of time at the Sorentino property since he and Amy had gotten together, and every now and then, Vaughn had no choice but to bite the bullet and venture into Rachel's territory.

Each time he made the turn onto their dirt road, he felt strung as tight as a wire, wondering if he'd catch a glimpse of her as she moved about her day's work. He never had, but every time, he wondered if she didn't see him coming and made herself scarce. Guess that wasn't always the case. At least this once, she'd been watching him.

The idea thrilled him. He shouldn't have allowed it to, but it did nevertheless. Eagerly, he clicked to the next photograph, but she was back to nature images. He did a rapid search of the rest of the pictures, but that single shot of him was the only non-nature shot in the entire fifty-image set before the pictures of the vandals.

He toggled back to it. It wasn't artistically rendered in the least. Almost out of focus and off-centered, like she'd snapped it in haste. He wondered if she ever looked at it, and if she did, what she saw in the picture—and in him. Wasn't like he'd ever done right by her to deserve the attention.

He'd never be able to fix the mistakes he'd made with Rachel, but now he had the opportunity to step up. It wasn't as much as she deserved, but he'd do everything in his power to keep her safe from Meyer and his network of bullies. He'd protect her the only way he could—with his badge.

He closed the folder of her camera images and opened Binderman's crime scene photographs. The graffitied boulder was the first picture. He studied it, but couldn't get his mind off the photo Rachel had taken of him. All of a sudden, his stomach dropped as the awful possibility occurred to him that Binderman and who-knows-how-many of his deputies had seen the photograph too. Maybe they hadn't taken the time to flip through her nature images, but then again, maybe they had.

Fingers unsteady, he pulled the picture up again and considered deleting it. He didn't want anyone to know about him and Rachel. He didn't want to explain why he was working a possible assault case involving his former lover. He moved the pointer over the image. If he erased this copy, then he'd have to delete it from her camera too, along with the copy on Binderman's laptop.

What a mess that would turn into, especially if he got caught. In fact, what the hell was he thinking? The truth floored him. He'd considered—seriously, honestly considered—tampering with evidence. What was wrong with him?

The *peal* of his cell phone ringing made him jump. With his heart racing and perspiration blooming on his forehead, he slammed the laptop closed and fished the phone out of his pocket. It was Stratis.

"Cooper here. What's happening?"

"Wallace Jr. is being moved to a suite on the second floor. His parents are demanding access, along with their lawyer."

"I'm on my way. Who's the lawyer? Anyone we know?" He unplugged the laptop to bring with him. He wanted to watch the look on Junior's face when he saw the photograph of him and his friends toting AR-15 rifles.

"Billy Tsai."

Didn't surprise Vaughn that Meyer had sprung for one of the premier defense attorneys in the state. Vaughn had given expert testimony in court against several of Tsai's clients over the years. The man was a shark in the courtroom, but Angela Spencer, the Quay County district attorney, was no minnow either. She could more than hold her own against Tsai and the Meyers.

Vaughn dropped his hat on his head, locked the car, and strode through the parking lot. "Go ahead and let the Meyers see their son, as long as you're in the room too. Maybe Junior will blab to his parents before Tsai has a chance to convince him he's better off staying quiet."

He'd press Junior for information until either Tsai or Wallace Sr. shut the conversation down, then he'd stand first watch on Junior's twenty-four-hour guard until

Kirby or Molina were available to relieve him. After that, he'd take on the job of guarding Rachel's door. Unadvisable, considering he'd probably spend the whole night torturing himself by watching her sleep. He wished he were stronger than to do that, but he knew, unequivocally, he was not.

It seemed that the harder he fought against her hold on him, the worse her grip around his heart got. Striding through the parking lot, then the lobby, he thought again about the secret picture she'd taken of him, and couldn't help but wonder if that feeling was mutual.

Chapter Four

Rachel's assessment of her suite being like a jail cell didn't change the next day. That is, it didn't change until she'd waited hours for the nurses to organize her paperwork and find a doctor to sign off on her release papers. By then, she'd concluded it would've been easier to get released from prison than checked out of a hospital.

Adding to her anxiousness to get home was her commitment to avoiding any more surprise run-ins with Vaughn. He'd made a brief, awkward appearance in the doorway that morning while a nurse was removing her IV. His eyes were tired, his expression gravely serious, and his uniform wrinkled, giving the impression he'd never made it home to change or sleep the night before. Even still, the mere sight of him sent her insides haywire. Then she'd jumped at the sting of pain as the nurse pulled the needle free of her arm, and her hospital gown slipped off her shoulder. She'd scrambled to cover herself, and when she'd looked up again, he was gone.

Amy drove her home and prattled the whole hour drive. Rachel was happy to let her talk, especially since she didn't seem overly concerned with whether Rachel was paying the least bit of attention to what she said, which gave Rachel plenty of opportunity to let her mind wander.

It was past lunchtime when Amy made the turn off the highway and under the wooden HERITAGE FARM INN sign that marked the road to their sprawling ranch house. A smaller sign on a fence post declared: INN CLOSED JUNE THROUGH AUGUST. LOCAL DISH RESTAURANT OPEN YEAR-ROUND. FRIDAY AND SATURDAY FOR DINNER, SUNDAY FOR BRUNCH.

Rachel rolled the window down and angled her face into the wind, inhaling her favorite scent in the world— her land. She could close her eyes and know the month by the way the alfalfa smelled, raw in its newness or crisp and ready for harvest, or by the bloom of cholla bushes. Even dirt smelled different in winter than summer, the scorched earth of August turning pungent with moisture by November as rain- and snowstorms swept through the high desert.

When Amy's conversation topic came around to the farm's safety, Rachel sat up a little straighter and tuned in.

"I've got to admit, I was worried about something bad happening last night, but it was quiet," Amy said. "Nothing out of the ordinary. Deputy Binderman stopped by this morning at first light to check on us, but he'd come and gone before the guests woke, so we didn't have to worry about explaining the presence of a squad car in the driveway."

"Good. I'm glad he checked on you. Remind me again what the guests' names are before we get home."

"The Westenbergs are Gary and Barbara, with their kids, April and Billy."

"Are those the teenagers?"

"No. You're thinking of the Moores. Howard and Elsie are the parents. Christina and Robbie are the teens."

Rachel grimaced, sorry she'd asked. She didn't mind sharing her home with the inn's guests as much as she'd thought she would. She wasn't inside all that often to begin with, and whenever she needed space, there was plenty of open pasture outside her door.

But with so many folks coming and going, she was hard-pressed to remember anyone's faces, much less their names. Amy gave her a daily briefing, but mostly, she got a free pass from being a hostess as long as she stuck to the role of resident cowgirl. She'd practically worked up a Texas drawl with all the howdys and y'alls she tossed around in front of the guests.

It was just her luck that when the travel magazine sent a journalist to review Heritage Farm in February, she highlighted Rachel as one of the main spectacles, or as the journalist called her, "A real live cowgirl who looked plucked from the history books of the Wild West." Rachel didn't think cowgirls plucked out of history would be carrying cell phones and GPS navigators on their belts, but there was no arguing with the uptick in business the farm received once the article came out. Never in a million years would she have guessed the financial future of her ranch hinged in part on her abilities as an actress. Such was life.

At least she'd get an acting break when the inn closed for the summer months.

"We've kept a real close eye on them," Amy said.

"Who?"

"The Westenbergs and Moores, silly. That pain medication you're on is making you loopy."

Rachel grunted. She didn't have the heart to tell Amy she wasn't on any pain meds, and her lack of focus was more because she talked so dang much that Rachel couldn't help but activate her mental mute button.

". . . and Kellan and I gave the workers a big speech

about not letting them wander off too far. Today they went on a tour of Chris and Lisa's dairy, then Mr. Dixon was taking them to Main Street for some shopping."

The inn had been Jenna's idea, the restaurant, Amy's. Their father's death a year and a half ago left the sisters with a pile of bills and no money to pay them with, so Jenna proposed the transformation of their home into a dude ranch as a way to save the property from foreclosure.

Rachel had vehemently opposed the idea. She'd argued that she needed solitude—her mental health downright required it—and having their home crawling with tourists sounded like hell on earth. More importantly, if the sisters got busy creating a new business, Rachel had argued, who would keep an eye on Mom?

What a bitter piece of irony that question turned out to be.

"What are you thinking about?" Amy asked, cutting into Rachel's thoughts.

She blinked, looking around. She hadn't noticed the car had stopped in front of their house. "Nothin'. Why?"

"You were staring at the porch, scowling. Don't tell me you're thinking of remodeling it. I know it could use a fresh coat of paint, but we've got enough going on with the wedding in less than three months."

She took the out Amy provided. "Needs more than a coat of paint. The wood's rotting through on some of those rails. You say it doesn't matter for the wedding, but half the Catcher Creek population is going to be here. For most of them, it'll be the first time they see our inn. I'll feel better if the place is up to snuff."

Amy waggled a finger. "No home improvement projects until your arm heals, got it?"

"Hmph."

"Promise me you'll take it easy for a few days. I want to hear you say the words."

Rachel unbuckled her seat belt with her left arm to prove the pain was no match for her iron will, but she could barely stifle a moan as a cloud of pain thundered along her shoulder and down her spine. "All right. I promise." She rubbed the pain from her arm. "Since when are you so bossy?"

"Since the resident bossy-pants got shot yesterday."

"I'm not that bossy."

Amy stepped out of the car with a *tsk* of protest and preceded Rachel to the front door.

Sloane Delgado and Tommy met them on the porch. Tommy, Jenna's five-year-old son, looked nervous. He held tight to Sloane's hand, his eyes as huge as coffee cups. Given the way Jenna and Amy had blubbered over her yesterday, Tommy probably thought her arm had fallen off or she was dying.

"Hey, Tommy," she said with her best smile.

"Are you okay, Auntie?"

She knelt and took his hands. "Never better, buddy. I got a scratch on my arm is all. The doctors put a Band-Aid on it." She held her bandaged arm up as evidence. "See? It's nothing. Doesn't even hurt anymore." He was a smart kid, so he probably didn't buy her flippant explanation, but he did relax at her words.

Sloane ruffled Tommy's hair. "We thought we'd say hello, but we've got to get back to the kitchen. We're making cookies as a welcome home present to you."

Tommy beamed.

"That sounds great. Thank you," Rachel said.

Sloane had come to work as a waitress at the inn's restaurant, but had morphed into an indispensable member of the family. She'd moved in a few months back to escape her meddlesome grandmother's house, and paid her rent by sitting for Tommy. The week before, she accepted the promotion Rachel and Amy offered her to become the overnight manager of their inn for the fall tourist season, even though she had her heart set on moving to New York City someday as a fashion designer.

Rachel knew diddly-squat about fashion, which was probably why Sloane's wardrobe looked to her like she'd hijacked the luggage of a circus clown. Today she was done up in a neon green blouse with a neon orange flower the size of a melon tacked in the center of her chest. Rachel half expected water to squirt from the center of it.

"I got to sleep over with Uncle Kellan last night," Tommy said, his chest puffed up with pride. "We set up sleeping bags in the kitchen, like we were camping."

"Wow," Rachel said. "Why the kitchen?"

He raised his arms, palms up, and looked at her like she was bonkers not to understand. "So we wouldn't bother the guests, of course."

"I bet you two had fun." Kellan was Tommy's absolute favorite grown-up in the world. Rachel wrote it off as a father figure issue, being that Kellan was the only daddy-age male in the little boy's life. Regardless of the reason, though, Rachel was grateful that Kellan lived up to Tommy's lofty expectations of him. Sounds like last night he'd surpassed them.

"Come on, Tommy. We'd better finish those cookies," Sloane said. "Otherwise they won't be much of a welcome home gift to Auntie."

Rachel watched them disappear into the house.

"In you go, Rach," Amy said. "You lie down and I'll bring you lunch."

"Think I'm going to stay out here for a little while."

"Nice try. Now get your butt in the house." Amy pointed through the open doorway.

Rachel backed up a step. "I've been cooped up in a hospital room. I don't think I can stand to go inside another set of walls quite yet."

To her relief, Amy didn't argue. Instead, she gave Rachel the stink eye. "All right, but don't do anything I wouldn't approve of."

Rachel grinned. "Isn't that what I always said to you? Never worked because you made it your life's mission to win my disapproval."

Amy grew taller, her expression one of mock indignity. "Not lately, I hope."

"Nah. You're right. Not since you moved home. I've been real proud of the choices you've made."

Amy winked. "Aw, thanks, Momma Two."

Rachel groaned. "Good grief. It's been a while since you or Jenna called me that, thank goodness. I'll be in after I get my fill of fresh air."

With a nod, Amy disappeared inside and left Rachel to her own devices, which was exactly what she needed at the moment. Or most any time, for that matter.

A raised splinter of wood on the armrest of the porch swing caught her attention. She wandered over and picked at it restlessly. As always, the swing reminded her of Vaughn—painful, arousing thoughts of the first night they'd spent together. The kiss he'd given her while they rocked on the swing in the darkness. The caresses that followed, along with the silent agreement to take it further. Right there on the porch.

The only reason she hadn't lugged the swing into the desert and burned it to an unidentifiable lump of carbon was that it served as a reminder of the devastation that could arise from selfishness, and of the vow she made to never let it happen again. At the time, she'd thought, *What the hell, I deserve a little happiness.* But look where that lapse in judgment had gotten her. Look where it had gotten her mom.

She gave the swing a shove and watched it jerk and dance on its chains. To escape the darkness of her thoughts, she wandered down the stairs and around the side of the house. The sound of a forklift diverted her attention. She waved to Damon and Rudy, her newly hired ranch hands and unofficial tour guides to the inn's guests, as they worked in the feed hold across the corral from the stable. Rudy took a few steps in her direction like he might try to talk to her, so she quickened her step. Most ranch hands she knew were strong, silent cowboy types, but Rudy could flap his lips as fast as both of Rachel's sisters, which was saying something.

In an effort to be a kind boss, Rachel endured daily conversations with him, but she didn't have it in her today to stand and nod while he rattled on about his singular passion—the weather. And, sweet Jesus, the man knew a lot about the weather. Not only in northeastern New Mexico, but on a global scale.

Before she realized where she was headed, she stood before the closed stable door. She slipped inside.

It was cooler in the stable than outside. Ventilation fans and swamp coolers whirred and rattled on the ceiling. Five horse heads poked over the doors of their stalls, clamoring for her attention. They stamped and shook their heads. As soon as she made eye contact with Growly Bear, he backed up with a huff and turned a circle, stamping anxiously.

Rachel approached him, her heart sinking. He'd been Lincoln's best buddy and next-door stall neighbor for years. She stroked his neck. "I know, Growly."

He whined quietly and pushed his nose into her neck. She nuzzled his cheek as she continued her methodical strokes. "You don't have to tell me. I know he's gone." Her gaze went to the empty stall.

Grief was nothing new to Rachel. She'd lost both her parents in the past two years. But the pointless loss of an innocent animal before its time hit her in an all-new way. Suddenly, nothing was more important than saying a final good-bye to Lincoln. She'd been too heartsick to ask Vaughn what was to be done with his body, but she suspected it was handled like any other livestock—cremated by Quay County Animal Control.

Rachel had never heard of a rancher holding a funeral for a dead horse, and she certainly wasn't going to broadcast that she was doing it, but she and Growly Bear needed closure, and Lincoln deserved to be cried over.

"Okay, Growly. You and I are going riding."

Saddling Growly offered its own challenges. The saddle blanket, halter, and reins were as easy as breathing to affix on the horse, but the saddle took three tries to hoist onto its back. The effort strained the skin around her wound, but despite the pain, she was too obstinate to seek help.

Once Growly was ready, she tucked a baggie of Fig Newtons in the saddlebag, along with a sky-blue ribbon from the accessory drawer Jenna had created for her horse, Disco. The plan was to stop by the west end pasture and gather dried wildflowers for a bouquet. Corny, maybe, but no one else would know.

She'd lost her favorite hat when she fell from Lincoln the day before, so she grabbed her back-up—a worn, soft cream felt Stetson with a braided leather band. She led Growly out, pausing at the door to reach above it and touch the smooth steel of the horseshoe mounted there, a gift from Kate Parrish's father many years ago, that her father had nailed over the door with the promise it would bring her luck.

When she mounted Growly, a particularly sharp pain shot through her left arm. She ran her hand over the bandage and her fingers came back bloody. Dang it all, she'd probably ripped the scab open. Amy would strangle her tonight when she helped Rachel change the bandage and saw the damage. Oh, well. Nothing she could do to change that now.

She walked Growly out of the stable yard, her thoughts drifting to the day the horseshoe was given to her. The day she'd come to consider the most liberating day of her life.

She'd been ten years old.

Her memory began in the bakery section of John Justin's Grocery Store on Main Street during one of her mom's most intense bipolar meltdowns. Back then, Rachel had never heard of the word *bipolar,* though she lived in a house held hostage by the illness.

Rachel and her sisters' reactions to their mom's depression were as different as their personalities. Rachel's anxiety was paralyzing. She clearly remembered, during Mom's outbursts, not being able to breathe or make her legs work. Standing there—frozen, her eyes riveted to the scene—her body became a sponge, absorbing the pain of everyone around her, along with the fear. She took it all in and made it her own.

Amy, almost four years younger than Rachel, took Mom's episodes as a personal affront. Maybe because she looked the most like Mom, or maybe because she'd been born with her heart on her sleeve, but for reasons Rachel didn't understand—and probably Amy didn't either—she'd exacerbate the situation, picking fights, goading Mom on. Having her own parallel meltdown.

Jenna, nine years Rachel's junior, seemed oblivious, like she'd been born with skin too resilient for their volatile home life to penetrate. When Mom would start into an episode, she'd wander off to play. For the longest time, Rachel thought Jenna would be the one to emerge into adulthood undamaged. Then Jenna turned thirteen and she turned wild—partying, drinking, running off for days at a time until a deputy, Vaughn most always, dragged her home kicking and screaming.

Rachel couldn't remember what Mom's trigger had been the day of her meltdown at John Justin's, or if there even was one, but she remembered Mom throwing loaves of bread at the store's baker, shouting obscenities. Then six-year-old Amy started clearing loaves of bread off the shelves while screaming at the top of her lungs. Jenna, one at the time, popped Cheerios in her mouth from the stroller tray and watched.

In the midst of the anarchy, Rachel, paralyzed and fighting the churning pain of her tummy, felt her fear dissolve for the first time ever. The scene before her narrowed until it seemed as if she were watching it on a small television at the opposite end of a long hallway. Then her legs unfroze.

She took a step back. Then another. Exhilarated by her newfound freedom of movement, she turned her back on her mom and sisters. And she walked away. Stepping through the sliding glass doors of John Justin's into the quiet, sunlit street was a feeling that would stay with her forever.

It was her moment of liberation.

Their farm was too far away for her to walk home, so she'd gone to the feed store. The Parrish family who owned it had always been kind to Rachel when she'd shopped there with her dad. They passed her sweets and told her jokes. That day, she walked into the feed store, and Mr. Parrish believed her lie that her mom had driven off and forgotten her, probably because everybody in Catcher Creek knew what Bethany Sorentino was like. Mr. Parrish gave her a peppermint and a horse-shoe that had been laying on the counter, explaining that it would bring her luck. Then he drove her home, where, horseshoe in hand, she set off on foot over the fields and pastures until she was hopelessly lost.

Hours later, her father, on his horse, found her sitting against a boulder. He sat with her for a long time, and when she asked if she could start working the farm with him in the mornings and after school, he hugged her and told her, *Of course you can, Jelly Bean.*

She missed her dad so much. Not the part of him who gambled and schemed their bank accounts dry, but the man who'd taught her to be a farmer. The man who found her when she was lost. This was her second spring without him, and though the loss wasn't nearly as acute as it had been a year earlier, her grief remained, tempered only by the anger and embarrassment she felt at how blind she'd been to his faults.

A mile into the ride, when she sensed Growly had warmed up enough to handle some speed, she nudged his flanks. They took off over the landscape, both woman and horse needing the exertion of a long, hard run to ease the burden of their grief.

From his vantage point at the top of the mesa, Vaughn looked at the gash in the dirt running along the twenty-foot drop of the mesa's face. The path Wallace Meyer Jr. took on his way to the valley. Stratis was on the scene with him, and the two had worked all morning to reconstruct a timeline of events from the previous day.

They'd begun in the canyon and followed the path of footprints around the south side of the mesa, where the slope was gentle enough to drive a truck up or walk. The footprints turned to scuffs once they reached the top of the slope, the marks of someone scooting on their knees. The scuff marks ended next to the imprint of a truck tire where, it seemed, Rachel stood and fired at the men. On the ground, scattered near the footprints, were six .38 bullet casings.

Not a good find. Not at all.

Which was why Vaughn was standing on the edge of the mesa, watching a hawk circle in the distance while he overcame his urge to kick something.

His interview with Wallace Jr. yesterday had lasted hours and yielded nothing except a grudging admittance—a demonstration of cooperation, his lawyer proclaimed—of the identity of the fourth man at the scene, the suspect currently at large with Elias Baltierra. Shawn Henigin. Henigin had a history of petty thievery and drug charges from Tucumcari to Santa Fe, the most recent arrest being a year earlier for possession of a stolen car. The charge hadn't stuck, as the car owner had a sudden change of heart and decided he'd allowed Henigin to borrow it.

Kirby and Molina were equally unsuccessful tracking down Henigin and Baltierra. At the county line to the south, they found a truck matching the one in Rachel's photographs as far as they could tell. Hard to determine exactly, given that it'd been torched to a crumbling shell. Four AR-15 rifles, also torched, were discovered in the backseat. That accounted for all the rifles in Rachel's crime scene photographs, but it certainly didn't mean Vaughn was going to amend the statewide APB out on the two suspects identifying them as armed and dangerous.

The state's forensic lab towed the truck to their facility in Albuquerque to process it, but Vaughn didn't have any high hopes they'd find a single trace of evidence in the wreckage.

Neither was Vaughn holding his breath in anticipation of Henigin and Baltierra's capture. Too often in border states like New Mexico, suspects found a way to skip out of the country, perhaps with the aid of one of the many illegal immigrant smugglers who haunted border cities in both countries and knew all the tricks to sneaking across the border undetected.

Stratis sidled up next to him after a few minutes. Despite the shade created by the brim of his brown hat, he squinted as he took stock of the valley, his angular features set in a hard mask, his arms crossed over his chest.

Stratis was an indispensible member of Vaughn's department, and with only a couple years separating their ages, everything on paper said the two of them should've been fast friends. Both were Quay County natives who'd worked for various law-enforcement entities for a similar number of years, and both were known for their unwavering commitment to professionalism and taking a hard line stance against police corruption, which were two of the main reasons Vaughn had promoted him to under-sheriff after his election.

Hell, Stratis would've made a top-notch sheriff if he hadn't had such a strong aversion to public attention. But, for whatever reason, their personalities had never quite meshed. They worked well together, but couldn't seem to have a real conversation about anything other than a case. Not that Vaughn was looking for more friends—he had plenty—but it would've been nice to feel like he knew more about the man than his arrest record.

"The footprints that begin in the canyon and continue up the south side of the mesa match Rachel Sorentino's shoe size," Stratis said.

"I know."

Stratis shifted to look at him. "She reloaded. Twice. You know what that means."

Vaughn chewed the inside of his cheek. Once the flare of frustration subsided, he regarded Stratis full in the face. "Not my first case, okay? I'm well aware of what that means."

The two shells in the canyon and the six .38 rounds scattered near the footprints meant she'd taken the time to manually remove the casings from the revolver and reload the weapon. Even more damning was that when he'd arrived on scene and took the revolver from her hand, he found six more empty casings inside. She'd fired fourteen rounds total, and even if the first two she fired from the canyon were heat of the moment shots, the act of reloading—twice—spoke of a conscious choice. Premeditation all the way. Thank goodness she'd taken photographs of the four men and their rifles, lending just cause to her actions.

"She needs to come in for another interview. Today." Stratis paused, then added, "I think I should handle it."

Hell, no. "Binderman called from the hospital. She was released a couple hours ago. I'll pay her a visit this afternoon."

Stratis's lips smashed into a straight line. Narrowing his eyes, he looked over Vaughn's shoulder. "She can't be here."

Vaughn pivoted, following Stratis's glare, and saw Rachel racing across the valley on horseback.

Her ever-present ponytail whipped in the wind beneath a cowboy hat that seemed to be staying on her head out of pure stubbornness, despite her speed. Today, as she usually did, she drove her horse hard and fast, eating up the ground they traveled over, her body a fluid, graceful wonder.

The first time they'd met in this valley, on an afternoon

two weeks into their affair, she'd ridden horseback. Vaughn had leaned against the hood of his patrol car, rendered frozen by awe and arousal at the tough, quiet command with which she moved through nature, the give and take of power, as if the land and sky and horse existed only for her, and in turn, she lived only for them. Watching her, he'd thought at the time, *She yields that power to me.* The thought had ripped through him like an orgasm. He loved controlling her pleasure, peeling away her inhibitions along with her clothes, making her as wild as the land surrounding them.

She'd made him wild too. With her, he'd become something other, something extraordinary—a part of the earth, just as she was. In this untamed valley, he'd clutched the soil in his hands as he rose above her. He'd spent himself onto the ground beneath the shade tree. Lying beside her on a blanket, he'd watched the reflection of the clouds in her eyes, the sun on her cheeks. He'd breathed in the fragrance of dried grasses and snow melting into the red earth.

But mostly, there had been Rachel—naked, open, blooming for him. Only him.

The tingling in his throat kicked to life, as if he'd swallowed bugs and they were crawling back up his esophagus. He looked away from her. Now, with his undersheriff standing next to him, wasn't the time to get a hard-on over memories of a former lover. And this valley wasn't a place of refuge and discovery as it once had been. It was a crime scene, and, as a person involved in the crime, Rachel wasn't welcome there.

"Did you know she was coming?" Stratis's voice was flat, but Vaughn read disapproval in his words, even though there was no way Stratis would know Vaughn and Rachel's history. They'd been so careful.

Then he recalled the photograph on Rachel's camera.

Maybe Stratis did have the right idea after all. Maybe he should've agreed to let Stratis conduct her interview.

"Something you want to say to me, Wesley?"

He never called Stratis by his first name, and it hung in the air between them, loaded with warning. Stratis held his ground. He met Vaughn's *don't-fuck-with-me* stare with one of his own in a face-off that went on long enough that Vaughn knew, sooner or later, the two of them would come to blows over Rachel.

Then Stratis's eyelid twitched. "I'm going to head to the office to touch base with my source about stolen AR-15s." He glanced at Rachel.

Vaughn did the same. She was still a solid five minutes out. "You do that. I'll be along shortly."

He followed Stratis from the mesa to the patrol cars parked in the valley. While Stratis fired up his engine and got organized, Vaughn reached through the open passenger window of his own car. He groped in the glove compartment for the pack of cigarettes he kept on hand.

Stowing a pack in the car was a mind-over-matter trick he'd started his first day of quitting. There was a certain power in having the substance he was addicted to within reach and making the conscious choice every time he got behind the wheel not to succumb to temptation. Problem was, every now and then the pull of addiction was too strong to resist.

Leaning against the hood, he held the sealed pack and watched Stratis's car disappear in a cloud of dust, his mind locked on Rachel and cigarettes. His fingers grew slick with clammy sweat, sticking to the cellophane wrapper as he tried fruitlessly to remove it. A few puffs would provide so much relief. He'd snub it out after that, but then maybe he could face Rachel without ripping his throat out to stop the tickle.

She'd smell it on me. If I took a quick smoke, she'd smell it on my breath and in my hair and on my clothes. Then again, if she got that close, I'd have bigger problems to worry about.

A glance over the top of the car told him Rachel was close. He needed to intercept her before she crossed into the crime scene.

He shook the box, listened to the cigarettes moving inside. Halfway through a deep inhale of the faint tobacco scent, he froze. "What am I doing?"

Sniggering in self-disgust, he returned the pack to the glove compartment and walked away from the car. Any other day, he might have felt good, noble even, about rejecting the lure of nicotine. But it was impossible to feel strong with his other, more powerful addiction flying across the desert valley on horseback, headed straight at him like a force of nature.

He positioned himself at the edge of the crime scene, his legs apart, hands on hips, bracing for impact.

Chapter Five

Rachel and her mount stopped several yards away from Vaughn. He didn't recognize the horse, a lean, muscular palomino with a golden mane, but it looked as though it had enjoyed the run as much as its rider did.

Tendrils of long, brown hair had pulled loose from their binding to frame Rachel's flushed cheeks and neck. Her position in the saddle accentuated the curve of her hips and small waist. A large white bandage peeked out from under the hem of her short-sleeve T-shirt, but otherwise, she looked as strong as ever, her body giving no indication that she'd been laid up with a gunshot wound until a few hours ago.

"You're home from the hospital already."

Way to state the obvious, jackass. He'd always prided himself on knowing exactly how to play any given situation, but not around Rachel. Her presence stripped him of even that basic skill.

She shrugged the shoulder of her good arm. "I don't know about *already*. Felt like it took forever to get out of that place."

During their affair, he'd lost count of how many nights he'd awoken alone in bed only to find her on his back porch, watching the stars. *The house is too small,* she always told him with a self-deprecating smile. "That's because you hate being stuck indoors."

"True enough." Her horse huffed noisily, like it didn't want to be left out of the conversation. She rubbed its neck and eyed Vaughn cautiously. "For some reason, I didn't consider the idea that anyone would be out here today."

It bothered him, her response. Got him thinking about premeditation and guilt. He'd already been wondering what she hoped to accomplish by revisiting the crime scene, but why had she hoped to find it unattended? What had she planned to do? "It's a crime scene. My deputies and I are still processing evidence."

"Guess I didn't think it through too clearly when I set out."

"Why did you come here?" He tried to keep the question from sounding like an accusation, but he had to know.

She watched him with a guarded expression and swung off the saddle. Vaughn felt the agility and power in her movement like a bare-knuckle punch to his heart. It was all he could do not to stagger back, clutching his chest.

She clipped a lead rope to the horse and guided it toward the irrigation spigot left over from the bygone days when alfalfa fields filled the valley.

Vaughn walked alongside them. "You didn't answer my question."

"Unfinished business, okay?"

"No, it's not okay. This is a crime scene. You can't be here."

The horse sniffed him curiously as it waited for water to fill the plastic tub below the spigot. He held his hand out for the horse's inspection. After a few sniffs, he licked Vaughn between the fingers, then pushed his nose into Vaughn's palm.

"This one's a kisser," he said, stroking his nose.

"His name's Growly Bear."

Vaughn scratched beneath his ear, which earned him a lick on the cheek. "Doesn't seem growly to me."

She shut off the water and tied the lead rope to the spigot. "He's not his usual feisty self."

"Something wrong?"

"He was Lincoln's best buddy."

Vaughn's shoulders sagged. In all that had happened in the last twenty-four hours, he'd forgotten that Rachel would be grieving over the loss of her horse. "I'm sorry about Lincoln."

She avoided his gaze as she walked to her saddlebag. Tucked inside was a bundle of dried grass stalks and wildflowers tied around the middle with a blue ribbon. "I wasn't trying to do anything illegal, coming here. I didn't consider it from the crime scene angle. I came, we came"—she gestured to Growly Bear—"to put these out for Lincoln where he died."

Vaughn longed to reach for her, to help her through her grief. But that was exactly how the mess of their affair started in the first place after her father's death. "What happened with Lincoln, nobody should have to go through that. But I can't let you down there."

She nodded, her expression distant as she crushed at a dried flower between her fingertips. "Was his . . . body taken away?"

"Yesterday."

She crushed another flower. The bits fell over the ground like grains of salt. "I need to say good-bye to him."

And he wanted nothing more than to let her. He pressed a hand to his throat and stalked away, unable to look at the sorrow in her eyes for another second without touching her.

He heard her footsteps trailing him. "Vaughn, please . . ."

He stopped and let his gaze sweep over the valley— anywhere but at her. He felt her warmth standing behind him, heard her breath, and knew if he turned around, he was a goner. "We can't have you adding things to the crime scene, even flowers. I'm sorry, but you'll have to find another way to say good-bye until the investigation's over."

"No one's here but us, unless one of your deputies is hiding behind the mesa or something. You could let me go down there. I won't leave this, but I could use a moment of silence for him."

"No one else is here, but I still can't." He'd compromised his professional ethics too profoundly with Rachel the first time around, and the guilt had eaten away at him ever since. He knew better than to make the same mistake again. But knowing better meant nothing with Rachel standing so close. "I'm trying to build a case against the men who hurt you and Lincoln," he ground out.

"I know."

The same hawk as before circled in the distance, coasting effortlessly, as if its will alone kept it aloft. "I can't keep you safe if I have to remove myself from the case because of our relationship."

"What we have isn't a relationship. It's a series of mistakes."

He winced. Her words stung, even though he understood the dark place of anguish that brought them forth. As much as he'd never let go of the guilt for sleeping with a witness during a possible murder investigation, she'd never forgive herself that her mom attempted suicide while she was in Vaughn's bed. "You and I were not the mistake, Rachel. The timing was. If we'd waited until the case closed. If we'd—"

"How many years have we known each other?"

Easy question, even if he couldn't see where she was going with her line of thought. She'd been haunting his world since his first week as a sheriff deputy. "Twelve years."

"Exactly. Took us more than ten years to do anything about the interest we had in each other, and when we did, we chose the worst possible circumstance, almost as though, on some level, we'd chosen the timing on purpose. Why did we do that?"

Hell if he had any idea. "I don't know why we sabotaged it. I've been wondering the same thing."

"I think it was because we knew, instinctively, it would never work between us. The night my mom overdosed, that's when I opened my eyes and took a good look at myself. I despised what I saw."

The bitter hurt in her words propelled him around to face her. She stood within arm's reach, her jaw set resolutely, her eyes hard. She clutched the elbow of her injured arm.

"What did you see?" he asked, knowing he was going to hate the answer.

"I saw a woman who sacrificed her every core value for a screw."

He swabbed a hand over his mouth, furious at her for disparaging what they'd had together. "We were more than that."

"Then how come, every relapse we've had since, all we do is sleep together? We don't talk, we don't laugh." She released her elbow and spread her arms wide, as though she were going to shout. But her voice only grew quieter, until she hissed the words. "We don't have a single thing in common except compatibility in bed. And if there's one thing I've learned, it's that we can't screw each other into happiness. Life doesn't work that way."

Frustration roiled through him with gathering intensity. Fisting his hands at his side, he fought to keep the wild gestures that came with his Irish-Italian blood under control. "You're only remembering what's convenient. We talked a lot, and laughed too. We sat in my truck or on your porch and talked all night long. Don't you dare tell me our time together didn't mean anything to you but a screw."

Her lips twisted into a sardonic grin. "And yet, you regret it as much as I do. What does that tell you?"

With those words, Vaughn's anger deflated. All he wanted to do was hold her, to ease the suffering he'd brought into her life from the moment he'd taken advantage of her grief so many months ago. To ease his own tortured heart. One step forward and he'd be near enough to trace the edge of her jaw with his fingertip, or slide his thumb across her lower lip. "Rachel . . ."

She took a step away. "Don't."

"Don't what?"

"Don't say my name like that, like you do when we . . ." She looked at the sky, like the words she was grappling with might be written there. "Vaughn, I can't . . ."

She didn't have to finish the thought—he knew exactly what she was trying to say. He wrapped a hand around her wrist and pulled her against him. His hand trembling with barely harnessed need, he removed her hat and tossed it behind her.

Threading his fingers through her hair, he held on for dear life. "I can't, either," he said softly. *I can't be with you, but I can't stop thinking about you. Most of all, I can't figure out a way to make us work.*

She clutched a fistful of his shirt. "We shouldn't be here alone."

"No," he said from behind clenched teeth. Because without the buffer of people around them, there was nothing stopping him from kissing her, or from taking her right there on the hard earth like he'd done more than once in the past. Desire, sudden and intense, knifed through his insides, so potent it made his bones ache.

"You've got to be stronger than me, Rachel. You've got to get out of here right now before anything happens." He heard the strain in his voice, and knew she could too.

Instead of walking away, she slid her hand up around his jaw. Her lips brushed the edge of his mouth. "I hate who I become around you. Weak. I'm so weak."

Weakness was something he knew all about. He worked a hand under her shirt, stroking the soft skin of her back. "I hate who I am around you too. You cloud my judgment, and I lose sight of everything I stand for. But I can't help it. . . ."

She pulled back and looked at him with eyes reflecting the same desperate longing that coursed through his veins. She trailed a finger along his temple. "I can't let you go."

There was nothing left to say. Dizzy with adrenaline, he wound her ponytail around his fist and dropped his lips onto hers, taking her mouth hard and deep like he knew she liked it. She surrendered to him, her hand gripping his shoulders, her breasts pushing against his chest.

The world apart from them disappeared, and all that was left in Vaughn's universe was Rachel's mouth, and her lean, lithe body pressing against him, and the way she made him feel.

He could have kissed her forever, but she tore her mouth from his and rested her forehead on his chest. Vaughn released her hair and wrapped his arms around her waist in an unmovable grip. He tipped his face toward the heavens, his eyes closed, praying for the strength not to beg her for more.

Of the two of them, Rachel was always the first to pull away, the first to remember the guilt and regret. The first to point out that their relationship would never amount to anything but a torrid affair. She was right, of course, but it damn near killed him every time she pushed away from his touch before he was ready to let her go.

She stroked the hair at the nape of his neck, which got him wondering how something as screwed-up as their relationship could feel so good. And, when she spoke, her voice was thick with agony. "Sometimes I think it would be easier if we were together. That maybe I could finally find peace. But you don't bring me any peace."

He pressed his lips to the top of her head. "There's too much past between us, too much damage done for it to work. And now, it's pointless to think about, because I don't trust anyone to look out for your interests the way I can in this case. Wallace Meyer wants your head on a platter. I won't let that happen, no matter what."

"We can't ever allow ourselves to be alone together again."

"No."

She pressed her palms against his chest until he released his hold on her. "I should go."

"Yeah." After adjusting his tie, he stuffed his hands in his pockets, trying to get his body and mind to work together again. "I'm going to need those photographs of the other graffiti incidents before too long, and we have a few more questions for you. I'll send a deputy to your place tonight to pick you up and bring you to the station house."

She scooped her hat from the ground and adjusted it

on her head, then walked toward her horse. "No need for that. I'll drop by your office this afternoon."

Vaughn kept pace behind her. "I won't be returning to the station house until at least five o'clock. Maybe it would be best if you came by before I got there."

She unwound the lead rope. "Why?"

"You took a picture of me."

That stopped her cold. "What?"

"On your camera. There was a picture of me."

She wrenched her head down and away, her lips pulled tight.

Shit. He hated for her to feel awkward, but couldn't see a way around it. "I'm only bringing it up because my deputies saw it. I'm afraid they're going to start to wonder what they don't know about you and me. I don't want to give them any more clues."

She blinked as though deep in thought, then gave a resolute nod. "I can't explain why I took that shot. I'm sorry if it embarrassed you in front of your employees. From now on, you have to do your job by the book, what-ever that means. Pretend I'm someone else if you have to. You're facing reelection this year and you can't risk your career because of this crazy, uncontrollable thing between us that won't go away. It's not worth it."

He stood back as she lifted into the saddle. He didn't have the heart to tell her there was no easy way to salvage his career in Quay County from the mess she and Wallace Jr. had created. All he could do was to keep Rachel safe from Meyer's reach and bring a reckoning down on Wallace Meyer for his sins.

Before she could race away, he took hold of the reins. "Rachel, I need you to understand that despite every-thing, being with you was worth it for me. There's a lot I regret about my past, but nothing more so than ruining my chance to prove that to you."

"You don't have anything to prove to me, Vaughn. Never did. It's better this way, for both of us." With a nudge to Growly Bear's flank, she lit off across the valley.

A pang of longing hit him. He wanted to ride with her. He wanted to change out of uniform, saddle a horse, and for a few hours forget about Wallace Meyer and reelection worries and all the reasons he and Rachel couldn't be happy together.

He watched the swish of her ponytail against her straight, proud spine, and knew—as certain as the passing of time—that even if he lived to be a hundred, he'd never feel more alive than in the stolen moments he'd spent with Rachel in his arms.

Rachel raced home, exhausted and defeated from the confrontation with Vaughn, cutting through the barren wasteland of weedy fields that had once been the dream she'd had for her life—still did, despite the shame she carried for being incapable of salvaging their alfalfa business from the mess her father had made of it.

Dollar signs in his eyes, he'd gambled away every penny of his savings and leveraged the value of the ranch to the limit on one get-rich scheme after another, allowing one field after another to go to weeds while Rachel had watched helplessly as her future went down the toilet. She knew he loved his family, but he'd never given her a straight answer any of the dozens of times she'd confronted him about why he'd done that to them.

To her.

Why he'd taught Rachel how to be a top-notch alfalfa farmer, and got her believing it was her future—the legacy she'd leave to her children and nieces and nephews—only to let it all go to waste. It was one of the many things she wanted to ask him, but she knew if he came down from the heavens today to stroll with her in the fields, she wouldn't dare waste time confronting him about his mistakes. Love didn't work that way, especially with those who'd passed on.

The discovery of oil under their southwest fields a few months back, when she and her sisters were on the verge of losing their property to foreclosure, provided her with the means to rebuild. Just about every property in Quay County had at least a couple derricks. Hell, royalties earned from oil leases was the only way most folks made ends meet on their ranches and farms, but, for decades, Rachel's family had thought their property was dry—a Catcher Creek anomaly—but it turned out the existence of the oil was one more truth her father had tried to take to his grave. The four derricks had been erected in January and were the new heart of the ranch, pumping petroleum that was the lifeblood for the farm.

Jenna and Amy took the oil discovery as a sign from above. Rachel reserved judgment about that, but she did seize on it as the opportunity it was for her to rebuild her dream one field at a time, as soon as they'd finished paying off the last of Dad's debts. They were so close to settling the last of the bills that she could almost smell the fresh alfalfa scent she grew up loving.

Inside the stable, she groomed Growly and tried her best not to look at Lincoln's empty stall. An inspection of his hooves revealed that one of his shoes had come loose, so she pried it the rest of the way off and fitted him with a soft boot to keep his weight balanced. Chuck, their farrier, usually came around on Fridays, and he'd reshoe Growly then.

Once she'd settled Growly in she was fresh out of excuses to postpone going indoors. The sooner she went inside, the sooner she could get on with her interview at the sheriff's department. If all went well, she'd be home in time to supervise the evening chores. She might even photograph the rising moon behind Sidewinder Mesa.

With a sigh of resignation, she washed her hands and headed out. She paused on the threshold and reached her uninjured arm above the door frame, running her fingers over her lucky horseshoe. The smooth iron fortified her, reminded her of what was important in her life—her sisters and nephew, the land that'd been in her family for sixty years.

The lesson she learned that fateful day she walked out of John Justin's wasn't one of self-preservation. It wasn't about the feeling of freedom from turning her back on her mom and sisters. The liberation she gained was the bond she'd forged with her dad, and her discovery of her true path in life as a farmer, as the keeper of her family's home and history. She learned that she could be the spine of the Sorentino clan without the paralyzing anxiety of standing in the thick of their drama. She could provide without the constant wounding to her spirit.

She pressed the pad of her finger into a nail hole of the horseshoe, fortifying her resolve. She had a way of life to salvage, along with a family to support—responsibilities that superseded her selfish desire to run from her problems or to seek comfort in a man's arms. She knew with unflagging certainty with whom her loyalties lay and what her core values were. The first and only time she had lost sight of those fundamentals had been catastrophic. Never again would she so egregiously disregard her responsibilities—no matter how tempting the vice.

No matter how heavily that choice weighed on her heart.

Stepping from the stable, she popped an antacid and watched Jenna direct one of the two families staying at the inn into corny poses for a picture with Tulip, Amy's flower-adorned pet cow. Dang. She nearly gagged, thinking the words. Who in their right mind domesticated a heifer? Only Amy would come up with such a ridiculous idea.

Of course, the farm's guests ate it up. Jenna had posted Tulip's photos on the Heritage Farm Web site, and she and Amy had changed the farm's logo to include the cow's silhouette.

Most of the time, Rachel was fine with this new path their family home had taken, but it felt like a scam, advertising their farm as a place for families to get a taste of authentic farm life when each day's guest activities included playing dress-up with the livestock, sleeping in until ten, and lazing around all day.

"There you are," Jenna said as soon as she saw Rachel. "Billy and April, this is our farm's number one cowgirl, my sister Rachel."

Oh, joy. Time for the cowgirl act. She tipped the brim of her hat at them and kept moving toward the house, hoping to avoid getting sucked in to a conversation.

"Wow," said a boy who looked a year or so older than Tommy. "You're a real cowgirl."

No dice. She stopped walking and turned around, smiling like she meant it. Wasn't the kid's fault she was having a rough week. "Sure am. And you look like a cowboy with that bandana and those shiny red boots."

He puffed out his chest. "I am."

Jenna crowded close to her and whispered, "You should be resting."

Rachel shrugged. "Yeah, so?"

Jenna rolled her eyes. "So, Amy had Kellan running all over the place in his truck looking for you."

"He didn't need to do that. It's not like I'm in danger of getting lost on my own ranch." Jenna got that mothering look in her eye, like she was winding up for a lecture. Time for a topic change. She gestured to catch the visiting kids' attention. "Did Jenna here tell y'all about Tulip's favorite treat?"

The two children vigorously shook their heads. "What's her favorite treat?" asked the youngest, a little blond girl of maybe three or four.

Rachel knelt next to the girl. "What do you think it is?"

"Cookies? That's my favorite."

Rachel nodded. "Good guess. Tulip doesn't have much of a sweet tooth, but she loves carrots. Jenna, why don't you help these cowpokes feed Tulip some carrots?"

Judging by the raise of Jenna's eyebrows, she knew she was getting played. Rachel smiled sweetly and inched away from the scene.

Pushing through the kitchen door, she was greeted by the aroma of baking sweets.

Amy's head shot up. She slammed her knife onto the cutting board. "Do you have any idea how worried I've been?"

Rachel surveyed the telltale mound of diced celery on the counter, Amy's favorite form of stress relief. "Yep. Pretty good idea. Sorry about that."

"Where have you been?"

She sat on the bench near the door and took off her boots. "I tried to leave flowers where Lincoln died."

That stopped her "Oh. You tried? Does that mean you didn't?"

Rachel buzzed by the table, where two trays of scones sat cooling, and snagged one. "Couldn't. It's a crime scene. The sheriff turned me away."

"It's just as well. You shouldn't have been out riding in the first place."

She bit into the scone. "I told you, I needed fresh air."

Amy dumped the celery in a bowl with a bit more zeal than necessary. "We've got fresh air right outside this door. There's no need for you to saddle a horse and go riding over the countryside to find it."

Quarreling was her and Amy's natural state of communication, but Rachel didn't have it in her at the moment. She edged toward the door to the dining room. "I promised the sheriff I'd bring in some photos of the ranch, so I'd better get on that so I can get to the evening chores."

"Rachel, you were shot. You need to rest. Let us handle the workload today. Kellan can take the photographs to Vaughn."

Tempting. Then there'd be no chance of her running into him inadvertently, no inquisitive looks by Vaughn's deputies or rumors to dance around. Problem was, she couldn't take a chance of her sisters or Kellan discovering the content of the photographs. She hadn't managed to keep the vandalism under wraps for four months only for them to find out by a careless slip-up on her part. "Nah, I'll take care of it. I think he's got more questions for me. Anyhow, I rested enough in the hospital. You know I don't have the temperament to sit around twiddling my thumbs."

Amy clucked in protest, but didn't press the issue, thank goodness. "Stop by the kitchen on your way out. I'll send scones with you for Vaughn. Cinnamon raisin is his favorite."

Rachel stopped midstride with her hand pushing on the kitchen's swinging door. "It is?"

"'Bout the closest thing to a fruit or vegetable he'll eat, in fact. Makes him impossible to cook for."

Rachel chewed the inside of her cheek as a pulse of ridiculous, misplaced jealousy rippled through her. This was her sister, not some romantic rival. Still, it hurt to think Amy knew something about Vaughn that she didn't. Hard not to wonder what else she didn't know—

what she'd never know since she'd never let herself get that close to him again.

"Are you feeling okay, Rachel? You look pale. Maybe you should sit down."

"I'm fine." She flashed Amy a smile to prove it. "When have you ever cooked for the sheriff? At Kellan's house?"

Amy leaned her butt against the sink, her brow creased with concern as she looked Rachel up and down. "Yes. Every Sunday he and Vaughn and the Bindermans get together to barbecue and watch sports on TV. I thought you knew that. And by the way, I'm sure he wouldn't mind you calling him Vaughn. He's practically family, as close as he and Kellan are."

If Amy only knew. She kept the reassuring smile on her face and shrugged the shoulder of her good arm. "Guess his title stuck in my head from all those years he hauled Jenna home in his cruiser after she'd been out whooping it up. Hard to think of him as family." Which was God's honest truth, even if it was technically a lie of omission.

"Oh, that reminds me! With everything that's happened, I didn't tell you we're moving the barbecue here this Sunday so I can try a new barbecue ribs recipe I'm experimenting with for the restaurant. Kellan and I debated about canceling it, with what happened to you, but we both agreed that in times like this, it's even more important to surround ourselves with family and friends. To celebrate all the things we're grateful for and show those trespassers that nothing slows the Sorentinos and Reeds down."

Vaughn. In her house—for an entire afternoon. The room started spinning. Rachel braced her other hand on the doorframe, squeezing the wood so hard it made her wound throb with renewed fury. "The inn's guests leave Friday morning, so I figured it was a good time to host.

Matt Roenick, Jenna, and Tommy will be here too. It'll be fun."

She heard Amy's footsteps approaching, but she couldn't make her body work.

Amy slipped an arm around her waist. "You're not okay. I'm taking you to the sofa."

She twisted out of Amy's grip and started toward the stairs. "I'm fine. Never better. I'll stop by the kitchen for the scones before I leave."

The stairs left her winded, her muscles achy. Closing the door to her room, she spied the double bed in the corner and exhaustion, sudden and swift, made her whole body feel heavy. Maybe a short rest was in order after all so she'd be at the top of her game when she delivered the flash drive to Vaughn's office.

She dropped her jeans and shirt to the floor, pulled the band from her hair, and crawled into bed in her underwear. Her room's window faced the afternoon sun. It speared through the cracks of the blinds, glowing yellow. She studied the pattern of light until the warm quiet dragged her into slumber.

Chapter Six

Vaughn's younger sister Gwen was a riot. A brazen loudmouth with a wisecracking sense of humor like the rest of their mother's side of the family, the Italian side.

Of the three Cooper kids, Gwen had received the highest concentration of Finocchiaro blood, complete with olive skin, curly black hair, and a fiery temper. Vaughn and his youngest sister, Stephanie, shared the black hair, skin tone, and loud mouths, but they'd missed out on the temper, thank goodness.

The way he and Stephanie figured it, the temper trait must be a hit-or-miss phenomenon because Mom was as mild-mannered an Italian as ever existed, while Vaughn's nonna was as much of a surly spitfire as one might expect from a four-foot-nothing grandma who, as a child, had immigrated from the Mediterranean climate of Sicily to the Texas desert. Then again, by some relatives' account, her temper hadn't truly triggered until her only daughter married Gregory Cooper, a local, poor-as-dirt Irishman.

Nevertheless, Gwen's temper came with her out of the womb and hadn't simmered down yet. When she got herself wound up real good, she even got to looking like

Nonna—her face red and scrunched, her gestures wild, and her long, curly hair tossing around like a black-leaf tree in a hurricane. Once, when she was a teenager, he told her as much, which nearly made her head explode from the pressure of her indignation. She'd given Vaughn the silent treatment for weeks.

No one knew who Gwen inherited her kleptomania from. It was the one Finocchiaro-Cooper family anomaly. First time she was ever caught stealing in public, at least in Vaughn's memory, she was four years old to Vaughn's ten. After a morning spent in the family's blacksmith shop on the campus of Tucumcari's farrier college, Gwen had come home with a pocket of horseshoe nails. During a lengthy interrogation by Mom, Gwen led them to the room she shared with baby Stephanie. Under her mattress, she dug out dozens of stolen shoe nails.

Shoe nails evolved into trinkets lifted from their nonna's house and odds and ends from her school. Their parents' reaction was abject horror. Vaughn remembered eavesdropping on a lot of whispered, heated discussions about Gwen and her *issue* through the years. He'd sense the mood shift on the other side of his closed bedroom door and creep out to listen.

Stealing from friends and family became shoplifting when Gwen was a teenager. That's when therapy started. What a waste of money those quacks had been, because no matter how many hours she spent on a counselor's sofa, no matter what kind of antidepressants they pumped her with, her impulse to steal only grew more powerful.

Vaughn earned his police badge with the Albuquerque City Police Department when he was twenty-two. That year marked Gwen's first arrest, after she shoplifted a necklace from a Tucumcari jeweler. Wallace Meyer himself did the honor. Didn't matter to him that

Gwen's parents had tended his horses every week for years. He recommended the maximum sentence to the judge for a petty misdemeanor—ninety days in juvenile hall and a five-hundred-dollar fine.

Vaughn pulled his patrol car into the driveway of the house he grew up in, parking behind his dad's four-by-four Chevy. He knew by the collection of beat-down, piece of crap cars lining the street that Dad was holding class in his workshop. He'd retired from service as a farrier and now taught at the college full-time. When the mood struck him, he held class at his personal blacksmith shop in the house's original garage.

Vaughn stepped from the car and adjusted the brim of his hat. The aroma wafting out of the kitchen windows told him Mom was home too, and baking cookies. Good timing on his part.

When Vaughn and his sisters were growing up, Mom worked alongside Dad as a farrier. They'd met while his dad was going through farrier college in Texas, and his mom had taken to the profession like a termite to wood. Eager to establish their own business, they'd picked up and moved west, to Tucumcari. A year later, Vaughn was born.

Mom gave up her career when she decided her first-born daughter needed more rigorous supervision. Vaughn sometimes wondered if she ever missed her job. He liked to believe she regularly stole away to the blacksmith shop when no one was paying attention to craft trinkets out of forged steel for her church's craft sales the way some women knitted hats or painted. Working with metal had been her favorite part of the job. Her hands looked too soft and fragile to handle the hammers and heat anymore, but a guy could dream.

Rounding the corner of the walkway that cut between the house and the garage, he saw a half-dozen folks gathered around his dad. Most looked college age, with a couple middle-age guys thrown in.

Small-time ranchers, when they scaled back their businesses or passed the work on to their children, sometimes signed up for farrier school. Probably the first time in their working lives they had time to learn how to shoe a horse. For the most part, professional farriers were called upon for horseshoe maintenance around ranch country. It was a skill that took a lot of know-how to master, and it was easier and more cost-efficient for a rancher to hire a farrier than learn the trade himself.

Vaughn leaned against the wood siding of the house, watching. He never got tired of listening to his dad teach, like he'd taught Vaughn so many years ago.

Dad bent over an anvil, tongs in one hand and a rounding hammer in the other, giving a lesson on shaping a toe clip. "Make the first blow a hard one. That'll seat the shoe against the anvil."

He demonstrated with a whack of the hammer that made the two older men in the class flinch from the noise.

"Hey there," his dad said when he noticed him. "My son, Vaughn," he said to his class in that proud father way that made Vaughn feel eighteen again.

He gave a two-finger wave.

Dad held out the rounding hammer. "Want to show them how a sheriff does it?"

"Nah, I'm on the clock. Besides, I never was as good as you."

Dad beamed at that, his bushy salt-and-pepper mustache curving up at the ends. "Are you staying for dinner?"

Vaughn shook his head. "Need to have a word with Gwen, then get back to work."

Dad paused, midswing of the hammer. Guess he read

Vaughn's tone and phrasing correctly. *Having a word with Gwen* meant she was in trouble.

Straightening, Dad passed the tongs and hammer to the nearest student. "Go ahead and take a few practice swings."

Walking to Vaughn, he doffed his gloves and wiped his hands on his leather apron. "Everything okay?"

His code for *What did she do this time?* Up close like this, he looked old, with more gray hairs than brown, and his skin grizzled from too many years working near high heat and smoke.

"Nothing new."

Dad nodded and smoothed his mustache, his eyes radiating a weary sorrow. Damn, Vaughn hated to cause his parents more grief. They'd suffered enough because of Gwen's illness. Not much he could do about it now though. Not with Meyer ready to punish Vaughn by lashing out at his sister.

"Class is almost over," Dad said. "Stop by the workshop before you leave. I'm forging a new sole knife tonight and could use your input."

What he really wanted was the scoop on Gwen, and Vaughn respected him enough to give it to him straight. "Will do."

As Dad resumed his lesson, Vaughn opened the kitchen door, then took his hat in hand. Mom was at the sink washing dishes.

"Hey, Ma." He bussed her cheek with a kiss as his eyes trolled for the cookies he'd smelled from the driveway. They weren't cooling on a rack, and they weren't on the kitchen table. He checked the cookie jar. Empty.

She shooed him away with her drying towel. "Get on with you, now. They're still in the oven."

"Aw, you didn't even give me a chance to use my advanced detective skills," he said with a smile and wink. "Gwen around?"

She eyed him suspiciously, her face turning guarded. "In her room."

He squeezed her hand. "Everything's fine. I need to tell her some news I heard yesterday."

A frown tugged at her lips, but she nodded and returned to the sink. Vaughn walked down the hallway, twirling his hat on his finger, his eyes passing over innumerable framed family photos. The trip they took to Texas when he was little. Vaughn in a big red cowboy hat sitting on a pony. Stephanie and Gwen sitting on Santa's lap, screaming their fool heads off. Pictures that had been hanging there his whole life, but that he couldn't resist glancing over every time he visited.

He stopped outside Gwen's door, wondering, as he had the whole drive over, what the hell he was going to say. Thirty years old and she was living in the same room that held her crib when she was a baby. She'd been in and out of this room her whole adult life, depending on the boyfriend of the moment or whether she'd been fired for stealing from the stores she worked at.

A television was on inside. He knocked three times and waited.

She opened the door and gave him the once-over. "I didn't do anything," she said. "I haven't left the house all week except to go to a party last night."

Great. A real high achiever. "Yeah, that's good. May I come in?"

Giving the door a shove to open it all the way, she turned and walked into the room. Vaughn followed, closing the door behind him.

At least she wasn't a slob. No piles of clothes on the floor, and her desk had only a stack of papers on one corner. She clicked off the television and perched on her neatly made bed. Vaughn took the desk chair.

"I've got a problem and I need your help," he said. Bullshit all the way, but as a cop he'd learned that everybody loved to feel important.

She rolled her eyes. "Spare me your condescending cop-speak."

Oh, sheesh. God help a man with sisters.

His throat reminded him that a cigarette would feel real good right about then, and really steady his nerves. He swallowed a few times. "A situation's come up at work, a disagreement between my department and the Tucumcari police on how to prosecute a crime."

That got her attention. "You and Wallace Meyer have hated each other's guts for years. What is it this time?"

"The crime involved his son."

"Junior? He wasn't at the party last night, and everybody had a different opinion about why. He's in jail, isn't he?"

Vaughn leapt to his feet, blinking fast and whipping up the air with his arms. "Whoa, now. You party with Wallace Meyer Jr.?"

"Not last night, I didn't."

Oh, hell, no. "He's . . . he's . . . a friend of yours?"

She shrugged. "Yeah. Why?"

Vaughn crossed the room in two strides to hover over her. "Gwen, listen to me. Junior's bad news. He's into some scary stuff that could get you in trouble or maybe even killed. What about his pals, Elias Baltierra, Shawn Henigin, and Jimmy de Luca? Are you friends with them too?"

"Jimmy, yeah, we're cool. Eli and Shawn come around sometimes, but I wouldn't call them friends."

He leaned in closer. "Any idea where I could find them right now?"

"How should I know? I only see them around parties, is all."

He hated that he had to ask this next question, but couldn't see a way around it. "Tell me the truth—are you using drugs?"

Sneering, she gave him a shove that backed him out of her face. "Don't be a jackass, Vaughn. Do I look like a junkie?"

He knelt, hands on hips, right up close to her, and gave her the same thorough looking over he might give someone he'd pulled over for erratic driving. Her skin was tan, not ashen, and free of scabs and sores. Her eyes weren't bloodshot. No dark circles under her eyes or weird bruising anywhere. But her hair smelled faintly of pot.

He fluffed her hair and took another whiff. Yep. Eau de Ganja.

"Hey!" she squealed, swatting at him.

Swabbing a hand over his face, he paced to the other side of the room and watched his dad's class through the window, reining in his fury. When he could speak without shouting, he rounded on her. "Damn it, Gwen. Pot? You're thirty, for Christ's sake! When are you going to grow up?"

She vaulted from the bed, and he knew by the fire in her eyes that he'd tripped her temper switch. Lovely. Just what he needed.

"You don't get to waltz in here with your fancy sheriff badge and that big brother smirk and boss me around," she yelled. "I have my shit together, and I don't need you or anyone else lecturing me on what I do in my free time."

"You've got nothing but free time," Vaughn hissed as quietly as he could manage. "You have nothing going for you at all."

"Screw you!"

"Kinda feels like that's what you're doing—screwing me over at my job, putting me in a position where I either got to sit on my hands while the police arrest you over and over again, or set aside my ethics as a sheriff to keep you out of jail."

"I don't need your help," she shouted, shoving him again.

He planted his feet right in the middle of her room, his hands in his pockets, and let her push on him. It wasn't like his little sisters hadn't beaten on him a million times when they were kids, and maybe it would wear her temper out faster. "Is that right? Then tell me how you're going to play it the next time Wallace Meyer or one of his gophers arrests you for possession of drugs or stolen merchandise? Because, right now, they want to catch you. They're on the hunt."

The head of steam she'd worked up deflated. "You don't know that."

Vaughn scoffed. "You know what I'm doing as soon as the warrant comes in from the judge? I'm going to the hospital to arrest Wallace Jr. for a violent crime. Chief Meyer knew it was coming to this, and the first chance he had, he got in my face with a threat against you."

She dropped to her bed again and wrapped her arms around her knees. "What?"

"That's why I'm here. You think I want to talk to you about this shit? Wallace Meyer told me straight up that if he catches you with so much as one foot stepping outside the law, he's putting the full power of his position into prosecuting you. I came here to warn you. If you feel the sudden need to go shopping, or however the urge starts inside you, do me a favor and head to Albuquerque, okay? Stay out of Tucumcari."

She hugged herself tighter. "I live in Tucumcari."

"Okay, well, don't go shopping. And for the love of God, no more parties with Wallace Jr.'s crowd."

"Fine."

"And while we're at it, how about you show a little respect for the people who raised you and hand over any pot you have in the house."

Her eyes turned wide and innocent. "I don't have any."

"Give me a break, Gwen. Hand it over or I'll search your room. Because I'd rather you be pissed at me than be storing drugs right under the noses of our parents."

After a minute's deliberation, she opened her closet and scrounged around in a drawer. Blank-faced, she handed a baggie to him.

He pocketed it, nodding. "Thank you. Anything else?"

"No."

"Are we clear about things?"

She picked at a fingernail. "Yes."

He put his hand on the doorknob, then stopped. "I know you don't think you need me, but I can list a hundred different ways you might get into hot water fast, now that Wallace Meyer has it out for you. If you have a problem, you call me, okay? If you think you're being tailed or harassed by the Tucumcari police in any way, you let me deal with it. Got it?"

"Yeah, I got it."

"If you ever get to thinking about doing stupid shit again, drugs or shoplifting—whatever—think about Mom and Dad, will you? Think about what this is doing to them."

She stalked up to him, indignation written all over her face. "You have no idea what I'm going through. No idea what it's like to have a problem you can't control."

He opened the door, the itch for a smoke burning in his throat again. "Yeah, sis. You're right. I have no idea what that kind of impulse control is like. You're such a special snowflake."

She threw something at him, a book or folder. He wasn't sure which because he ducked, then scrambled out, shutting the door. A second something thunked against it.

"Were you two arguing?" It was Mom in the living room, her apron bunched in her hands, her face anxious.

Turning on his brightest smile, Vaughn swatted the air as he walked to her. "Sibling squabble. I suggested she work with Dad at the college to earn her keep around here. She told me to butt out of her life." He slung an arm across her shoulders and guided her to the kitchen.

"She doesn't want anybody's advice, Vaughn. You know that. I've been praying for guidance, but that's about all she'll let me do to help her."

Seems like Gwen was letting Mom do plenty, providing her with free boarding and food, and probably doing her laundry too, but he'd never call Mom out about it. "You get any answers from the Big Man on High yet?"

"Not yet."

He rubbed her shoulders. "Whatever you do, keep trying." He glanced at his watch. Five o'clock. "Any chance you've got some extra cookies to spare? I'm going to check in with Dad, then I've got to get on patrol."

In a six-man department, the sheriff was on the hook for patrol as much as the most junior members of the team. There simply weren't enough bodies to cover the shifts while the sheriff sat behind his desk. It was one of the many things Vaughn loved about being a sheriff of a rural county. He loved getting his hands dirty on the job, keeping his finger on the pulse of the community. He hadn't gone into law enforcement to work a desk job.

"I already packaged them for you." She presented him with a bag full of snickerdoodles.

"Thanks, Ma." He took the bag and bussed her cheek. "I've been craving cookies since the last time you sent a batch home with me."

She followed him to the door. "If you had a girl of your own, I'm sure she'd make you cookies whenever you wanted."

He couldn't help but smile at the singsongy nag, relieved her anxiety over his argument with Gwen had passed. And yet, he didn't know how to break it to her that he wasn't all that attracted to domestic types of women. He didn't want a rancher's wife—some cute little thing who stayed home to cook him dinner and wash his clothes. It was a certain truck-driving, ride-the-range sort of cowgirl who'd captured his interest.

He wondered what his mom would think of Rachel. He could almost reconcile it in his head, the two of them bonding. Not over cookies or knitting, but horseshoes and grain feed.

He opened the bag and popped a cookie into his mouth. "You're not going to rest until I get hitched, are you?"

"I need grandchildren."

Bam! There it was—Mom's favorite topic. Uncanny, how she'd weaseled the conversation in that direction. Still, he had the good grace to look surprised by the suggestion. "Wait a gosh-darn minute. Stephanie gave you three grandchildren. Frankly, I thought I was off the hook years ago. I sent Steph a fruit basket to thank her."

Mom got that twinkle in her eye that only showed up when she found him charming. "You did not send your sister a fruit basket for having a baby."

"Sure I did. When she popped the second one out and it was a girl. I figured my keister was covered because she'd had one of each, so I sent her another fruit basket. Actually, more like a fruit tower. Boxes of apples and pears and oranges—a whole tower of fruit."

He'd reeled her in good now. Chuckling as she was, she'd forgotten all about the fact he hadn't brought a girlfriend around in a long, long time, or that her middle child was a petty thief and all-around loser.

"I've always wanted one of those, like from the catalog," she mused.

He gathered her in a bear hug. "That's good to know." He kissed her hair. "See you soon, Ma. Thanks again for the cookies."

He found his dad alone in the workshop, sharpening a hoof knife. He afforded Vaughn a sideways glance. "Did I hear your mother hassling you about grandchildren again?"

He opened the cookie bag and popped one in his mouth. "Brings her great joy to nag me about it, so I'm hard-pressed to complain."

"That a boy," Dad said with a grin. "'Course, if you're really interested in bringing her great joy, it wouldn't kill you to bring a woman around for dinner every now and then."

Vaughn rubbed his eyelid, grimacing. "That might kill me, actually."

Dad grinned. "Aw, now, I'm teasing you. Don't get your undies in a bunch."

Vaughn grinned and nearly choked on the snickerdoodle he was swallowing. "*Undies?* What am I, eight?"

Dad chuckled and went back to sharpening his knife. "Does that mean you avoided upsetting her with Gwen's trials, I hope?"

Vaughn settled on a bench. "Tried my best not to, even though Gwen makes that near impossible most days."

Dad tested the knife edge with his thumb, then

sheathed it in a worn leather scabbard. "I take it today was one of those days?"

"I don't know where you and Mom find the patience to deal with her."

"It's called love, son. No use loving someone if you can't be patient with their shortcomings."

Snorting softly, Vaughn opened the nearest drawer. The divider tray of horseshoe nails was a mess, with no rhyme or reason to its organization. He set the tray on the counter and got busy sorting.

"Tell me what's going on with Gwen," Dad prompted.

Vaughn sighed, "I've got something going on at work. A case involving Wallace Meyer Junior. And Meyer told me out-and-out that if I arrest his son, he'll be looking to repay the favor next time Gwen has a problem." Out of the corner of his eye, he watched his dad perch on a stool, shaking his head. "Makes me want to treat her to a month-long cruise in the Caribbean so I can concentrate on the case without having to worry about her."

"What kind of case are we talking about here?"

Vaughn swept a pile of No. 5 nails into the largest section of the tray. "Junior trespassed onto private property in Catcher Creek along with some buddies. They shot the homeowner and a horse."

Dad whistled. "That boy never was worth his salt."

"None of the Meyers are."

"Watch your tone. The Meyers were our clients for a lot of years. They, along with the rest of our clients, put food on the table and put you through college."

He laid the No. 4 nails in a line on the counter, checking for size inconsistencies. "Yet Wallace and Kathryn treated you and Mom like crap the entire time. Don't even get me started on the way they treated their horses."

"They weren't the most pleasant people."

He sifted the imperfectly sized nails from the line and

set them aside, then gathered the rest by the handful and dropped them in the tray. "Aw, Dad. You can't say an unkind word about anyone, can you? It's like you're physically incapable of verbalizing a person's faults."

"That's not true. The other week I was grousing about Sal Dias forgetting to fill my weed whacker up with gas after borrowing it."

Vaughn flashed him a bemused grimace. "You're a real hard ass, all right." They could joke all they wanted about Dad's good-naturedness, but it irked Vaughn that he refused to speak the truth about Wallace Meyer. It was a disingenuous way of living, to sweep every unpleasant reality or thought under the rug. He took up a metal file and one of the too-long No. 4 nails. "Grousing about your neighbor is a start, but there's a big difference between leaving a weed whacker on empty and beating a horse bloody because it threw your child, who didn't have the handling skills to ride it in the first place."

"We don't need to dig that up—now or ever. It has no bearing on the trouble Wallace Jr.'s gotten himself into." Vaughn registered the offense in his tone, the warning to back off.

"Yes, it does," he countered quietly. He dropped the filed nail into the tray and started on the next one.

His dad appeared at his side, a file in hand. He chose an irregular nail and got to work. "The past only haunts us if we let it, son. I've chosen to let it go, and I suggest you do the same before the bitterness eats away at you."

The only bitterness eating away at Vaughn was the fact that nobody'd ever succeeded in challenging Wallace Meyer's unchecked power. He intended to be the one to change that statistic, but he respected his dad enough not to press the subject. He finished shortening the last of the No. 4 nails, and repeated the process with the No. 6 nails, laying them in a row on the counter.

He nudged Vaughn's shoulder with the back of his hand. "Who is she?"

Vaughn sent him a sidelong glance. "Who's who?"

"The homeowner Wallace Jr. shot. I'm right about it being a woman, aren't I?"

"How'd you know?"

Dad tapped his file on the lip of the counter. The nails rattled. "Because you're reorganizing the nail drawer. You only do that when you've got a person of the female persuasion on your mind."

Vaughn huffed. Helluva poker face he'd crafted for himself. "Guess we've had our share of chats in the workroom over the years, haven't we?"

"Yes, we have. So who is she this time?"

None of the No. 6 nails were irregular, so he swept them into the tray. "She is Kellan's soon-to-be sister-in-law, Rachel."

"Hold on—Wallace Meyer's son shot Rachel Sorentino?"

"I don't have proof it was him. Could've been one of his associates." He ran his tongue over his teeth before asking, "What do you know of Rachel Sorentino?"

He held his breath, weirdly anxious about what his dad might say. What if he didn't like her for some reason? That was baloney, though, because the man had never made a disparaging comment about anyone in his entire life.

"I farriered for the Sorentinos back when Gerald Sorentino's father, Albert, ran the place. Rachel is Gerald's firstborn, if memory serves. She was a quiet thing. Apple of her daddy's eye. I hear she's grown into a fine farmer."

"That she has." He reached into the tray, turning all the nail heads in the same direction.

"What kind of designs do you have on Rachel Sorentino?" Dad asked.

Vaughn's hand stilled. He kept his head down, knowing better than to look Dad in the eye when he lied. "No designs."

Dad held up a nail as though presenting the evidence to a judge. "The nail drawer doesn't lie."

Vaughn stuffed his hands in his pockets and pushed off the bench. He paced to the far end of the room. "Look, just because I've got Rachel Sorentino on my mind doesn't mean I have designs on her."

"Mm-hmm. If you say so."

"Dad, you know I can't have a relationship with someone involved in an investigation. It's unethical and immoral, and, in this case, it would be illegal because there's a decent chance she's going to face charges for possessing an unregistered firearm. Hell, Wallace Meyer wants me to charge her with attempted murder because she shot Junior in the back."

"Are you going to charge her with that?"

"Hell, no. She had a right to defend herself on her own property."

"If that's all there is to it, then why is my nail drawer the neatest it's been in over a year, when you told me about some girl—who, I might add, you never saw fit to bring around for dinner—breaking it off with you? You had your head in a storm cloud for a good long while after that."

Dad had a hell of a memory for a man who didn't like to remember anything unpleasant. Vaughn dropped to the bench again and looked him in the eye, ready to stop skirting the truth. "Same girl."

Dad rubbed his mustache. "Well, now, that complicates things."

"Tell me about it."

They both reached for the cookie bag at the same

time. Vaughn let Dad choose first, then dipped his hand in for two.

"How does she feel about her ex working her case?" Dad asked.

Her ex implied they'd had more than a scorching four-week fling. It implied that they'd dated, when in reality he'd never so much as taken her to dinner. The realization hit him like a loss. What he wouldn't give to go back in time and do things differently with her. "Hard to say. I think she's as torn as I am. She seems relieved I'm looking out for her interests, but, like me, isn't much enjoying the reminder of all the reasons why we didn't work out."

"What are you going to do?"

Vaughn released his breath in a long, slow stream. "Only thing I can. Use my badge and my position to protect her from Meyer. That's all I've got left to offer her, and she needs it because Meyer could make her life a living hell if he got it in his mind to."

Dad gave his shoulder a squeeze. "I know you'll do your best to be fair. You don't have anyone to answer to but your own conscience, and you don't have anything to prove to me or your mom. With everything on your plate, and Rachel needing your help, don't give another thought to Gwen. I know you want to save her from herself—we all do—but you're her brother, not her keeper. She's in therapy, and on meds, and she's a grown woman. All any of us can do is love her no matter what."

"Yeah, I know." He stood and stretched his legs. "I'd better get back to work."

Dad gave his shoulder another squeeze and shake. "Things'll work out. You've grown into too good a man for them not to."

He gave his dad a skeptical grin as he sealed the cookie

bag. "I don't see how that would matter, but thanks nonetheless."

Dad stood, motioning to the bag. "I'd better swipe a couple more of those before you leave."

Vaughn tucked it in the crook of his elbow and covered it with his hand. "I don't think so. You've got trays full of cookies in the kitchen. This is all I've got to tide me over."

"I didn't raise you to be helpless. You could bake cookies."

The idea had Vaughn belly laughing as they walked to his patrol car. "That's a great idea in theory, but you're talking to the guy who uses his oven as file storage. I think my best option is to start visiting Mom more often on her baking day."

Vaughn opened his door, tossed the cookie bag on the passenger seat, then shook his dad's hand. That or a shoulder squeeze was the closest they got to hugging, but that was fine with Vaughn. If there was one thing he could count on besides death and taxes, it was his folks' love and support. A hug couldn't tell him anything he didn't already know.

But as he drove, his mind got stuck on something his dad had said. *You don't have anything to prove to me or your mom.*

Funny, that. Because at the crime scene, Rachel had made a point to remind him he didn't have anything to prove to her either. But wasn't that what life was about? Proving your worth to the people you love. Proving your mettle as a man. Before Vaughn's career in law enforcement was over, he was going to prove that wealth and power didn't also come with a free pass to abuse it.

And he was starting with Wallace Meyer and the Tucumcari Police Department.

Chapter Seven

Rachel woke achy and disoriented after dreaming of Vaughn, her body wet with perspiration and arousal, her mind filled with visions of bound wrists, merging bodies, and unbearable pleasure.

She'd always had that type of dream, even in high school. What an odd thing for a country girl to crave, she'd thought. What a strange, wicked fantasy. But it wouldn't leave her alone. Sometimes, not all the time, she liked it rough. She liked not to be in control. In that one sliver of her life, she wanted someone else to be in charge.

None of the lovers she'd had over the years understood that about her, or shared the same proclivity. No one except Vaughn, who seemed to know instinctively what she needed, and made no issue of giving it to her. Expertly, passionately, perfectly.

The clock read four A.M., which meant she'd slept thirteen straight hours. No wonder she felt disoriented. She sat, pushing the covers away, but the top sheet stuck to her left arm and pulled at her bandage. She clicked on her reading lamp, blinking until her eyes adjusted.

The gunshot wound had oozed though the bandage and crusted on the sheet. Nasty.

Gingerly, she peeled them apart, then, bleary-eyed, stumbled to the bathroom that adjoined her bedroom. Removing the bandage, she inspected the wound. It was a couple inches long. The scab tugged at her swollen skin. Double nasty.

With a grimace, she popped three ibuprofen and turned the shower water on. She didn't feel much like doing farm chores at the moment, but, really, did four o'clock ever come around to find her fresh as a spring daisy, ready to work?

The shower helped. Not because she found it refreshing, but because the streams of water hurt like the devil on her wound. That woke her up good.

Back in her room, she did her best to apply a new bandage. Then it was to the kitchen for coffee. Amy was at the stove, stirring something. Mr. Dixon, a retired navy cook and local farmer who worked as Amy's sous-chef, sat at the kitchen table nursing his own cup of coffee.

"Morning, Mr. Dixon. What're you doing here so early? I thought eight was more your speed."

"Howdy, Rachel."

"He slept over," Amy said mysteriously.

"What for?" Rachel asked him. "Problems at your place?"

"Problems at your place is more like it. I heard about the trouble in the valley on Monday, and figured the more folks around here, the safer it'll be until the sheriff gets it sorted out. A shame, the way kids these days treat violence like it's a video game."

His assessment of the situation was predictably geezeresque, but it was easier to take the path of least resistance than correct him. She nodded noncommittally and sipped her coffee.

Amy plopped into a chair. "He's sweet on Tina. Stayed over so they could watch television together in the living room late into the night."

Rachel grinned at him. "No kidding."

Tina was Kellan's mom. She'd been skin and bones when she'd arrived last December, a recovering junkie and alcoholic, looking for Kellan's forgiveness. He'd given it to her, and Rachel and Amy had provided her with a place to stay and a job while she found her footing. Douglas Dixon was doing his part, driving her to daily AA meetings in town and being a sympathetic ear. Guess Rachel had underestimated *how* sympathetic he was.

He swatted the air. "Aw, now, you know it's not that way. I'm too old for those kind of shenanigans."

"You're sixty-one. That's too young to use words like *shenanigans,* much less give up on your love life," Amy said.

"Pshaw. Love life indeed. I had a love life for a lot of good years before my wife passed on. Lord knows I'm not looking to start down that path again."

Amy's eyes turned dreamy and lovesick. "You don't always get to choose when or who you fall in love with. Sometimes love sweeps you off your feet and there's nothing to be done but to go along for the ride."

Rachel snickered. "Says the blushing bride-to-be."

"Mm-hmm," Mr. Dixon added. "She thinks everyone should be in love because she is."

Amy tossed her hair. "You should. It feels great."

Oh, boy. "I can't believe we're discussing the merits of falling in love at four-thirty in the morning. Ames, I know you get up early these days, but isn't this pushing it a bit?"

"Kellan stayed over last night again, but he has work to do at his ranch. He left a few minutes to four. Are you feeling better? You slept straight through dinner. Vaughn called, wondering why you hadn't come to the station house like you two had arranged. I told him you weren't looking so good and that it'd have to wait until today. He said that was no problem. You must've needed the sleep because I checked on you every hour or so until I went to bed, to make sure you didn't get feverish, and you were out cold every time."

"Thanks for doing that. I'm feeling much better today." Which was sort of true, so long as she didn't take her throbbing, seeping gunshot wound into account.

"You're not working today, just so you know."

Rachel set her mug down with a clatter. "Not to be rude or anything, but I don't see how you're going to stop me."

She quirked a brow. "I have my ways."

"Which means what? You gonna chain me to the table?"

"Maybe I'll call Vaughn."

Rachel leaned back, her hands gripping her thighs. "What the hell is that supposed to mean?"

"Calm down. I was teasing about having him arrest you to keep you from working. You need to learn how to take a joke."

She sipped coffee to hide her relief. "I'll get right on that. Right after I feed the livestock." She rose, mug in hand, and walked to the bench her boots were under.

"I'm telling you, there's no sense putting those boots on."

She stuffed her feet in the boots, donned her work jacket and hat, and headed outside. Rudy and Damon were in the stable yard, tinkering under the hood of the tractor along with a clean-cut young man she recognized as one of Kellan's ranch hands, though she couldn't recall his name.

Whereas most young ranch workers tended to blow off steam at Smithy's Bar after quitting time, she couldn't ever remember seeing this guy outside of Slipping Rock Ranch. When he noticed Rachel crossing the stable yard toward him, he removed his cream-colored cowboy hat. His eyes were wide and anxious, his light hair was buzzed short enough that she got an accurate reading of the shape of his head.

"Morning, Rudy, Damon." She touched the brim of her hat in greeting, then stuck out her hand to the newcomer. "Rachel Sorentino. You're one of Kellan's workers, right?"

His handshake was firm, his hands as calloused as hers. "Yes, I was, ma'am. Ben Torrey."

"What can we do for you, Ben?"

He pulled back, blinking, then chanced a look at Rudy and Damon, like the question had been in a foreign language and one of them might be able to translate. With his head turned, she could make out the circle of early pattern baldness that his shorn hair rendered barely perceptible, but didn't completely mask. As young as he looked otherwise, she'd bet he'd started balding in high school. Poor guy.

"Go on and tell her," Rudy said, grinning like a salesman. Maybe the global weather was especially rousing that week.

Ben curled the brim of his hat in his hands. "I work here now, ma'am."

He said it like it should clarify things, but his answer only got Rachel to believing he wasn't the sharpest barb on the wire. "How do you figure that?"

Behind him, Damon closed the tractor hood with a *bang*. Ben jumped out of his skin and his hat fell to the ground. He picked it up and dusted it off, then went back to curling the edges. "I'm the new foreman. Hired yesterday." He paused and looked expectantly at her as though hoping he'd jogged her memory.

Amy's doing, no doubt. Good grief. "Who hired you exactly?"

"The other Miss Sorentinos and Mr. Reed, ma'am. Before yesterday, I worked at Slipping Rock Ranch for three years, second in command to Mr. Reed's foreman."

Did Kellan think she wasn't handling the farm well enough? So much so that he needed to step in without discussing matters with her? It'd be a cold day in hell before she let anyone waltz in and take over her life's work, even someone she admired as much as Kellan. "Go on," she prompted through gritted teeth.

"Mr. Reed told me you and your sisters were looking to hire a foreman who knew about growing alfalfa. He sent me here yesterday to interview for the job. Your sister, Miss Sorentino—"

"Which sister, now?"

"Miss Sorentino."

Rachel took a long, slow sip of coffee, and silently counted to ten. "What's her first name?"

"Oh. Amy, ma'am."

She'd called that right, though it didn't mean she was going to strangle Amy any less for being predictable. Amy could spot a needy soul waiting to be collected into her menagerie of misfits from miles away.

"Congratulations, sis." Amy's smug voice sailed down to the stable grounds from behind her. Rachel whirled around to face her, a whole batch of fighting words on the tip of her tongue. Before she could let them fly, Amy added, "As of yesterday, you've been promoted from worker to full-time manager of Heritage Farm."

Even in the dim light of predawn, Amy's smile shone down on the stable grounds.

"What do you mean?"

Taking a cue from the annoyance in her voice, and knowing better than to get between Amy and Rachel when they were fixing to butt heads, Rudy and Damon slunk off toward the stable with a wheelbarrow of feed. Ben watched them go with an expression of longing.

Amy sauntered toward Rachel, clearly feeling proud of herself. "It means that from now on, you only have to get your hands dirty when you want to. It means the entire burden of the farm work doesn't fall on your shoulders anymore. It means you can delegate, and maybe even take a day off every now and then."

"But I . . ." Tulip, Amy's damnable pet cow, nudged Rachel's hand with her wet nose. Absentmindedly, she reached up and scratched it between its ears. "But I like getting my hands dirty. I don't want to take a day off. Why didn't you consult me on this?"

Amy's expression turned serious. "When you were in the hospital, Jenna and I realized how dependent the farm is on you. I mean, we knew it already, but you being injured really drove the point home. Kellan pitched in, but he's got his cattle business to contend with. We need some permanent help. You, Jenna, and I had debated about hiring a foreman since the oil was discovered, and Jenna and I had already decided to surprise you for your birthday. But then you were shot, so we thought, what the heck. Early birthday present."

Tulip raised her head to position her nose right under Rachel's palm, so she took to scratching the wiry hair of the cow's face. "You can't give me a person for my birthday. It doesn't work like that."

Amy crossed her arms over her chest. "Who says it doesn't?"

"Miss Sorentino, with all due respect." Ben had curled his hat into looking like a taco shell. "This is the job opportunity I've been waiting for. A chance to use what I've spent my whole life learning. Working on

Slipping Rock was great, but my know-how is all about growing premium alfalfa."

"Did you grow up on an alfalfa farm?"

"Yes, ma'am. Lucky Fields Farm over in San Ysidro."

"Why aren't you working there?" Rachel had no use for a man who turned his back on his family's farm to seek his fortunes elsewhere.

He nodded gravely, though his eyes glittered with pride and he stood up straighter. "I would if I could. The dream I had was getting a degree through New Mexico State University in agricultural business. My folks made it happen with the understanding that I'd eventually take over their farm, but three years into the program, my dad got injured and the money ran out. I went home to work as soon as I learned of it, but the place was past the point that I could do much good."

A stab of sorrow sliced through Rachel's gut. Ben's was a story she'd lived herself. She nodded, trying to put his defensiveness at ease. "Once the alfalfa starts to go, it's gone. Happened to this place much the same way."

He swallowed. "After we lost the farm to the bank, that's when I took the job at Slipping Rock."

Rachel scrubbed her face with her hand, frustrated by what Ben had gone through, what they'd both gone through. "You tried to grab hold of something for yourself by going for your degree, and the whole world exploded when you were turned the other way."

His jaw grew tight. "Yes, ma'am."

Rachel had never thought seriously about getting a degree while she was young. She couldn't afford the time away from the farm, and anyhow, she didn't think she'd have tolerated being indoors that many hours and years. Still, she never quite forgot about the disadvantage her lack of formal training put her at in the alfalfa industry, especially after her crops started dying off. A part of her would always wonder if things would've turned out differently if she'd had a better education. "You went through all that and didn't get to finish college anyhow. That's a shame."

"Actually"—he tipped his head and raised an eyebrow, his pride restored—"I earned my degree through night school. Took a lot longer that way. I was already working for Mr. Reed by the time I graduated. But I did it. He helped me with the tuition and books, even. That's why I'm perfect for the job as your foreman, Miss Sorentino."

Hard not to admire that sort of determination. "How's your dad's injury?"

He stuck his curled hat on his head. "Thank you for asking after him. He's coping, but he never did get himself back to what he was before. He and my mom moved into an apartment in town."

No way she could deny him the job now. Not when she understood what he'd gone through, or his qualifications to help her get her alfalfa crop thriving again. So young, so much responsibility. She knew all about putting what you want on hold to take care of things. Crops and livestock were the hands that never stopped reaching for help, never stopped needing. Relentlessly. The thought made her tired all over again, despite her thirteen hours of solid sleep.

"Please tell me Amy offered you a decent wage at least."

He smiled a big old toothy smile full of rows of crooked teeth. "Yes, ma'am. She was very generous."

"Did Damon and Rudy go over the morning routine in the stable yet?"

"No, ma'am. We were seeing about getting the tractor running."

"That tractor's engine hasn't turned over in two years. There's no point paying a mechanic to fix it until we're ready to plant our first crop. Go on ahead to the stable and I'll meet you inside. I need a quick word with the other Miss Sorentino first."

"Thank you, Miss Sorentino, ma'am."

"Rachel will do. And you're welcome."

With a nod at Amy, he made his way to the stable.

Amy angled her gaze around Rachel to watch him walk away and gave a little whistle under her breath.

Rachel elbowed her hard in the ribs. "What the hell are you doing? You can't ogle our employees. Besides, you're engaged."

"Technically, he's your employee, not mine. Kellan knows good and well he's all the cowboy I need, but just because I've got a ring on my finger doesn't mean I've lost my appreciation for all the glories life has to offer."

Against her better judgment, Rachel tipped her chin over her shoulder and snuck a furtive glance at the particular glory Amy was admiring. Damn it all, she was right. Ben Torrey knew how to fill out a pair of jeans just fine. Still, Rachel didn't much care for younger men. Didn't matter how good they looked, they never seemed to know what to do with a woman's body, at least in her experience.

The peek she took must not have been all that furtive, because Amy started chuckling. "You're checking him out, aren't you? Go, Rach! There might be fire in you after all."

There was plenty of fire in Rachel, but none she cared to reveal to her sister. "I was only curious if he found the stable, is all."

"Sure you were." Amy stuck her hands on her hips and gave Rachel a cockeyed look. "I've been getting the feeling lately that there's more to your personal life than you've led me to believe."

"My personal life is none of your business."

"It is so my business, because I'm making it my business.

I'm going to find you a man to bring to my wedding. Consider yourself warned."

Rachel pinched the bridge of her nose and said another slow count to ten. "Back to Ben Torrey. Are you sure we can afford a foreman? That's a huge expense."

"Jenna crunched the numbers. She says we can. She's starting him off at a decent salary, with bonuses in his contract for crop harvests and sales. I'm sure she'd show you the figures if you want. Your dream is to get the fields producing again. You've worked your whole life to help me and Jenna and the farm, so this is the two of us saying thank you and returning the favor the best way we can."

"I appreciate it. Thank you."

Amy threw her arms around her and hugged her hard. "Love you, sis."

Rachel never knew what to say when Amy or Jenna got demonstrative with their affection. *I love you* sounded corny coming out of her mouth. Her sisters knew how she felt, even if she didn't ever find a way to say it right.

She patted Amy's back. "I'd best get into the stable before the horses get concerned about their unfamiliar visitor."

Amy grinned and stepped away. "See you around noon for supper. Tell Ben he's invited too. And I'll see if Kellan has any eligible bachelor friends for you that might join us."

Oh, boy. "How about you save yourself from a wasted effort by focusing your matchmaking skills on Jenna?"

Amy paused in the doorway, a sassy smile on her face. "Jenna already has a man set in her sights. It's you who needs some sisterly guidance."

By midday on Wednesday, Jimmy de Luca was cleared by his doctors for transfer to the medical wing of the county jail. Vaughn served his arrest warrant, then oversaw the transfer paperwork, and provided backup until de Luca was secure in the back of Reyes's cruiser in the basement of the hospital parking garage.

Vaughn had executed a number of successful hospital-to-jail transports over the years, but he'd never seen a prisoner as nervous about it as de Luca. He *asked* for a flak vest. He wanted to know the details of where and how he was getting from his room at the hospital into the safety—as he put it—of the jail.

"Who are you afraid of, Jimmy?" Vaughn asked him in the elevator.

"Everyone and no one," Jimmy answered.

Helpful. Real helpful.

Figuring it wouldn't hurt to take de Luca's anxiety seriously, he pulled Kirby and Molina from patrol to escort Reyes's car along the one and a half miles to the jail.

"Should we be on the lookout for Henigin and Baltierra? Do you think they'd want to get you, like maybe they figure you've turned on them?"

Jimmy swallowed hard, but didn't answer. Yet his eyes were shifty the whole way down the hospital's service elevator. He hunkered in the wheelchair like he was trying to melt into the vinyl seat, and when he climbed into the back of the patrol car, he slid so low in the seat he was practically sitting on the floor cross-legged.

Whatever de Luca was nervous about, nothing ever came of it. The transfer went off without incident. The prison guards and staff settled Jimmy de Luca into his new home in the medical wing to await sentencing, while Vaughn remained at the hospital for his daily date with Wallace Meyer Jr. and his lawyer.

Binderman stood watch inside Junior's open door. He nodded at Vaughn from across the hallway, but maintained his guard posture. He was taller than his older brother Chris by an inch or two and had the same eager youthfulness that Vaughn had when he first started his career, though in Nathan it was tempered by the same natural even-keeled temperament all the Bindermans had been blessed with. Great qualities for a sheriff deputy to possess. With that attitude and his background in crime scene forensics, Nathan had already proven an invaluable addition to Vaughn's department.

Billy Tsai sat in a chair in the hall, angling an entire muffin into his mouth. It didn't quite fit, so crumbs rained over his dress shirt and tie as he chewed through partially open lips. When he saw Vaughn, his mouth snapped closed, his Adam's apple bobbing as he swallowed. Ever the professional, he stood to shake Vaughn's hand, and Vaughn tried to ignore the crumbs raining from his clothes onto the floor, Tsai's loafers, and Vaughn's boots.

Thankfully, Wallace Meyer and his wife weren't in sight. Meyer knew the score, that a detainee wasn't allowed visitors—even police chief fathers. Still, it didn't mean Meyer wouldn't try to push the limits. All he needed was a local news crew to film Vaughn turning him away from visiting his own son and suddenly Vaughn would look like asshole number one to his voting constituency.

After greeting Tsai, Vaughn nodded to Binderman. "Lunch break. See you in an hour or so. Heavy on the *or so.* The diner across the street makes an excellent pot pie, but they're slow about it."

"Thank you, sir. That would hit the spot today."

"Come on in, Tsai," Vaughn said, opening the hospital suite door. He propped it open with his backside and tapped the papers he held. "Let's get this over with. I'm serving Junior his arrest warrant today."

Wallace Meyer Jr.'s lanky body stretched to the end of

his hospital bed, though the lack of meat on his bones left plenty of room for Tsai to sit on the bed at his side. His eyelids were half closed and obscured behind the mass of shaggy brown hair that fell over his face. Tubes and wires were suspended between his body, the bed, and an IV pole on which three bags hung. His arms and legs were restrained to the bed rails with soft cuffs.

His earlobes had huge floppy holes in them from the rings Junior had stretched them out with. All his jewelry was now sitting in a bag at Vaughn's station house, including the blunt metal dowel he wore through his nose like a bull and another through his left eyebrow. Reminded him of Gwen, who damn near gave their mom a heart attack during her pierced tongue and pink hair phase several years ago. He'd seen enough of that kind of costume on the job to realize that sort of body art was all about kids advertising their insecurities, wanting people to see the freak and ignore the vulnerability underneath.

Didn't explain what Junior had to be insecure about. His whole life, everything he wanted had been handed to him on a silver platter. Then again, Gwen had led a pretty vanilla life, but that didn't stop her from having problems as deep as an oil well—and just as black.

Vaughn walked around to the opposite side of the bed from Tsai, poking the bottom of Junior's foot through the blanket with his pen as he moved. "How's it going, Junior?"

Junior turned his head away from Vaughn and closed his eyes.

He whacked Junior's stomach with the stack of papers. "Hello? Anybody home?"

A second whack and Junior's eyes cracked open. "What?"

Vaughn leaned in. "That's more like it. Having fun yet, Junior?"

"Screw you."

"I'll take that as a yes. You think of anything else you want to share with me about the shooting on Monday? Like where you got the guns?"

"Don't answer that," Tsai said.

Vaughn didn't miss a beat. "See, we looked up the firearms registered to you. Two hunting rifles. No AR-15s."

Junior's eyes popped open. His lips curled into a sneer. "You can't register an AR-15. They're illegal, dumbass."

"I told you to keep your mouth shut," Tsai hissed.

"Who brought the guns to the party?" Vaughn tried again. "All I want is a name to give to the prosecutor. Maybe help your case out, show how cooperative you are. So who was it? Henigin? Baltierra? De Luca?"

Junior raised his right hand as far as it would go given the cuff and flipped Vaughn the bird.

"Fair enough," Vaughn said. "New question. Why were you in the Parillas Valley?"

"That's not a new question. You asked me that a million times already."

"I'm still waiting for an answer."

Junior shook his head. His stretched-out earlobes wiggled like worms.

Vaughn flipped through the case file until he found the picture of the graffitied boulder and dropped it on Junior's chest. "*We warned you bitch.* Who was the message for?"

Junior turned his chin up, eyes to the ceiling. "You don't even know I was the one who sprayed that."

Vaughn shot Tsai an exasperated look. "Your client isn't getting it." He reached into the case file and grabbed the stack of photographs from Rachel's camera, shaking it in the air over Junior's stomach. "We have pictures of you shaking the aerosol paint can, then pictures of you painting every letter of every word on the boulder. There are so many pictures of you in action, I could flip through the stack and animate it for you, like a movie."

A frown of irritation settled on Tsai's face. "Junior has said from the beginning that he has no knowledge of why he was taken to the valley. He was coerced into acting as he did, fearing for his life."

Yeah, right.

"Coerced by whom? If Junior here is so innocent, then why can't he share with me who did all this coercing he's swearing by?" He tucked the pictures away and slapped the papers on the counter behind him, then turned to Junior's bed. "Who are you afraid of?"

"I ain't afraid of nobody."

Vaughn mashed his lips together, watching Junior's eyes. Looking for the telltale signs he was lying, but Junior's face was a mask of defensiveness and immaturity. Nothing for Vaughn to work with. "Your pal Jimmy thinks someone wants to kill him. He was all twitchy today when we transferred him to the jailhouse. Any idea who's got him so rattled? Someone who's bold enough to pop de Luca in front of a bunch of cops. Know anyone like that?"

"How the hell would I know what Jimmy's scared about? I barely know the guy."

"Is that so? 'Cause I'm wondering if whoever he was spooked about could also be after you. What do you think of that theory?"

"I think you can suck my dick," Junior said.

Vaughn shifted his gaze to Tsai. "This case isn't looking so hot for your acquittal record, Tsai. If your client can't keep his vocabulary and hand gestures respectable, I don't see how he's going to win over a jury."

"Worry about your own job, Cooper, and I'll worry about mine."

"Sure, sure. The problem is, my gut's telling me that Junior is withholding critical information on two dangerous fugitives. When that information comes out, which it will, do you honestly think I won't add it to the list of charges against him? You'd best be advising him to answer my questions."

"We're done here," Tsai said, rising. "Serve the warrant."

Vaughn bit back his simmering frustration. "See now? It sounds like you're starting to worry about my job, and what did you just tell me?"

"My client needs his rest," Tsai grumbled.

"Don't get your undies in a bunch." Vaughn could see why his dad liked the phrase. Rolled off the tongue real nice. "We've got a cozy room for him at the jail as soon as the docs clear him for transfer. He's got a lifetime of leisure ahead of him."

"Get on with it," Tsai said.

Vaughn fished the arrest warrant out from the stack of papers and handed it to Tsai. Then he placed his hand over his heart. "I've been waiting years to say this to you, Junior. You should know, from the bottom of my heart, I mean every word." It was a shame Junior's wrists were already cuffed to the bed, because Vaughn had always wanted to do the honors. "Wallace Meyer Junior, by the power vested in me by Quay County and the state of New Mexico, you are hereby under arrest . . ."

Chapter Eight

As the afternoon sun glinted orange off the windows of the squat, nondescript sheriff's office perched on the edge of Catcher Creek's four-square-block downtown, Rachel pulled her rusty red pickup into the parking lot. She walked to the building with grim resolve, the flash drive of graffiti photographs in her pocket, a folder stuffed with hate mail and the petition against Heritage Farm tucked under her arm, and a foil-covered plate of scones in her hand.

Such were the ways of a small town, she thought wryly. God forbid someone arrive at a gathering empty-handed, even if that gathering was a police interview. At least Vaughn's patrol car wasn't parked out front. Thank God for small favors.

She'd called ahead and spoken to Irene Beckley, the sheriff's department dispatcher-slash-office manager, inquiring about when Irene thought the sheriff would return to the office because she had a file to deliver. Irene estimated his return at five or six, so Rachel made sure to arrive at four.

Irene sat behind the welcome desk. A pillar of the Catcher Creek community, she'd worked at the sheriff's department as long as anybody could remember, doling out divine guidance to near about every person who called or walked through the door. More than once, when Rachel had retrieved Jenna from the station house after she'd been caught for underage drinking and partying, Irene was sitting with her, working to sober her up with black coffee and a stern lecture on the perils of sin.

Undersheriff Stratis was the only other person in view. She'd never been comfortable around Wesley Stratis. He was around town a lot, and from all accounts, he was excellent at his job, but she couldn't shake the impression that when he looked at her, it was with harsh judgment in his eyes. He'd never been overtly hostile to her, and for the most part, she chalked the sensation up to an effect of the lingering guilt she harbored from her affair with Vaughn.

When Stratis saw her, he rose from his seat, his expression curious. "Ms. Sorentino."

"I promised Sheriff Cooper I'd bring in photographs of vandalism around my farm."

Stratis approached her, tapping a handful of files against the palm of his left hand. "I heard about that. Thank you for bringing them so promptly. What's under the foil?"

"Scones," she said, feeling like a moron.

He reached for the plate.

On instinct, she pulled it out of his reach. "For the sheriff."

The second the words crossed her lips, her face turned hot. Stratis's expression turned sharp, like he knew all about her history with Vaughn and he thought she'd brought him a treat she'd baked. "No, I don't cook. They're from my sister—Amy, the chef. It's nothing, really. You can have one." She pushed the plate into his hands.

He peered under the foil skeptically. "Okay . . . Now, about those photographs?"

"Yes." Relieved for the topic change, she handed him the file, then produced the flash drive from her pocket. "The folder's full of hate mail the farm's received since opening the inn, and the photographs are on the drive, along with a record of dates and locations."

He nodded toward the hallway. "Why don't we go over those dates and locations right now so our department has all the facts straight?"

She glanced over her shoulder, through the glass door at the lowering sun. It was later than she hoped. The evening chores would need to be started soon, and who knew when Vaughn might appear.

"Looking for Sheriff Cooper's car? I guess you had your heart set on talking to him instead, is that it?"

The way he said it made her hairs stand on end. Maybe he did see her sins when he looked at her.

She raised her chin, defensiveness setting her mouth in a tight line. "I didn't have my *heart* set on anything. You or the sheriff or any other deputy—doesn't matter to me who I talk to." That was absolute horseshit, but how dare Stratis turn nothing into something.

"Well, then. After you."

Oh, he'd played her, all right. Tapped right onto her rawest nerve, and she let him do it. Irritated with herself, she brushed past him and stalked down the hallway. He followed her into the conference room and, leaving the door open, took a seat on the far side of a dark brown rectangular table. Rachel settled into the nearest chair.

After she'd declined his offer for a glass of water, Stratis propped his elbows on the table and pressed his hands together. "Before we talk about the information on the flash drive, I'm confused on a few points regarding the events that took place on your farm on Monday. I'd be much obliged if you could fill in some of the blank spots in my mind."

Slick police work, to throw her a curveball like that as soon as he had her trapped in the room. Her fingers fidgety with nervous energy, she reached for a scone and broke off a bite. It tasted like cardboard in her dry mouth. She pushed it around with her tongue, wishing she hadn't declined the water. "Undersheriff, I don't mean to be a pain, but I have a lot of work to do before sundown. I agreed to talk about the contents of the flash drive, nothing more."

"So, for the record, you're declining to cooperate with our investigation?"

"I didn't say that. I—"

"Then you don't mind going over the timeline of events again. I appreciate that. Start at the beginning."

Oh, he was good. She plucked a raisin from the scone in her hand and squished it between her fingers, wondering why she felt so trapped and defensive when she hadn't done anything wrong and the sheriff's department was on her side. Besides the time lost for her evening chores, she had no valid reason to deny Stratis's request.

Thus resigned, she gathered her memories with a slow inhale, then launched into the story at the start of the trouble, when she and Lincoln first spied the truck on the mesa. As she talked, she picked at the scone, gathering the crumbs into a pile on the table. Stratis listened intently, scribbling notes and prompting her when she paused.

"You thought these were the same vandals you'd encountered before on your ranch?"

"Exactly."

"What was your theory on why the vandals were targeting you?"

She sniffed. "Turning our farm into a tourist destination has been a sore point for more than a few townsfolk."

"Like who, in particular?"

She gestured to the file she'd handed him. "All the names are on the copy of the petition I gave you."

Stratis opened the folder, tapping his pen against the paper as he scanned the petition with a blank expression. "Why didn't you notify the sheriff's department about this sooner? You might've been able to prevent what happened Monday."

"It would've been bad for business if word got out about the trouble, and I thought if that happened and we lost business because of it, I'd be giving the protestors what they wanted, especially when I knew I could handle it."

He scratched his neck. "You thought you could handle it? Isn't that the same flawed logic that got you into trouble Monday, Miss Sorentino?"

Her hackles raised at the accusation in his words. "I suppose it is, Undersheriff. Are you planning to arrest me for using flawed logic?"

His face broke out in a hard smile. "If that were a punishable offense, we'd have every citizen of Quay County behind bars at one time or another." He lifted a scone from the plate and took a huge bite.

"True enough. Look, as I mentioned, I've got a lot of work to do before sundown, so may I go on with the story?"

Stratis set the scone down. "One more question. Why didn't you call 9-1-1, instead of firing off those warning shots?"

Didn't she just answer that? She thought she could handle it. What more did he want her to say? "Because I have the right to defend my property and my family, and a warning shot had been effective with the other vandals. One shot and they got in their cars and beat it off my land."

"Not this time."

"Obviously." She kept her expression blank, though her heart rate picked up its pace. His hostility was throwing her off balance. Her stomach acid flared, demanding her attention, but she refused to eat an antacid, not when doing so might tip Stratis off to her inner turmoil.

More than anything, she wanted to leave. To bid Stratis a good day and go. In fact, the more she contemplated the urge to flee, the brighter it burned inside her. She'd give this five more minutes and then she was out of there—no matter what.

He took another bite of scone, then gestured with it in his hand. "Go on with your story, Ms. Sorentino. Please."

He listened silently. Rachel found herself omitting certain details—her fear, her pain over shooting Lincoln. Her instincts warned her against trusting Stratis with her feelings. When she got to the part where she stuffed her pockets with extra ammo, she did not admit to her desire to kill the four men. She never would have done it. Even though she wanted them dead, as soon as she'd snuck up on them and had one in the sights of her revolver, she knew she'd never shoot to kill, no matter how enraged she was, or how much the men deserved to die.

Stratis raised a finger, a puzzled look on his face, and Rachel stopped talking. "When the four trespassers drew their weapons and you realized you were in over your head, why didn't you flee?"

"I was hidden from view in the canyon. If I'd have run, I'd have given them a clear shot at me and my horse."

"As it was, they did have a clear shot, didn't they? They shot your horse."

Rachel wiped her hand on her jeans. "Anyone who's ever fired a gun knows there's a difference between a clear shot and a lucky shot."

"But you still didn't call 9-1-1, even after the men proved they were different from previous trespassers, that they were violent and wanted to do you harm. Instead of dialing dispatch so Irene could get the nearest patrol car to your property, you dialed Sheriff Cooper's personal cell phone. Why did you do that?" His tone, though matter-of-fact, had a flinty edge to it, like his professionalism barely won out over his urge to shout the words.

Rachel opened her mouth to speak, not that she had any idea what she'd say. She couldn't very well admit he was the first person who came to mind when she needed help. "I don't know. I can't remember why I made that choice."

Stratis stood so abruptly that his chair tipped and thumped against the wall. He towered over the table, his hands braced near the scone plate. "Can you remember why, even after you phoned the sheriff and knew help was on the way, you didn't sit tight? Instead, you went on your own violent rampage."

Rachel flinched, surprised by his sudden and aggressive movement. When had the conversation turned into an interrogation? Using her feet, she pushed her chair away from the table and stood, reestablishing the boundaries of her personal space. Though her legs were weak and shaky with adrenaline from the sudden change of Stratis's mood and her stomach ulcer burned in protest, she forced herself to be bold. Leaning over the table, she met him nose-to-nose. "What I did was no rampage."

She willed her lips into a brazen smile.

He countered her smile with a tight-jawed smirk. "No, you're right. It was premeditated. You reloaded twice—"

"That's enough, Stratis."

Rachel's spine snapped straight. Relief and exhilaration whipped up inside her like a dirt devil in a field. Vaughn stood in the doorway, his expression stoic. The gear belt hugging his waist shifted as he propped his shoulder against the doorframe and smoothed a hand over his pressed blue shirt. He devastated her, wearing that uniform. Drove the breath from her lungs and made her head spin.

He gave Rachel a terse nod, then let his eyes rove over her body, his expression morphing to one of concern, like he expected to find her harmed. "Ms. Sorentino."

She nodded, too rattled to speak.

His focus shifted past her, to Stratis. "What's going on here?"

Rachel shifted, positioning her body to keep both men in her line of sight.

Stratis stiffened defensively at Vaughn's question. "Ms. Sorentino stopped by with a plate of cookies for you"—he gestured to the table—"along with a flash drive of photographs from the vandalism incidents she failed to report initially. It seemed a prime opportunity to ask her some of the questions I had about Monday's incident."

She ground her molars together. Wouldn't do her any good to get defensive about his phrasing like she was tempted to. "Scones," she bit out, not meeting Vaughn's eye. "From my sister."

Just like that, she'd never eat another scone for the remainder of her days.

Vaughn barely glanced at the plate. His boots clomped on the floor as he made his way around the table toward Stratis. "I'll take over from here, Stratis."

With his narrowed eyes on Rachel, Stratis rolled his tongue along the inside of his lower lip. "Fine with me, Sheriff, but the thing of it is, I still don't understand why Ms. Sorentino didn't sit tight after she called you for help. She was outnumbered and outarmed." He stopped and leveled his gaze at Rachel. "What made you do it?"

"Stand down, Stratis." Vaughn's tone was tight with warning.

If Stratis hadn't already insinuated that he knew something was going on between her and Vaughn, he sure would now, with Vaughn springing to her defense like that.

Determined to prove otherwise, she raised her hand to quiet Vaughn. "No, that's okay. It's a valid question. What made me take action, you want to know?"

"Yes, ma'am," Stratis answered.

"Because if they'd started firing again, and landed another lucky shot, they might've killed me. They might've gone after my family next. We may never know what their plan was. So instead of sitting there, hoping on high that they wouldn't kill me or my family, I decided to make sure they couldn't. By wounding them."

Stratis's brow raised. His lips twitched. "Good answer."

Asshole.

She shifted her gaze to Vaughn. "I'm done here. You have the flash drive and folder. We can set up an interview for another time if you have questions about the contents."

Vaughn looked like he wanted to ask her another question. Too bad. She was getting the hell out of the building. She fast walked down the hall. Irene looked at her like she hadn't missed a word of the conversation. Her Bible was open on her desk, her finger pressed to the words on the page as though holding her place while she watched Rachel. Rachel glared at her until she looked away.

"Ms. Sorentino. Rachel," Vaughn called. She heard a

jangle of keys and gear that meant he was hustling to catch up. "I'll walk you to your truck."

"No, thanks," she tossed over her shoulder, rounding the corner to the waiting area between the welcome desk and the door. She pushed the door open and angled her footfalls toward her truck. Let him chase her down if he had anything to say.

Chase her down, he did. Before she could get her key out of her pocket, his hand closed on her elbow.

"Rachel, stop for a second. Please."

Like she had a choice with the near-painful grip he had on her. She ground to a stop and yanked her arm away. "What?"

He wiped the hand he'd touched her with on his pants, then shoved both hands in his pockets. "Stratis was out of line. I'm sorry."

"I can handle myself around Stratis." *It's only you I fall to pieces around.* She opened her truck door.

Vaughn's hand clamped onto the door. His body heat and energy snuck up against her back, his nearness a palpable force between them. "What did he say to you?"

His breath puffed against her neck, calling forth the memory of his hands and lips on her, and she shivered. Goddamn, she was a hot mess. Of all three sisters, who would've thought she'd be the one to completely unravel in the presence of an attractive man? Pathetic.

She pulled her body up into the driver's seat. "Ask Irene. She heard it all."

Cursing under his breath, he released the door.

Rachel tugged the door closed and started the truck. Despite the pull Vaughn had on her, she managed to navigate her way out of the lot and down the road without once searching him out.

Chapter Nine

The shrill beep of the treadmill grated on Vaughn's nerves like it always did as he ramped his speed up to a hell-for-leather sprint. A sports newscaster prattled with his co-host on the television in the corner. He'd stopped listening more than two miles earlier, his attention fixed on the map of the Sorentinos' farm taped to the wall in front of him.

After a mile sprint, his lungs screamed. Not bad. Two years ago, he would've stopped jogging after five miles, and he never would've attempted a sprint. Since he quit smoking, he relished his daily runs as an opportunity to give nicotine the big *Fuck You* first thing in the morning. He scaled down the speed to a comfortable jog, then focused on the map again, this time on the black dot he'd added at the location of the first vandalism incident, on one of the property's newly installed oil derricks.

The day before, after Rachel dropped the flash drive off at the station, he'd been too pissed off to talk to Stratis rationally. Instead, he'd taken the flash drive home and fired up his computer. The photographs of the vandalism left his blood cold as ice. Graffitied messages that all threatened the same thing. Someone wanted Rachel and her sisters to leave town. What a preposterous demand, even if folks were peeved about their new dude ranch venture. Vaughn checked, and the Sorentino family had owned that land since 1952.

According to Rachel's records, the first time the vandals hit was the week Gulf Coast Petroleum broke ground on the wells. The graffiti message was scribbled on a leg of the derrick, as it waited near a large hole to be installed. The second message was on another derrick two weeks later. Intrigued by the possible connection between the vandalism and the discovery of oil on the property, he'd dug through his work files for a map of the county and made an enlarged copy of the Sorentino property on his printer.

With a black Sharpie, he'd spent the next hour mapping the locations of the vandalism incidents. If he included Wallace Meyer Jr.'s vandalism, there were six occurrences all together, spread in a line that reached from the southwest corner of the acreage to the southeast, in the Parillas Valley. Catcher Creek cut through the eastern corner of the line. With fatigued, midnight logic, he'd been absolutely convinced he was on to something. He would've bet his house that the vandalism trail followed the bed of oil underground.

He went to bed pretty damn proud of his detective skills. And woke up just as proud—right up until he stepped on the treadmill and asked himself, what does the son of a police chief and his gang of ingrates care about the Sorentino family's oil?

He didn't have an answer to that. Epiphanies on open investigations often came to him while he ran, so he'd taped the map to the wall in front of him. Ten miles later, he had nothing. He punched the STOP button on the treadmill and caught his breath, swabbing his sweat-drenched neck and forehead with a towel. The sky outside his workout room's curtained window was lighter. In another few minutes, the sun would pierce the morning haze.

Maybe Wallace Jr. wasn't the key. Maybe it was one of the other guys. Jimmy de Luca and Shawn Henigin were local boys, like Junior. But Elias Baltierra was a convicted criminal. He was most likely the leader of the group, despite Wallace Jr.'s money and connections.

He glanced at his watch. Binderman would be on shift by now, until midafternoon. As soon as Vaughn's breathing returned to normal, he dialed Binderman's number.

"Hey, Cooper here. What's the rundown for the night?"

"Quiet," Binderman answered. "A domestic in Devil's Furnace that Molina took, and Reyes made a routine traffic stop for speeding, which turned up a man with a warrant for his arrest in Tucumcari. We transferred him to the Tucumcari police's custody an hour ago."

The domestic wasn't surprising. Devil's Furnace, on the north side of Highway 40, was Quay County's only real slum. The site of a massive, sprawling new home development project two decades earlier, the entire five-mile area had gone up in flames before the owners had the chance to pay their first mortgage bills.

Vaughn had been fifteen at the time and still recalled the eerie orange-gray smog that settled over the county during the week of the fires. The rubble of the burned homes had only partially been cleared, to make way for trailer parks and low-income housing. The perfect petri dish for breeding druggies and criminals.

"Any news on Baltierra or Henigin?"

"Two anonymous tips came in to Lea County. Molina worked the graveyard shift, so I passed them on to Kirby. She's on the swing shift with me today."

"Good. Thanks. Listen, I've got some crime scenes

that need processing. Do you have much of anything on your plate today, or could you meet me at the Sorentino house at, say, eleven o'clock? I want to run forensics at the sites of the other vandalism incidents, see if we turn up any evidence. Maybe someone left a fingerprint we can salvage."

"Roger that. Happy to help."

"Good." He swabbed his face with a sweat towel. "By the way, I'm reassigning you to be my second on this case."

Long pause. "I thought Stratis . . ."

"Stratis is busy tracking down the source of the AR-15s." An executive decision Vaughn had made about two seconds earlier. No way would Stratis get near Rachel again anytime soon if Vaughn had anything to say about it. Binderman was still pretty green, but he'd proved himself to be an eager apprentice at the job. This was an ideal opportunity to kick his training up a notch.

"Okay. Thanks on that."

After the call ended, he folded the map of Sorentino Farm and set it by his car keys on the table in his entryway. En route to the bathroom, he stripped out of his workout shorts and started the water for the shower.

While the water heated—slow business in a house as old as his—he braced his hands on the lip of the sink and stared at his reflection in the mirror.

The scar on his jaw shone bright pink, usual for after a workout. He didn't mind its presence, and in fact felt lucky to have escaped with such a minor injury from the junkie who'd pulled a rusty switchblade on him during a routine traffic stop in Devil's Furnace the year before. He rubbed at it absentmindedly, then angled his head to study his hair. It needed a trim. He leaned in closer and scowled at the sprinkle of gray hairs at his temples. Job stress and genetics—two of life's inescapable constants.

Not that Vaughn had anything in his life worthy of complaint. At thirty-six, he had it pretty damn good—a great job, a house he owned, loyal friends, and a solid relationship with his folks.

He didn't have Rachel, and he wished that didn't bother him as much as it did.

There were other women, something he kept reminding himself of. In the year and a half since Rachel broke off their affair, he'd been on a few dates. Nothing that got past dinner and a kiss on the cheek. No one he ever wished he knew more about, or wished they wanted to know more about him. It kept coming back to Rachel.

More than once, he'd forced himself to consider the possibility that his preoccupation with her stemmed from the same source that made him love his job as a cop—there was something intoxicating about learning people's secrets and solving the mysteries of their lives. No one on this planet was as big a puzzle to crack as Rachel Sorentino.

Then again, maybe he was fooling himself to boil his attraction down to such a simplistic reason. She was a mystery, all right, but a beautiful, passionate one. When the two of them crashed into each other, the result was euphoric. Nothing he'd ever done in his life felt as good, as extraordinary, as connecting with Rachel, bringing her pleasure and finding his pleasure with her.

A month had passed since the last time they'd succumbed to the unyielding pull of each other. The memory stirred his body to life, his cock rising to nudge the cold porcelain sink.

He stared at his reflection, thinking about Rachel and their last time together, until the mirror steamed over. Then he stepped into the shower, adjusted the heat, and, bracing a hand on the tile wall, ducked his head under the stream of hot water.

The meeting with Rachel hadn't been planned. Never was, even though he put himself in her path as often as opportunity allowed, which was easy enough in a town as small as Catcher Creek. The diner, Parrish Feed & Grain, the vet's office. They knew each other's trucks, and knew what it meant when one approached the other. When Rachel wanted him, she let him know it loud and clear, and he took the reins from there.

The last time she wanted him, last month, she found him at Smithy's Bar. She'd sat across the room and never once looked his way, but he paid the tab for her single beer on the sly, then followed her out and helped her into the passenger seat of her truck. He'd pulled her truck into his garage. No need to set tongues wagging with her truck parked out front.

He fisted his erection, remembering the way she'd undone his pants right there in the truck the minute the garage door closed. The wet heat of her mouth on him, the dragging friction of her tongue and lips.

Every tug of his hand on his flesh brought the memory into sharper focus. The silky soft feel of her hair in his hand when he'd brushed it away from her face. The way the back of her throat felt on the head of his cock, the hint of teeth. Her hands working his balls.

They'd spilled out of his truck, a tangle of clothes and skin. In his head, he heard the mewling cry she gave when he bound her wrists with his tie and looped it over the hook on the wall. They didn't always play that game, but she seemed to need it rough that night.

He drizzled soap over his hand and worked his fingers over the ridges of his shaft in long, pumping strokes. His teeth gritted, he relived the taste of her wetness when he'd dropped to his knees and buried his head between her thighs. Her exquisite pussy, pink and swollen, opening for him. He'd rolled her flesh between his lips, then suckled her clit as he worked his fingers inside her wet, hot body. She'd whimpered his name.

Damn, he loved the sound of his name in her husky, desperate tone of arousal. Knowing it wasn't just sex for her—it was him. It was all the things he could do to her that no other man could. He replayed the sound. The breathy whimper of his name on her lips that signaled her surrender to pleasure.

Build up came too swiftly at that particular memory. Panting, he backed off, sliding his hand to the base of his erection. He fluttered his fingers over his balls, taking a break to fast-forward the vision to the moment he'd wrapped her legs around his waist and entered her, pushing inside until her tits hit his chest and his balls smacked her ass. He slid his fist along the length of his shaft, squeezing hard, mimicking the feel of entering her body.

Bracing her back against the wall, he'd removed the tie from the hook so she could drop her bound hands around his neck. They'd kissed openmouthed, violently. She'd bit his lower lip hard enough to draw blood, then licked it away. His eyes shut tight, he rubbed the sensitive flesh behind the head of his cock, recalling the wicked look in her eyes as her tongue had darted over her lip to lap the blood. She'd used the tie binding her wrists to pull his face to hers for a second taste.

Fuck, he couldn't hold back anymore. He pumped hard and fast, Rachel's voice echoing through his head, whispering his name when she came. Release swept through him, buckling his knees, summoning a grunt from his throat, as it had that night. Only this time, instead of spilling himself into a condom buried deep inside Rachel, his seed fell to the shower floor.

Instead of collapsing into the warm, soft body of the

sexiest woman he'd ever been with, all he had to lean into was the cold tile wall.

Parrish Feed & Grain sat smack in the middle of Main Street, straight across from First Methodist Church and two buildings down from Smithy's Bar. A square, single-story building with a two story façade of wood shingles done in a Wild West, frontier style, the store had probably looked sharp and fresh thirty years ago, but now looked old and tired.

Rachel admired the family's ability to keep their doors open despite years of a downward spiraling economy, family deaths and squabbles, and the opening of a new feed supply superstore in Tucumcari the previous year.

At nine-thirty, Rachel pulled into their parking lot, which sat empty save for the company's old beater of a forklift and one other truck Rachel recognized as belonging to Kate Parrish. This time of day, most farmers and ranchers were still busy mucking stalls and tending to livestock. Thanks to the hiring of Ben Torrey, Rachel was at liberty to make this trip to town for supplies without worrying about falling behind on her work.

She came armed with a long list she and Ben had written out that morning, supplies to prep the fields for the first alfalfa crop, as well as a credit card she hoped carried a high enough limit to pay for it all. Ben had all kinds of good ideas on getting the farm up to snuff as a competitive alfalfa grower, and neither he nor Rachel could wait to dig in and get started.

Growing up, Rachel and Kate had been a few years apart in school, with Kate being Amy's age, and so hadn't really had a good reason to be friendly until Kate took over as the feed store manager five years earlier, leaving her dad more time to make deliveries to bigger farms and ranches. The two sometimes walked across the street to the Catcher Creek Café for lunch or a slice of pie if the store was slow, and Kate regaled her with stories from her time in Washington, D.C., where she'd gone to college and briefly tried to make a living in politics. Sometimes she talked about her sister, Chelsea, who was a rancher's wife in Clovis, or her younger brother, Carson, a deployed marine.

Rachel wasn't sure what had brought Kate home to Catcher Creek, and Kate never got specific. Maybe she'd grown tired of politics, or maybe something happened in the Parrish family that Rachel wasn't aware of.

The front entrance of Parrish Feed & Grain chimed when Rachel entered. Kate smiled at her from behind the counter, on which a thick ledger book was open. A fancy calculator held one side of the book open. Her curly, reddish-blond hair had been wrangled into a braid that had fallen forward over the shoulder of her denim shirt.

She propped an elbow on the counter and smiled. "Well, hello, stranger. I heard tell you were shot, but you don't look very shot."

Rachel grinned. "How, exactly, does a shot person look, do you think?"

Kate got a saucy look in her eye. "Horizontal, with IV tubes and a pale complexion from all the blood loss and pain."

Chuckling, Rachel showed her the bandage on her arm. "I was only grazed by a bullet. It's going to leave me with an impressive scar, but that's about it."

"Girl, that's the weakest story I've ever heard. You need to manufacture yourself a real tall tale. One about your bravery and sacrifice. How you threw yourself in front of a bullet to save a child's life, then rose from your deathbed and endured great pain in the name of working on your farm. That's what this town likes—a good story."

They shared a laugh.

Rachel leaned against the counter. "I'll work on it, but my imagination isn't all that creative."

"You already have the start of a good story, what with all the talk about Vaughn Cooper swooping in to save you. Word is he carried you into the hospital in his arms."

Rachel pushed her tongue against the roof of her mouth until her shock faded enough that she could speak. "Is that the rumor going around?"

"By my word." She arched a brow and leaned in closer. "But I know that's not true because cowgirls like you and me, we don't need no saving. All we need is a loaded Smith & Wesson and a direction to aim it in."

Rachel's mouth went dry. "Anything else people have been saying about me?"

Kate fiddled with the turquoise rings on her fingers. "There's been talk."

"What else is there to say? I got in a shootout in Parillas Valley and took a bullet in the arm."

"Not about the shootout." She stared at her hand, where her fingers were busy sliding a ring up to her first knuckle and back.

Her frustration mounted at Kate's silence. Why the hell was she making Rachel dig the information out of her one spadeful at a time? "About what then?"

Kate stopped working her ring and pressed her palms on the counter, meeting Rachel's gaze. "We've been friends a long time. I'm telling you the talk I've heard, woman to woman, even though you know I don't have the stomach for hearsay and rumors."

Seemed to Rachel that her stomach was doing just

fine with hearsay and rumors at the moment. "Spit it out, Kate. What are people saying about me?"

"Not only about you, but you and Vaughn Cooper. They say you're having a secret affair."

Rachel wouldn't have been more surprised if a unicorn had come trotting out of the darkness of the stock room. She gripped the counter, lightheaded.

"You know," Kate said. "Sheriff Cooper is one of the most eligible bachelors in the county now that Kellan Reed's off the market. You'd snuff out the dreams of a lot of girls around here if you landed him, including mine. I thought I was making headway when your name started popping up during conversations about him at the beauty salon."

Rachel's temper flared. She crushed the list in her hand. "Has Sheriff Cooper returned your interest?"

Smiling like a fool, Kate cocked her head. "We've been out a couple times."

Goddamn it. She wrung the list in her hands until she heard the rip of paper.

Kate heard it too and pointed at Rachel's hand. "Ah-ha, so there is something going on with you two. Linda Klauss was right."

Whether or not Kate was being malicious on purpose, Rachel couldn't tell. Either way, Rachel liked her a whole lot less than when she'd walked through the door. "Do I look like the kind of woman who has time to mess around with a cop? There's barely enough time in the day for me to breathe with all the work I have around the farm."

Drumming her fingers on the counter, Kate's smile grew even wider. Rachel wanted to hit her. Not bad enough that she'd actually let loose with a blow, but it felt really good to visualize her fist making contact with Kate's cheek.

"I don't know about that, Rachel. When a fine figure of a man like Vaughn takes a liking to you, you make time for him."

Kate was right about that, even if it didn't bear admitting. "Kate, you've lived in Catcher Creek most of your life. You know better than to believe everything you hear in this town, don't you?" Her tone had a forced quality to it. She bit her tongue, wishing she had a better poker face.

Kate shrugged. "Whatever you say."

Rachel counted down from a hundred in her head as she worked to flatten the paper she'd crushed.

But Kate wasn't quite done. She leaned clear over the counter and arched a brow. "That's fine, that you don't want to talk about it. But would you do me a favor?"

Oh, boy, this ought to be good. "What?"

"When Vaughn gets done with you, will you at least give me the courtesy of a heads-up, so I can have a try at roping him in before word gets around that he's available again?"

As far as backhanded compliments went, that one had a whole lot of knuckle to it. Rachel ran her tongue along the inside of her teeth, working up a response. She should've said, *He's available now. Go ahead and take your best shot.* But the words wouldn't come out.

Instead, something lit up like a flame inside her. It wasn't plain old jealousy, though. Kate would make a fine match for Vaughn. She was pretty and fun, smart as a whip, and from a good, solid family. There was no toxic history between them, as there was between herself and Vaughn, no deep regrets or blame for grievances suffered.

But no one could match the raw heat Rachel and Vaughn generated when the two of them came together. Everything else about their lives was incompatible, but not that. Standing there, staring at Kate through slits of eyes, Rachel's indignation turned her spine to steel. She knew without a doubt that no experience he'd ever have with Kate Parrish or any other woman would compare to the two of them.

It was that knowledge that made her say, "Then I feel obliged to inform you, Kate—woman to woman—that when I get through with him, *if* I ever get through with him, he ain't gonna be good for much. Not after being ridden that hard for that long. A cowgirl like you should know that. But if you've got a thing for sloppy seconds, go ahead and get in line."

She unwrinkled the list and slapped it on the counter. "Here's the supplies I need. I'll send my foreman to pick them up tomorrow."

She left an openmouthed, stupid-faced Kate Parrish gawking at her as she walked away.

From the window next to his desk, Vaughn watched the flow of customers at Erskine's Barber across the street from the station house as he dialed Gwen's cell phone. He wasn't all that certain she'd take his call, but she picked up on the second ring. "Oh. My. God. What are you, my parole officer?"

Nice manners. "Good morning to you too. How's my favorite klepto doing?"

"How dare you treat my illness like it's some kind of joke." He rolled his eyes and picked up a pen to doodle with until she finished her tirade. She ranted a bit longer, then ended with, "You don't think I've had enough people making fun of me for it throughout my life? I've been through hell, Vaughn."

She had a point. High school had been rough on Gwen. Tough to be part of the in crowd when hanging out at someone's house or attending a party gave her the itch to steal her friends' parents' collectibles or silverware. On a memo he'd received on grade school outreach, he colored in the *d*'s and *a*'s. "With the way it's ruined your life and our folks' lives, trust me, nothing could be less funny."

"Got that right," she muttered, pacified.

"I didn't call to pick a fight," he said, filling in the *o*'s. "I wanted to make sure you were okay."

"I'm fine. You don't need to check up on me."

"You and I will have to agree to disagree on that point." She growled, but he pressed on. "You're staying home? No shopping or parties?"

"No, Officer," she deadpanned. "I'm behaving myself like a good little criminal."

He drew a bouncing line to connect the letters he'd filled in. This next question would make her mad, but no more so than he was for having to ask it. "You're not using drugs either, are you? You gave me the last of your stash, and you're not out replenishing your supply, right? Because nothing will get you behind bars faster than—"

"Oh, gawd. I'm hanging up. Get a life, Vaughn. And leave mine alone."

The phone clicked over to dead air.

"Love you too, sis," he grumbled, tossing his pen down.

He swiveled in his chair to stare out the window once more. The parking spots in front of Erskine's were empty. He watched a few minutes more to be sure he and Dale would be alone, then, after a word to Irene, walked across the road for a haircut.

Dale Erskine was a bear of a man. Thick in the middle and hairy all around, from his bushy red beard to the back of his hands and neck. The frizzy red hair on his head was in a constant state of crisis, as though he cut it himself using a funhouse mirror. But he was handy enough with other people's hair, even if he shortchanged Vaughn's sideburns every time.

Haircutting expertise was not why he patronized Dale's shop, one of two in town.

"Hey, Dale."

Dale looked up from sweeping. "Sheriff! Have a seat here. You want the usual today?"

"Sounds good. I'd like my sideburns longer than last time, if you don't mind." Never hurt to ask. One of these years, maybe Dale would heed his instructions.

He swung a plastic cape over Vaughn's body. "No problem, man. Long sideburns are hip."

Dale set to work, spraying water and combing, keeping busy. Vaughn's hair was thick and a veritable minefield of cowlicks, but Dale wrangled it into submission easy enough. "How's the keeping-the-peace business going, Sheriff? Need any help from me?"

No beating around the bush today. Vaughn liked that. "I've got three names for you. Jimmy de Luca, Shawn Henigin, and Elias Baltierra." He'd bring up Wallace Jr. in good time, but for now, he wanted Dale to concentrate his mind on the other players. The sixties and seventies hadn't been kind to Dale's mental capacity, and Vaughn had learned to pace their discussions.

"Haven't heard much talk about Jimmy de Luca. His folks run a pawn shop in Tucumcari that's talked about as being a great place to unload merchandise of questionable origin, if you catch my drift."

If Vaughn missed an insinuation that blatant, he'd be the world's worst sheriff. "I'm with you. What about the others—Baltierra and Henigin?"

"Elias Baltierra is bad news. He runs product for a drug cowboy across Highway 40."

Bingo. He had a hunch Dale would be the right informant for this case. "He's a supplier for Devil's Furnace?"

"Among other places. There's an element of Santa Fe who appreciate the service."

"Who's the drug cowboy he works for?"

"Not sure. There's been whispers of a new player in the county, someone called El Diente."

"The Tooth? What kind of nickname is that?"

Dale shrugged. "I think it's kind of hip. Like, that's his trademark. When people mess with him, he takes a tooth. Cool, right? I mean, every businessman needs a trademark."

Vaughn's mind flipped through the past four years' worth of investigations. A handful of times over the past few years, bodies had been found with missing teeth. Not so surprising for drug addicts and gang members, but Gerald Sorentino had been missing a molar. "What about Shawn Henigin? Did he work for El Diente too?"

"You don't have to worry about him. I heard he bit the dust in a car crash a while back."

Whoa, now. He watched Dale's reflection in the mirror, strategizing the best way to coax more information out of him. Time was a tricky topic for Dale, and *a while back* in his world could mean anything from a few hours to a few years, but Vaughn knew better than to ask him to clarify. He didn't have the patience to sit through one of Dale's mind-bending monologues. "Did you hear where the crash took place?"

"Hard to say." He buzzed the hair around Vaughn's right ear.

"Think harder."

"Hmm. Okay, I've got it. Down in Chaves County. He drove off a cliff along Hoja Pass."

An image of Gerald Sorentino's flattened, overturned truck at the bottom of Hoja Pass flashed through Vaughn's mind. Good God. "Hold that thought, Dale. I need to make a call."

He strode out the front door with the vinyl cape still around his neck, fishing his phone out of his pocket as he walked. "Stratis, it's Cooper. I need you to check on a couple things for me in Chaves County. A car crash on Hoja Pass that would've happened in the last day or two. Dale thinks that's how Shawn Henigin met his end."

"At Hoja Pass? You mean like . . ."

"Yeah, same place as Gerald Sorentino died. If Chaves County confirms the car crash, ask them if the deceased is missing a tooth."

"Like Gerald was," Stratis added.

"Exactly. According to Dale, there's a new dealer in town who goes by the street name El Diente. He might be the link between the criminal activity on the Sorentinos' farm and Wallace Jr. I'm going to pump Dale for more information, then I'll get back to the office to tell you the rest of it and figure out where we go from here."

Dale was standing as Vaughn left him, buzzers and comb in hand, looking unperturbed. "Did I do good with that information?"

"For sure. Like you always do." He waited a few beats to allow Dale to get back on track with the haircut, then asked, "Was Shawn Henigin running drugs for El Diente too?"

"Maybe. He was buds with Baltierra. They were here for haircuts once with Wallace Meyer's son, Junior."

Good boy, Dale. His idea for the haircut was getting bigger and bigger. "Tell me more about that."

"Well, uh, okay. Baltierra takes a number three attachment on the buzzers for his haircut—"

"I don't care about their haircuts. Did they say anything interesting while they were here?"

He pressed the buzzers to Vaughn's right sideburn and buzzed it clean off. "Right on. I dig you now. They were asking me questions about the dude ranch out there on the Sorentino land. Shawn was telling a story about taking his girl there for an overnight stay."

Vaughn nearly leapt from the chair. He twisted to look Dale in the eye. "What did you say?"

"He said he took his girl there. Him and Junior laughed about it real hard, about how the Sorentino place was nothing like a real farm. More like a tourist trap. So I told him, what did you expect from a dude ranch? And Shawn said, at least the food was good."

Vaughn swabbed a hand over his face. One of the shooters had spent the night in Rachel's house. Holy mother of God. The cape around his neck closed in, suffocating him. He ran a finger between the plastic wrapper and his neck, trying to breathe. "When were they here? Last week, last month?"

Either oblivious or unconcerned about Vaughn's state of disturbance, Dale came around the side of the chair and buzzed his left sideburn. "You know, time is weird, man. What's to say we're not living the same day over and over again. Like right now, I look out the window, and the street looks the same as it did yesterday. Or maybe it really wasn't yesterday. Maybe yesterday is really tomorrow—Hey!"

Vaughn clamped a hand over Dale's wrist. "Dale, listen to me. Do you know where Elias Baltierra is right now? This is important."

He scratched his head like it might loosen up his memory as it had earlier. "Hmmm. I knew you'd ask that, as soon as you got that crazy look in your eye. I haven't seen him since he was in here with Shawn and Junior. I s'pose you could ask Junior."

"I'll do that," Vaughn said, his mind distant, trying to fit puzzle pieces together that didn't seem to even be from the same puzzle, much less match up.

Dale set the buzzers aside in favor of scissors and a comb. Vaughn blinked falling bits of hair away from his eyes.

"Speaking of Sorentino Farm," Dale said. "Charlene Delgado says you and Rachel Sorentino are an item."

Vaughn grunted. Hard to care about Charlene blabbing rumors of Vaughn's private life when a dangerous criminal who'd shot at Rachel and may have connections to the death of her father was still at large. And he couldn't even go to the place in his head that would allow him to accept that Shawn Henigin had spent the night in her house.

Dale rattled on. "I asked Rachel out a few years back. She's a classy lady. When she declined my offer, she was real sweet about it. Said she wasn't in the market for a relationship, but thank you anyway. Guess she changed her tune, eh? Hard for a guy like me to compete with the sheriff." He gave Vaughn's shoulder a good-natured nudge with his elbow.

"Are we done here?" Vaughn asked.

"Near abouts. Let me get the hairs on your neck." He unbuttoned the cape and Vaughn took his first deep breath since the Sorentino name was brought into the conversation.

Felt like an hour passed by the time Dale finished. Vaughn tossed him forty dollars. "Thanks for the cut and the conversation, Dale."

"Come around anytime, Sheriff. I'm happy to help keep the peace."

Back in the station house, he swung by Stratis's desk. "What did you find out?"

"Chaves County confirmed. Late last night, a body was found in a car that crashed off the I-70, right off Hoja Pass where your informant told us to look. The description matched Henigin, so they sent pictures. We'll need family for an official ID, but it's him."

"Any drugs or alcohol in the vehicle?"

"No. Car was clean except for the body."

"Evidence of foul play?" If the vehicle had been tampered with, it might be weeks before the forensic lab could determine that, but it was worth asking anyway. Especially in an unidentifiable car that had been wiped clean of prints.

"Nothing they could determine at the scene. His skull was a mess, teeth included, so it'll take a formal autopsy to determine if any teeth were ripped out prior to the accident. The initial finding was that the accident was caused by steering mechanism failure. The steering gear bolts were sheered off, and I know you get what that means."

Vaughn's gut twisted. Everyone in his department, save Nathan Binderman, who transferred in after the fact, was intimately aware of every detail of Rachel's father's car crash. From day one of investigating the crash, he and Stratis had suspected foul play, but had no other evidence to support their gut-level instinct—until now. "It means it's time to take a second look at Gerald Sorentino's closed case file." He released a weary exhale. "Has the Chaves County Sheriff's Department heard of this El Diente guy?"

Stratis tipped back in his chair and joined his hands behind his head. "No, but his name came up in another conversation I had today with a border patrol buddy of mine. Last week his team seized a shipment of AR-15 rifles near the border, and the serial numbers match up with those recovered in the torched truck Kirby and Molina found. The two men who were arrested squealed, said they worked for a man named El Diente."

Why was a drug dealer terrorizing Rachel's family, and how had Gerald Sorentino been involved? The Parillas Valley shootout case was unraveling into too many threads to hold on to all at once, with each passing day bringing more questions than answers.

Kirby and Reyes were on double duty at the hospital guarding Meyer Jr., which left either Stratis or Molina to chase the lead with the arrested drug runners, and Molina was fresh off the graveyard shift. Not only that, but he needed a third person at Rachel's farm, now that the ranch house needed to be processed for evidence of Henigin's purported visit. Despite his goal of keeping Stratis away from Rachel, he had no choice but to bring Stratis with him to process evidence on her farm.

"I'll send Molina to the state pen to interview those gun runners. Maybe we can get a better handle on El Diente's business plan and how it involves Wallace Meyer Jr. and his associates."

"That was my thought, but both squealers got themselves killed in a prison yard fight," Stratis said.

"Well, hell. That was fast."

"You could say that again. Border Patrol's e-mailing me a copy of their interview notes. Did Dale Erskine have anything interesting to share with you?"

Vaughn dropped into the chair facing Stratis's desk. "As a matter of fact, he did. Which is why I need you at the Sorentino Farm in an hour to process evidence."

Stratis picked up a pen with both hands and rolled it between his fingers, avoiding Vaughn's eyes. "I'm sure Rachel Sorentino would rather see you than me."

Vaughn ran his tongue over his teeth. They were back

to that, were they? Tired of Stratis's passive aggressive bullshit, he had half a mind to drag Stratis into his office to hash it out, but now wasn't the time.

He stood, glancing behind him, to where Irene was pretending to read her Bible while she listened in. "Don't you worry, I'll be there too. In the meantime, get on the horn with other departments across the state. El Diente just became the most wanted man in New Mexico." He leaned over Stratis's desk and added in a low voice, "Consider this fair warning that if you ever again talk to a victim of a crime like you did to Rachel Sorentino yesterday, be prepared to look for work elsewhere. Are we clear?"

Stratis's jaw rippled. His eyes glinted with disgust. "Then you can consider this fair warning that I'm putting my name in the hat for sheriff come the November elections."

As pissed as he'd been at Stratis, he hadn't seen that curveball coming. Between Stratis and Meyer both gunning for his departure, the odds weren't looking good for Vaughn to keep his job, but there were a lot of months between May and November, and Vaughn was smack in the middle of the biggest case of his career. His legacy.

He stood to his full height. "You'd make a top-notch sheriff. Don't get me wrong, I'm going to fight like hell to beat you, but if you win, you'll be great at it. Until that time comes, though, you're still my employee, and you'll follow my rules. Understood?"

Staring at the wall behind Vaughn, Stratis sniffed. "Sir."

"Good. See you in an hour."

Chapter Ten

Rachel gave new meaning to the term *breakneck* as she barreled over the dirt road leading to her family's homestead. She was only going thirty, but with her truck's negligible shocks and the uneven road surface, she was surprised her head didn't pop clean off her body. It felt good, driving recklessly, beating herself and her truck up. What had she been thinking, saying what she had to Kate Parrish?

Why couldn't she have kept her mouth shut? Or smiled and offered a "Bless your heart"? But *sloppy seconds?* Where had she come up with such a nasty barb?

There it was, though. No doubt Kate was already down the street at the beauty salon, sharing the story with her friends. If word got back to Vaughn about what she said, she would die. She would lie down in a dusty field and let the buzzards have her.

If damage control were possible, only one person in Rachel's life would know how to go about it. Which was why she was heading straight to Catcher Creek's number one gossip maven. She spied Amy at the chicken coop, along with Mr. Dixon and Kellan's mom, Tina, helping the two guest families gather eggs and feed the hens. Mr. Dixon and Tina looked cozy, cuddling and whispering off to the side of the coop. Funny how Rachel hadn't noticed how close they'd gotten over the past few months since Tina came to live with them until Amy brought it to her attention the day before.

When her truck got close, she slowed to a stop and stuck her head out the window. "Morning, y'all," she called, lapsing into her cowgirl act without even meaning to. "Finding many eggs to gather this morning?"

She really didn't give a flying pig if they had, but after putting her boot in her mouth with Kate, she figured it wouldn't hurt to indulge in a minute of polite conversation.

The teenage girl in the bunch rushed to the truck, showing off a basketful of eggs.

"Wow. Neat! What are you going to do with all those?" she asked, pulling off a smile she hoped looked genuine.

"This afternoon, Amy's giving us a cooking lesson. We're going to learn how to make a real cowboy supper."

"With eggs, huh?" Rachel's idea of a real cowboy supper involved beef and potatoes, but it looked like tonight she'd be making do with eggs. She'd have to give Rudy, Damon, and Ben a heads-up so they could skedaddle to town before they got roped into the meal. "Sounds yummy. I can't wait to try it." As the girl returned to the coop, Rachel got her sister's attention. "Amy, may I have a word real quick?"

Amy wiped her hands on her jeans as she walked. She pulled Rachel's sleeve up and inspected her bandage, frowning.

"It's fine, Ames. Geez. It's been four days since I got hurt."

Amy *tsk*ed judgmentally. "True, but you're doing a

terrible job taking care of yourself. The scab's already torn once. And you're looking pale." She set the back of her hand against Rachel's forehead. "Are you feeling okay? I've got a nice list going of available bachelors in the area, so we've got to get you well. You're going to be on the arm of a good man for my wedding if it's the last thing I do."

What a pain in the ass sisters were. "God blast it, Amy. I don't want your help."

"Too bad. You're getting it."

She swatted Amy's hand away. "I've got enough stuff going on in my life without worrying about what schemes you're cooking up."

"Chef humor, that's cute. If you'll excuse me, I've got to attend to our guests."

"Wait. Do you know where Jenna is?"

Amy hooked her thumb over her shoulder as she walked back toward the chicken coop. "She's at her house, last I heard."

A quarter mile and a foothill separated Jenna's house from the main house, which had been originally constructed for the farm's foreman. Seeing as how they hadn't been able to afford a foreman since Rachel was a child, the house became Jenna's as soon as Tommy got old enough that he made their mom anxious with his little-boy energy. Better for all parties involved, Rachel and Jenna decided, that they put a couple acres of buffer between Tommy and his grandma.

In an ongoing project that took nearly a year to complete, the two of them had spruced up the exterior of the house, transforming it into a neat little cottage with a garden of succulents out front, along with a smattering of kid toys and a metal A-frame swing set. Rachel was proud of the work they did. Even as completely opposite personalities as she and Jenna were, they worked well together and rarely argued, which was more than she could say about her perpetually prickly relationship with Amy.

She parked her truck behind Jenna's white sedan. The door and all the windows of the cottage were open. Rachel checked her watch. Ten-thirty. Jenna had another two hours before she met the school bus bringing Tommy home from the pre-kindergarten class he'd started attending in January. Plenty of time for Rachel to grill her for information.

Figuring Jenna had heard Rachel's truck, she didn't bother to knock before walking into the comfortably cluttered living room. Jenna sat at her desk in the corner, typing on her laptop. Books were scattered and stacked everywhere. Some novels, but mostly manuals and how-to books, along with too many kids' picture books to count. Seemed that Jenna was always reading about how something mechanical worked, or studying up on the history of one invention or another. Door stoppers, Rachel jokingly called the thick books. But Jenna loved that kind of thing almost as much as she loved her computer.

"Hey, Jenna. What'cha up to?" She sidestepped an especially tall stack of books and sat on the long yellow sofa she'd helped Jenna haul home a few years back from an estate sale in Tucumcari.

Jenna glanced away from the screen with a smile. "Hi. I'm adding a testimonial page to Matt's Web site with quotes from satisfied clients."

Matt was Matt Roenick. He'd been Kellan's good buddy long before Rachel and her sisters hired him as their oil rights attorney after the oil was discovered on their property. When he'd taken a peek at the sisters' new Heritage Farm Web site, he'd asked for a referral to the Web design company to spruce up his law practice's site. Rachel had been there when he'd asked that question, and she didn't think she'd ever seen Jenna look prouder than when she admitted it was her handiwork.

In no time flat, Jenna and Matt had worked out a barter system. In exchange for a reduced fee on legal services rendered to the farm, Jenna signed on as his . . . "What do they call the person who designs and runs a Web site?" Rachel asked.

"A Web mistress."

Rachel snickered. "You're his Web mistress? That sounds . . ."

Jenna swiveled her desk chair to face Rachel. "Dirty, right? Trust me—I wish it wasn't as innocent a relationship as it actually is."

Jenna had a huge crush on the man, which Rachel didn't understand in the least. He was a nice enough guy, and supersmart, but his hands were callous free, and he was too white-collar to be useful around the ranch.

Rachel picked at a crust of mud in the seam of her jeans. "I have to ask you something random."

Jenna cupped her knee in her joined hands. "Random works for me. What's up?"

"Have you heard anything around town about me? Rumors or whatnot?"

Jenna pulled her bottom lip into her mouth with her teeth. "I've heard all sorts of stuff these past few days. What do you want to know?"

Rachel took a deep breath and surveyed the walls. This kind of conversation was uncomfortable enough without it happening in the close confines of a tiny room. Oh, well. Time to face the music. She pushed up from the sofa and walked to the window, bracing her hands on the sill to look outside. Even though she'd never said his first name aloud to either of her sisters in her lifetime, she said, "About me and Vaughn Cooper."

Saying the words made her dizzy. She clutched the windowsill and focused on a scrub tree in the distance.

"Yes, I have." Jenna paused and let the revelation hover in the air.

Rachel hunched into her arms as her gut lurched. "Go on. Don't make me pull it out of you. Tell me what people are saying."

She heard Jenna's chair creak, but kept her eyes locked on the window.

"People are saying that you and Vaughn are having a hot and heavy secret affair."

All the desperate hope she'd felt that Kate Parrish was exaggerating about the gossip deflated. She squinted until all she could see was the scrub tree. "Why didn't you warn me that people were talking?" Her voice sounded distant, calm like the eye of a tornado was calm.

Footsteps grew louder, until Jenna materialized next to her, leaning her shoulder on the wall. "I didn't want to spook you."

She cranked her head to the side and drilled Jenna with an exasperated glare. "What the hell is that supposed to mean?"

"Rach, what I heard in town this week is the first time I've ever caught even a whiff about you having a love life. I figured you and Vaughn were happy thinking no one was noticing what you two were up to. Seeing as how this was probably your first time, I was afraid you'd stop if you knew people were talking."

Rachel blinked. That was some effed-up logic. She was afraid to ask the next question that came to mind, but she did anyway. "My first time doing what?"

"First time doing *IT*. Duh. You lost your virginity to Vaughn, am I right?"

Rachel turned to face her sister head-on. Still, she had to open and close her mouth several times before any words would come out. "What you said is so wrong in so many ways, I don't know where to start."

"Are you saying you and Vaughn Cooper aren't having a not-so-secret affair?"

Rachel folded her arms over her chest. "I'm not telling you anything until you tell me where you got your information."

Jenna took a deep breath. "When I was at the Diamond Diva Salon getting a manicure, Linda Klauss was there, and I overheard her dishing with Nancy Tobarro while they got their hair done."

She paused and looked at Rachel like she'd just provided irrefutable evidence to a trial jury on one of those courthouse television shows.

"Keep going," Rachel prompted with a sweeping wave of her hand.

"Linda Klauss was one of the nurses who admitted you to the emergency room after the shooting, and she said Vaughn carried you in."

Rachel thought back to the haze of that morning. She remembered him carrying her, but couldn't collect enough details from her memory to know if it happened in the Parillas Valley or the hospital, or both. "Maybe. But I was injured, and woozy from shock. What's the big deal? Linda's reading an awful lot into things if something that inconsequential got her tongue wagging."

Jenna's expression turned solemn. "She said he fretted over you like a scared husband. She said he didn't let go of your hand for more than an hour."

Her mouth went dry. *He did that for me?*

Pushing away the wild elation stirring inside her, she shrugged. "I don't remember any of that. Everything about that day is pretty foggy. I had no control over what Vaughn did or didn't do. That's his business anyhow, not mine."

Jenna pressed her lips together like she did when Tommy was feeding her a line. "Mm-hmm. Except that, as it turned out, that day in the hospital wasn't the only time folks had spotted you two together around town."

"We weren't together around town, like on a date or something. I got shot. I was in the hospital. He was investigating. Sounds to me like folks are working awfully hard to squeeze water out of a rock."

Jenna ignored her valid point. "So after Linda told her story, Nancy piped up. She saw you get in Vaughn's truck a couple months ago out back of John Justin's. Late at night."

Shit.

"And then Marti, while she was doing my nails, she was listening too. She saw you and Vaughn leave Smithy's Bar together last month."

Ha! She had this one covered. "I never left Smithy's with him." That was the honest truth. Even if they did have the occasional well-timed exit.

"She said she saw you two making eyes at each other across the room, before getting up and leaving one right after the other."

"That doesn't mean anything."

She plowed ahead. "Maybe it wouldn't have, except that Gloria, the bartender at Smithy's, is friends with Marti and she said the sheriff paid your tab. Marti had asked her about it because the night it happened, when she went out front of the bar for a smoke, she recognized Vaughn's truck in the parking lot, but you were both gone."

She'd never been the subject of gossip before, and it felt like she'd been dropped in the middle of a rodeo arena full of bulls. "Well, goddamn, if no one in this town has anything better to do than gossip. No wonder the New Mexico economy's suffering."

"You want to hear the rest of it?"

She smacked her forehead with the palm of her hand. "There's more?"

"Charlene Delgado lives down the street from Vaughn, and she can count at least a half dozen times over the past two years that—"

"Stop. Enough. I can't listen to this anymore." She stormed through the living room and pushed out the door, worming her hand into her jeans pocket for the fresh roll of antacids she'd snagged that morning.

Behind her, the screen squeaked as it opened. She stole a glance over her shoulder to see Jenna hot on her heels. Knowing Jenna would never let the conversation go now that the dam had broken, she flopped onto a rock to give in to the inevitable.

"Well?" Jenna prompted, standing over Rachel with her hands on her hips.

She picked open the paper wrapper of the antacids and popped one in her mouth. "What do you want me to say?"

"I'm right, aren't I? You lost your virginity to Vaughn."

She pushed the antacid between her teeth and cheek. "Jenna, I haven't been a virgin since I was seventeen."

Jenna dropped onto the rock next to her. "What? Who? Why didn't you tell me?"

"Because when I was seventeen, you were eight. Plus, it's none of your business."

"And . . . and . . . there've been men in your life since then? Boyfriends and such?"

Rachel shrugged. "I've been on plenty of dates, but not with anyone I ever cared to call my boyfriend, not even many I'd consider my, uh, lover." Good grief, that was a clunky word. Tripped off her tongue as smooth as a lump of peanut butter. "I'm no prude, as you and Amy have so much fun believing."

"Why am I only now hearing about this?"

"I didn't realize I was supposed to clear my every romantic relationship with you."

"Who are these guys? Certainly no one around town or someone would've heard tell. And where do you find them? You never leave the farm."

Rachel yanked a blade of wild alfalfa from a clump growing at the base of the rock and twisted it around her finger. "I leave the farm all the time. I go to a lot of livestock auctions and supply stores, and I used to deliver alfalfa to ranches all over the county. I've been surrounded by men every day of my life." She paused, shaking her head. "Why am I telling you this?"

"I'm not sure, but I'm spellbound. Tell me more. I want details. Lots of details."

Good grief. "I think you and I are better off never confessing our sexual histories to each other, Jen. I don't want to know who and what you've done, and I'm sure as hell not going to give you details about who and what I've done." She unwound the grass from her finger and snapped it in half, wincing as a new possibility hit her. "Did you share any of the rumors about me with anyone, like Amy?"

Jenna huffed. "Nah. You're my sister. I'd never gossip about you to anyone except Amy, and right now she's too busy with the restaurant and her wedding plans to think of anything but her own happiness."

Thank God for small favors.

"Vaughn's totally hot, by the way," Jenna added. "I'm not into the whole cowboy lawman vibe he's got going on, but he's still drool worthy."

A smile tugged at Rachel's lips. "Yes, he is."

Jenna picked her own blade of wild alfalfa and tied it in a knot. "After Dad died, there were a few times when I stopped by the main house and Vaughn's patrol car was parked out front, but neither he nor you could be found. With so much going on at the time, I forgot about it until I heard Linda and Nancy gabbing at the salon. Is that when it started, this thing between you two?"

"He and I had been circling each other for a while, but after Dad died is when it finally happened."

"He was at the hospital when Mom died."

Rachel knew where this railroad track led, knew she no longer had the luxury to hide behind her cowardliness. Admitting her affair with Vaughn meant confessing to her deepest, most painful sin. She pulled another blade of alfalfa from the ground and cinched it around her finger until the pool of blood in her fingertip throbbed.

How could she say it? How could she explain to Jenna how their mom's death was her fault? How did one find the words to admit to the negligent homicide of a parent? She had to try, though. Her throat constricted. "Yeah, he was."

"And he was at the hospital the night mom tried to kill herself."

How did Jenna do it? Blew Rachel's mind the way she could get to the heart of the matter so intuitively. Rachel ground her fist into her stomach to quell the burning. "How did you know that?"

"I went to my car looking for my cell phone and saw you two talking in the parking garage. I figured he was interviewing you in an official capacity about what happened. But that's not why he was there, was it?"

"No." She shoved off from the rock and paced to the decorative picket fence she'd constructed for Jenna around her orange tree so Tulip couldn't get at it, swallowing a bunch of times to ease the tightness in her throat. "Jenna, I owe you an apology. I owe you more than that, but it's all I have to give. That and my vow to you and Tommy and Amy that I'll never let anything like that happen again."

"I'm confused. I thought we were talking about you sleeping with Vaughn."

"If I'm going to tell you about my private life, and the mistakes I've made, I'm going to start at the beginning." She pushed another antacid from the roll onto her tongue. "You remember the day of Dad's funeral, the day the bank called?"

That was the day she and Jenna discovered their parents had been flat broke, their land mortgaged to the hilt, their retirement funds empty, and their bank accounts overdrawn. Amy had been off preparing to film a cooking competition TV show, and though she'd come home immediately on learning of Dad's death, she'd had to rush back to the show as soon as the funeral ended. Mom spent the day in her room, heavily sedated under doctor's orders.

"That was a rough day," Jenna said.

"To say the least. After you went home to put Tommy down for the night, I was too agitated to be indoors. You know how I get."

Jenna offered a melancholy smile. "You got that from Dad."

"One of many things. So anyway, I snagged a six-pack of his beer from the fridge and headed to the porch. Two beers later, the sheriff—" She winced. Old habits died hard. "Vaughn showed up."

She stopped talking, lost in memory. He'd parked his patrol car next to her work truck. She'd never forget the sound of his boots crunching on the gravel driveway, nor the look on his face when he got close enough for her to see it in the light of the full moon. For the first time, he didn't look at her like she was troublemaker Jenna

Sorentino's older sister, or a grieving daughter, or a member of his voting constituency.

She'd never before seen desire burning in a man's eyes like it had in his that night. Hunger and need darkened his expression, making his body tense, his movements sharp.

How did he know?, had been her first thought. How did he know she'd wanted him that same way for years?

"I was so angry at Dad, for the finances and for dying on us like he did. And I had a beer buzz going. I couldn't help myself. Vaughn, he—" Damn, she couldn't say it. Besides, what had happened next wasn't any of Jenna's business.

Right there on the porch of her parents' house, while her mom slept off her drugs, she and Vaughn had done wicked, wonderful things to each other. He was everything she needed, the escape she'd been longing for. It was such a relief to let her guard down, to give up control and surrender to baser feelings. To not think at all.

He was so damn skilled at what he did. And she'd wanted him for so damn long.

"You don't need to rationalize it," Jenna said quietly. "Grief does funny things to us all. A man wanted you and you wanted him, and that's really all it takes, isn't it? Nothing complicated about that."

Rachel squeezed her eyes closed, jarring loose the tears that had been pooling in her eyes. "But it *was* complicated. Because Mom was sick and I wasn't around. I had responsibilities to her. And I turned my back on her for a few fleeting moments of pleasure."

"I still don't understand what you have to apologize for."

Rachel's legs grew unbearably restless. Pushing away from the fence, she stalked up to Jenna, swiping at the tears on her cheek. "Because the night Mom tried to kill herself, I was at Vaughn's house. I wasn't home when she needed me. I left her alone in the middle of a bipolar meltdown so I could screw the town sheriff. It's my fault she's dead."

Jenna was crying silent tears, same as Rachel. But she didn't look angry. Not in the least. She hugged her knees up to her chest and sniffed.

"Do you hear what I'm saying?" Rachel said more loudly, her voice cracking. "It's. My. Fault." She choked on a sob.

Why wasn't Jenna horrified?

Instead, Jenna pulled a whole clump of weedy grass up by the roots and let it sprinkle from her hands like grains of wheat. Tears fell over her cheeks and dripped onto her shirt. She wiped them with her sleeve.

"Talk to me, Jenna. I need to know what you're thinking, even if you can't forgive me."

The glassiness disappeared from Jenna's eyes as she met Rachel's gaze. "It's hard, thinking about that month. Worst month of our lives."

Rachel nodded. "It was. And I made it worse. You and Tommy and Mom were counting on me, but I let the unimaginable happen." A fresh cascade of tears fell from Jenna's eyes. Rachel slid to the ground and knelt before her, covering Jenna's hands with her own. "I am so sorry for the mistakes I made. I'm sorry I let you all down. I don't think I'll ever forgive myself, and I certainly don't expect you to forgive me, but I need you to know I'll live the rest of my life trying to make it up to you all."

Jenna threw her arms around Rachel's neck. Rachel hugged her middle.

They trembled and cried together.

"All this time, you've been holding that inside you?" Jenna whispered. "My God, how did you function, carrying that around?"

"I was scared to tell you. Scared of what you'd think of me."

With her voice muffled against Rachel's shirtsleeve, Jenna said, "No wonder you have ulcers, sis. You've been hurting worse than the rest of us, and we didn't even know it."

"I don't understand why you aren't furious."

Jenna set her hands on Rachel's shoulder. The look she gave her didn't have a hint of anger to it, but was full of love. "When I got pregnant with Tommy, I cared more about your judgment than both Mom's and Dad's combined. I thought for sure you'd never forgive me."

"I was spitting nails for weeks when you confessed why you were sick as a dog every morning."

"True, but you didn't send me packing, or insist I get an abortion or marry the baby's father—all the things that had me terrified of telling you."

"Of course I didn't. It wasn't my place to force you into making another hasty choice that would affect the rest of your life. Now, I'll admit I would've killed whoever dared knock up my little sister, but seeing as how you never saw fit to tell me who I should aim my shotgun at, I was prevented from landing myself in jail for murder."

Jenna chuckled. "Oh, the gossip that would've stirred up in town."

"You know what, Jen? As hard as those first couple months of your pregnancy were, Tommy was a real miracle for this family. Especially for you."

"He deserved a mom who had her act together. But I turned my life around for you too. I didn't think it'd do to repay your support by sticking you with my baby while I went off partying like I didn't have a care in the world."

Rachel climbed up to sit on the rock. "Why are we talking about this now?"

Jenna slung her arm across Rachel's shoulders. "Because you're more of a mom to me than Mom was. You raised me more than anyone else did in this family. My whole life, I watched you work your butt off around this place, and I never helped you out. All I did was cause you grief, getting in trouble with the law, getting drunk and running with the wrong crowd. And when I topped my own list of screw-ups by getting pregnant right out of high school, you told me everything would be okay. And it was. Because you made sure it was. What kind of person would I be not to forgive you? Not the person you raised, that's for sure."

Jenna's words wrapped around Rachel's heart, numbing her to the crippling pain her confession had brought on. She dried her cheeks on her shirtsleeves and gritted her teeth to keep them from chattering.

Jenna pulled her close and dropped her cheek to Rachel's shoulder. "Do you have any idea how much I love being your sister, Rachel?"

All Rachel could do was sit there and tremble and try not to lose it. She reached across Jenna and took her other hand in hers. This was why Rachel lived as she lived, toiled over her land as determinedly as she did—because she loved her sisters and nephew so much, she'd do anything for them. All these years, she wasn't sure Jenna had noticed how Rachel tried to watch over her and provide for her, to make up for all the many shortcomings of their parents. But Jenna had noticed after all. That acknowledgment alone was a great and powerful gift.

Jenna stood and opened her arms. "Give me a proper hug, will you?"

Rachel embraced her tightly. "I'm so sorry I wasn't there to keep Mom safe," she whispered into Jenna's hair.

"I know you need to hear me say it, so I forgive you."

They pulled apart, sniffling. Jenna walked to her car and ducked inside, coming out with a box of tissues and offering one to Rachel.

She thanked her and blew her nose.

"I still have some questions," Jenna said, dabbing at the streaks of mascara under her eyes. "What ever happened with you and Vaughn? Have you two been an item all this time?"

"No. I broke it off with him after Mom's overdose."

Setting the tissue box on the rock, Jenna let out a halfhearted laugh. "Your idea of breaking it off with a guy must be different from mine, if half the accounts of you two running around town are true."

Rachel rubbed her neck, wondering how to explain the complicated back and forth she and Vaughn were locked in. "I don't know what to do about him. I can't let him go like I should. I think about him, about being with him, all the time. Every day. But then, when I snap and give in to temptation, as soon as it's over, all that guilt about Mom and my farm responsibilities comes rushing back at me. It's torture."

"Sounds like it. What's Vaughn's side of the story?"

She reached for a second tissue and used it to dry her eyes. "He doesn't want a relationship with me any more than I want one with him."

"How do you know? Has he told you as much?"

"The affair started during Vaughn's investigation into Dad's car accident. There was no way he should've been messing around with me. The accident turned out to be just that—a freak malfunction of his truck's steering mechanism during a rainy night that Dad should've never been out driving in. But at the time, when the sheriff's department was still entertaining the possibility of foul play . . ."

Jenna nodded, getting the picture. "Vaughn could've

gotten in a whole heap of hot water for having an affair with you."

"We had to keep it a secret for the sake of his job and the investigation. Not that I wanted anybody to know, either. Not after what happened to Mom. And now, with the shooting in Parillas Valley, if anyone found out about our history, he'd have to recuse himself from the case. So you can see why our relationship can never amount to more than a dirty little secret. We've been doomed from the start." She heard the sneer in her words as certainly as she felt it tugging on her lips.

"Problem is, people in town are starting to figure it out on their own."

"I thought we'd been more careful than that, but I was in town this morning, and I had it out with Kate Parrish when she brought Vaughn up."

Jenna's mouth opened on the word *No* and stayed there.

"Oh, yeah. She asked me to let her know when I was done with him so she could have a crack."

Jenna gasped, wrinkling her nose. "What a slut! How'd you answer?"

Rachel wrung the tissue between her hands. "That's the problem. Instead of denying it, I added fuel to the fire."

"I'm sure it's not that bad. What did you say?"

Despite her remorse over her reaction to Kate, she felt the hint of a smile in her cringe. It had felt pretty dang satisfying to knock Kate down a notch, even if it was the wrong course of action. "I told her if she had a thing for sloppy seconds, she could go ahead and get in line."

Clapping her hands, Jenna let out a *whoop* of laughter that echoed off the foothill. "That's cool, Rach. I love this new side of you."

"I don't. Now I'm screwed. Kate's probably spread the news to every corner of the county by now."

Jenna patted her knee. "Sweetie, there's no such thing as secrets in Catcher Creek to begin with, so there's no sense wasting your energy worrying about discovery. What's done is done. Next time you go into town, keep your chin up and act like you know what you're doing."

Rachel bit her tongue to keep from bringing up the irony of Jenna's words. There was no such thing as secrets in their town. At least one big one, anyway. As far as Rachel and Amy could tell, not a soul in the town had any proof of the identity of Tommy's father. Everybody had a theory, including Rachel. But it didn't do any good to press Jenna on it because she was as tight-lipped as a kid confronted with a plate of spinach.

"He might need to recuse himself after all, in that case," Rachel said. "I know he wants to put Wallace Meyer Jr. and the others behind bars, but it's not worth jeopardizing his career over."

"Do you love him?"

There it was—the fifty-million-dollar question. She rubbed her hands together, choosing her words carefully. "I always thought if I settled down, it would be with a farmer. I've been doing this job alone for a long time. A partner would be a welcome change."

"True. That would be nice. Too bad life doesn't work that way. It's funny how often we get what we need instead of what we think we want."

She raised her brows, huffing. "That's the damnedest thing about it all—I don't *need* Vaughn. No one in their right mind needs that kind of hurt, where you can't live with someone, but you can't live without them either. Vaughn's brought nothing but pain and upheaval into my life. He's the last thing I need."

"Okay, but do you love him?"

Rachel puffed her cheeks full of air. She'd answered that question for herself the last time she and Vaughn had slept together the month before. But knowing the answer and feeling good about sharing it with her sister were two entirely different animals. She walked to the side of the house and picked at the chipping paint. The cottage needed a new coat. Maybe she and Jenna could tackle the project together now that Ben was here to manage the daily chores.

Jenna's searching gaze felt heavy on Rachel's back.

When she'd built up the nerve to speak, the power of confessing her deepest secret hushed her voice to a whisper. "Yeah. I do. Makes no difference because nothing will ever come of it, but yeah, I'm crazy in love with him."

Jenna joined her at the siding. Rachel watched her gaze travel past the house and up the hill that split her valley with the main house. "Speak of the devil."

Rachel whipped around. Sure enough, Vaughn's squad car, followed by a sheriff's department patrol truck, then another squad car, paraded down the road in the distance. At the fork, they turned toward the main house.

Rachel dusted her jeans, praying her eyes weren't as red and puffy as Jenna's. At least she didn't wear makeup so she didn't have to worry about having the same raccoon eyes Jenna was sporting.

Rachel handed her a tissue. "Here. Your makeup's running."

Jenna wiped the smears. "Thanks. You should know I'm not going to tell Amy any of this. It's your story to tell when you're ready." She set her hands on Rachel's shoulders. "Remember, you didn't owe me an apology, and you don't owe Amy one either. What you need to do is figure out what you want with Vaughn."

"That's what I'm trying to tell you, Jenna. What I want is for things to be the way they were in simpler times. Before Dad died and Mom's depression took a turn for the worse. Before we had to peddle our way of life for a tourist dollar. The way things were before Vaughn."

Jenna tossed the tissue box in her car. "Despite the way you've got it pictured in your head, our lives were never simple. They were predictable, and that's a big difference, but you're only fooling yourself if you think we ever had it easy." She draped an arm across Rachel's shoulders. "C'mon, sweetie. Let's go see what's brought your sheriff out to the farm today."

Chapter Eleven

The first thing Vaughn noticed when Rachel stepped out of her truck was that her eyes were rimmed in red. Her cheeks and nose were red too. So were Jenna's, he saw after she walked around from the passenger side of the truck.

It threw him off something fierce to know Rachel had been crying. He was dying to know what would push her to such an openly emotional state, though he didn't dare ask. The ways of women when they got together weren't meant to be understood by mankind, his dad used to say when the two of them retreated to the workshop on Bunco night or during his sisters' innumerable sleep-overs.

Stratis and Binderman were busy organizing their evidence kits and preparing for the task at hand, so Vaughn met the sisters to explain the reasons for their visit. Rachel's gaze barely touched on him as she looked at the vehicles and Binderman before resting her gaze on Stratis, who was digging through his trunk. She frowned at him, her eyes wary.

He hated that she was uncomfortable, but there wasn't a whole lot he could do about it.

"Good morning, Sheriff," Jenna said.

He touched the brim of his hat in greeting, then turned his focus to Rachel, "How are you feeling today, with the gunshot wound?"

"Better, thanks. It's healing nicely." Her response was as woodenly delivered as his question. They were quite a pair.

Maybe that was why Jenna was staring at him like she was trying to read his thoughts telepathically. Maybe she could. What the hell did he know? Of all the Sorentino sisters, Jenna was a complete mystery to him, though it hadn't always been that way. When Jenna was in high school, he'd had her figured out to a fault, a product of hauling her butt to school or Rachel's door near about every week. But this new Jenna, the single mom, he didn't know a thing about her except that, from all accounts, she had a whip-smart mind that rivaled her older sisters'.

When she wouldn't stop staring at him, he extended his hand in greeting. "How are you, Jenna?"

"Doin' fine, Sheriff."

As he was scouring his brain for a bit of small talk to engage her with, Binderman chose that moment to walk up, for which Vaughn was eternally grateful.

"This is Deputy Binderman, and Undersheriff Stratis is over by the truck. We're here to gather evidence and ask you all a few more questions."

"You've already been all over the Parillas Valley. What more do you need?" Rachel asked.

"Oh, I meant at the other graffiti locations."

"We haven't . . ." Jenna rounded on Rachel. "What's he talking about, Rachel?"

By the way Rachel's expression turned wide-eyed and panicky, it was clear she hadn't been forthcoming with her sisters on what had been happening around the farm. He did a mental cringe. Bad call on her part. She had to know it was going to be public knowledge sooner or later.

"If I say it's not important, will you let it go?" Rachel asked her.

"I don't think so," Jenna answered in a peeved tone.

"It's nothing. Really."

"Spill it, Rachel." Geez, she sounded like Vaughn's mom when she'd caught him or one of his sisters up to mischief. There must be some sort of secret mom school where they all learned to do that.

Rachel huffed and threw her arms up. "*Spill your guts, Rachel.* Isn't that just the theme of the day?"

Vaughn looked at Nathan and they both took a step back, then another. And one more for good measure.

"You and Chris don't have any sisters, so you're not altogether familiar with this sort of sisterly battle?" he asked.

"Nope. Just us three boys. Our oldest brother, Tom, has two girls."

Vaughn watched Rachel explain the other graffiti instances to Jenna, whose face got redder and madder with every detail Rachel revealed. "I have two younger sisters. My only word of advice is never get caught in the middle of two sisters fighting. It ain't pretty. Especially when they live close together and their monthly cycles match up." He shuddered, remembering some of the hair-pulling, shrieking battles his sisters had gotten into growing up.

Nathan balked. "Aw, now, don't talk about woman stuff. Ugh."

"Spoken like a man who doesn't have sisters. There's no escaping the topic when you live with three women. You become numb to all the tampons and crying and ice packs and late-night chocolate ice cream runs. You'll have to take my word on that."

Nathan looked horrified.

Vaughn chuckled. Nothing wrong with razzing your greenest deputies every so often.

His smile vanished when Jenna stalked up to him. "Is this true? Twelve times people have come onto our property and defaced it? Once even as close as behind our stable? That's way too close for a criminal to be to my son. Can't you arrest Rachel for failure to report or something? Teach her a lesson about keeping every damn thing inside herself instead of sharing the information with her family, of all people?"

"I'm not going to arrest Rachel. She thought she was doing the right thing, keeping you all in the dark."

Jenna's mouth twisted in disgust. "Oh, perfect. Of course you're taking her side. I should have guessed you'd back her up."

"Don't you dare bring him into this," Rachel hissed, low and menacing. The two went back to snapping at each other.

Binderman leaned over and whispered from the side of his mouth, "What happened to your advice to never get caught between two sisters fighting?"

Vaughn glanced sideways at him, then held up his palms and said in a booming voice, "We have bigger problems. I received information today that one of the suspects, Shawn Henigin, has actually been a guest at your inn." That got their attention.

Rachel and Jenna gasped. Jenna reached to Rachel and gripped her forearm, shaking her head. "No way. I would've recognized the name."

"He probably used an alias," Vaughn suggested. "I know your farm mainly serves families, but have you had any couples stay with you lately?"

Jenna nodded. "Three pairs in the last few months."

Rachel's jaw tightened. "I didn't recognize him on Monday, but then, I don't have much interaction with the guests, especially the couples without kids."

"Understood," Vaughn said. "While Deputy Binderman and I interview you about the graffiti, Undersheriff Stratis has a picture of Henigin to show Jenna and Amy, along with some questions to ask them. Would that be all right with you, Jenna?"

Jenna nodded and swallowed.

Stratis nodded to her. "Let's get started, Miss Sorentino."

But Jenna didn't move until Rachel gave her a subtle nudge that kick-started her into action. Stratis opened his arm, guiding her toward the front porch.

When they were out of sight, Rachel asked, "What would this Henigin man gain from staying with us? None of the graffiti has been close to the ranch, except for the one time behind the stable. As far as I know, nothing was stolen, so it's not like he was casing the joint."

"I don't know, but it chills me to the bone to think of you, Amy, and everyone else sleeping under the same roof as that man. I hope to God my source was wrong."

Rachel nodded and jammed her hands into her pockets, her jaw tight, her shoulders tight—everything about her tense and scared. She looked so shaken, he was overcome with the need to hold her. He shook the thought away. "Let's work on getting out to the derricks as fast as possible. We'll puzzle out the rest later. I'm assuming the locations of the graffiti incidents are accessible by truck?"

Rachel shook her head. "All but the second to last one, on the boulders overlooking the western edge of the Parillas Valley. It's only reachable by horse or ATV."

That didn't make for a fast or quiet getaway for the vandals. He filed that bit of data away.

"How many ATVs do you have on this place?" Binderman asked.

"One is all we've got working right now. Most of the revenue from the oil has gone toward paying debts and our workers' wages. Plus, I'm saving for a new tractor engine." Shaking her head, she bit her lower lip. "And I don't know why I'm telling you that. Sorry."

"No. That's understandable. A new tractor is important." *Understandable?* What a moron. For once, he wished he could talk to Rachel in front of other people and not sound like a robot with a broken circuit board. He took a deep breath and tried again. "I'd like you to come to the crime scenes to tell us more about the vandalism and show us exactly where the graffiti occurred. Does the ATV hold two?"

An unwanted thrill stirred to life in him, imagining Rachel straddling the ATV behind him, her arms around his waist, her face near his shoulder. Good Lord, why had he suggested such an outrageous idea?

If the idea of sharing an ATV affected Rachel as it did him, she didn't show it. "It's a one-seater. I can ride horseback. Follow you there."

On Tuesday, he'd longed to ride with her. To be near the wild strength she harnessed when she moved in the saddle. The circumstances today weren't ideal, but it might be as close as he ever got to that dream. "If you've got a second horse up for the task, I'd like to ride too. My evidence kit's small enough for a saddlebag."

Though riding double on an ATV hadn't sparked a fire in her eyes, this new notion did. Flushing, she turned away from Nathan's line of sight.

"That would be fine." Her voice was throaty and low.

She pressed her hand to her chest. "Jenna's horse, Disco, hasn't been on the trail in a while. You'll like him."

He nodded to Nathan. "Binderman, you take the truck and process the derrick for evidence. After Rachel and I get you started there, we'll move over to the other scenes and leave markers for you to find them."

"Yes, sir."

"Rachel, would you point Deputy Binderman toward the derricks?"

He waited near the stable door while Rachel gave directions to Nathan, then followed her through the sliding double doors. She beelined for the tack box.

"What's going on with Jenna?" he asked, joining her.

She pulled out a saddle blanket and handed it to him. "What do you mean?"

"Before I brought up Shawn Henigin, she was acting . . . odd. She wouldn't stop staring at me." He wished he had the guts to add, *And you two had obviously been crying.* "I couldn't tell if she hates me or if she was trying to flirt with me. Either one would be bad."

Rachel snickered, coming up from the tack box with a halter and bridle combo. Brushing past him, she fitted the halter and bridle onto a gorgeous black horse with white diamonds on its legs and nose, then led it from its stall.

"Jenna's not flirting with you." She stroked the horse's neck, and Vaughn had to wonder if she were deliberately avoiding his gaze. He came up next to Rachel to let the animal sniff its fill of him. "Vaughn, meet Disco."

"Hey, buddy. Wanna go for a ride?" He reached in front of Rachel to stroke Disco's neck.

"How long has it been since you've ridden?"

It was a fair question. "Kellan and I go trail riding on

his land fairly often. I was practically born on a horse, though, with my parents being farriers."

Disco nudged Vaughn with his nose, then gave his cheek a little nibble and knocked his hat off. Vaughn snatched it out of the air and tucked it under his arm, then scratched Disco's neck near his chin. "How come you don't think Jenna was flirting with me? You think that's so impossible? I'll have you know I get flirted with all the time."

"I believe it. Kate Parrish considers you Quay County's most eligible bachelor now that Kellan's off the market. She told me so today."

"She did, hmm?" Had to wonder what else Kate said, seeing as how they'd muddled through a couple awkward dates before Vaughn had gentlemanly, but firmly, let her know a third one wasn't in the cards. Kate was nice enough, and pretty in a former prom queen way, but he didn't feel a thing for her except neighborliness. "Then why is it so hard for you to entertain the idea that Jenna might think of me the same way?" He smiled so she'd know he was teasing her.

Rachel took the blanket from Vaughn and placed it on Disco's back. "Because she told me she's not into your whole cowboy lawman vibe."

A chuckle bubbled up from low in his belly. "That's a good thing, because I'm not into her whole younger sister of my—" He froze, stuck on wondering what Rachel's title would be in his life.

"Former lover vibe?" Rachel provided, tossing the words over her shoulder as she walked to the tack box.

Oh, doggie. Time to let that uncomfortable conversation thread die. He wandered past the rows of stalls, stopping in front of Growly Bear, and offering the horse his hand to smell.

"You want me to get Growly Bear out?"

"No. I have to take Amy's horse, Nutmeg, today. Growly threw a shoe and our farrier couldn't come by until tomorrow."

Vaughn peered into Growly's stall. The horse's left hind leg had been fitted with a cloth boot.

Rachel appeared next to him. "Lincoln was my trail horse. Growly didn't see much trail time, so we didn't know his shoe was compromised until . . ." Her voice trailed off.

He was anxious to save her from having to vocalize about Lincoln's death. "Understood. Who's your farrier?"

"Chuck Harring."

The farrier community was a small one. Chuck was a longtime friend of his family and an all-around decent guy. "He's good. When he comes by, make sure you tell him Growly's going to be seeing a lot more trail time. He might need to adjust all the shoes. Were you able to recover the thrown shoe?"

"Yes."

Vaughn smoothed his hand along Growly's neck. "I keep a basic farrier kit in my trunk. You'd be surprised how often it's come in handy over the years in my line of work. Chuck wouldn't mind me stepping in, if you'd like me to take care of it real quick."

"That would be great, but I know you have a lot of work to do and the day's not getting any younger. I could ride Nutmeg no problem."

For reasons he didn't care to analyze right then, he wanted to help Rachel out, get her riding her preferred horse. He wanted to make her happy, sure, but he suspected his offer was more about the way he felt watching her gallop with Growly across the Parillas Valley earlier that week. "Bring him out of his stall. I'll get my kit."

The grounds were quiet, save for two of Rachel's

farmhands who were tinkering under the hood of a tractor. They didn't notice him, so he kept moving.

Back in the stable, he and Rachel exchanged cautious smiles. She watched from a stool as he took off his tie and utility belt, leaving them in a pile on a workbench. He hesitated with his fingers at the button of his uniform shirt's collar. It wouldn't be professional to get it smudged while shoeing, but stripping to his undershirt in front of Rachel was the start of a story that invariably ended with them both naked and breathing hard.

He solved the issue by turning away from her until he'd taken off his shirt and replaced it with his leather farrier apron. Still, he felt her dark eyes studying his every move. When he snapped and glanced her way, it was to see her raking her eyes up and down his body, her lower lip snared in her teeth and her eyes dark as midnight, as if the sight of him in a white T-shirt and apron was the sexiest sight she'd ever witnessed.

In college, when he worked for his parents farriering, he'd definitely managed some dates with various ranchers' daughters using this look, but that was a solid fifteen years ago, when he was a whole lot younger and fresher faced.

He moved a stool near Growly's tail and laid his tools out. Then he smoothed his hand over Growly's back, then his hindquarters, until he was certain the animal was comfortable with him. Maintaining contact with his shoulder against the hindquarters, he slid his hand down Growly's leg. In a quiet voice, he asked Growly to lift his leg as he patted his leg above the hoof. Growly complied and Vaughn pulled it onto his apron, to rest on the ledge made by his bent knees.

From the corner, Rachel let out a ragged breath that left the air in the room crackling with tension so brittle he could've snapped it like a stick of toffee.

Don't look at her. Do the task at hand and keep your mind out of the gutter.

He picked up his hoof knife and took to cleaning the hoof, prepping it for the shoe. Ignoring Rachel.

He was doing fine with that until he asked her to bring him the shoe. Because then she came too close and said in a husky voice, "You might not be a rancher by profession, but your heart is pure cowboy."

Don't look at her. "Cowboy lawman, according to your sister."

She let out a throaty laugh and strolled toward her perch in the corner. And then, as if he weren't having enough trouble keeping his thoughts virtuous, he watched the sway of her ass until she resumed her seat. Their eyes met, and the look she gave him singed him where he stood.

Forcing his focus to shoeing, he tested the smoothness of Growly's hoof with the pad of his thumb, filed down a couple rough spots, then fitted the shoe on. Before he had enough sense to restrain himself, he blurted, "Unlike Jenna, you dig my cowboy lawman vibe, don't you?"

"What do you think?"

Actually, he wasn't sure what the hell he'd been thinking, asking her that. He selected a No. 5 nail and a hammer, then tapped the first nail in place. Hoping to defuse the tension with humor, he painted on his best self-deprecating smile and said in an exaggerated Texas drawl, "Darlin', how about I show you my six-shooter?"

Rachel snickered. "I bet that's the line you use on all the ladies."

"Hey, a guy's got to work hard to earn the title Most Eligible Bachelor. My pretty face alone don't cut it." He tapped the next nail in place.

"I hate to break it to you, but I get the impression that

the only requirements for Eligible Bachelor status in Quay County are: one, that a man's single; two, that he has a steady job; and three—this one's optional—he owns a house."

He raised a brow and glanced her way. "That's all women want these days? Seems simple enough."

"You'd be surprised how hard it is for a woman to find that winning trifecta in a man."

Oh, hell, no. She better not be saying what he thought she was. Try as he might to keep it in place, the smile wiped from his features. When he spoke, the timbre of his voice had a sharp edge of irritation. "You been looking?"

She was silent for a beat, but he refused to look up from his work, afraid of what she'd see in his expression.

"No, I'm not out looking. Just been listening to my sisters bitch about it for years."

He hammered another nail in place, annoyed that her answer hadn't done much to quell his jealousy. It was hypocritical of him to be bothered in the first place, since the two of them had already broached the subject of Kate Parrish. But the thought of her with another man made him want to kick his boot through the stable wall. Real mature, Vaughn. He selected another nail and concentrated on not taking out his anger on the horse.

They lapsed into a tense silence while he nailed the shoe in place. Growly had the calm disposition of a well-cared-for horse that was used to being shoed. He affectionately nibbled the back of Vaughn's neck every so often, but otherwise stayed still. When he finished, Vaughn lowered Growly's leg and rubbed his hindquarters, satisfied by how straightforward the shoeing had been. "Done. I'll repack my kit and we can get moving."

He watched Rachel's approach out of the corner of his eye and braced himself to resist her.

"Thank you for doing that," she said.

Still avoiding her eyes, he shrugged. "Why don't you prep the horses to ride while I get myself put back together?"

"Sure."

She moved away from him, toward the tack box on the far side of the stable. He released the breath he'd been holding, then walked to the washbasin and scrubbed his hands. He removed the apron and folded it. His undershirt was dotted with circles of perspiration. The damp cotton clung to his chest and rendered his dusting of black chest hairs visible. Embarrassing.

With a grimace, he ran a hand over his stomach and reached for his dress shirt. Once his shirt was on, he fixed his belt in place, then reached for his tie. As soon as he took it in hand, a flood of memories washed through him—of the times he'd blindfolded her with it, or bound her wrists. Once, he'd used it as a gag. She'd come so hard that day, he'd gone out and bought a proper one, not that he'd ever had the chance to use it on her. She'd broken their affair off the next day.

A *clunk* caught his attention. A pile of tack sat on the ground next to where Rachel bent over the box. He followed her worn brown work boots up her legs to the supple curve of her backside, then higher, to the sliver of black panties showing above her jeans.

Before he even realized he was moving, he was behind her, his hand on her hip, testing the curve of her body beneath the denim. Rather than flinch away, she pressed that curve more firmly into his palm as she stood. He lifted her hat off and hung it on a nail within reach. She let him do it, so he took a chance and ran the tip of his tongue over her earlobe, then bit into the curl of flesh at the top until her body shuddered.

Her upper teeth pressed onto her plump, rosy lower

lip, a move that blinded him to all the reasons kissing her was wrong. He angled in, desperate for a taste of her.

With a breathy gasp, she jerked her face away and folded forward to rummage in the box, a move that presented her backside to him again. She was too smart to not be aware of what she was doing. The erection pressed against her thigh should've been enough to tell her his control was fraying. He cupped his hand over the firm flesh. Was she testing him? Making him prove his resolve to resist her? This was one test he'd have no qualms about failing at the moment.

She twisted up and looked over her shoulder at him, carnal awareness battling with self-control in her eyes as surely as it was battling in his mind. Then she handed him a halter combo and a leather rein.

Damn, the leather gave him impure thoughts. He tucked the halter under his arm and stretched the rein between his hands.

Two seconds. That's all it would take for him to bind her wrists to the handle on the side of the box and stretch her across the top as tightly as strings on a guitar. Wouldn't be the first time he took a leather strap to her body. His blood throbbed beneath his skin, imagining all the ways he could bring her pleasure in that position.

He closed his eyes, his breath coming in starts and fits, gripping the rein hard enough that it cut into the fleshy part of his palms. "Tell me to get away from you. Tell me to leave you alone."

As he stood frozen, torn between ravenous need and his integrity, Rachel stood. Her hips shifted to stroke him in the cleft of her buttock. Her fingers found his jaw, and she scraped her nails over the stubble of his neck and chin. "And if I don't?"

He stroked the back of her arm with the rein. "If you

don't do what I tell you, then you're going to pay the price."

Rachel molded her body into his. She tipped her head back to rest on his collarbone, her breathing ragged. "We should not be here like this."

True enough, but he was too far gone to care. "Close the lid, and don't say another word." He hadn't used that voice in a while. The low, fierce command. Threatening to anyone's ears but Rachel's, who knew from experience that there'd be no repercussions if she didn't follow his command, that despite the force behind his words he'd never get dangerous with her. She obeyed him because she wanted to, and he never forgot that. Even when he was so aroused that he couldn't remember his own name. The power was Rachel's to give or take back as she pleased.

He waited for her to make the choice, his hands clutching the rein, listening to the rustling sound of the horses and the surge of blood in his ears.

She bent forward and closed the lid.

He gritted his teeth as a wave of arousal crashed through him. *Game on, baby.*

Dropping his arm to his side, the leather strap unfurled from his hand. He shook it out and gave Rachel time to change her mind.

She remained tipped forward over the box, her hands braced against the closed lid, her legs apart. She glanced sideways at the rein, breathing in even, shallow breaths through parted lips. She knew what was coming, and it turned her on as much as it did him. He leaned in and brushed his lips across her cheek before taking her mouth in a hard, ravishing kiss.

He broke away, gasping for air. They didn't have time for this. People were waiting. It was nearly noon and the stable sat in the center of Rachel's bustling family enterprise. Not too far away from the stable, he heard the sounds of the guest families. Chatting, their children laughing and playing. Somewhere nearby, an engine revved. That would be Rachel's farmhands working on the tractor.

Screw it all. He needed this. Rachel needed this. Besides, no one would know. And that made what they were doing even more intoxicatingly wicked.

A bowline knot came fast for his practiced fingers. Sliding his hand down her arm, he waited for the resulting shiver to leave her body before taking her wrist in hand.

"Other wrist too," he commanded.

She brought it to meet her right wrist and held still, allowing him to slip the loop over both. He jerked the end of the rein, removing the slack, binding her arms together. She whimpered, the little mewling sound she almost always made when she was close to orgasm.

His brain and his cock screamed, *AGAIN*.

That morning, he'd jerked off in the shower to the memory of her making that sound. And here he was, a few hours later, hearing it fall from her lips. He hadn't even touched her but a little, and nowhere near her erogenous zones. If she were that close to coming already, then maybe she needed this even worse than he'd suspected.

"Turn around and face me."

His cock pulsed as she obeyed. There was no more battle in her eyes as she looked at him. Arousal had won the day.

"Lie back."

She hitched her ass on the edge of the lid and reclined. He grabbed hold of the knot binding her wrists to support her weight as she lowered. When she'd settled, he kicked her boots as far apart as her legs would go. The end of the rein in hand, he walked to the far side of the box and threaded the leather through the handle, pulling it tight, stringing her torso across the box. The act brought out a moan from her, but it wasn't the sound he needed to hear again.

She watched his face as he secured the rein to the handle with a second bowline knot. He brushed hair away from her eyes, then traced over the cinnamon freckles of her cheeks. She was so damn pretty, and the fire of life and intelligence in her eyes glowed so damn bright. His flame. His beautiful, complicated flame.

She drew his finger into her mouth and held it in place with her teeth as she suckled it, flicking the end with her tongue.

Given the position and angle she lay at, he could brace his knees on the box and feed her his cock. He knew she'd take it greedily. She'd do whatever he asked of her—suck him off, swallow. Whatever he wanted. The knowledge of his power nearly had him unzipping his pants. But then, if he did that, she wouldn't make the sounds he craved, nor experience the sharp, sweeping pleasure he wanted so fervently to bring her before they got to anything else.

"Stay," he growled.

His senses dazed, he stumbled away from her and snagged a rope hanging from a nail in the wall. His vision tunneled on the sliding stable doors.

At the door, he glanced sideways at her. She lay where he'd left her, her legs apart. Beautiful, strong, gifting him with the power to command her pleasure.

He threaded the rope through the door handles and knotted it. No one would get through the door now. Unless lightning struck, or the world collapsed beneath them, nothing was going to interrupt what he was about to do to Rachel.

He stopped by the washbasin to scrub his hands again, deliberately slow, letting her lie there, letting the tension build between them until he couldn't stand it anymore. Then he advanced on her, adjusting his rock-hard erection to run diagonally along his hip within his briefs. Out of the corner of his eye, he watched Disco stroll lazily into his stall. None of the animals seemed to be paying them any mind. Good. He didn't have the patience to deal with them now.

He stopped near her head and lowered his lips onto hers, kissing her deeply. Beneath her T-shirt, her small, gorgeous breasts thrust toward the ceiling, beckoning to be touched. He cupped one, loving the way it felt in his hand. Breaking the kiss, he moved his mouth to her chest, pulling the shirt up and the bra down to gain access. Her freed breast jiggled beneath a nipple drawn up so tight, hardly any areola remained around it. He set his mouth over her, curling his tongue around her taut flesh. He flicked it with the slightest touch, knowing she preferred it harder.

"Suck it," she whispered, panting. "Please."

Her plea laid waste to the last vestiges of his control.

He tore away from her nipple and loomed over her, cupping the back of her head in his hand. With his mouth close to hers, he said quietly, "Are you telling me what to do? I think you were. You know what that means?"

"What?" she breathed, her eyes dark with passion.

"It means I'm going to touch you so lightly you won't be able to stand it."

She shivered.

He pulled her other breast free and traced her nipple with his fingertip. She arched up to him, but he stayed with her, adjusting his pressure to her squirming, desperate body. Closing his mouth over her nipple, he brushed the tip with his tongue as gently as a feather

might, then he traced her areola with his tongue as his
finger had. When it was good and wet, he lifted his
mouth and blew on it.

Rachel groaned.

He fixed his mouth on it again and captured her
nipple in his teeth. But instead of flicking it with his
tongue, he simply held it there and breathed on it. Her
groans became a panting cry, but still not the sound he
wanted to hear from her again.

Holding her nipple in his teeth, he pressed a hand
between her legs along the seam of her pants until his
hand was over where her clit would be, two layers of
fabric below. With his fingertip, he tapped hard and rhyth-
mically against the warm denim, willing the sound he
wanted to hear into being. Though she squirmed and
arched, she remained silent until he wound his hand
back and unleashed a single, forceful throttle against
her crotch as, finally, he sucked her nipple as hard as
he could.

That brought up the mewling whimper from her throat.

After several more forceful sucks on her nipple, he
repositioned himself between her legs. Steeling his hand
into a flat paddle, he let rip with another hard hit right
into the seam of her jeans.

"More," she begged.

So demanding. He unsnapped the button of her fly,
then rolled her to her stomach and yanked her jeans
and panties down as far as they'd go with her legs spread,
which wasn't all that far. Still, the round swells of her
bottom were exposed. Taking her soft, willing flesh in his
hands, he parted the cheeks to catch a glimpse of the
secrets her body protected. The places he wanted to sink
his fingers and tongue and cock inside.

He ran his thumb inside the crease, delving deeper,
lower, until he hit the honey of her arousal. Whew, she

was wet for him. He dipped lower still, and she bucked the second his fingertip hit the swollen rise of her clit. She squirmed, clearly trying to increase the pressure of his touch. He lightly pinched her clit, plumping it between two fingers.

There was sound again, a primal, guttural whimper that meant she would come as soon as he allowed her to. He backed off, slipping two fingers into her wet, swollen opening. She squeezed his fingers and his mouth went dry. When he got around to fucking her, it was going to feel out of this world. It was going to blow his fucking mind.

First things first.

She wanted him to spank her again. Harder, And, well, that was one demand he was happy to oblige. He unlatched his belt one-handed.

It sagged in his hand, much heavier than he'd expected.

Shaking his head to clear it of the fever dream he was operating within, he looked down. This wasn't his off-duty belt. It was his equipment belt, complete with radio, firearm, utility knife, and all the other trappings of his job as sheriff.

He blinked at it, reality hitting him hard.

What, in God's name, was he doing? Had he gone crazy? He'd come to Rachel's ranch with two of his employees to process crime scenes for evidence. And not an hour later, he was knuckle-deep inside her in the middle of the day. In uniform. With his squad car sitting out front. And with her sisters home.

My God. He had no integrity at all. He'd become a sheriff to fight against Meyer and the other good old boys who abused the power of their positions. But look where he was—getting his rocks off with a victim in an open case while he was on the clock. Could he ever feel superior to Meyer again? Because he sure didn't now.

The instinct to pull his hand away from her was a strong one. The only thing stopping him was the knowledge that she was close to release. So utterly close. And the damage was done. There was no taking back the choice he'd made any more than he could take back all the other terrible choices he'd made involving Rachel.

Remember this, you rotten prick. Because this is the last time you'll have her like this. Never again. You'd better brand into your memory her sounds and the way she feels on your hand when she comes. Because this is it.

He rocked forward, set the belt on the box next to Rachel's hip, and braced his hand on the lid as he leaned over her, as close to her ear as he could get.

"Rachel?"

Her eyes, blissed out and half lidded, regarded him dreamily.

He dragged his fingers from her depths and swirled them over her clit. Smashing her eyes closed again, she whimpered and panted, her hips straining toward his touch.

He stared at her beautiful face, her freckled nose and long lashes, the tightening of her jaw as he swirled and stroked her. "Say my name when you come."

She lifted her head and opened her eyelids all the way, questioning. He thought she was going to ask him why, but then one corner of her lip turned up, and she whispered, "I always do."

Then her body tensed. Her eyes rolled back and she dropped her cheek to the box lid. That mewling whimper spilled out of her throat, and then, as her back practically levitated from the box, she chanted his name.

He watched, unblinking, trying not to miss any detail

of her orgasm. Her pulsing muscles, her wet heat, the sound of his name. Her wild, bucking body coming apart all around him.

When her release subsided and she stilled, he almost said, "I love you." Except it didn't matter that he'd finally figured out that's what he felt for her. Because she'd told him in so many words, too many times to count over the last year and a half, that she couldn't love him, not after what happened with her mom. Even if she could grow to return his feelings, what could they do about it? Some things weren't meant to be, and, clearly, he and Rachel were doomed to keep looping back to each other in the same vicious cycle of impulse and denial.

The bowline knot released easy enough from her wrists, though she'd tightened it considerably since he'd bound her. That was the kinky thing about a bowline—the harder the bound person pulled against it, the tighter it got. Rachel's wrists were red and raw.

She straightened her bra and shirt, then stretched up, tugging her panties and pants in place as she stood. "Why did you stop?"

"I wanted to take care of you. That's all I need." He rubbed her wrists. "These marks look bad. Do they hurt?"

She pulled away from his touch. "I'm fine. Give me a real answer. Why did you stop?"

He snagged his belt and held it up as proof of his sins. "I'm on the job and I should've never . . . we should've never . . . You put that rein in my hand and I forgot who I was."

Nodding, she hugged herself. "You should have thought about that before you chose to go by horse with me."

"You're right." His chest grew tight, seeing the defeat in her expression. So much for an afterglow. Shunting the pain aside, he reattached his belt, then went in search of his hat. When he found it, he pulled it low over his forehead so she wouldn't see the storm in his eyes. He almost didn't elaborate, the truth hit so close to home. But he owed it to her because she was right. He tipped the first domino when he decided to accompany her. "But I couldn't pass up my one chance to ride with you."

She swallowed, her eyes locked on a spot near his feet. Then she rubbed her wrist and he had to wonder if the binding had hurt her, after all. "I've always wanted to ride with you too."

He let out a hard laugh. "We are so screwed up, you and me. My God, we are a mess."

She swayed, like all the energy had drained from her in one mighty whoosh. He reached for her, but she caught herself on a post, sagging against it. He smoothed a hand over her back. "You all right?"

"No, I'm not." She turned her eyes up to his, resolve as hard as steel glinted in them. "Recuse yourself from the investigation. For me. For us."

Chapter Twelve

The stuffy heat of the stable pressed down on him. The buzz of flies he'd previously been oblivious to filled his ears. He ran a finger between his collar and his neck to combat the heat and the excruciating tickle in his throat.

Why the hell had he ever thought it was a good plan to quit smoking at the same time he tried to quit Rachel? He would hand over the deed to his house if a cigarette would materialize in his hand. Stupid thought to flit across his mind, but he couldn't have possibly heard Rachel right. Because that would mean she felt something for him besides blinding lust, besides infuriating resentment for that lust—which, he'd decided a while back, were pretty much the only two feelings she harbored for him.

"What?" he croaked.

She straightened. "Remove yourself from my case. I want to try for something real. With you."

Oh, God, no. Why now? Why couldn't she have been ready a month ago, before the shooting? Feeling as if he'd been struck with a cane, he sunk into the arm he'd braced against the post, closing his eyes. "Don't you think I've considered that already? I haven't thought of one other thing since Monday except how I can possibly make everything work. There's no easy answer."

She shoved away from the post to pace the length of the stable, her hand on her forehead. "You were expecting the answer to be easy? Because I can tell you from experience, nothing in life worth having is easy. Look around you on my farm, Vaughn. Every valley used to be covered in alfalfa. My crop. It's all gone. I've been fighting for my place in the world since the day I was born. You think anything's supposed to be easy?"

"Damn it, Rachel. Listen to me. I didn't mean *easy* like you think. Look, the Meyers have been acting above the law since the day I met them. My whole goal in becoming a cop was to one day put myself in a position to hold them accountable for their crimes. That's what I've been working toward for the last twenty years. Since I was sixteen, that was all I wanted."

He flicked the brim of his hat higher, no longer wanting to hide himself from her. "Then, after twenty years of waiting for the right moment and the right case to come along, Wallace Jr. and his friends trespassed onto your property with drugs and automatic rifles. They shot you. They shot your horse. It was the perfect opportunity for me to bring justice down on the Meyer family. It was the case I'd been waiting for."

She sucked her cheeks in and looked so lost he thought she might start crying. "Forget I asked. I can't compete with revenge."

"That's what I'm trying to tell you—everything's changed for me, but I'm trapped. If I recuse myself now, the first thing that'll happen is Meyer and his men will start digging around to find out why. And they won't have to dig far. People in town are already spreading rumors about you and me."

"You'd lose your job."

"Maybe, but I don't even care about that anymore. What I have to care about is that the people of this county entrusted me with enforcing their laws. If the truth came out about our involvement, all the interviews and evidence I've collected against Meyer Jr. and Jimmy de Luca could be labeled as tainted in the eyes of the court. If a judge threw it all out, a conviction would be nearly impossible.

"Elias Baltierra will have other charges to contend with when my men catch up with him, but if Meyer Jr. and Jimmy de Luca were released due to lack of admissible evidence, and they went off and committed another violent crime, I would've failed the people I vowed to protect. I can't live with that. I've been wracking my brain since the afternoon of the shooting, but I can't see how it's possible to do my job the way it needs to be done and still have what I want."

Rachel dragged her eyes away from the horses to fully regard him. "What is it that you want?"

Oh, baby. "Do you really have to ask?"

"Yeah, Vaughn, I'd really like to know because I can't figure it out."

How could she not know? Maybe she needed to hear it from him, was all. Wouldn't change a damn thing, but if she needed it said out loud, then he could cowboy up and lay bare his heart, the same as she had. He strode to her and settled his hands on her shoulders. Her proud, stubborn chin raised a notch. Her brown eyes were glassy with moisture, but just as stubbornly set.

"I want you. I've always wanted you."

Saying it didn't feel freeing, as he'd thought it would. All these months he'd wanted to tell her how he felt. He thought if he ever got the chance to, it would ease his burden. But it felt like shit.

Her glassy-eyed gaze shifted to the space over his

shoulder. He tried to pull her against him to embrace her, but she remained rigidly upright.

He tucked an errant hair behind her ear. She flinched, but let him do it. "The afternoon you were shot, all I wanted was to make the men who hurt you pay. When I found out a Meyer was involved, it was like the only two things in my life I'd ever wanted were slamming into each other while going a hundred miles an hour. I had about a split second to figure out how to react. I never thought it was possible—"

His throat closed, snuffing his words, as the truth hit him hard.

She wanted him to recuse himself because she had feelings for him. She wanted to give a real relationship a try.

And, oh, it hurt worse than saying the words to her had. It felt like sinking headfirst into quicksand. He sucked air in through his nose, long and slow, struggling against the ache in his lungs and heart.

Lightheaded, he tried again to explain. "If I had thought for one minute that you felt something real for me, I would've given the case to Stratis from the get-go, and we wouldn't even be having this conversation. But in the last sixteen months, you'd made it clear to me, over and over, that you didn't want anything except a roll in the hay when the mood struck you." Shaking her head in protest, her face crumpled. He pressed on. "I thought you and I had no chance in hell of ever working out. So I vowed to take care of you the only way you'd let me— with my badge. I thought, if I make the Meyer family pay, then at least I will have gotten one thing I wanted. The only thing I was at liberty to have."

Hugging herself, she stared as hard as she could at the space over his shoulder.

"Talk to me, Rachel. Please."

She drew a tremulous breath. "When my mom's doctors told us that the overdose had left her with so much brain damage she'd never be the same again, I was hurting so bad. It was like what I'd been through with my dad all over again, except that my mom's life was over because of the choice I made to be with you."

He put his arms around her and she resisted, but he was done with her pushing him away. He locked his arms around her and tugged hard until she acquiesced and stumbled into his chest. The rigidity of her spine surrendered and she melted into his embrace.

"I stood at Mom's bedside that night before you got to the hospital and it was like I was watching my family crumble to dust in my hands. I was afraid that the next time I took my focus off my family, another disaster would happen. And we couldn't take any more hits, as fragile as my sisters and I were. I ended things between us that night believing I was cutting off an infected limb so the rest of me could survive. I didn't expect—" Her words cut off as her whole body was overcome with a violent shudder.

He held her head in his hand, his other arm like a vice around her back. If he could've gotten closer to her, he would've. He wanted to crawl into her skin and pump her heart for her, breathe for her, anything to take away the lonely, defeated pain in her voice.

She turned her face into the hollow of his throat. "I didn't expect that a year and a half later, I still wouldn't be over you. I was managing my feelings okay until this week."

That about said it all, right there.

He could see it plainly now, how they'd gotten to this state of total and utter fuck-up. Didn't make it any easier a pill to swallow, though.

He smoothed a finger across her cheek. "Nothing like a crime to bring the two of us together, huh?"

She raised her head and offered him a melancholy smile.

"Like you said, we are one hell of a mess."

He returned her sad smile. "It bore repeating."

"How long until the case against Wallace Meyer Jr. and the others closes?" she asked.

Vaughn sucked his cheeks in and bit down on them until he'd gotten a solid grip on the wild hope that she'd be willing to wait for him. "Until their cases are settled in court? A year. Probably more like two."

She thunked her forehead on his chest. "Okay. Two more years."

He bit his cheeks harder. Until he tasted blood.

"You ought to get on with your job, then. If we're going to deny ourselves what we both want, let's at least make sure something positive comes of it."

She was so strong, so resilient. No wonder he'd fallen hard for her. She was incomparable.

She wiggled, trying to break loose of his grip, but he cupped her chin in his hand and turned her face up toward his. "I'm going to kiss you first."

She met him halfway, pressing her lips into his. They fit so perfectly together. She yielded her mouth to his tongue. He slid it along hers, tasting her, merging with her, body and soul. Unlike the other good-byes they'd said to each other over the last year and a half, this one felt official. Permanent.

At least for a year or two.

Damn.

He suckled her lower lip before letting her go.

When he turned away from her, his heart felt as empty as his arms.

* * *

They saddled Disco and Growly Bear in heavy silence, their eyes averted, together but alone. A thousand different feelings whipped through Rachel, images of her life, of her family. That day in John Justin's that she was liberated. The day she broke her arm when she was seventeen. The first glimpse of her father's body when she identified him at the morgue. Her mother lying in a field next to an empty bottle of vodka. Tommy's birth. Vaughn standing on her porch in the darkness, his eyes smoldering with desire. Field after field gone to weeds and dust. Thirty-two years and this is what it came down to.

One man. And the hardest choice she'd ever had to make, but also the clearest. She would not jeopardize public safety by compromising the case against the men who shot her, at least, any more than she already had. It was a line in the sand she should've recognized from the get-go, as he should have. But at least they were crystal clear about it now.

At least, finally, they were being honest about their feelings for each other. It was a hard-earned peace that was settling over her, but at least it was peace, even if it was nestled within grim reality.

She lifted the lead ropes for both horses. "Let's get this over with. You've got evidence to collect and we're wasting daylight."

He untied the knot he'd locked the stable doors with and opened them, rubbing his throat. He'd done that a lot this week, and she wondered when he'd picked up the nervous habit. While she led the horses to the heat and blazing sun at the edge of the stable yard, he swung by his squad car to exchange the farrier kit for his evidence kit.

Once they were on the horses and clear of the yard, Rachel relaxed a bit. Without turning her head, she darted a look at Vaughn. Disco was used to new riders, and men in particular. He was the horse Mr. Dixon and Kellan rode, and sometimes the most skilled horsemen of their guests. This was the first time Rachel had seen Vaughn handle a horse, and she didn't work all that hard to mask her admiration of his exceptional skills.

Having already unbuttoned his collar, he was rolling up his shirtsleeves. His tie was nowhere in sight.

"Where's your tie?"

"In my pocket. I figured my choices were to either let some air flow in or dissolve in a puddle of sweat."

Rachel tried a smile on for size, hoping he'd relax into one of his own. "You chose wisely. It's a hot day."

He adjusted the brim of his hat to shade his eyes, his lips not even close to smiling. The same awkward silence in which they'd prepped the horses descended over them. After about a mile and a half, Rachel decided the horses were warmed up enough to get moving. Maybe she and Vaughn could outrun the day's heat along with their mutual heartbreak.

"Well, Sheriff, you wanted to ride with me, so how about we kick it into gear? You up for some speed?"

He stared at her, his lips twitching the way they always did when he was deliberating between choices.

She broadened her smile. "I can't see anything wrong with having some harmless fun at this point."

He swallowed, then seemed to rouse himself from his melancholy. "Disco and I are ready for anything. Aren't we, Disco?" He scratched the horse's side.

"Come on, then. See if you can keep up." She spurred Growly faster. Disco followed close behind.

Gradually picking up speed until the horses ran at a

full gallop, they thundered across the valley. In no time flat, Vaughn proved himself her equal in horsemanship.

She stole as many glances his way as she could manage. Drinking in this fantasy come to life. Her cowboy lawman, with horse handling skills as long as his legs, dressed in that devastatingly handsome sheriff uniform that turned her to putty, complete with a holstered sidearm, worn boots, and a hat.

Then he smiled at her. Flying across a long stretch of desert, their horses neck and neck, he'd turned her way and smiled. Boyishly, without reservation or the anguish that came with their broken relationship. Love bloomed in her heart.

For the first time that she could remember, she didn't feel guilty around him. Guilty that she was doing something wrong, shirking her responsibilities, that disaster was waiting to strike because she'd let her guard down to laugh and relax. She didn't feel lost, either. She supposed that's what their hard-earned peace had given her. The ability to breathe and smile in his presence.

She could live with that trade-off—for a year or two, anyway.

Once, coming around a rocky bend, he and Disco found a shortcut between two scrub trees and snuck into the lead. His *whoop* of laughter floated to her on the wind. "Disco takes the lead," he called.

"This isn't a race!" she hollered, laughing right along with him.

He pointed to a lone scrub tree a couple acres away.

"It is now," he shouted over his shoulder to her as he put pressure on Disco's flanks. "To the tree!"

Their horses churned over the dust and dirt. Rachel lifted out of the saddle, bending low over Growly's neck to whisper encouragement in his ear. She clutched his mane, and kept up the string of sweet nothings to

Growly until he was nose-even with Disco. Her method worked, and soon, she and Growly pulled into the lead.

"You don't play fair, cowgirl," Vaughn shouted. "Get that ass in the saddle so I can concentrate."

Smiling so hard her facial muscles ached, she stayed standing until Growly passed the tree. Then she circled to slow down, shaking her hands in the air in a show of victory, and giggling the whole time. "You didn't think you could actually beat me in a race, did you?"

Vaughn laughed and shook his head. "You caught me. I'm all bluster."

She brought Growly to a stop. "That was fun. Let's get these guys a drink of water before we go on."

"Sounds like a plan."

They dismounted. Vaughn found the water while she pulled two water bowls from her saddlebag.

"How much farther to the derricks?" he asked.

"They're right behind that ridge." She gestured west, to a small rise.

"I haven't seen the road Binderman would've taken."

"The road follows the fence line around to the west. This way takes longer, but it's more fun. I figured since you wanted to ride, and this is probably the only time we'll get to, we might as well make the most of it."

"I'm glad you reasoned it out like that."

She wanted to kiss him in a bad way, but for once, she overcame his temptation without too much effort. "Me too."

While the horses drank, Vaughn looked south, surveying their surroundings and getting his directional bearings. Rachel snuck her camera from the saddlebag. He'd hear the click, so if she wanted a candid image of him, the first shot would have to be perfect.

She inched around the front of the horses, framing Vaughn with Sidewinder Mesa to the left and a prickly pear cactus ten yards out to the right. His arms weren't visible, crossed over his chest as they were, which didn't make for the best image. She held the camera to her face, her finger on the button, waiting.

Disco snorted, spraying water on her legs. She held the camera steady, even as Disco moved to block Vaughn from view. She had a hunch that would be worth waiting for if it happened. Sure enough, Disco headed straight for Vaughn. He gave Vaughn a nibbling kiss on the nape of his neck.

Vaughn jumped in surprise, then threaded his fingers into Disco's mane and smiled at him.

Click.

As she knew he would, he shifted his gaze over his shoulder to look at her. His smile dropped to a flat line. His eyes turned serious, searching.

Click.

She lowered the lens. No sense apologizing or explaining it away. She was a photographer, and catching Vaughn looking at her like that—standing with a horse, her land in the backdrop—opened her heart so wide she could barely breathe.

Capturing a moment like that with a picture was like grabbing hold of a flash of lightning. Only after you froze the image could you pick out all the intricacies that made the moment beautiful. The complicated threads of energy curving and breaking, the play of light and shadow, the incomparable power. Photography was the only way she knew how to harness the world's power, to understand time and all the forces of the universe beyond her control.

No force was more beyond her control than the love she felt for Vaughn.

He didn't say anything about the photographs, but

silently shook the extra water from the bowls and replaced them in the saddlebag.

She stole a quick peek at the shots she'd taken. They looked good, but she'd have to develop them before she knew for sure. She packed the camera in its case and dug for a bag of horse treats.

"Ready to ride again?" Vaughn asked from across Growly's rump before swinging onto the saddle.

"Sounds good." She gave the nibblies to Growly and Disco, then followed suit. Anxious to keep their fledgling camaraderie alive, she nodded her chin in the direction of the derricks. "Race you the rest of the way?"

"You're on, cowgirl."

Chapter Thirteen

The Sorentinos' string of four beige oil derricks sat in a valley near an old, dry irrigation canal, each pumping at the same rate, but out of sync with each other. Vaughn's first thought on seeing them was that it was a good thing he hadn't brought Deputy Reyes along. The lingering symptoms of his post-traumatic stress disorder wouldn't have handled the lack of synchronicity well. He would've managed, but his blood pressure would've shot through the roof.

A crude road ran parallel to the canal and the derricks. Nathan Binderman stood behind the squad truck, his evidence kit spread across the open tailgate along with copies of photographs Rachel had taken of the graffiti.

He handed Disco off to Rachel to tend and sidled up to Binderman. "Find anything of interest yet? Prints, I hope?"

"The graffiti was painted over, so there weren't any prints to get."

Annoyed, he kept his focus on Binderman when Rachel offered a sheepish "Sorry."

"But I did find some older tire tracks preserved in

dried mud, smaller than a vehicle or ATV tires. Looks like dirt bikes."

Odd. He opened his mouth to ask Rachel about the tracks, when she volunteered, "The morning I found the graffiti, the ground was covered with dirt bike tracks, but we don't keep dirt bikes."

"Damn it, Rachel. I wish to God you would've called me when you found those. We'll be lucky if we end up with a single piece of valid evidence out of this day."

She bristled. "Not fair, Sheriff. This is rural country. We don't go crying to the police every time someone trespasses on our property any more than we report every case of missing livestock on the chance that some-one's stealing from us. That's not our code, and you know it."

She was right, but it still ticked him off something fierce how she'd handled it. "I'll give you a pass on the first couple, but when you decided to start carrying a firearm around to scare the vandals away, that should've been your first clue to get my department involved."

"I can't change my past mistakes any more than you can, Sheriff."

That shut him up. Well, that along with the searing glare she drilled him with.

"Did you find similar tire tracks at the other vandal-ism sites?" Binderman asked.

She squinted, thinking. "Not the one on the backside of the barn, but the rest, yes. Not only around the van-dalism areas, but all over this west end. I figured illegal immigrants were making use of the land as a trail north."

Binderman shook his head. "I'm not sure that's a rea-sonable assessment, with all due respect. On illegal im-migrant trails, there's a lot more debris. Food wrappers, water bottles, dirty socks, smashed-up prepaid cell phones, used diapers. Nasty stuff. In Chaves County, where I worked before I transferred to Quay, we called them Trash Trails. You could pick them out in a helicopter."

Binderman was right. Vaughn had dealt with a lot of scuffles between immigrants and the ranchers whose land they crossed through, and the trash stuck in most property owners' craws more than anything else. "Immigrants on the move don't usually use dirt bikes, either," Vaughn added. Drug runners did, but he wasn't prepared to open the idea up to Rachel until his department had more evidence to back up that theory.

"Was the canal shut off from water because of the derrick placement?" Binderman asked Rachel.

Vaughn cringed. The drying up of the fields due to her father's mismanagement was a prickly topic for her.

"No," she said, frowning. "That one was already dry. It's the same canal the second graffiti message was written on, about a mile south. This whole part of our alfalfa operation was the first to go. The flow vents between the canal sections broke and we didn't have the money to fix them. We do now, and we hired a foreman this week, so this'll be the first field we plant come fall. I know this whole area is a crime scene, but the foreman, Ben, and I were planning on coming out this way tomorrow morning, to assess the plumbing and take inventory of what we need to fix."

"I don't see a problem with that. We'll be done gathering evidence today," Vaughn said as his phone rang. It was Stratis. "What'd you find?"

"Henigin stayed overnight at the property two months ago, March 15th through the 17th, under an alias, paid cash. Jenna Sorentino recognized him in the photograph. Looks like the girlfriend used an alias too. No DMV records. Jenna had a picture of the two of them for the inn's photo album, so I put out an APB on the girl, then dusted the room they'd stayed in for prints. Got a few. The biggest surprise came when I searched the rest of the house. The lock to the storage under the house's raised foundation had been jimmied open. The storage had been tossed up pretty good, like someone was in a big hurry to find something. The ground's dug up in a half-dozen places. I'm down there now, dusting for prints. I'll upload the photos to your phone."

Times like these, Vaughn wished he could clone himself. "Good work."

"I'm checking the rest of the property now, with an eye for broken locks or hasty searches."

"Keep me posted." He replaced the phone on his utility belt. "Rachel, what do you and your sisters keep in storage under the house?"

She blinked, surprised. "Nothing but old, broken farm equipment and Christmas decorations. Why?"

"Stratis found proof that Henigin was on your land, and it looks like he searched your storage area. When was the last time any one of you were down there?"

Covering her mouth, she stumbled back and braced her hand on the squad truck. "He was going through our stuff?"

His arms twitched with the need to hold her. He hitched his thumbs on his belt, fighting the feeling. "I can imagine how violated you must feel right now, but you and your sisters were lucky. Obviously he wasn't there to harm you, and we can all be thankful for that."

Hugging herself, she looked into the distance as if gathering strength from the land. "January. Me and Jenna were down there in January putting away the holiday decorations. What was he looking for?"

"We don't know yet. But we're going to keep looking until we have the answers." He directed his attention to Binderman. "On that note, we need to get on down to that second site. Do you need anything else from either Rachel or me?"

"I've got this, boss. Go ahead."

"Check in with me when you're done. We'll leave markers at the canal so you can find the graffiti locations easily. I'll process the boulder, then work my way back to you."

Scared the shit out of Rachel that a man had been in her home, digging through their things. Scared her so bad that she felt herself shutting down, which wouldn't do at all, not with her family's safety at stake. Vaughn and his men were working to capture the criminals who were terrorizing them, so she didn't have the luxury to fall apart.

She dissolved an antacid on her tongue, working to dig out from the panic and fear by looking on the land she loved, visualizing neatly plowed rows and fields full of green. Soon, she vowed. Every day she was taking small steps toward a brighter future. For her farm, and—she glanced Vaughn's way—for herself.

They rode south from the derricks. Vaughn set small yellow flags at the two spots in the dry canals where the graffiti had been written, before they crossed through a canyon en route to the west side of Sidewinder Mesa, where the final graffiti incident had taken place.

Once they reached the bottom of the canyon, the trail opened up into one of the dry tributaries of Catcher Creek, dipping deep into a canyon that was one of Rachel's favorite spots on her farm to photograph. The canyon walls, smoothed by wind, rippled to the sky in a series of rust red and brown ribbons, each a marker of the passing of time—the history of Earth captured in the ground like a layer cake, reminding her of how temporary her efforts as a farmer were. She nudged Growly close to the wall and ran her finger along a dry layer of sand that crumbled at her touch.

The ground on the canyon floor was wide and even, not requiring a great deal of horse-handling skill, so Rachel decided it was time to broach the topic with Vaughn she'd been wondering about for a few days. "Amy told me you don't eat any fruits or vegetables. What's up with that?"

"What?" She could see his brain doing a one-eighty to catch up with the direction of the conversation. "Oh, no. I don't. Plants are disgusting."

"That's really unhealthy of you."

He shrugged. "I take a multivitamin."

"How did that get started? I mean, most kids aren't into vegetables—Tommy's sure not—but fruit? What's wrong with fruit?"

"I don't know. I don't like it. The texture, the taste—bleh."

"What about fruit pies? Everybody loves apple pie."

He shook his head. "Not me."

"Not even Catcher Creek Cafe's triple berry cream pie? I dream about that pie."

"Disgusting."

Rachel gasped at his blasphemous remark. "If I were dying, I'd eat that pie for my last meal, no question about it."

He scratched his chin. "I'll keep that in mind."

"Didn't your mom make you peanut butter and jelly sandwiches when you were a kid?"

With his index finger, he pushed the brim of his hat higher and gave her a lopsided grin that made her heart tighten. "Peanut butter and honey."

"Well, damn."

"It's not such a big deal. Isn't there a food you hate?"

Rachel didn't give much thought to food in general, so long as it was hot and she didn't have to make it. There was one food she couldn't stand, but she'd never breathed a word of her distaste to anyone. "All right, I'll tell you, but you've got to keep my secret. You can't let it slip to Amy because it would break her heart."

"Your secret is my secret."

"Okay." She dropped her voice to a whisper. "I don't like pasta. The texture makes me want to barf."

He slapped a hand on his thigh. "What? No way. How can you not like pasta?"

"Shhh! Don't say it so loud."

He rewarded her confession with a belly laugh. "That's criminal."

She scoffed. "No more than your warped opinion of triple berry cream pie."

"Amy doesn't know? When she fixes pasta, you eat it anyway?"

"Mm-hmm," she said with a cringe. "I don't have the heart to tell her. She's so proud that she makes it from scratch."

He laughed again and this time she joined in. "You're a better person than me because there ain't no way, no how, I'm letting a plant cross my lips." He twisted his fingers in front of his lips like he was locking them closed with a key.

"I didn't know that about you until Amy told me the raisins in her scones were the only fruit you'll eat."

"Yeah, I guess raisins are okay in sweets." He scratched his neck. "You don't like pasta. I would've never guessed. Tell me something else I don't know about you."

Fiddling with the rein, she considered the request. "I think you know everything about me, actually."

"That's a cop-out answer. Put your mind to it and you'll think of something."

They ascended from the canyon floor onto the western slope of Sidewinder Mesa, within a mile of the graffiti boulder. She wracked her brain for something to tell Vaughn about herself. Her life was so simple, so straightforward. She got up every morning, worked the farm until sundown, sometimes later, and got ready to do it again the next day. Her only hobby was photography. She didn't watch much television, or keep up with the latest in music, but . . . "I like to whistle."

"Really?" He seemed genuinely charmed by the discovery. "What do you whistle?"

"When I'm out riding by myself, sometimes I whistle old Glen Campbell songs, the ones my dad played when I was a kid. Back then, we had a tractor with a tape deck—we thought we were living like kings with accessories like that—and he'd play Glen Campbell while we worked."

"Let me hear you whistle some Glen Campbell right now," he said. "How about 'Southern Nights'?"

She should've guessed he'd lobby for a performance. "I can't do it with someone else around. It's embarrassing."

"Okay, I'll start. You join in."

He puckered his lips, but stopped short of whistling, a stumped look on his face. "I can't remember how it goes."

She gave him a chastising look. "You're trying to bait me into whistling first. It's not going to work."

"No, really, I can't remember."

Rachel hummed the opening bars.

He nodded. "Okay, I got it now." Even though she'd hummed the melody for him, it took him a few tries to get the first note right, but then he dove straight into a decent rendering.

Rachel was smiling so big, it was tough to pucker her lips enough to whistle, but she managed it halfway through the first line of the chorus.

They hit most of the notes correctly, and even managed a bit of accidental harmony during some of the verses. The horses plodded up the trail toward the top of the mesa, side by side, undisturbed by their riders' music. Rachel couldn't take her eyes off Vaughn, who was staring right back at her. What a crazy thing to do— whistling an old country tune on the trail like two fool cowpokes without a care in the world.

It felt sublime.

Not even a photograph could bottle lightning as powerful as the way she felt, making music with the man she loved. Two years. Yeah, she could handle waiting to be together, as long as she kept this memory of whistling with him fresh in her mind. A carrot to look forward to again when they reunited. In two years, she'd be on the cusp of thirty-five, still young enough to have a couple kids if they were quick about it. Then again, she didn't know how he felt about kids. But she certainly wasn't going to break the mood by asking him about it.

Vaughn forgot the coda at the end, and his expression was so panicky, Rachel stopped whistling to let her laughter escape before she plunged into the final chorus. Vaughn caught up with her by the final notes.

She held the last note for as long as she could, watching a rabbit dash across the valley to take refuge in a creosote bush. Smiling so wide she thought her lips might crack, she looked Vaughn's way, expecting him to feel as bubbly good as she did.

But the look he pinned her with cut straight through her heart like a knife.

Pain like grief dragged his features down. His whole body, from his tense shoulders to the blue eyes that had turned glossy with wetness and the down-turned mouth that was the window to his thoughts, radiated the same kind of implacable longing Rachel knew all too well. If she'd ever doubted whether he felt about her the same aching love she harbored for him, she didn't any longer.

She winced and tore her gaze away to stare at her saddle horn. Her heart—no, her whole chest—hurt. Her throat tightened. "We can do it. We can wait. We've been apart for this long, right? Two more years is a flash in the pan."

Vaughn's hand reached across to grab hold of her horse's reins, commanding it to stop along with his own horse.

"Look at me, Rachel."

She squeezed her eyes shut, praying for the strength to hold his gaze without breaking down. Reopening them, she met his gaze.

The grief had diminished, replaced by an unreadable mask. He took her left hand in his. "The day I quit smoking, the day you broke things off with me, I left a pack of cigarettes in the glove compartments of both my vehicles so that every time I got in a car, I had to make the choice not to light up. It was torture at first. It almost killed me to say no to my addiction a dozen times a day, every single day. But little by little I got stronger, and denying myself got easier. I'd stopped thinking about lighting up on a daily basis, which was a major milestone for me. That is, until you were shot on Monday. I've been dying for a cigarette ever since, but that's a different issue. My point is, it's not like that for me with you."

He swallowed, and Rachel's heart plunged. She tried to pull her hand away, a futile act of self-protection.

"It doesn't get easier to say no the more I'm around you," he said. "It gets harder. It's getting damn near impossible."

It sounded like a breakup. His tone, his expression, and his body language mirrored the breakup she issued him seventeen months ago in the hospital parking garage. She shook her head. *This can't be happening. Not now, after I've found peace with my feelings for you.* "Vaughn, please don't—"

He cut short her plea. "You've got to let me get this all out, Rachel, before I lose my nerve. Because one minute we're whistling Glen Campbell. and the next, all I can think about is ripping your clothes off and making love to you right there on the ground. Doesn't matter that I'm working a case and my employees could drive up any minute and see us, because I'm sitting here in the saddle, watching you, and running arguments through my brain trying to justify it, like I did in the stable. I don't know what's wrong with me, but I'm helpless to fight my need to be with you when you're nearby."

When she was nearby. That meant he wanted her to go. The realization enraged her as much as it devastated her. "Say it," she said. "You have to say it or I'm not going to believe you could really be asking it of me, after all we've been through."

His jaw tightened, and when he spoke, it was through gritted teeth. "I need to ride the rest of the way alone, and when I get back to your house to return Disco, you need not to be anywhere I can find you."

Rachel wrenched her face over her right shoulder, as far from Vaughn's scrutiny as she could manage. She yanked her hand again, and this time he let her pull away.

Her stomach lurched so violently saliva pooled in her mouth like she might throw up. "This is what you want?"

"No. But it's what I have to do. I know it's too much to ask, but I need you to help me be strong, Rachel. Please go."

Time slowed down. Rachel heard every jingle of the horses' tack, every rock they kicked as they shifted their feet. Her heartbeat boomed in her ears.

"This trail will lead you straight to the graffitied boulder. You should find it, no problem," she said, each word carefully measured so as not to reveal her utter anguish. "Rudy or Damon will help you get Disco settled in the stable." Stretched to the limit of her endurance, she couldn't say the word *good-bye*. Couldn't even turn her head to look at him one last time. She turned Growly downhill and urged him into a trot.

A year. Probably more like two. It had seemed such a manageable challenge. But now, she couldn't imagine a worse fate.

What would've happened if he hadn't stopped himself from pulling her off the horse into a passionate kiss? What if he'd really made love to her on the ground like he wanted? In the end, it would've made it even harder for them to stay away from each other, and the pain of separation would've hurt her even worse than this moment did. But she couldn't stop wishing he'd done it anyhow. It would've been worth it to hang on to the peace and happiness she'd felt for a few more fleeting moments.

Chapter Fourteen

Vaughn hated the idea of crawling into his empty bed enough that he only stopped by home for a quick shower after leaving Rachel's property before holing up in his office with paperwork until three o'clock in the morning rolled around.

At three, he unlocked his safe and added a Sig 229 to his ankle, backup for his S&W side piece. He readied his favorite M4 rifle and added two magazines to his belt. After locking up the office, he made the twenty-minute drive to Tucumcari, where he was meeting the rest of his team. The time had come to transfer Wallace Meyer Jr. from the hospital to the jail.

When he arrived, Deputies Kirby and Molina were already standing guard at the entrance to the hospital's underground employee parking garage. Reyes patrolled the aisles of cars, his sidearm drawn. Vaughn pulled to the curb adjacent to the elevators and stepped from his car, leaving the engine idling. He adjusted his flak vest and snapped a magazine in place on the M4. He and his team had worked out the details of this transfer days ago, beefing up their usual transfer security so that every single member of his department was involved. If El Diente made an appearance, they were ready for him.

Stratis and Binderman were assigned to transport Wallace Meyer Jr. in his wheelchair via elevator. The parking structure was dead silent as Vaughn and Reyes waited, save for a drain on the east wall, which dripped every thirty seconds or so into a pothole filled with water. He hadn't noticed until Reyes pointed it out, but now he was counting the time between drips, like some of Reyes's neurosis was rubbing off on him.

Great.

Vaughn's radio chirped. It was Stratis.

"We're at the elevator."

"Roger that," Vaughn answered, gesturing to Reyes. Showtime.

Vaughn alerted Kirby and Molina through the radio that they were a go, then opened the back door of his squad car as the elevator mechanism whirred behind the closed door. In another minute, the door opened. Stratis exited first. He nodded at Vaughn, then stepped aside for Junior's wheelchair, pushed by Binderman. Junior wore a flak vest like the rest of them. Unlike de Luca, though, he didn't look the least bit nervous or scared.

Vaughn stood outside his closed driver's side door, surveying the lot along with Reyes while Binderman and Stratis loaded Junior.

Stratis closed the door. "Clear."

So far, so good.

Binderman abandoned the wheelchair curbside to walk to his squad car, then he and Stratis walked to their respective squad cars as Vaughn slid behind the wheel of his.

He glanced at Junior in the rearview mirror. He looked pale, weak. His hair was plastered flat against his head and the holes in his ears sagged toward his shoulders. "Morning, sunshine."

Junior grunted. At least he was listening.

Vaughn pulled away from the curb and followed Stratis up the exit ramp, and past Kirby and Molina's squad car. Traffic was nonexistent. In another five minutes, they'd be at the jail and Vaughn could breathe normally again. Behind him, his teams' squad cars pulled into view. They drove without lights or sirens, nice and easy through the dark, empty streets.

"We brought the whole gang out to drive your ass four miles, Junior. Are you ready to come clean to me about who you're working for and where Baltierra is?"

Junior remained silent, staring dully out the window.

Stratis turned left onto the street that led to the back entrance of the jail. Vaughn followed, as did Binderman, Reyes, and Kirby and Molina. Two more miles on a straightaway road until touchdown.

"I've got a question for you."

Junior huffed.

"Shawn Henigin was scoping out the Sorentino place. He stayed there a couple months ago. Any idea why?"

"What do I look like, his mother?"

Vaughn drummed his fingers on the wheel. "Are you using the Sorentino property to move drugs toward Devil's Furnace?"

"I'm not saying another word without my lawyer."

"Ah, your daddy trained you good."

"Screw you."

He watched through the mirror for Junior's expression when he said, "We caught up with Henigin yesterday. Did you hear about that?"

Silence.

"Yeah. Personally, I was excited by the opportunity

to cut him a deal to flip on you and Jimmy, but he's not talking."

"Nobody flips on me."

He said it with such authority, an alarm sounded in Vaughn's mind. Junior was the leader of the group, not Baltierra and definitely not Jimmy de Luca. "Especially a dead man."

Junior didn't flinch. His eyes didn't register surprise or remorse. Maybe—and this could've been Vaughn's imagination—they took on a hint of satisfaction.

"It's too bad about him, really. Freak car accident," Vaughn continued as he pulled into the jail's underground parking and prisoner transfer station. "If my gut's correct, you have better odds of surviving while you're in my jail than you would on the street, because I have a feeling El Diente's cleaning house."

He twisted in his seat to smile condescendingly at Junior, who wouldn't meet his eye. "That's who you work for, right? El Diente, the new drug cowboy in town?" He faked speculation, scratching his chin and rolling his eyes to the car's ceiling. "Hmm. I sure hope he doesn't get the wrong impression that because I'm on the street tossing his name and your name around together that you flipped on him and gave me his name. I don't think he'd like that, do you?"

"I've got nothing to fear from El Diente." The way he said it, coupled with the smug look on his face, Vaughn believed him.

"Any time you want to chat about El Diente or Baltierra, you let me know. District attorneys and judges appreciate a man who steps up to help us catch more bad guys. Never know what kind of deal your cooperation might get you."

A gate closed behind his car, sealing the entrance. Still, Kirby and Molina set up position on the street. Four prison guards met them and waited curbside with cuffs and a fresh wheelchair. He stepped from his car and saluted the guards as he walked around to the passenger side. The guards stepped forward with the shackles and wheelchair.

He opened Junior's door with a flourish, then stepped aside to let the guards have access. "Welcome to your new home, son. On behalf of the Quay County Sheriff's Department, I hope you enjoy your stay."

"Rachel? You need to take a look at this."

Ben stood in the dry canal, leaning against the grate that separated the canal sections. He'd pried off the lid to the electronics and was attempting to open the flow valve. He'd sworn to her he was mechanically minded and could most likely fix it without calling in an electrician, but he'd been working for over an hour in the hazy glow of early morning, and it looked to Rachel like all he'd accomplished was coating himself in a thick layer of sweat and dust.

Rachel stood a half acre away, shoveling muck onto the embankment so that once they started the water flow, the debris wouldn't get snagged in the grates and create a dam. It was hard work, and now that the sun had crested the land to the east, the temperature was climbing. According to Rudy, the air would touch ninety-five degrees or more. In other words, the labor and heat were the ideal remedy for the foul mood Vaughn had left her in the day before.

"Did you figure out why you're having so much trouble?" she called.

"Yes. It's a little tough to get a flow valve working if it's not actually a flow valve."

Huh? Propping her shovel against the canal wall, she

slogged to where Ben stood. "What do you mean? What else could it be?"

The air around Ben stunk, like a dead animal was rotting in a nearby bush. The entire flow mechanism had been removed and sat on the embankment. Where it had been sat a dark, square hole that disappeared into the earth. "Ugh. That smell is something awful."

"The machinery was tampered with so that it looked like a flow regulator, but when I pried the vents off, I could tell right away that's not what it is."

"Go on."

He leveled an earnest gaze at her. "You're not going to believe me, but it's a swamp cooler."

"What? That's crazy."

"Rachel, ma'am, I know machines. This is a swamp cooler."

"Why would anyone do that?"

Squinting into the sun, he shrugged. "Beats me. Who had access to it around the time the canal stopped pumping?"

"Only me and my dad. Technically, Jenna had access too, but she never had the temperament for farm work."

"Any farmhands?"

"No, by then we'd let them all go."

He scratched his head under his hat. "I can't see any reason why a farmer would tamper with his own equipment, especially something as important as the main irrigation canal. Especially to go to the trouble of jury rigging a swamp cooler to look like a flow mechanism."

"I'm telling you, Ben. You have to be wrong about this. What good would a swamp cooler do out here in the middle of nowhere? There's nothing to cool."

Ben looked at the canal. He stomped the heel of his boot against the concrete. "Could be my imagination, but that sounded hollow."

Rachel threw up her hands. "Oh, now there's a secret room underneath the canal. Great theory. Where's the door?"

Rubbing his chin, Ben looked around. Rachel followed his gaze. In the dirt adjacent to the canal sat the covered box of the pump that took water from the canal into the field. The second Ben zeroed in on it, Rachel's stomach dropped. A nagging voice told her he was on to something, despite how preposterous the idea was.

Ben pulled himself out of the canal, then offered his hand to Rachel. She accepted his help and followed him to the pump.

He pulled the lid off the box, and Rachel expected to see a hole or a hatch, but all she saw was the pump.

"Nice try," she said.

He squatted and tinkered with some of the parts, his brow furrowed in concentration. Then he stood, wiped his hands on his jeans, and pulled the entire pump system up while Rachel gasped in shock.

The tops of the pump valves and tubes had been bolted to a steel plate. They weren't connected to anything. A façade. Beneath it, a hole that disappeared into darkness. And it stunk so bad of chemicals and rot that Rachel's eyes watered and her stomach threatened to unload its contents. As a born-and-bred farm girl, she'd spent her life around unpleasant smells, so turning her stomach was a tough ticket to sell.

What have you done, Dad?

From his back pocket, Ben grabbed a flashlight and pressed it into her hand. "I suppose we ought to look inside."

She wanted to say no. She wanted to say, Cover it up and let's pretend this doesn't exist, but there'd been too many secrets on this farm already, and she'd had enough. She dropped to her belly and peered into the space with the flashlight.

The walls were lined in concrete and angled toward the canal.

Too numb to think, she stood and handed the flashlight to Ben. He lay flat and ducked his head inside. "Any ideas why it was built?" he asked. "Maybe a fallout shelter or something?"

Rachel hugged herself and looked at the clouds on the horizon. "He wasn't the type of man to see a need for a fallout shelter. He was more of an eternal optimist type." Then again, she was beginning to feel like she didn't know him well at all. Her hair stood on end. Something was wrong. Never mind the whys of it—when would he have had the opportunity to build an underground passage, complete with swamp cooler, without Rachel knowing? It would've taken at least a week and a whole construction crew, depending on the size.

It hit her in a flood of memory. After the water stopped in this field and the alfalfa crop died off before it was ready for harvest, her dad had put her to work in the fields on the east side, and when she'd made noises about getting back to the west side fields to fix the canal, he'd sent her to a week-long agriculture convention in Colorado. She'd crowed that they couldn't afford it, and that the money would be better spent fixing their irrigation system, but he'd been adamant, and she'd dreamed of taking a vacation for years, so she went along with it.

But still, wouldn't she have noticed when she returned that the ground around the canal was disturbed?

Maybe the structure was older than she was assuming.

"This canal runs the entire western and southern length of our farm. My dad built it when I was a kid to replace the antiquated system his father had used since the early fifties. I wonder if this is the only hidden set-up like this."

"Easy to find out, now that we know what to look for. Let's go down there and check it out. Maybe it'll give us some clues about why your dad built it."

They'd driven in Ben's truck that morning. He walked to it and found a second flashlight. He left his hat sitting on the seat of the cab. Rachel walked over and did the same. "One more thing," he added, digging under the seat.

He brought a rifle out. "My dad taught me to always be prepared."

"Like a Boy Scout farmer?" It was easy to joke because the rifle made her feel better, as did Ben's presence. But she was still rattled to the core by their finding.

He loaded rounds into the chambers. "Boy Scout farmer—I like the sound of that. Let's check out the tunnel."

He squeezed through the narrow opening first. His broad, brawny body almost too big to fit. She handed his rifle down to him, then followed, grateful she wasn't claustrophobic like Jenna because they were standing in a narrow tunnel barely wider than Ben's shoulders.

He shone his flashlight in, and Rachel's beam of light joined with his. The stench of rot made her dizzy. She plugged her nose. Ben did the same, taking the lead through the tunnel.

Twenty paces in, the tunnel opened into a low-ceilinged, long concrete lined room about the size of their kitchen with doors on either side that led into more darkness. Rachel shone her beam of light over the ceiling, searching for where the swamp cooler vent would be. She found one in the upper left corner, then another vent on the right. They were standing directly beneath the irrigation canal.

Ben's beam of light was searching the floor. Having

finished examining the ceiling, she joined him. Two long tables were littered with buckets and tubes. Two bathtubs sat against one wall.

"Do you ever watch that cable TV show *Real LEO?*" Ben asked, his voice barely above a whisper.

"Never heard of it."

"In the show, television cameras follow cops around on arrests and raids and stuff. It's a cool show. My roommate tapes it and I've watched it with him a lot of times. Last week, they followed this SWAT team in Texas that raided a house. The basement looked like this."

Rachel's heart filled with dread. "What was that room for?"

He shone the beam of light off to the side so as not to blind her. His eyes were wide with disbelief. "It was a meth lab. I think your dad was cooking meth."

Ninety-nine times out of a hundred, filling out paperwork was Vaughn's least favorite part of his job. Not today, when that paperwork was admitting Wallace Meyer Jr. to jail. This morning, he took his time, watching the prison guards walk Junior through his print and DNA collection, waiting outside the medical exam room while Junior underwent evaluation and a body cavity search and personally escorting him to his cell in solitary.

He would've loved to parade the smugly confident boy past the rows of cells first, but alerting them to the presence of the police chief's son would've been advertising for trouble. Just about every prisoner had a grudge against Wallace Sr. and the rest of the Tucumcari Police Department, and would like nothing better than to introduce Junior to their fists or shivs, or worse.

Standing at the counter in the jail's office, he watched

the sun rise through the window and filled out the paper-work at a leisurely pace, relishing every minute of it.

The prison warden sidled up to him, setting his coffee mug and an elbow on the counter. "I haven't heard that song in a while."

"What song is that?" Vaughn asked.

"The one you were whistling. 'Southern Nights.' Great song."

Vaughn hadn't been aware he was whistling, much less "Southern Nights." Damn, Rachel, to sneak her way into his subconscious like that.

The office secretary rolled her chair to the small television in the corner, which had been running through the local news on mute. "He's on, everybody."

Vaughn glanced at the screen. Wallace Meyer stood in dress uniform behind a podium. With all that had been happening, he'd forgotten all about Meyer's conference to tout his impressive drug arrest record.

The prison warden sipped his coffee, then gestured with the mug toward the television. "It's a strange day for Chief Meyer to hold a press conference. Everyone here expected him to cancel it given what's going on with his boy."

Vaughn's cell phone rang, but Meyer had started to speak, and Vaughn couldn't wait to hear what he had to say so he turned the volume off.

"Over the past twelve months, the Tucumcari Police Department has staged a city-wide crackdown on drug dealers and users. We have the numbers to prove that our tough new stance on drugs is paying off."

He prattled on about arrest statistics, and Vaughn smiled a private, ironic smile knowing Junior's tox results were in and he'd been loaded on meth at the time of the Parillas Valley shooting. That would change Meyer's tune once word got out.

"In our continuing effort to protect and defend the citizens of our fine city against the criminals who would use it as a playground for their unlawful and immoral conduct," Meyer continued, "today marks the beginning of a new city-wide crackdown on another type of criminal behavior, one closely linked with drug abuse—shoplifting."

So that's how it was going to be. All this time, Vaughn had expected Meyer to go after Rachel for shooting his precious son, but he'd decided instead to attack Vaughn's family. He'd been joking about the idea to his dad, but maybe he would spring for a nice, long cruise for Gwen and his folks after all.

"Shoplifting, even petty shoplifting, hurts our community, bleeds revenue from small businesses, and damages our already-struggling local economy. Times are tough, and we can no longer issue ineffective slaps on the wrists of those who violate the law. This morning, I'm calling for the city council to adopt stricter penalties for shoplifters, most importantly, serial shoplifters. I have a message to those among us who have no respect for this country's laws, their neighbors, or local businesses: be warned. We will catch you and you will pay."

Meyer looked directly into the camera, hellfire in his eyes. Vaughn's stomach lurched. He fumbled for his cell phone.

"As I speak," Meyer continued, "the Tucumcari police are searching the home of one of Tucumcari's most flagrant serial shoplifters after receiving an anonymous tip this week that this individual is responsible for a rash of larceny across our city."

Vaughn couldn't hear what Meyer said next over the pounding of his heart. His hands unsteady, he brought his phone out to look at the display screen. He'd missed ten calls in the last five minutes. All from his dad's cell phone.

He dialed his dad's phone, but it went straight to voice mail. He hit the speed dial for his parents' land line. The answering machine clicked on. Gwen's phone did the same. Mom didn't have a cell phone, which left him out of options.

No. Please, God, no.

His legs felt like they were trapped in concrete. The weight of the universe pressed down on him, smothering him where he stood. Scrubbing a hand over his hair, he clutched his phone and tried to concentrate on the words of the local news anchor who'd returned to the screen.

"Our sources here at Local KQSN News believe the arrested suspects to be the family of the Quay County Sheriff, Vaughn Cooper . . ."

He stumbled away from the desk, fighting for air. The room had gone dead silent. He tore his gaze from the screen to look at his employees. Every one of them was staring at him, some with pity, some with shock, others with cruel judgment.

". . . Sheriff Cooper's parents, Greg and Maria Cooper, along with their daughter Gwen Cooper, who has a long history of petty shoplifting charges. Our cameras are on the scene of the breaking news this morning. Whitney Numos is standing by with a report."

The image snapped to a field reporter standing in a street, the home behind her instantly recognizable.

"No." Panic, like thousands of needles digging into him, almost dropped him to his knees. He spun in place, searching for the door. He couldn't remember where it was, but he had to get out of this room. Had to get to his parents before the unimaginable happened, if it hadn't already. Oh, God, he had to save them. Digging through his pocket for his car keys, he rubbed his eyes as his vision grew dark around the edges. Someone was talking to him, their voice muffled by the *whoosh* of blood in his ears, the taste of acid on his tongue.

". . . This dramatic footage was filmed moments ago, when Tucumcari police surrounded a local area house, their battering ram ready should the owners refuse them entrance."

In a trance, he forced his eyes to the screen. Police in SWAT gear ran around the perimeter of his childhood home. The sight of a long, black metal battering ram jolted his system. With a strangled gasp of horror, he turned and ran. He must've found the door because the next thing he remembered, he was in his patrol car, the sirens and lights on, blazing down the road to his parents' house ten minutes away.

The only thoughts in his head were, *This is my fault. I did this to them. I failed my family.*

He ground to a stop as close to the police barricade as possible and fought his way through the crowd. Gwen sat in the back of a squad car, sobbing. He couldn't find it in himself to feel sorry for her. He scanned the scene for his parents, and when he saw them near the open garage door, he tipped over the edge of sanity.

"Get those off of her!" he bellowed, jumping the barricade. He evaded the officers lunging at him as he ran toward the man handcuffing his mother.

"Get those off of her! You son of a bitch, that's my mother."

He was tackled halfway up the driveway, dropped to his stomach by someone dressed in black, the wind knocked clean out of him.

"Sir, stop. Don't make this any harder than it has to be."

Like it could get any harder.

"Vaughn, don't worry," his mom called. The quaver in her voice cut his heart out. "We're going to be okay once this is sorted out."

Oh, hell, she was trying to comfort him. His mother, while being cuffed and read her rights, was worried about him. It was more than he could take. He dropped his forehead to the concrete and swallowed the bile rising in his throat. Let this be a nightmare. Please, God.

But when he looked up again, it was to see his mother being walked past him toward the squad car. "No, no, no."

His dad marched past his line of sight next. "Don't lose it, Vaughn. We need you to keep a cool head. Keep it together for your mom."

Keep it together? He'd already spiraled into hell.

But Dad was right. Whatever had happened to bring this on, he couldn't do his parents any good in his current wretched state. He squeezed his eyes shut, breathing into the ground.

You've failed them so completely that somehow you must find the will to pull it together and right the wrongs you've caused.

"Let me stand," he said to the person holding him down. "I won't make a scene."

Maybe because of his title, or maybe it was because the officer accepted the resignation in his voice, but he moved his knee away from Vaughn's ribs and stood aside for Vaughn to push himself up. He kept his back to the patrol car his parents were being led into, knowing that if he saw his mom, he'd lose it again.

Pressing his palms to the sides of his head, he pushed his tongue around his mouth, digging deep for the strength to speak calmly. "On what charge are they being arrested?"

The officer looked on him, but didn't say anything. He glanced around, as though anxious that his colleagues would notice him fraternizing with the enemy.

"If it was your family, you'd want me to tell you."

The officer continued to look around, speaking out of the corner of his mouth. "Thousands of dollars in stolen merchandise, along with methamphetamine and marijuana."

"That would be Gwen. Why my parents?"

"The drugs and drug paraphernalia were found in the master bedroom and kitchen."

Vaughn wasn't sure who he hated more at the moment, himself or his sister. Either way, she was lucky to be driving away in a squad car right now so she didn't have to face Vaughn's wrath. Yet. "They're being taken to the Tucumcari station house?"

"Yes."

Vaughn nodded. "Thank you."

He patted his pockets for his keys, but didn't find them, so he retraced his steps from his car. The Tucumcari police on scene were giving him a wide berth, but watching his every move. With his eyes on the pavement, looking for his keys, he slipped between barricades and pushed past his parents' gawking neighbors, who whispered to each other and darted looks at him. The lights were still flashing on his patrol car, the keys still in the ignition and the engine running.

At least he'd managed to throw it in park.

Reaching across the dash, he opened the glove compartment. After a few attempts to peel open the cellophane wrapper from the cigarette box with his unsteady fingers, he ripped it off with his teeth and hung a cigarette from his lips. Even before lighting it, he felt steadier, more able to cope with the horror and fury coursing through him. The lighter took him a minute of rummaging to find, but find it he did, and clicked a flame into being.

He drew deeply on the cigarette until he felt it settling into his bones and brain. His radio squawked at him, so he snapped it off. He didn't want to talk to anyone in his department. Not until he had a handle on the situation. Another flick of his fingers turned his sirens on.

Exhaling, he watched the smoke swirl and dissipate in the closed confines of his car, making his eyes water. Fuck it. He wasn't even going to bother opening a window. It wasn't as if he had anything more to lose in his life.

With another slow, deep inhale, he pulled away from the curb and tried not to think about the sight of his mother's face when she'd seen him, nor the look of the metal cuffs on her wrists. Instead, he concentrated on the image in his head of Wallace Meyer's sneering, walrus face, and imagined all the ways he'd make the bastard pay for his sins.

Chapter Fifteen

Rachel paced on the ground adjacent to the canal, her cell phone to her ear.

Restless and curious, Ben had left the notifying to her while he examined the flow mechanism on the far end of the canal section. There'd been two vents in the underground room, so that was most likely the second swamp cooler.

She didn't want to talk to Vaughn, but couldn't see a way around it. Even if she requested to speak to Deputy Binderman, Vaughn had made it clear that he wasn't going to hand the case over to anyone else. So, as seemed to be their eternal fate, they couldn't escape each other no matter how hard they tried. Life kept pulling them together in painful, impossible ways.

When his home phone went to the message machine, she pressed END and drew a fortifying breath. He hadn't answered his cell phone either, so her only remaining option was to phone his office. Irene picked up.

"Hello, Irene. Is Sheriff Cooper in?" Her heart was pounding out of her ribs, but there was no getting around this call, no matter how it would hurt her to hear his voice.

Irene was silent for a beat, then, "You haven't heard?"

"Heard what?"

"Nothing, dear. It's not my place. The officer on duty is Deputy Binderman, but he's on the other line. Would you like me to leave him a message to call you?"

"It's urgent. I'll wait."

"If there's an emergency, you'd best explain it to me so I can dispatch someone right away, get you the help you need."

If only it was that easy. But there was no way to save her from the shattered illusions of her past. What could she say?

My father isn't the man I thought he was. He wasn't a lazy dreamer and a cheat. He was far, far worse. Everything I thought I knew about my life was wrong.

"Urgent, but not an emergency."

"Of course, dear. Bless your heart. I'm going to put you on hold."

Ben was farther away now, walking through the next section of canal.

She kicked a clump of wild alfalfa and felt the first cracks in her composure. Deputy Binderman had better not dally because she wasn't sure how much longer she could keep it together. The horrible truth about her father had been stewing in her mind too long as it was. Rage simmered inside her, close to boiling. She wanted to scream at the heavens or beat her fists against her truck.

She wanted to find her sisters and tell them, "You were right. He did ruin our lives. I'm sorry I ever defended him."

She kicked another clump of weeds. Damn him.

Damn him to hell for his lies. He'd known full well Rachel had staked her life on this farm, on the alfalfa crop. She hadn't gone to college; she didn't have a backup plan. All she had was this farm and her dream to keep it running. He knew that, yet he'd sabotaged the irrigation and ruined her chance on purpose. He'd brought drugs and criminals onto their property. He'd bankrupted Rachel and her sisters' future. And for what? If he'd been running a meth lab, where was the money from it? He certainly hadn't shared it with his children or wife. Where did the oil drilling fit in with his illicit schemes and drug trade? Where did Wallace Meyer Jr. and his buddies fit in?

She wasn't sure she wanted the answers to those questions. Wasn't sure she cared anymore. She reached down, into the dry dust, and ripped the weeds up by their roots, growling with the effort.

She'd believed in her father, despite his many faults. She'd convinced herself she felt lost because she'd lost him—first, to his shortcomings and addictions, and then to an untimely, accidental death. But now she knew the truth.

She ground the heel of her boot into another wild patch, releasing the cut grass scent she used to love. Her father hadn't been the man who rescued her when she was lost, but the one who set her adrift. All this time she'd thought their alfalfa business died because she'd failed as a farmer, as a daughter. But that wasn't it at all. It was he who failed her. In every possible way a father could.

"Ms. Sorentino? It's Deputy Binderman. What can I do for you?"

Her mind was caught in a flurry of noise and hate too toxic to speak. "Yes," she said, her breathing labored. "Yes."

"Ms. Sorentino, are you hurt?"

Yes, I am. "No. Out of breath." Resting her hand over her forehead, she fought to get a grip. "My foreman and

I found something this morning at our irrigation canal." She took another pained breath, so enraged that her lungs felt like they were collapsing in on themselves. "Near where the graffiti had been written. We don't know much about these things, but we think it might be a . . ." Another breath. *Goddamn you for doing this to me, you son of a bitch.* "A meth lab."

"Oh." Binderman paused, like her words were still sinking in. "Oh. Get away from it. Far away. Meth labs are unstable. You said it's by the graffiti sites?"

Her arm started shaking, so she cupped the phone with both hands. "Yes."

"That's far enough away from the house that we don't need to worry about evacuating. I'll meet you in your driveway in twenty minutes, and I'm calling for backup and a fire truck."

"Whatever you need to do is fine."

Binderman clicked off the line.

Ben was far enough away that it made more sense to call his phone than holler at him. "We've got to get to the house to meet the police."

"On my way."

She closed her eyes and let her ulcer flare, sizzling her body from the inside out. How was she going to explain this to her sisters? She was so damn tired of giving them bad news. All she wanted was peace. All she wanted was not to feel lost or hurt anymore. But the hits kept on coming.

Screwing her mouth up, she bit back a fresh scream of rage and pivoted, hurtling her phone into the canal. It shattered into pieces. Good riddance.

Ben backed up, his eyes wide.

She sniffed, swiping a hand across her dripping nose. "I'm riding in the back. Fresh air." Head down, she stalked to the truck, grinding every blade of alfalfa with her heel along the way, and climbed into the bed.

At least Ben was smart enough not to say anything. He settled in the driver's seat and set off toward the house.

She stood with an arm hooked around the bar strung across the cab, holding her hat. She released her hair from its band and let the wind whip it around her face as the truck bounced down the road, her gaze settling over the terrain. The browns and oranges of the burnt ground, the deep greens and yellows of the trees and shrubs that were as much survivors of the harsh, unforgiving high desert landscape as she was. Scrappers who defied the odds, even with all the forces of nature and man working to destroy them.

When they pulled around the side of the stable into the yard between the stable and the main house, they weren't greeted by squad cars and fire trucks, but by Amy, Jenna, and Sloane, along with Mr. Dixon, Tina, the farmhands, and both of the inn's guest families. Everyone was hugging and laughing and snapping pictures with Tulip, who'd been dressed to the nines with a funny little red hat and a wreath of flowers.

Rachel's heart sank to her knees. She'd forgotten about the big group send-off.

When they noticed Ben's truck pulling into the yard, everyone clapped and cheered. Rachel cursed under her breath and replaced her hat on her head.

"There's our cowgirl," Jenna said in a perky voice.

"Here I am." She forced a smile as she leapt over the side of the truck bed. "I need to have a word with you, Jenna, Amy."

Amy looked at her like she'd lost her marbles. "Now?"

"Right now."

She stalked toward the stable, her sisters in tow, then slid the door closed behind them.

"Now's not the best time, Rach," Amy said. "We've got a yard full of people."

"I know that. Which is why we need them to leave. Now! Is Mr. Dixon driving them to the airport?"

Jenna waved her arms. "Hold on. What are you talking about?"

Rachel opened her mouth, but the sound of sirens approaching cut through the air.

"Ben and I had no choice but to call the cops. We found something bad out on the west end field. Another one of Dad's secrets."

Jenna and Amy nodded, getting enough of the point to spur them to action. They pushed past Rachel and threw the door open as a fire engine and three squad cars barreled into the yard. Rachel had trouble getting her legs to work. Her eyes turned up to look at the space above the door.

Her lucky horseshoe.

Another illusion she'd held on to for too long.

She couldn't stand the thought of leaving it there one moment longer to gloat at her. She banged the stable's tool closet door open and found a tire iron. Maybe she'd take the shoe to her father's grave and bury it right alongside her false memories of the man she'd idolized. Then again, that would be too much effort expended on the man who obviously hadn't loved her all that much.

Three pries with the tire iron and the nails gave way. The shoe flipped from the wall and sailed over Rachel's head to fall into the scoop she used to muck out the stalls. A fitting end for a rotten lie of a story.

Cursing loudly, she tossed the tire iron aside. It clattered to the ground as she marched from the stable, ready to face her new reality.

* * *

It took the sheriff deputies and firefighters a solid eight hours to assess and process the new crime scene on Rachel's farm. Ben had been right—what they'd found was indeed a meth lab. Undersheriff Stratis and Deputy Binderman estimated it'd been used as recently as the previous winter. Right about the time the oil derricks were installed.

The timing baffled Rachel as much as it seemed to baffle the sheriff deputies. She would've figured it'd gone out of use at the time of her dad's car crash, which the sheriff's department was no longer calling an accident. When she pressed for details, all they would tell her was that the case had been reopened due to new evidence.

As if Rachel and her sisters could handle any more tough news.

Then again, if her dad had gotten himself killed, she'd bet the house it had something to do with the drugs. There wasn't a drug dealer or cooker on the planet who ever died of natural causes, that was for sure.

The whole day long, she kept her eyes open for a sign of Vaughn, but he never showed up. Not to her farm, and not to the station house, where she'd followed Stratis's squad car for a more formal interview in the late afternoon. She'd been certain he'd at least want to make sure she was okay, but his silence broke her heart all over again.

Her interview with Stratis at the station house was free of the unpleasant tension and innuendos of wrongdoing that had plagued their first interview. Probably because Rachel was too far mired in her pain to care, but also because Stratis was all business. His features and words were wooden, his demeanor stoic. All the questions he'd asked her earlier, he asked again, along with a dozen more. Questions mostly about her dad's last few years of life. She answered the best she could, but nothing about her memories of her dad seemed real anymore.

He never once brought up Vaughn. None of the deputies did, for that matter. Save for the name plaque on his office door, it was as though he'd ceased to exist.

When Stratis released Rachel at a few minutes to five o'clock, she nearly stopped by Irene's desk to ask after Vaughn's whereabouts. She simply couldn't reconcile the idea that he'd heard about what she was going through and had chosen not to check on her. But Stratis was on her heels, walking her to the front door, so she kept moving.

In the parking lot, she climbed into her stuffy truck and rolled the windows down. She sat, at a loss of where to go or what to do. What she really needed was wide-open space, but the places she'd always found solace in reminded her of her father. If she went to her house, she'd have to deal with her sisters, and she didn't have the strength for that yet.

She started the truck's engine and cruised down the main road. Old habits died hard; and she couldn't help but scan for Vaughn's truck or squad car in every parking lot she passed. Three blocks down, Smithy's Bar came into view. No evidence of Vaughn in the lot, but she turned in to the parking area anyway.

She needed the company of Catcher Creek locals like she needed a hole in the head, but a cold beer might be nice. And Smithy's had a pay phone out back if she worked up enough courage to call Vaughn out on his neglect of her.

The air inside the bar was cool and smelled of cleaning products and spilled beer. A Merle Haggard song poured from the jukebox in the dark corner to her left. The place was crowded, being after normal workday hours on a Friday. Rachel squeezed onto a bar stool between two older men she didn't recognize, hoping no one would bother to notice her except Gloria, the bartender.

After a few minutes, Gloria worked her way and sailed a cardboard coaster in front of her. "The usual, hon?"

"That'll do. Thanks."

She tapped the coaster on its side against the bar and kept her head down while she waited, hoping to avoid catching anyone's eye.

Gloria returned with a bottle of beer, but instead of setting it down and leaving, she lingered. "Surprised to see you here, Rachel."

Rachel set her hand on the cold glass bottle and looked at Gloria's overdone face and bouncy, peroxide blond hair.

"Why's that?" Rachel asked, too grumpy for small talk.

Gloria arched one of her drawn-in brows. "Because of what happened today with Sheriff Cooper's family. We all figured you'd be consoling him. Are you two on the outs?"

Rachel sat up straighter. "What happened to his family? Is someone hurt?"

"Only their pride," Gloria said.

"Tell me what happened. Please. I didn't know."

She got a saucy twinkle in her eye that turned Rachel's stomach. "Early this morning, the Tucumcari police raided his parents' house. It was all over the news. They arrested his sister and both his parents on shoplifting and drug charges."

Gossip like that was too horrific to be true. Even still, her hand itched with the urge to slap Gloria, she sounded so gleeful at the revelation. "That can't be right."

Then she thought about Vaughn's contentious rivalry with Chief Meyer and the possibility didn't seem so outlandish.

"My cousin lives on his parents' block," Gloria said. "She told me the sheriff had to be restrained when they took his mother away in cuffs."

Oh, hell. Lightheaded and entertaining the possibility of being sick to her stomach, she pushed off the stool.

"That's enough, Gloria."

Rachel whipped her head around to see Kate Parrish standing, her arms crossed over her chest, her expression livid.

"Is Gloria right? Vaughn's parents . . ."

Kate nodded.

"Told you," Gloria said.

Refusing to look in Gloria's direction, Rachel reached into her front pocket for her coin purse. Every cell in her body screamed with the need to get to him, to throw her arms around him, and forget the cruel world they lived in.

Kate set her hand on Rachel's arm. "I've got your beer. Go to him."

Rachel searched Kate's expression, expecting malice, but saw only the friend Kate had always been to her before that week. "Why would you help me?"

Remorse flickered across her features. "Jealousy is a funny beast, you know?" She nodded toward the door with a sad smile. "Get out of here."

"Thank you." She took off in a fast walk for the door. She'd have to process Kate's turn-of-mood some other time. Right now, her mind didn't have room for anything else but Vaughn.

She parked across the street from his house and shut the engine down. His truck sat at the curb, his patrol car in the driveway. Now that she was here, she was chickening out. Maybe he didn't want to see her. She wasn't sure she could bear that. The only thing she ever had that was all hers was Vaughn, and their damaged, pain-filled connection to each other. If he turned her away, she wouldn't have anything left in the world to hold on to.

The blinds in his exercise room were closed, but with the falling shadows of late afternoon, a faint glow of light was visible behind the blinds. The metal knocker on the blue front door was rusty and falling apart, but he'd explained to her that he'd never replace it because his parents had gifted him with it when he bought the place. It had been the door knocker on his grandparents' Texas farm. His work boots sat on the porch, and she could just make out the stuffing in his roof from the sparrows that wintered there, and that he didn't have the heart to evict. Outgoing mail had been clipped to the front of his mailbox with a clothespin.

The longer she sat and stared at his place, the deeper into loneliness and longing she sank. He had this full, rich, moment-to-moment life that she wasn't a part of, and it hurt, knowing that. Every day he woke up and worked out and went through the motions of his day—without her.

Tonight, at least, she knew on an instinctive level he needed her as much as she needed him. But it scared her to death that maybe her instincts were wrong about that, as they had been with everything else.

So what? So what if he rejected her. If she got to the point where there was nothing in her life, then at least she'd know she'd finally hit the bottom of the well. She slid out of her truck, locked up, and crossed the street.

Three concrete steps and she was eye-to-eye with his door knocker.

She rang the doorbell. Hugging herself, she fought to

ignore how vulnerable it felt to stand there, waiting for his judgment.

Footsteps on his hardwood floor preceded the rattle of the deadbolt.

He opened the door dressed in a gray T-shirt drenched in sweat, blue nylon workout shorts, and sneakers. The shirt clung to the muscles beneath, outlining the hard points of his nipples. A white towel was slung over his shoulder.

His expression was dark and despairing. Absolutely lost. He took a deep breath through his mouth.

When it became clear that he wasn't going to say anything, or invite her in, she hugged herself tighter. "I heard what happened to your family."

He gave a terse nod, the line of his jaw rippling as though he were clenching his teeth.

"I had a bad day too. And I need . . ." She raised her eyes to the eaves. Christ, could she feel any more pathetic? "I need you tonight."

He must have known what it cost her to say that because, after a beat of hesitation, he opened the door all the way and moved aside to allow her entrance.

She closed and locked the door, then stood against it.

As wretched as she felt, he looked even worse. He had yet to say a word, but she read the hurt and need in his eyes plain enough. She wanted to give herself over to him, to be the balm for his troubles as he'd been to hers once upon a time. Gripping her shirt at the hem, she tugged it over her head and tossed it aside.

His expression remained unchanged, save for the flaring of his nostrils and the curling of his hands into fists.

She doffed her boots and socks next, lining them up along the wall next to the door. Holding his gaze, she worked the snap and zipper of her jeans. They dropped to the ground and she kicked them toward his sofa.

Her undergarments were black cotton, simple and functional. Maybe he wished she weren't so ordinary. She'd wager that the other women in town jockeying for his attention wore silky, lace lingerie, but all she had to offer was herself. And fancy underwear wasn't who she was. She hoped, tonight, she'd be enough.

He stared at her body, taking slow, silent stock of her breasts, then stomach, then legs.

She was greedy to see the physique hidden beneath his clothes, so when he didn't make a move to undress, she reached for his shirt.

His left hand snapped from his side and locked around her wrist. She gasped, surprised.

Stepping into her, he pinned her wrist near her ear, pinned her body flat against the door with his own. His right hand splayed over her hip and he pressed his forehead to hers. His breath was shallow, his eyes closed tight. Though his mouth brushed hers with a feather-light touch, he did not kiss the parted lips she offered.

His body was cold sweat, all male. The burgeoning length of his arousal beneath the flimsy nylon shorts grew harder, pushing into her stomach. She cupped his jaw and stroked the stubble of his cheek with her thumb. Reckless, incinerating need blazed through her body. Not the need for sexual release, nor comfort, but for connection with the one man she'd ever loved. For a glimpse into the life with him she'd been denied, the happiness she'd wanted so badly she'd let it burn her.

His breath fanned over her face, and she detected a hint of cigarette smoke, a scent that took her back to their original affair. Knowing what she did about the hurt he'd suffered today, it was an easy guess as to why he'd fallen off the wagon with his addiction. Wasn't that the same reason that had compelled her to his door tonight? Allowing her pain to justify giving in to impulse, to the thing she needed despite all the reasons it was bad for her.

With quickened breath, she arched into him, clutching his head with her hands, her mouth reaching for his.

He evaded her efforts, turning his face to nuzzle the side of her head with his nose. But then the hand gripping her wrist slid up, his palm over her palm. She curled her fingers down over his hand, twining her hand with his.

And it was like something snapped inside her.

Her whole life, everything she wanted, everything she tried for, she never got any of it. She never got her father's attention or love, and didn't even have a real understanding of the man he'd turned out to be. And she'd failed to grow into a successful farmer like her grandparents had been. To sustain something for herself and her family. To breathe the air in a field of grass and know it belonged to her.

She didn't have Vaughn's love either, at least in any real way that made him care enough to fight for her. But tonight he'd accepted her into his house and he held her hand like he loved her back. Exactly how she needed to be loved.

Her throat tightened with the surge of a sob. She was powerless to stop the welling of moisture in her eyes or a rogue tear from escaping down her cheek. Goddamn, she felt raw.

She drew a labored breath that quaked and stuttered in her throat. Vaughn opened his eyes, concern registering in them.

Please don't ask me why I'm crying. Don't make me speak the pain aloud. And whatever you do, please don't let go of me.

He didn't. He swiped her tear away with his finger. Clutching even tighter to the hand he held, he angled his lips over hers and took her mouth in a slow, deep kiss.

Chapter Sixteen

Vaughn just wanted to look at her. He wanted to gaze on something beautiful, and God, Rachel's beauty awed him. That someone like her wanted him was astounding, humbling. She was too pretty to touch, standing in his entryway in her bra and panties. All he could do was drink her in.

He was so fucked up in pain tonight. He'd failed his family, he'd failed Rachel. And what he was doing right now—laying his hands on her body, deliberating which part of her to put his mouth on next—that was the failure of his integrity as a sheriff. Having failed at everything, he was just a man now. A fucked-up, scared, failure of a man.

Never once had he done a thing right by Rachel, but she'd come to him anyway tonight. She'd undressed for him, the tenderness in her eyes slaying his soul. Had she any idea what she did to him when she looked at him like she loved him? Then she let him touch her, and when she cried, all he could think was, here in his arms was the toughest, most capable person he knew, and she trusted him enough to let him see her cry.

He didn't know the reason for her tears. Something

bad had happened to her, she'd said, but he had no earthly clue what it was, as wrapped up in his own shit-storm as he'd been. She could be crying about that, or maybe, like him, who she was and the pressure that came with it, had become too much to bear.

His tongue claimed her mouth, stroking against hers as his lips consumed her. She melted into his kiss, her warm, soft body wrapping around him, stripping him of his pain. Stripping him of his failures. Maybe tonight, that's all he needed to be—a man who needed a woman, this particular woman. Nothing more, nothing less.

He wrenched his mouth away from hers and tore his shirt off, then kicked off his shoes. Given how long and how rigorously he'd been working out when she knocked, he probably stank, but Rachel was already seeing him at his worst in every other way, so he tried not to care. After pulling off his socks, he unceremoniously lowered his shorts and briefs, then removed his watch.

Then he stood before her—a man, and nothing more.

She swallowed hard and reached for him, smoothing a hand up the ridges of his stomach. His muscles contracted under her cool touch, and his breath froze in his lungs when her hand flattened over his heart.

It was a move that proved his undoing.

Covering her hand with his, he gritted his teeth against a welling of love for the woman who accepted him, failures and all. To stand before her, stripped to his most elemental self, and know that it was enough. He wanted the same for her. To free her from the pain of her day, from the pressure of being Rachel Sorentino.

He unhooked the watch from her wrist and set it on the table, then pulled the rubber band from her hair and admired the way her sun-kissed brown locks tumbled around her shoulders.

The bandage on her left arm caught his eye. He

peeled an edge of the medical tape away and studied her injury. The jagged-edged, three-inch gash had scabbed, and the bruises on the skin surrounding it were fading.

"It's better every day," she said quietly.

"May I take the bandage off?"

When she nodded, he peeled the tape as carefully as he could manage, then dropped it to the table and covered the wound with his hand. Of all the things he reckoned she'd gone through that week, the gunshot injury seemed like the wound to be healing the quickest.

She angled her chin up, inviting him to kiss her. He drew her lower lip into his mouth and suckled it, feeling her reach between them. She took a firm hold of his erection, and he nearly bit her lip, it felt so right. He reached behind her and unclasped her bra. She hunched her shoulders, relinquished her grip on him so he could free her arms from the straps.

Her breasts fit perfectly in his hands. But then, he already knew that. He knew how her nipples beaded when he rolled them between the pads of his thumb and index finger. He knew the weight of them, the silken texture, and the angle of her back arching when he pulled a hardened tip into his mouth.

He ran his hand down the curve of her spine, settling atop her panties.

He dropped to his knees, prostrate before her, and grazed her belly with his nose and lips and cheeks. She was so soft, so exquisite.

The panties were black and stretchy. Sitting back on his heels, he burrowed his face between her thighs. The panties were damp. Jutting between his legs, his cock pulsed and hardened at the proof of her desire. He pulled one edge aside and lapped at her smooth, wet outer folds. She tangled her hands in his hair. After one taste, he stopped. There would be time enough to bring her pleasure that night, but for now, he wanted to finish the job he'd started.

He peeled the damp panties away from her body and helped her step out of them.

Standing, he took her hand in his and led her to the shower. Time to wash it all away—the sweat, the smoke from the cigarettes he'd lit up before deciding that exercise was a more fit punishment for his sins, the dirt of Rachel's workday. Her tears. The mistakes they'd both made. The carelessness with which they'd treated each other.

He kissed her—slowly, venerably—while the water warmed. When it had, they stepped in, a tangle of limbs. Angling so her wound was out of the stream of water, he held her, rocking her in a slow dance. She rested her head on his shoulder and buried her face in his neck. He washed her back like that, slid his soap-slick hands over her bottom and up her spine.

"Tip your head so I can get your hair."

All he had was cheap dandruff shampoo. Shaking some into his hand, he remembered how, during their initial affair, she'd stocked girlie shampoo in his shower. After she'd ended things, he'd gone through the house with a trash can, erasing her from the surface of his life. The memory strung him so thin and raw, his eyes watered. He'd fought to forget about her, to make his feelings for her disappear. What a fool he'd been to think that was possible.

He worked his shampoo into her hair. Supporting her with his left arm around her waist, he tipped her back to rise. She took over the rinse job and he held on, his right hand exploring her breasts and ribs, watching the water and soap bubbles cascade over her creamy skin.

With a fresh round of suds on his hands, he reached one around to her backside and the other between her legs. She propped a leg on the edge of the tub and gasped in pleasure when he swirled his finger over her clit. He dipped lower and pushed two fingers inside her as the hand on her ass slid into the cleft, teasing her entrance there until she arched, pressing her hips back until he slipped his finger inside her. With a whimper of ecstasy, she fisted her hands in his hair and brought his lips to hers in a hard, wet kiss that told him exactly how much she loved what his hands were doing.

His cock was right there, so close to her wet heat that he could shove into her if he moved his hand. Arousing, the idea of claiming her body with his in that way, but he respected her too much not to use a condom. The more he thought about what that skin-on-skin friction would feel like, though, the faster his self-control began to fray, until his only choice was to ease his fingers away from her body and give himself the space to regroup.

She made a noise of protest, but took the hint, watching him duck his head under the water with dreamy, half lidded eyes. The next thing he knew, she was behind him, bar of soap in hand. Her mouth kissed along his spine, reaching higher until her teeth clamped onto his shoulder near his neck, a sensation so fantastic that he sucked a gulp of air in through his clenched teeth. Then she reached around to his front and took his cock and balls into her sudsy hands, driving his willpower to the brink of destruction.

All that stopped him from dropping her to the floor and unpacking their orgasms right then and there was the knowledge that in a few minutes—as soon as he wanted—he would have her on her back in his bed. The image gave him enough strength to clamp a trembling hand on her wrist to stop her. "Enough. I want you in my bed, in my mouth—right now."

He made quick work of drying them both, as quick as

he could, given that he couldn't stop kissing her or watching the wicked fire dancing in her eyes. She must've felt the same because she never let go of the hold she had around his shoulders the whole way to his bed. They toppled together onto the duvet.

He spread her knees and dove into her swollen, wet flesh with his lips and tongue. Goddamn, she tasted good. Sweet and thick and uniquely Rachel. He got his fingers working again inside her body and, in no time, found a rhythm that turned her wild, quaking and whimpering and clutching at his ears.

He could've touched her like that forever, but she grew still and stroked his hair, whispering in a tremulous voice, "Get up here. I don't want to come until you're inside me."

And damn if he'd ever deny her that.

Levering up on his elbows, he reached across her body into the nightstand for a condom. He was all thumbs trying to manage the rubber, dropping it twice before securing it over his erection. The whirlpool of emotions vying for space inside him made him clumsy and shaky. He tried to fool his mind by telling himself this was just Rachel. He'd fucked her brains out in his bed many times over, and had even made slow, fierce love to her on occasion, but this time with her felt different. Profound in a way that frightened him.

He pressed inside her in a slow drag of flesh-on-flesh that had his whole body tensing with pleasure. A sensation so rapturous, he couldn't help but whisper her name. His own personal prayer. His everything. She met his gaze, her dark eyes shining as fiercely as his heart screamed. He found her arms behind his neck and brought them over her head, locking their hands together. And then his body took over. His hips surged and retreated as they rocked together in the dance they'd begun in the shower, a fluid union of heat and friction and wetness.

Vaughn had no idea what he was going to do to fix his life. No clue what the future held, but inside Rachel, in that moment, he didn't feel like a failure. He felt strong and worthy, capable of anything. And when she found her release, holding tight to his hands, her body trembling and her breath a staccato of gasps against his neck, he felt indestructible.

He pushed up and back, kneeling, bringing her hips with him. When he came, he wanted to do so while looking at Rachel's beautiful, sated body, framed in the glow of the bathroom light. With every thrust, he felt their vivid, eternal connection coursing through him. It shamed him that he'd thought he could break free of the hold she had on his heart, if only he tried hard enough. What a fool.

Taking her backside in his hands, he thrust harder, burying himself deep within her, feeling his balls tighten with impending release. At least tonight he'd cherished her the best he could. He'd been the man she deserved.

A final thrust and he came with a growl, holding fast to the only woman he'd ever loved. There would be no getting over her. He recognized that now. With everything else about his life destroyed, he knew as sure as the cruel sun would rise in the morning that the way he felt about Rachel was the only real part of himself he had left.

Rachel woke in silent darkness.

She felt Vaughn's absence before she opened her eyes. It whispered to her like the winter wind through a canyon, hollow and cold. This was the worst part of falling asleep in his bed—waking to the harsh reality that the fantasy of their togetherness was over. The next part was good-bye. A hundred good-byes they'd said to each other over the last sixteen months. A hundred good-byes, and each time, she vowed it would be the last.

Vaughn's pillow smelled like him, spicy and male. Closing her eyes, she hugged it to her body and inhaled. Why did she keep putting herself through the hurt of having to say good-bye? It didn't make sense why a woman would torture herself over a man who didn't love her enough to fight for her.

Maybe because that's what she'd expected of him. To treat her with as much careless disregard as her father had. She'd loved her dad with her whole heart. Loved Vaughn in a totally different way, but just as ardently. Didn't seem to matter to men that she gave them the gift of her love. It was clear now that she'd never be anyone's first priority but her own.

Then again, maybe she wasn't giving Vaughn enough credit. Making love tonight had felt different than every other time they'd been together. Maybe he'd sensed it too. Even though she'd made terrible choices of whom to trust and what to believe—the fallout of her hopelessly flawed intuition—she owed it to Vaughn not to give up on him without giving him a chance to prove that her assessment of him was wrong.

She threw back the duvet and climbed from the bed.

The nearest fix for her nudity was in his closet. She fumbled with a hanger in the darkness, then pulled a white T-shirt over her head. From a drawer, she pulled on a pair of his boxer briefs. Like the shirt, the underwear was a loose fit, but good enough.

She padded from the room in search of him, following the smell of cigarette smoke toward the dark kitchen. He wasn't in the kitchen, but the door to his backyard had been left ajar.

Dressed in sweatpants and a black T-shirt, he sat on the steps looking at the darkness, a cigarette between his lips. He didn't turn to acknowledge her until she stood on the top step, breathing in the dense odor of burning tobacco. She wasn't a fan of the smell, but it evoked a comforting familiarity she welcomed tonight.

"Hey," she said.

"Hey, yourself." He made no move to snuff the cigarette. Maybe he was past caring what she thought.

She sat cross-legged on the small concrete landing, leaning against the side of the house so that she looked at him in profile. The night air was a tad cool on her legs, but not enough that she was uncomfortable.

He let out a slow stream of smoke into the black night. It danced, illuminated by the moon, before dissipating into the air. "I'm going to quit after this one."

"That'd probably be for the best."

He nodded and took another drag. The cigarette was nearly gone, with barely enough for him to pinch between his fingers. "I've got a half marathon in three weeks. The United New Mexico Law Enforcement Charity Run."

"You run it every year?"

"Yup. Me and my deputies run as a team. It's good fun, good press, that sort of thing. Last year was the first race since I'd quit smoking and, big surprise, it was my fastest time ever." After a lingering inhale of the cigarette, he flicked it into a rusted coffee can, then handed her the rest of the pack. "Hide this from me, would you? Otherwise I'll start right back up as soon as you leave."

She tucked the pack in her lap. *As soon as you leave.*

There was her answer.

She hadn't put it all together how desperately she'd wanted him to invite her to stay until he said that, but now the only thing she wanted more than to wake up with him in the morning, farm chores be damned, was for him to want her there.

Her heart aching something fierce, she brought her knees up and hugged them. "What happened to your family today? I heard talk at Smithy's that your sister and parents were arrested, but all I heard were rumors."

"That sounds about right for this town." He shifted, twisting his fingers together as though, now that he was done smoking, he had no idea what to do with his hands. "My sister, Gwen, she has a disorder. Been cursed with it all her life. She steals things. From people's houses, from her job or retail stores, all over the place. Used to be, the compulsion only seized her when she was nervous or scared. Last few years, though, she's gotten worse."

"That sounds like it would be tough on the whole family."

"That's the cold, hard truth. My folks, over the years they've been through way more than any parents should. I can't tell you how frustrating it's been for me to watch. I've done what I could to look out for Gwen. Wallace Meyer and I had an unspoken agreement that he'd look the other way with her shoplifting as long as I looked the other way with Junior's, shall we say, hiccups with good citizenship." He looked at her lap with hound dog eyes.

She set a hand on top of the cigarette pack. "Not on your life."

He offered her a weak smile. "Fine. Be that way."

"Was Gwen arrested for shoplifting today?"

"No." He shook his head. "I mean, yes. But that's not how the mess started. It started with Wallace Jr.'s trespassing and assault on your property."

"You violated the unspoken agreement between yourself and Meyer when you arrested Junior, didn't you?"

He scoffed. "Hell, no. Junior violated it the minute he brought rifles onto your land. That was no hiccup I could overlook. Even if I didn't already have it out for Meyer, or if Junior had shot a stranger instead of the woman I—" He picked restlessly at his fingernails, scowling. "The details of who and what are immaterial. Junior's guilty of assault with a deadly weapon, and no handshake agreement can save him from his crimes."

"But Meyer didn't see it that way."

The statement roused a sardonic huff from Vaughn's throat. "Meyer issued the order for his officers to search my parents' house at the exact time I was transferring Junior from the hospital to the jail so I wouldn't have the chance to interfere. The police found meth under my parents' bed, weed in the cookie jar, and thousands of dollars of stolen goods in Gwen's bedroom. I arrived at home in time to watch them cuff my mother and father and read them their rights."

The despair Rachel felt that day came tumbling over her again. Vaughn's foundation had been shaken as much as hers. More so, because unlike Rachel's dad, his parents had been innocent victims. But she knew better than to show him sympathy for his experience. The kind of man she knew him to be, his only concern would be for his parents' pain. "I'm so sorry they had to endure that."

He scrubbed a hand over his nose and mouth. "The looks on their faces, of their hands cuffed behind their backs, will haunt me until the day I die. Nothing I ever do or say can make up for what I allowed to happen to them."

She nearly argued that point, almost reminded him there was nothing he could've done. Then it hit her that she would've felt the exact same way. That she did, in fact, feel the same burden of guilt about what happened to her mother. Could it be that she was never actually capable of protecting her mother? Could that have been part of the illusion she'd bought into for too many years?

Her mother had spent many unsupervised hours in the house every day while Rachel worked on the farm. She was unsupervised all night long, as she and Rachel slept in different rooms on opposite sides of the house. Her mother could've overdosed without even leaving her room, if she'd had a mind to. How had Rachel managed to convince herself it had happened because she'd spent the night with Vaughn? Her guilt suddenly seemed ludicrous and self-indulgent.

Vaughn rubbed his throat. "Let me have that box, would you?"

Rousing from the trance of her epiphany, she fell forward, cigarette box in hand, and crawled behind him. She'd leave him as soon as she gathered the strength to do so, but for a few more minutes, she wanted to be near him. Resting on her side, she tucked the cigarettes behind her, hooked her arm around his shoulders, and dropped her forehead to the back of his neck. "Don't do that to yourself. If you give in again, it'll only give you something else to regret."

With a soft snort, he grazed his lips over her forearm. "That's the story of my life, Rachel."

Was he implying that he regretted giving in to her tonight? Probably, but she certainly wasn't going to apologize about asking for what she needed. "Were the drugs found in your parents' house planted by the police, do you think?"

He shook his head. "Gwen confessed to hiding them when she heard the police coming through the front door. She figured they only had a warrant to search her bedroom, not the whole house."

"After she confessed, were the charges against your parents dismissed?"

"The drug charges, yes. But Meyer's still sticking it to them on harboring and abetting a known criminal. A judge released them on their own recognizance a few hours ago and I drove them home. Their house was trashed during the search, so I offered to put them up in a hotel while I cleaned or hired someone to, but they were too stubborn to let me."

"Will those lesser charges stick?"

"They'd better not," he said. "I've got to somehow convince Meyer to drop them, but I have no idea how I'm going to manage that within the purview of the law."

"What about Gwen?"

"Gwen needs to pay her dues and get clean. Prison might be the best place for her right now. I hooked her up with a top-notch defense attorney and she'll be sentenced early next week. My folks are sad about it, but seem to be taking it in stride."

They settled into silence. He stroked her arm absentmindedly while she kept her cheek pressed to his back, concentrating on the rise and fall of his lungs beneath his ribs, the muscles of his back shifting, the unyielding tension in his shoulders. Beneath the residual smell of smoke, she caught a hint of soap and sweat on his skin.

"Something happened to you today too," he said.

She unwound her arm from his neck and propped her back against his. "In the southwest field, Ben and I found an underground meth lab, of all the goddamn things."

He craned his neck to look at her. "You're kidding."

"I wish."

She could almost hear the wheels turning in his mind. "How was it ventilated?"

"Swamp coolers disguised in the irrigation flow vents."

"How did you discover it?"

The prospect of answering that question for the

hundredth time made her weary. "No offense, but I can tell you're going into sheriff mode, and let me tell you, I spent the whole day answering questions like that for your deputies and Undersheriff Stratis. I could use the night off. I'm sure Stratis will fill you in tomorrow."

"Stratis called me this morning, but I was too wrapped up in getting my parents out of custody to hear what he was saying. I designated him in charge of everything that came in and turned off my phone. I can't believe the one day I was off the grid, you needed me and I had no idea." With a groan, he shook his head, and Rachel swore she felt his shoulders hitch another notch toward his ears.

She did need him, but not in the way he was prepared to help her. More than anything, she needed him to ask her to stay. She needed strong arms around her that wouldn't let go no matter what. But she wasn't going to ask. She was done giving her heart over to men.

She cleared her throat. "There wasn't anything you could've done differently from your deputies. When you didn't come to investigate along with your men, and then you weren't at the station house, I assumed it was because"—the truth hurt to think, much less say in a neutral tone of voice—"because you didn't want to have contact with me." She registered the strain in her words and, panicking, added, "Which was fine because you have a really great team of people working for you and they did an excellent job. Even Stratis was polite, which was a nice surprise."

He cursed under his breath.

"I can't tell you what it was like today, learning that my father destroyed my career, my future, and my ability to provide for our family. All these years, I thought our business went under because I wasn't a good enough farmer. And he let me believe it."

"You're a great farmer."

She scoffed. "Not yet, but I'm going to be someday."
Picking her fingernails, she added, "Did I ever tell you
how I got into photography?"

He didn't answer right away, like it took him a few seconds to make the mental U-turn. "No. I've always wondered."

"I was seventeen. Riding along the northwest fence
line with Cressley, the American Paint horse my dad got
me for my tenth birthday. Going through an alfalfa field,
I spotted a coyote crouched along the edge. Right there
in the heat of the day. I figured he was sick or hurt, but
before I could steer Cressley away, it sprang at us. Cressley reared and I fell."

Vaughn eased away from her slow enough that she
had time to shift her weight. He repositioned on the step
so that his back was propped on the railing and he was
looking at her. He patted the concrete next to him. "Sit
here with me."

She settled next to him, their shoulders touching. She
fought the surge of affection the gesture evoked, but that
proved impossible once he took her hand and cradled it
in his.

"That's better. Keep going. You fell . . ."

"I hit the ground hard and face planted in the dirt.
I knew right away something in my body had broken,
but couldn't tell what." The pain had radiated through
her, tightening her throat, constricting her chest. It was
the moment that marked the first time in her life she'd
experienced real fear. The kind of bone-deep, suffocating fear that leaves the soul scarred. The soil had vibrated with the energy of hooves churning over the
ground as Cressley fled. Then the world went silent but
for the beating of her heart and the rustle of alfalfa in
the breeze.

"What did you do?"

"I rolled to my back and held my right arm up for inspection. My hand dangled limp. The broken bone had cut through the skin near my wrist." She spared him the gory details, but she saw them as plain in her mind as she had that day.

Vaughn sucked a breath in through his teeth and squeezed her hand. "Damn."

"I couldn't stop thinking about what the broken bone meant. I had responsibilities. I didn't have the luxury to nurse a broken wrist. I was terrified for the future of the farm, and who was going to do the laundry or fix meals or get Amy and Jenna to school."

"You were a child, but you were already running the show around there."

She shrugged. "I didn't have a choice. Somebody had to. I sure didn't know how I was going to manage with my right arm out of commission. Not to mention the coyote was out there, and it wasn't going to chase Cressley for long, not with a smaller, more helpless creature on the ground. I remember praying, Please don't let me get bitten by a rabid coyote."

"You would've died. Out there in the middle of nowhere, in the time before cell phones. Did anybody know where you were, at least?"

She rested the side of her head on his shoulder. He was so warm, so solid, it was hard not to crawl into his lap. "Not a soul, or so I thought. The longer I lay there, the more my fear subsided. Probably due to the shock I was in. I was at peace with the reality of the situation, you know? I settled into my fate. It was a typical June day, beautiful but hot. I remember looking up at the sky, framed as it was by alfalfa shoots. I remember breathing in their baked grass smell. Used to be my favorite smell in the world."

He released her hand to wrap his arm around her, pulling her tight against his side. "Why's that?"

Thinking about it made the smell tangible. She inhaled deeply through her nose. "That was the smell of survival for another crop season. It meant we were going to be okay."

He drew lazy circles on her arm below her injury. "For me it's the smell of metal heating in the forge fire of my father's workshop. Best smell ever."

"I don't know that smell."

"Guess I owe you an invitation to dinner at my parents' house."

Her throat constricted. What was she supposed to do with a loaded comment like that? "Does their house smell like a forge fire?"

He let out a soft laugh that vibrated against her ear. "Pretty much. My dad turned the original garage into a blacksmith workshop before I was born, so yeah, everything from the furniture to the carpet smells like a forge fire."

"I'll bet." Before he could reiterate his offer or push the issue on dinner, she steered the conversation to neutral territory. "You want me to tell you what my long-winded story has to do with photography?"

"I was curious, but I didn't want to rush you."

"I was lying on the ground, looking at the sky. It was peaceful. I could make out the peak of Sidewinder Mesa in the distance. A smear of clouds pulled vertically behind it, like taffy, and I wished I'd had a camera."

His hand stilled against her arm. "Seriously? Your arm bone was exposed and a possibly rabid coyote was lurking nearby, and you wished you'd brought a camera?"

She grinned. "Yeah, you're right. It was an absurd thing to think about, but it's the truth. Funny how the mind works when it's in shock. Nevertheless, after that day, I was never without a camera again." Knowing it would get a reaction out of him, she added, "End of story."

"Whoa, whoa, whoa. Hold on a minute. That's not the end of the story. What happened next? Did the coyote come back?"

She smiled at his indignation. "Yes, it did. It walked right up to me and sniffed my injured arm."

Vaughn gave a low whistle.

"Right when I was sure it was going to start chowing down on me, I felt more vibrations in the ground. Horse hooves. The coyote sensed it too, because it raised its head, listening." She'd stared, unblinking at it, not breathing. Its chin whiskers were coated in her blood. "A loud *whoop* sounded. The coyote lit off in a flash. Then my dad fell to my side and examined my break, all the while firing questions so fast, I had to interrupt to answer."

Bitter grief rocketed through her. That had been one of her favorite memories until today. She'd adored her father in that moment. Worshiped him.

"How did he know where to find you?"

"Cressley had run home, and Dad sensed right away something was wrong. I never found out how he knew where to look for me. I was too busy idolizing him." Had he been cooking drugs even that far back? While she was laid up with her injury, afraid for the farm's future, was he already actively working to destroy it?

"You'd been afraid of how the farm would stay running while your arm healed. Did that end up being an issue?"

"Not as much as I'd feared. Dad stuck close by me for a few weeks. I thought he'd turned over a new leaf."

"It didn't last?"

"Not much in this world does." A shiver started at her

legs and crawled its way through her body. She pressed her face into his neck as her body trembled.

He hooked a hand under her knees and pulled her onto his lap.

She thought about protesting, but it was such a relief to be held tight, to feel loved. "I don't know how to reconcile what I've learned about him with the man I thought I knew. I'd been so wrapped up remembering the times he saved me, I was blind to the lying, cheating criminal he really was. I'm not sure he ever really loved me."

He stroked her hair. "Of course he did, and he's still the man who found you when you were lost and hurt. Nothing can change that. But all this talk about him saving you makes you sound like a damsel in distress, waiting for your knight to ride up and slay the monsters for you. That's not who you are. All those times your dad failed you, you know what was really going on? You figured out how to slay your own monsters. You learned how to save yourself. It's one of the things I admire most about you. Someday, after your grief fades, you'll be able to see it better."

Maybe, but she sure didn't feel strong at the moment. She didn't want to be. She wanted to stay curled on Vaughn's lap forever.

He smoothed a hand along her calf. "Your legs are cold. What are you wearing down here, shorts?"

"Your underwear."

His head lolled and he groaned. "You shouldn't say stuff like that to me. I might have a heart attack picturing you walking around in my underwear." His hand crept higher on her thigh until his fingers snuck beneath the hem of the briefs. "I always thought I was a leg man, but I'm starting to think I'm more of an ass man, because I can't get enough of yours."

She grinned. She'd known that about him from the get-go.

Then he placed a finger on her chin and tilted her head, aiming his lips for hers, and she knew what would happen next. Exactly what she'd promised herself she was done doing.

She evaded his efforts. "It was two-thirty on the alarm clock when I woke up, which means it must be after three now. That's not enough time for us to start something new and still allow me to make it home before my workers show up. And I'm sure as hell not going to drive up with them standing there to watch me get out of my truck in the same clothes I wore yesterday."

That cheap, filthy feeling bubbled up inside her. She was so sick and tired of sneaking around with him.

"Let me love on you a few more minutes."

She pressed her palms against his chest and scooted away, feeling strong for the first time in too long. "Either ask me to stay through morning or let me go. The choice is yours."

Chapter Seventeen

Vaughn's hands fell away from her. He looked out at the darkness for a long beat before turning to face her once more. "What do you want me to say, Rachel? They took my mom away in handcuffs. I can't afford to make selfish choices like sleeping in with you or taking a chance that someone would see your truck parked out front come morning. I thought you understood that. You and I agreed to wait until the case is settled. I can't tell you how frustrated it makes me that it has to be that way, but there it is. I'm sorry."

The lack of sting she felt from his words didn't surprise her. She'd already known what he was going to say. What floored her, instead, was the realization that she'd said almost exactly the same words to him after her mom's suicide attempt. *I can't afford to make selfish choices.*

What was it with the two of them that they valued their own happiness so little? Whatever it was, Rachel was done with it. Time to start over. Time to focus on herself and being happy. Because, damn it all, Vaughn had been right when he said she was no fainting damsel. No one was going to save her but herself, especially not a man, even if she did love him like crazy.

She stood, her legs strong and capable. No more trembling. No more weak knees.

"I know what we agreed to, but I thought maybe things had changed. You don't owe me an apology. You don't owe me anything." She'd spouted that line so often to him it'd become her mantra, but this was the first time she knew in her heart it was true.

"Of course I do."

She straightened the T-shirt and briefs, feeling more powerful with every breath she took. "No, you don't. All you need to worry about is taking care of your parents and running your investigations. I'm going to go live my life, and see if I can make sense of everything that's happened. And I'm going to plant a crop of alfalfa this year if it kills me. When the case is settled, you know where to find me."

She walked through the kitchen, stripping off his shirt and briefs en route to the front entryway, where her clothes sat in a pile. Vaughn followed. She felt his eyes on her while she dressed, but kept her back to him until she was fully clothed.

When she faced him, his expression was guarded as he handed her his folded shirt and briefs. "I'd like to imagine you wearing these when you sleep. Would you do that for me?"

Refusing to engage in a conversation about it, she took them. He set the box of cigarettes on top.

"I'd forgotten about those," she said.

His lips curved into a pained smile. "Believe me, I hadn't."

"Any other smokes you want to send with me before they tempt you?"

He shook his head. "I already smoked all the rest. That was my last box. You want to borrow a jacket for the drive?"

"I'll be fine." She unlocked the dead bolt and stepped outside, Vaughn behind her. They crossed the street to her truck in silence.

He held her door while she climbed in and buckled up, then stroked her cheek with his thumb. "You'd never before wanted to stay until morning. If I'd have asked you, would you have?"

Turning her face into his hand, she smoothed her lips over the inside of his wrist. "Yes. This time I would have."

He released her and stepped away, his jaw tight. Looking down the length of the dark street, he nodded, his lips twitching like he was torn about what to do. Maybe he was going to change his mind and invite her to stay after all.

Then he returned his world-weary gaze to her. "Good night, Rachel."

Okay, then. Enough was enough.

She closed the door, fired up the engine, and rolled down her window. "Good-bye, Vaughn."

She felt empowered, saying the words and meaning them. Freer and lighter than she had in years. She wasn't a failure as a farmer. She wasn't to blame for her mom's death. And, for the first time in sixteen months, she didn't feel like her happiness hinged on Vaughn. She'd hit rock bottom this week, sure, but that only meant there was nowhere for her to go but up.

The drive home was uneventful. One lonely road after another. Her headlights picked up a coyote dashing across the road into the bushes near the turn from the highway, and another time, her truck's radio started playing Glen Campbell's "Rhinestone Cowboy." Less painful than "Southern Nights," but she still couldn't stand to listen to it. Other than that, she made it to the dirt road into their property without incident.

An unfamiliar black sedan was parked on the south

side of her house. She didn't see it until she was right up
on it, given the blackness of the night. Who knew which
new misfit or lost soul Amy had invited to stay? They
were already housing Tina, Sloane, and Ben. More and
more, Mr. Dixon or Kellan stayed over too. The last time
Rachel went to Tucumcari to have new keys made, the
man at the hardware store had joked about giving her a
bulk discount.

She pulled into her usual spot in front of the porch,
grabbed Vaughn's clothes and cigarettes, and stepped
outside, stretching her back. She had an hour until
Rudy, Damon, and Ben showed up for work. Plenty of
time for a shower and a cup of coffee. The coffee might
get her through morning chores, but given how little
sleep she'd gotten, there wasn't enough caffeine in the
world to keep her energized until the end of the day.

Movement to her right made her turn.

A man in dark clothes flew at her, hitting her to the
ground, the air knocked clean out of her lungs. He
backhanded her across the cheek, and she was too
stunned and hurt to react. He was so strong, crushing
her with his body. She pedaled her boots against the
gravel, but couldn't break free. He wound back to hit
her again, so she flailed her hand, smacking his face
with her ring of keys.

He grunted, like maybe she hurt him, so she swung
again and he grabbed her arm. But his weight had
shifted enough so that she was able to push her boot
against the ground and roll him off her. Scrambling to
her feet, she sucked in her first real breath of air and
screamed. Less than ten yards away was a house full of
people. If she was going to go down, she at least needed
to warn her family of the danger.

The man lunged at her again and she tripped back,
running for Ben's truck across the yard. Desperate for a

weapon, she had the driver door open when the man slammed into her back. He knocked her head against the side of the truck. She elbowed him, catching him in the soft part of his belly. Her movements were imprecise and unskilled, but got the job done.

She pulled herself away from the attacker by sheer will and flung her upper body onto the floor of the cab. Ben's rifle was easy to find under the seat. The ammo sat behind it in a box. She grabbed some, but didn't have time to load. So she pivoted, swinging the rifle around like a club.

That's when she saw the flames, licking up toward the sky in a swirl of black smoke.

The porch was on fire.

She gasped. Amy was in the house. Ben, Sloane, Tina too. Maybe Kellan. Oh, God. They hadn't reacted to her screams. Did that mean the assailant had gotten to them already?

In that moment of blind terror, the assailant grabbed the rifle from her hands and knocked her across the skull.

She crumpled. Her mouth pooled with blood and her head pounded so bad she couldn't move her eyes. The smoke alarms were sounding in the house now, loud and out of rhythm with each other. The attacker grabbed her by the boots and dragged her facedown across the gravel driveway, past her burning house.

He shoved her into the trunk of the black sedan, and she was too weak to defend herself beyond flailing her arms. In the blackness of the closed trunk, once the engine rumbled to life and the car took off, her fear and pain subsided enough for her to think.

Whoever the man who'd kidnapped her was, he had to be connected to Meyer Jr. and the meth lab. It all went back to her father, and the terrible choices he'd made. Fear and rage battled inside her. Rage at her father for dragging them into hell. But also at herself. Her epiphany about her actions being consequence-free was a load of crap. What happened tonight was her fault alone.

The message the universe had been trying to get through to her was finally sinking in, though it was too late to matter. All that week, her farm and family had been under siege by druggies and violent criminals, two of whom were still on the loose. But instead of staying home to watch over her family, she'd been off screwing the sheriff—again. Her mom had already paid the price for her selfishness, and now she, along with the rest of her family, were going to die.

Vaughn's cell phone rang. He tore his gaze from the case file he'd been poring over to look at his watch. Three-forty-five. With no cigarettes to take his mind off Rachel or his parents' grim situation, he'd thrown in the towel and gone to the office.

The overnight dispatch calls were patched through Irene's home line for another three hours, and Deputy Reyes, the on-duty officer, was on patrol. Grateful for the silence, Vaughn had dug into research on El Diente, pulling every unsolved injury and fatality case in the county involving victims who were missing teeth.

The display on his phone said the call was from Kellan's cell. If he'd found out Vaughn had slept with Rachel and was phoning to tell him off for it, then he could go to hell. It was none of his business. He pressed ACCEPT and propped a boot on his desk. "Hey, what're you doing up this early?"

"We can't find Rachel." Kellan's words rushed out in a blur of speech. His voice was strained with fear.

Taken aback, Vaughn dropped his foot and snapped his chair up. He wasn't thrilled to admit he and Rachel had been together, but he couldn't let Kellan go on worrying. "She left my house about a half hour ago. She should be home any minute."

"Her truck's here, but she's not. With the fire, we didn't notice right away—"

Vaughn stood. "Slow down. What fire?"

Kellan drew a breath. "I stayed the night with Amy. A few minutes ago, the smoke detectors went off. We came downstairs and the porch was covered in flames."

Vaughn sprinted down the hallway, digging for his keys. His phone chimed with another incoming call. He held the phone out and read the display. Irene. He ignored it and put the phone back to his ear.

"Everybody's out of the house," Kellan said. "Ben and I got the hose going from the emergency tank." Holding the phone with his shoulder, Vaughn locked the front door and jammed himself behind the wheel of his squad car. "They're still trying to put the fire out, and the fire department's on its way, but we can't find Rachel anywhere."

He flipped his lights and sirens on. "On my way. I'm assuming you've called her cell phone?"

"Her foreman said she smashed it yesterday morning after they found the meth lab."

Vaughn cursed. She'd driven home from his house alone in the middle of the night without a cell phone. Why in God's name had he let her take such a risk? "Are all the horses accounted for, or could she have gone for a ride?"

"They're all here. Amy and Sloane went through the stable and moved the horses to safety, along with the other livestock." He let out a stressed-out exhale. "I have to get off this thing, get back to helping with the fire."

"I'll be there as fast as I can."

The second Kellan disconnected, Vaughn called Irene and instructed her to send all four deputies and Stratis to Rachel's place. With the accelerator to the floor, he made it to the dirt turnoff to Sorentino Farm in ten minutes flat, with Stratis, Binderman, and Reyes right behind him. The whole drive, he kept busy talking himself down from looming hysteria, bargaining with God that he'd change his ways, he'd be a better man, if only He'd let Vaughn find her unharmed. But he couldn't escape the possibility that she might've died in the fire. She might've suffered, alone in the dark, not knowing he loved her.

When his parents were arrested, he thought he had nothing left to lose. He thought he'd never experience a worse moment in his lifetime. What a crock of shit. Failing as a son and sheriff, losing his dignity, was nothing compared to the idea of losing Rachel forever.

He threw his car into park behind the fire trucks and ambulance in the driveway and sprinted toward Kellan and the volunteer firefighter he was talking to. "Tell me she wasn't in that fire," he shouted as he ran. "Tell me you didn't find her in there."

Kellan caught him by both shoulders. "She wasn't in the fire."

"You didn't find any . . ." The word *remains* lodged in his throat. He sagged into Kellan's grip.

"No, man. No. Nothing like that." He gave Vaughn's shoulders a squeeze, then turned him toward Rachel's truck. "Look there. We think she might've been taken by whoever set the fire."

On the ground next to her open truck door, the contents of Vaughn's cigarette pack were scattered over the gravel, the box crushed. The T-shirt and underwear he'd sent home with her lay in a crumpled wad nearby. He moved, like floating, to her truck.

The efforts to douse the fire had compromised the scene, soaking the ground and trampling over potential evidence, but the gravel was overturned and cut to the dirt below with gashes. Clearly there'd been a struggle.

Stratis brushed by him to examine the evidence. "Cigarettes? Could those be the perp's?"

Vaughn scrubbed a hand through his hair. Finding Rachel trumped everything, his career, his standing in his employees' eyes—everything. He met Stratis's eyes. "No. Those are mine. I gave them to her so I wouldn't be tempted to smoke. The clothes are mine too. She left my place about three-fifteen this morning. She couldn't have been here more than a few minutes before trouble started."

Stratis nodded, his expression unreadable save for the tightening of his eyes. "Maybe trouble was already here and she drove right into the middle of it."

"That's what I'm starting to think," Kellan said.

Vaughn braced his hands on his knees. He should never have let her drive alone in the middle of the night. He should've followed her home. He should've asked her to stay through morning.

"El Diente or Baltierra? Or both?" Stratis asked.

"There's another truck with an open door over here," Binderman called. "Unspent ammo on the ground."

Vaughn and Stratis strode over.

"That's my truck." It was Rachel's foreman, Ben. "Looks like my ammo too."

"You keep a rifle in there?"

"Yes, sir. A .22. Under the driver's seat."

Binderman ducked his head to look. "It's missing. Did Rachel know about it?"

"Yes, sir. She did."

Vaughn pulled his focus back to take in the scene all at once. Jenna and Amy, trembling in each other's arms, holding Tommy together. His deputies puzzling over a trail of upturned dirt. The fire engines, the smoldering porch. Just like that, everything in his life fell into focus. He'd always accused Rachel of clouding his judgment, making him second-guess himself, but never in his life had he been more crystal clear about what he needed to do—professionally, personally—than he was at that moment.

"You're in charge here, Stratis," he said. "If you find any other evidence, call me. Binderman, meet me at the jail in a half hour."

He took off in a jog to his car.

"Where are you going?" Stratis called after him.

Vaughn called over his shoulder, "Wallace Meyer's ranch. It's time to settle the score once and for all."

Chapter Eighteen

Wallace Meyer lived at the end of a long, single lane road that shot off north from Highway 40, five miles and a canyon away from Devil's Furnace. Vaughn had no trouble gaining entrance to Meyer's property. The ungated driveway was a point of pride for Meyer, who regularly reminded his adoring public that he refused to erect any barriers that would separate him from the people he served. As if money and power weren't barriers enough.

Vaughn hadn't set foot on Wallace Meyer's property since the age of sixteen. His father had farriered for Meyer for another few years after that, but Vaughn refused. No way would he work for a man who beat his wife and horses, and raped the maids. He'd learned that gem by accident, while washing his tools in a spigot near the side of the house. Through the open window, he'd heard two women whispering to each other about why the latest maid had left town in the middle of the night.

The Meyer estate gave off an air of plastic perfection, like a woman who'd indulged in too many facelifts. The buildings were too clean, too new. The lush, manicured lawn as wastefully indulgent and out of place in Quay

County as the six-door garage that stretched across the circular driveway.

Vaughn left his car running and sprinted up the steps. He banged on the door with his fist and rang the doorbell simultaneously, shouting, "You son of a bitch, open this damn door."

He kept it up until a light turned on behind the beveled glass. Meyer's revolver preceded his bald head out of the opening door.

Vaughn's body reacted instinctively to the sight of the gun pointing at him, his shooting hand popping the strap of his sidearm holster before he even knew he was doing it. He caught himself before he'd inched the gun clear of the holster and slid it back down, though he kept his hand on the grip and watched Meyer's trigger finger for the slightest twitch.

Meyer screwed his cheeks up like he was collecting a wad of saliva to spit at Vaughn. "You've got some nerve, frightening my wife in the middle of the night like this. What the hell is wrong with you, Cooper?"

"Junior's associates kidnapped Rachel Sorentino tonight. You're going to make Junior tell us where they took her."

Meyer lowered his gun and stepped outside, closing the door behind him. "Do you honestly expect me to help you find the woman who tried to kill my only child?"

"Give it a rest with your bullshit melodrama, Meyer. A woman's life is in danger." *Please, let her still be alive.*

"She should've thought of that before she aimed her gun at my son."

"Junior brought that on himself. You know it as well as I do, damn it. Like we both know you're not going to stand by while a woman's life is at stake, if for no other reason than it'll crush your public image if word gets out."

Meyer propped a shoulder on the door frame and folded his arms over his chest. "It's fun watching you squirm, Cooper. Like a worm on a hook, helpless. I could get used to this."

Vaughn ground his teeth together. Every second ticking away dimmed Rachel's odds at being rescued alive. Time to play the only ace up his sleeve. "If you don't come with me and tell Junior to cooperate, I'm going to make his life a living hell, beginning with a move to the general population. And I'll make sure that every single criminal you put away knows your son's inside. How long do you think he'll last before someone makes him their bitch or kills him?"

Meyer straightened. "You do that and you won't believe the wrath that will come down on your family."

Vaughn slid his body forward, getting up near Meyer's face. He'd move his parents to Canada if he had to, but there wasn't a threat Meyer could levy that would derail this, Vaughn's only hope of recovering Rachel. "You drive to the jail with me right now or I make the call to move Junior out of solitary. Your choice."

Meyer's lips twitched into a vicious grin. "If you want my help"—he spit the *p* out, spraying Vaughn with spittle—"it's going to cost you."

Vaughn looked into the eyes of the man he'd hated for twenty years, an abuser of people, animals, and power—the man who'd given orders to arrest Vaughn's mother and father. None of it mattered anymore. "Name your price."

"If Junior cooperates, he pleads out on the assault charges. Parole, no jail time."

Vaughn curled his hands into fists. "Fine, but only if you drop all charges against my parents."

"All right. Then I should add that you'll need to drop the other charges against Junior while you're at it."

"Okay."

Meyer licked his lips. "One more thing. After you find the girl, you're going to resign."

Vaughn didn't hesitate. "Done."

Meyer grinned, satisfied. "I'll get my keys."

Vaughn phoned Binderman on his way to the jail, so by the time he arrived, Junior was set up in an interview room.

Acutely aware that forty-five minutes had passed since Kellan had called him about Rachel's disappearance, he watched with mounting nerves through the one-way mirror while Meyer talked to his son. Angela Spencer, the district attorney, slid up next to him, dressed to the nines like she was fresh from a hearing at the courthouse, despite the fact that it was four-thirty in the morning.

"Hey, Angela. Sorry to put you in this position. I didn't have a choice." It hadn't been Vaughn's place to bargain for a plea agreement. He'd banked on her support by virtue of the professional camaraderie they'd cultivated over the years.

She offered him a sympathetic smile. "Glad it doesn't happen all the time, but I've got your back."

"Thank you." Vaughn turned his focus to the interview room. The dynamic between Meyer and Junior caught him off guard. Junior didn't once make eye contact. His whole body, from his eyes to his feet, turned into stone the way teenagers did when lectured to. Vaughn had expected smugness, maybe even a celebratory hug. But the hostility Junior exuded had Vaughn making a one-eighty with his interview strategy.

When Meyer gave the signal that they were done,

Vaughn brushed by an exiting Meyer and settled into a chair, working hard not to appear as terrified as he felt about Rachel's fate.

"Did your father tell you the deal? Help me find Elias Baltierra and El Diente, along with the woman they kidnapped, and you plead out."

Staring vacantly at the table, Junior's lips twitched into a hateful smile that made Vaughn's stomach drop. He'd staked Rachel's life on Junior's cooperation, but he couldn't shake the feeling that Junior wasn't going to make it easy. It was all he could do not to glance at his watch.

"Let's start with the Parillas Valley shootout. Where did you get the rifles?" he asked, to test Junior's veracity.

"Dealer in Chaves County."

So far, so good. "Was it El Diente?"

Junior's chest trembled with a silent chuckle.

Vaughn's patience was unraveling fast. "You can tell me. Remember? You help us and we'll cut you a plea deal. Tell me where I can find El Diente."

Junior turned his smirking face up to Vaughn. "You're looking at him. I'm El Diente."

Vaughn wanted nothing more than to smack the smile off Junior's face. Instead, he punched the table. "Stop it with the bullshit answers. If the woman El Diente and Baltierra kidnapped isn't found alive, the deal's off. You'll rot in jail for the rest of your life as some prisoner's bitch. Start talking."

Junior sat up a little straighter. "I told you, El Diente's my street name. I set it up for myself four years ago when I started dealing weed. If somebody was kidnapped, must have been Elias who did it."

"How'd you decide on a name like that?"

The smirk returned. He looked Vaughn straight in

the eye. "Because when people cross me, I take a tooth as payment."

The way Junior said it—the boastful gleam in his expression, the conviction in his tone—convinced Vaughn he was telling the truth.

Mother of God. Wallace Meyer Junior was no junkie or small-time dealer or petty criminal. He was a mass murderer. And all those cold cases and unsolved murders bearing El Diente's signature that Vaughn had pulled to reexamine had a new number one suspect. He rolled his gaze up to the one-way mirror, knowing Angela was conducting her own mental search of past cases.

He could interview Junior about past crimes all day long, but it wouldn't get him any closer to saving Rachel. "I'm confused. If you're El Diente, then who killed Shawn Henigin? Elias?"

"How should I know?"

"Because Shawn was missing a tooth when he died. And Elias is the only one of your gang who could've done that. I'm betting he's running the El Diente show, and you're riding his coattails. Know how I'm so sure?" He fell forward over the table and drilled Junior with a glare. Time to go for the jugular. "Because your daddy didn't raise no leader. Even tonight, he was certain you'd do whatever he told you. He pulls the strings and you dance like a puppet."

Junior waved his hands. "That's not true. I'm El Diente."

Vaughn painted a look of skepticism on his face and drummed his fingers on the table. "My first memory of you was the day you were bucked from that horse, when you were five. Do you remember?"

Junior scrubbed a hand over his face, the air of superiority wiped clean away. "Don't talk about that."

"Your horse threw you, and your daddy was all over that. Took you aside, real fatherly-like, and told you it was time for you to learn how to command respect from those you governed. You remember what happened next?"

"Shut up."

"He put a whip in your hand. You cried, and he slapped you, called you a girl. Told you if you wanted to be a man like him, this was what you had to do. I left and called the sheriff, hoping to save that horse's life, but the sheriff told me to shake it off because no one crossed the Meyers, especially a nobody like me. You liked whipping that horse, didn't you? Felt real powerful—just like your daddy."

Junior leapt to his feet. "I hated doing that. Dirt Devil was my best friend."

Vaughn set his palms on the table and pushed to standing. "Don't kid yourself. You're daddy's puppet through and through."

Junior kicked the leg of his chair. "I am not!"

"When I told your old man you could help me find the kidnapped woman, he said, 'My son, the screw up? No way.'"

Something triggered inside Junior. Shaking, tears sprang to his eyes. He looked like a kid again—the scared, angry son of a monster. "He doesn't know anything about me. He only sees what he wants to."

"He doesn't see how smart you are."

Junior whirled around and glared at the mirror. "He never has."

"He thinks Elias is in charge. He figures you're too stupid to run a business. Daddy's puppet—you're probably Elias's puppet too."

"That's bullshit. I'm El Diente. Just me."

"A fucked-up daddy's boy like you? If you're El

Diente"—he added air quotes to the name—"you need to prove it to me. I want to see this jar of teeth. Tell me where to look."

Junior turned away from Vaughn and stalked to the mirror. A growling rumble emanated from his throat, then he spit a gigantic wad of phlegm at it. He stood, watching it drip, sneering at his reflection. "Corner of Troy and Allison. In Devil's Furnace. Used to be a Laundromat. The teeth are in the dryer nearest the back door. Elias will be there too, if he took the girl."

There was nothing left to say. Vaughn shot toward the door. He had a hand on the knob when Junior asked, "I get to plea out, right? That was the deal."

Vaughn looked at him over his shoulder. "Sure. You can plea out on the Parillas Valley charges. That was the deal. Then again, my deputy's going to arrest you right now for Gerald Sorentino's murder, so we don't care so much about the other charges anymore."

He hustled into the hallway, his walkie-talkie at his lips. Before he could signal Stratis on where to meet him at Devil's Furnace, Meyer intercepted him, his expression pained. Vaughn had to give him credit; at least he had enough humanity to look disturbed by the revelation that his progeny was a mass murderer.

"Change of plans, Meyer. I'm not resigning." He kept moving, thumping Meyer's shoulder hard with his own as he ran past. He turned and walked backward, affording Meyer one last flinty look. "Oh, and congratulations on singlehandedly creating a sociopath. Way to go, Dad."

Meyer stared after him with an expression of utter despair. Vaughn turned forward again and sprinted to the exit. *Rachel, I'm coming for you.*

* * *

The crumbling Laundromat in which Rachel sat, her wrists tied behind the chair back, was coated in a thick layer of yellowish dust, most likely from the shredded insulation spilling from the ceiling. The dust swirled through the air like toxic snowflakes as her captor paced. She recognized him as one of the four who'd shot at her—Elias Baltierra.

Hard to say what part of her hurt the worst. Her skull throbbed. Her arm was wet with blood. Somewhere along the line, the scab from her bullet wound had ripped clean off. And her heart ached so bad she couldn't see how it was still beating. Amy might well be dead. Kellan, Sloane, and Ben too. With a house as old as theirs, who knew how fast the frame and roof would burn? At least Jenna and Tommy lived far enough away to escape the blaze. That is, if Baltierra hadn't paid them a visit first.

"Oh, Christ," Baltierra muttered. "What the fuck am I supposed to do with you? Oh, hell."

Rachel twisted her arms and slipped her thumb into the knot of the rope around her wrists. She'd had her wrists bound enough times to know when a knot would hold, and this one was as unsophisticated as they came.

Hope, wild and ridiculous, sizzled through her. If Baltierra left the room, she'd have herself free in seconds. Maybe she could find a phone and call to get help to the farm before it was too late. But scrambled as her brain was after the battering she'd endured, coming up with a plan to get him out of the room wasn't revealing itself easily to her.

"I've got an ATM card in the wallet in my back pocket. If you need cash, I'll tell you the code. There's got to be an ATM around here." Every word clawed at the inside of her parched throat.

"Nice try, bitch. But the money I need is a lot more than I can take out of your bank account."

"Is that what you were looking for at my house? Drug money? Is that the reason for the graffiti too? You wanted us out of the way of your drug operation?"

He whirled around and pounced on her, his hands on the chair back, his body odor flooding around her like a fog, his funky breath on her face. "What do you know about that?"

"I know my dad was cooking meth. Were you one of his customers or his business partner?"

He pulled back, his body tense, hands fisted. Rachel braced herself for a punch, but instead he resumed his agitated pace. "Gerry cashed out of our arrangement before we was ready to let him. Junior got mad. He don't like to be told no. We was still cooking in Gerry's lab until the oil people came around, and then your stupid, fuckin' dude ranch screwed everything up."

She grew cold all over. Her father was murdered. "Junior's your leader?"

"Was. Didn't have no choice at the time. Junior was the only one who knew how to cook meth. He and Gerry had it all worked out. But it's changed now. I'm in charge."

"What about Shawn Henigin? Is he still your partner?"

He offered a wheezy laugh and rubbed the knuckles of his right hand as he prowled. "Shawn's not doing nothing anymore. He was getting twitchy, was going to turn himself in and blab to the police. But from now on, I'm El Diente, and there ain't nothing him or Junior can do about it. I saw to Shawn, and I guess I have you to thank for taking care of Junior."

Rachel had never heard the name El Diente before. Didn't much care who he was, or what Baltierra had done to Shawn Henigin, as long as they weren't a threat to her family. "How about you thank me by letting me go?"

"Naw, naw. That's no good. You could lead the police to me, easy. Or worse, the Burque dealer waiting on the payment we owe. Maybe I could trade you to him instead."

Raw, real fear for herself seized a hold of her gut. She'd rather die than be passed as a consolation prize to another drug dealer—probably a bigger dealer than Baltierra if he was based in Albuquerque, probably even more deadly too.

"That's just passing trouble to the other dealer," she said, trying to sound logical. "People will be looking for me. I'm dating the sheriff. He's not going to take kindly to it if I'm hurt."

"Shut up. I'm trying to think." He pressed his palms to his temples and strode to one of the windows, peeling the yellowed newspaper away to gaze outside.

It was a gamble to admit her connection to Vaughn, but she couldn't see any other choice, even though it disgusted her to feel so helpless that her best chance of survival was to throw a man's name around and wait for him to rescue her. Then again, maybe Vaughn had been right—she was no damsel in distress. She'd learned the hard way that no one was going to save her, or her family, but herself. She didn't need a man.

What she needed was a weapon.

She scanned the room. Every space was jammed with a rusted washer or dryer. To her left was a sagging hanger rod on one of those rolling baskets. It wasn't a sure bet that it would pull off easily, but she didn't like the way Baltierra was nervously petting his gun.

A tug, then another, and the rope fell away. Sucking in a breath, she stood. Baltierra didn't turn around. Three silent steps to the side and she was at the rolling basket. Carefully, carefully, she gripped the rod. It didn't budge at her light touch. She'd have to yank, which would make a sound. But any second, Baltierra would turn around and see her standing there. Instinct told her he wouldn't hesitate to shoot.

She took a moment to send her love out to her sisters and Tommy, along with a prayer that they be taken care of if she died. Then she sent her love out to Vaughn, for all that was worth. Even if she did make it out of this room alive, she knew their relationship was over for good. Wasn't sure she'd ever open her heart to a man again, after all the disappointment and hurt she'd been dealt. Then she tightened her grip on the rod.

"I know what I need to do with you. You and I are going to go for a drive," Baltierra said in a louder voice. He looked over his shoulder at her. "You ever see the view from Hoja Pass?"

Rachel yanked the rod down with her as she ducked behind a washing machine. It gave way from the rolling basket. But she was too late. Baltierra opened fire.

Chapter Nineteen

Rachel made herself as small as she could. The washing machine danced and quaked as it was pummeled with bullet after bullet. Any time now, he was going to change angles to get a clear shot at her. Cornered as she was, there wasn't anything she could do to stop him.

The window was too high off the ground for her to break the glass with the metal rod and escape. She shoved at the next washing machine, hoping to squeeze behind it. But Baltierra's head came into view, then his shoulders. Another two steps around and he'd have a point-blank shot.

He rounded the corner of the washing machine, sneering at her. "Guess we're not going to need to go to Hoja Pass together after all."

He leveled the gun at her face, and she thought, *This is it. Might as well go down fighting*. She rose, the rod feeling heavy in her quivering hands as she wound back. Laughing, he squeezed the trigger and at the same time she swung.

Click.

The gun was empty. Baltierra's mouth fell open, his eyes widened. Rachel threw her weight into the swing, releasing a primal growl as the rod connected with the side of his skull.

He fell backward and hit the ground.

At that moment, the door banged open and four helmeted men dressed in black and holding rifles poured in. SHERIFF was written in white block letters across their flak vests. Hope flared anew inside her. If they'd found her, then they must be aware of the fire too. Could it be that her family was safe and alive?

She recognized Vaughn instantly. He rushed to Baltierra's prone body and kicked the gun away from his hand. A second member of his team joined him, aiming his rifle at Baltierra's body. The other two officers, one of whom Rachel now recognized as a woman, rushed past, searching the room.

Vaughn ripped his helmet off and stepped around Baltierra to Rachel, rifle in one hand and the other arm open wide, as though to embrace her. She stepped back, flattening against the wall, the rod out in front of her, distressed at the idea of touching him. She couldn't allow herself to fall into his arms, because then she'd be back to that needy state, back to wanting Vaughn more than was safe or healthy for her. She refused to walk into that trap again.

He was panting, like he'd been running for miles. She could tell the instant he realized she wasn't going to let him hold her because he lowered his arm to his weapon and stared at her in disbelief. "Are you hurt?" he asked between gasps.

"My family. Are they . . . were they lost in the fire?"

"Oh, baby, no. They're all fine. Everybody's worried about you."

The beginning of a sob of relief tore from her throat. She couldn't stop nodding. He reached for her again, but she held the rod steady. "Stop, please," she croaked. "You were right about me last night. Right about everything. I have to save myself. I can't lean. I won't. Never again."

His hurt was written plainly on his face. "What?"

She gritted her teeth and looked past Vaughn, blinking her tears away. Stratis had rolled a semiconscious Baltierra to his stomach and was cuffing him.

"I need to see my family," she said.

"Okay. The EMTs are going to check you out first, make sure you're not hurt. Then I'll take you home."

She let the rod fall to the ground and smushed her face into her palms. He wasn't getting it. She had no choice but to hurt him again, like she had that night in the hospital parking lot so many months ago.

He stroked her arm. "Rachel, talk to me. Are you hurt?"

"I'm not hurt. I don't need the EMTs to look me over. I have to see my sisters right now!" She swallowed hard and met his gaze. "And I don't want you to be the one to take me."

He flinched, and she felt wretched, bringing that pain down on him. But it was the only way they could move forward. He'd already told her he couldn't be with her, couldn't even spare her one morning when she'd been desperate for his comfort. And that had hurt her something fierce, but it had taken being kidnapped for the lesson to truly sink in. All along, she should've planted her feet and stood tall and proud and alone instead of wasting time wondering if the men in her life were going to come through for her.

"I'll take you," Undersheriff Stratis said. He shot Vaughn a sidelong glance. "It's the way it should be anyway."

She nodded. "Yes. The way it should be. Thank you." She lurched toward the door.

"Don't do this," Vaughn called after her. "Rachel, please . . ."

Then she was outside, stumbling through the early-morning darkness, Vaughn following close, Stratis at her side. The street was crowded with patrol cars, fire trucks, and ambulances. Beyond the vehicles was a gathering crowd of onlookers.

Stratis directed her to his squad car.

"Let me drive you home, Rachel. Don't cut me out like this," Vaughn said, his voice strained, desperate. "Please, give me a chance to talk to you."

With her hand on the passenger door of Stratis's squad car, she met Vaughn's gaze. "We're out of chances. When I'm with you, my life falls apart. Bad things happen. Like when I leaned on my dad. You and me, we're really over this time."

She thought she might throw up, saying it. Mashing her lips together, she lowered into the seat and closed the door. When Stratis pulled away from the curb, she chanced a look out the rear window.

Vaughn was on his knees in the road, his head in his hands.

She closed her eyes and hugged herself tight. Her family was safe, the bad guys would never bother them again, and she was alone. From here on out, her life was family and alfalfa. When she felt lost, she'd have to find her own way out from under the feeling. No more waiting around for men to slay her monsters. No more leaning.

No more Vaughn.

It took all day long for Vaughn and his deputies to sort through the case against Elias Baltierra. Nathan Binderman and Torin Kirby spent the day at the Sorentino farm processing the scene. Damn near killed Vaughn to hold back from asking them how Rachel was faring.

When he'd found her at the Laundromat, all he'd wanted to do was hold her, to feel her breath and heat, and assure himself she was okay. But she'd pushed him away. On some levels, he understood her fear. Twice now, terrible events had happened after she'd been with him. But the hour he'd spent not knowing if she were alive or dead brought Vaughn's priorities into stark focus.

Nothing mattered to him as much as Rachel. But proving to her that his love was worth facing her fears was an overwhelming proposition. He had no idea how to go about it. What he needed was some solid advice.

He pulled his squad car into his parents' driveway around dinnertime, hoping he wasn't interrupting their meal. He didn't smell any tasty dinner aromas wafting over the front yard, so there was a good chance he'd timed it right.

He knocked on the kitchen door as he opened it. His mom looked up from dusting the window blinds. Dad was at the kitchen counter, tossing a nasty-looking salad.

With a wave to his dad, he went straight for Mom and snagged her in a hug. "What are you doing, cleaning the blinds? You already cleaned the house from top to bottom yesterday. You should be relaxing, maybe watching one of those daytime talk shows you tape, a glass of wine in your hand."

She patted his arm. "I know, I know, but the house doesn't feel clean yet. Maybe when I'm done with the living room I'll take a break."

It was no wonder the house felt unclean to her. The police had invaded her private space, pawed through her clothing, touched everything in the house. Every time he thought about it, his anger toward Meyer started winding up again.

"Why don't you let me hire some cleaning people to come in and scour the place?"

She shrugged. "You already offered that, and it's sweet of you, but the thought of more strangers in here doesn't sit well with me."

Vaughn hugged her tighter. "I'd do anything to go back and prevent what happened to you yesterday."

She reached up and cradled his cheeks in her palms. "You already told me that too. What you're forgetting is that my people are from Sicily. So I know how to handle hard times. It's in my blood. I'm no weakling, honey. Don't insult me like that."

"Of course you're not, Ma. I didn't mean to imply—"

His dad clapped a hand on his shoulder. "Vaughn, here's a lesson about dealing with women. Keep your head down and say I'm sorry. Don't try to explain because you'll only dig yourself deeper into a hole."

He arched a brow at his dad, masking his pain with a grin. "You learn that the hard way, old man?"

Dad chuckled. "You don't know the half of it. We're having a salad for dinner, so I'm not even going to bother inviting you to stay."

"Appreciate that. It looks terrible." He pulled a face that made his mom smile and playfully slap his arm.

"How's the investigation going on Monday's shootout at the Sorentino property?" Dad asked.

"That investigation turned into a whole web of charges against Wallace Meyer Jr. and his cohorts. I handed the cases over to Nathan Binderman and Wesley Stratis about an hour ago."

His dad narrowed his eyes. "I thought you wanted to stick it to Wallace Meyer."

Vaughn rubbed his chin. "I've had a change of heart."

He hooked his thumb in the direction of the workshop.
"I reshoed a horse a few days ago, so I'm low on No. 5
nails. Do you have any you could spare?"

His dad nodded, taking the hint. "Let's go see."

In the workshop, Vaughn settled onto a stool and
opened the nail drawer. It was still neatly organized from
the last time he'd visited. Dad set a bucket of nails in
front of him. "My students made these. How about you
see if any of them are salvageable?"

Vaughn grinned and dumped the contents onto the
counter.

Dad motioned to the pile. "All right. Start talking."

Good plan in theory, but Vaughn wasn't sure where to
start. He spread the nails out, considering. Things between him and Rachel had been so screwed up for so
long that untangling the truth didn't seem possible without starting at the beginning.

"I am . . ." He'd never said it aloud before, and it
shocked him, how profound the statement felt, sitting
there on the tip of his tongue. He swallowed and started
again. "I am in love with Rachel Sorentino. I've been
heading in that direction for quite a while, since my first
year as a sheriff deputy, actually. But I didn't think . . .
Our lives weren't compatible. I don't know why I didn't
ask her out anyway, but it never seemed like the right
time. Everything changed after her dad died."

Leaving out the intimate details, he told the story,
even the parts he was ashamed of. As he talked, he felt
the weight of the secrets and lies lifting off his shoulders.
Dad listened attentively, sorting nails right alongside
Vaughn.

The hardest part of the story to tell—the part that
had emotion squeezing his heart and gut, and his throat
tickling with the need for a smoke—was that morning's
events. "She told me we were over for good, but I can't

lose her now. My gut's telling me I should leave her alone until things calm down, but I don't know if that's the right move."

With a huge sigh, Dad dumped the small pile of hopelessly irregular nails into the bucket. "The most important choice I ever made was to fight for your mother's hand."

That pulled Vaughn up short. "I thought you two fell in love right away."

"Falling in love doesn't necessarily make forging a life together easier."

That was the damn truth. He laid two No. 5 nails side by side to compare the length, then tossed the short one in the bucket. His dad's class had done a terrible job on the nails. Must be a beginner's course.

"Your mother's parents hated me. I was Irish, and from the wrong side of town, and your mother was an Italian girl from a wealthy family. Back then, those were impossible odds. I almost didn't fight for her."

"I find that hard to believe."

Dad shrugged. "I'm not a combative person. The Finocchiaros scared me to death. Your mother's father and brothers are not small men, and they've got tempers that rival your nonna's. It would've been easier to let her go, but I knew I'd never be as happy with someone else as I was with her. So I faced my fears, and I thank God every day I had the wherewithal to make that choice."

"But I'm not the one who's afraid. Rachel is."

Dad scooped a handful of warped nails into the bucket. "That's hogwash. Your whole life, you've been afraid of not measuring up. Measuring up to what, I don't know. Some impossible standard you set for yourself. Even as a kid, in school or sports, you were always harder on yourself than anyone else was. Your mom and I didn't need to get on you about homework, and we never had to give you a lecture on trying your best because you were born with this chip on your shoulder. We don't know where it came from any more than we know where Gwen's issues came from. Tell me that doesn't come from a place of fear."

Okay, no. His dad was the wisest person he knew, but he was way off. "That's not true. I ran for sheriff. People who are afraid of not measuring up don't stick their necks out like that."

Dad picked a nail up and tapped the point on the counter. "They do if they've made it their life's mission to prove that rich and well-connected people don't deserve to hold all the power. You ran for sheriff because you wanted to prove you were a better man than Meyer."

Vaughn's hand stilled over the nails. "Okay, I'll give you that. But what does that have to do with my situation with Rachel?"

"That's easy. You're terrified of not measuring up in her eyes, so you're not even trying to prove yourself to her."

Vaughn huffed. "I did try. I've been trying for a year and a half."

"No, you haven't. Not really. According to your story, whenever you had to choose between her or something else, you chose the something else. And when you're around her, all you're doing is haunting the corners of her life without really being a part of it. How's Rachel supposed to think she can count on you when you don't put her first and you're never really there?"

"I am there." He'd rescued her from a kidnapper and cleaned up so many crime scenes at her property he'd lost count.

"When her mom overdosed, did you stick around?"

"No, but she told me to leave her alone."

"Last night, you said she was hurting over something

about her dad and she wanted to stay at your house through morning, but you told her she had to go."

Vaughn rolled his eyes to the ceiling and sucked his cheeks in to chew on them. He sounded like a real bastard when his dad summed it up like that. "Right."

"What're your instincts telling you to do about her now?"

He closed his eyes. Oh, God. Dad was right. Every time the going got tough, he dropped out of her life. "I was trying to do what she wanted. She's a solitary person. Her whole life, she's stood alone—strong and alone."

"Why do you think that is—because she's a natural hermit or because she's never had anyone she could count on? Which scenario do you think is more likely, given what you know about her family?"

Vaughn rubbed a hand over his chin and mouth, processing. Her words that morning returned to him . . .

When I'm with you, my life falls apart. Bad things happen. Like when I leaned on my dad.

She was lumping Vaughn into the same category as her father—the man who'd let her down so miserably and completely that she'd decided she couldn't rely on anyone but herself. Life had taught her through one hard lesson after another that if she let herself lean, she'd fall, and no one would be there to catch her. Sitting on his back porch with her, Vaughn had seconded that theory. Had told her straight up that he admired the way she took care of herself without anybody's help.

And if his dad was right—if Vaughn really was afraid of not measuring up in her eyes—then the two of them had created the perfect storm. They were the living embodiments of each other's worst fears. Holy shit.

No wonder he and Rachel were so fucked up.

"I see the wheels turning in your head, son."

Vaughn shook himself back to the present and looked

his dad in the eye. "You're right. About everything."
With a strangled sound, he pushed up from the stool
to pace the room, scrubbing his hand over his throat,
letting it all sink in. "But it can't be too late for us. I can't
let it be. What can I do to get her over her fears? It seems
impossible."

"Everyone talks about steel like it's unmalleable. But
you and I know that's not true. So let me ask you: how do
you bend steel?"

What the hell did that have to do with anything? "Are
you comparing the woman I love to a piece of metal?"

Dad chuckled. "No. Rachel's not the steel; her fears
are. How do you bend steel?"

"You heat it up."

Dad waved off his answer. "Before that."

Vaughn scratched his eyebrow, then gestured to the
forge. "You have to build a fire and wait for the ideal
temperature before you put the steel in."

"Once the metal's hot enough, what do you do?"

Vaughn shrugged. "You bend it."

"Yes, but you have to use the right tools. Is it easy?"

Grinning with burgeoning awareness, Vaughn shook
his head. "No. It takes a lot of muscle and know-how and
patience."

"Does it happen fast?"

"No." His grin broadened. Dad was a genius. The
Dear Abby of the blacksmith world. "You have to coax it
a little at a time. Sometimes, you have to keep tapping
on it until it decides to give in to the direction you want
it to go."

"That's right. You have to keep tapping on Rachel's
fears until they give way, but you've got to go about it the
proper way, and you've got to be patient. That means
you need to be a consistent presence in her life, prove to
her over time that she can count on you to put her first.

Instead of rushing into something, court her. I know you think I'm a fuddy-duddy, but there is nothing wrong with an old-fashioned courtship."

Vaughn dropped onto the stool. "Okay, I like that plan. But you're forgetting—she doesn't want me around."

Dad folded his arms over his chest. "Your best friend is marrying her sister. I think you can work out some excuse to be near her."

Then he remembered. Their weekly barbecue was taking place the next day at Rachel's house. Chris Binderman had called to let him know it was still on, despite everything the Sorentinos had gone through because Amy and Jenna wanted to be surrounded by their family and friends. Bingo.

Chuckling, dad tapped his temple. "The wheels are turning again."

"Big time." He looked at his watch. Six o'clock. He leapt from the stool. "I've got to run if I'm going to make this work. Catcher Creek rolls its carpets up early on Saturday nights. Will you tell Ma I'll check in with you guys before church tomorrow?"

"You don't have to do that."

"Sure I do." He offered his hand and they shook. "Thanks, Dad."

"Anytime. You know that."

Vaughn looked at the piles of nails sitting in disarray on the counter. Dad waved it off. "Don't worry about this mess. You have a woman to win over. Out of curiosity, what does this plan of yours involve?"

Vaughn grinned and hustled toward the door. "You know the expression, 'easy as pie'? I think that's my ticket back in to Rachel's life."

Chapter Twenty

Sunday afternoon, on the drive to Catcher Creek after accompanying his parents to their church for morning worship, Vaughn's cell phone rang. One look at the caller ID had him jerking the truck to the shoulder of the road and scrambling to answer, his heart beating like mad.

"What's wrong? Did something happen?"

"Everybody's fine," Jenna Sorentino said with a chuckle. "But I can understand the panic in your voice. My family's had more than its fair share of problems lately."

"I'll say." He let out a slow, steady exhale to combat his pounding pulse. "Plus, I don't think you and I have ever had a conversation outside of official police business."

"Aw, that's not true. I say hello to you every Sunday at church."

He supposed she was right, but everybody said hello to him at church because he was the sheriff. His Sunday mornings passed in a blur of handshaking, cheek kissing, and listening to people's grievances against their neighbors. "Good point. What can I do for you?"

"You weren't at church today, and Kellan told us

you're not coming to the barbecue, but you have to come." Before he'd sought his dad's advice, he'd asked Chris to let Kellan know he wasn't attending. "There's only two and a half months until Kellan and Amy's wedding. You might have heard I'm planning it for them. Today we're gathering the whole wedding party at the barbecue to have the cake tasting, everybody except Kellan's brother because he's out of town. You need to be there. You don't want Kellan to think his best friend can't be bothered."

Vaughn felt a grin spreading on his lips. "You play dirty, Jenna. Only a mom could lay a guilt trip on that thick."

"And you don't want to disappoint the bride, either. If ever there was a woman who'd turn into a bridezilla, it'd be Amy."

"You can't talk about her that way. It's unsisterly."

Jenna *tsk*ed into the phone. "It's true, and you know it."

Amy did seem to fall on the high-strung end of the emotional spectrum, but he hoped it'd take more than him missing a meal for her bridezilla switch to flip, otherwise Kellan was in for a long and taxing life. "Okay, but—"

"Think of all the cakes we'll be tasting. If you won't do it for Amy and Kellan, do it for the cake."

"Jenna, time out. I'd already decided to come. But I'm glad you called because I could use your help with a couple things."

"Oh. Sure."

He braced himself for the inevitable questions that would follow, then asked, "Would you make sure Rachel's there this afternoon? If someone doesn't trick her into attending, I'm not sure she'll show up."

Jenna didn't miss a beat. "I'm way ahead of you in that department."

"Did you lay the cake testing/bridezilla guilt trip on her too?"

"You betcha. Are you hitching a ride here with someone so she doesn't see your truck and get spooked?"

Apparently, he and Jenna were on the same page. And the fact that she didn't question why he wanted to see Rachel told him a whole lot about what Jenna knew of their relationship. "I'm on my way to the Bindermans' now." He was all set with a tall tale about the broken suspension on his truck not being able to handle the Sorentinos' dirt road so Lisa didn't get suspicious.

The phone practically vibrated with the sound of Jenna's belly laugh. "I like you, Vaughn. I think the plans you and I are cooking up have a lot in common."

"I think you're right. Which brings me to the second thing I need your help with." He glanced at the stack of pastry boxes on the passenger seat. "About that cake tasting. Is there room in the mix for one more dessert?"

Two hours later, the Bindermans' minivan pulled into the gravel driveway of the Sorentinos' sprawling white and yellow ranch house. The porch was little more than a black gash of burnt wood that streaked up to the wood siding of the second story. He'd learned from the firefighters after the fact that the house hadn't suffered any structural damage from the fire, only water damage to the front room from their efforts to douse the flames.

Vaughn scanned for any sign of Rachel before crawling out of the backseat. The only folks in sight were Douglas Dixon and Kellan's mom, Tina, who were rocking lazily on a swing in the yard, cans of cola in their hands and looking awfully cozy.

"Hi, you two. Nice day to sit outside." He opened the back of the minivan and filled his arms with pastry boxes.

"Sure is," Douglas said. "Good to see you under happy circumstances, Sheriff."

A large brown cow wearing ribbons and flowers and a huge bandana around its neck chose that moment to trot around from behind the stable. The Bindermans' six-year-old daughter, Daisy, squealed and intercepted it. The bizarreness of the cow's get-up had him shaking his head as much as its behavior.

"What's up with the cow in the costume? It has Kellan's brand on it."

Douglas and Tina burst out laughing. Chris was busy unhooking their baby, Rowen, from his car seat, but Lisa went around the back of the minivan to unload all her mommy bags filled with diapers and God-knows-what. "That's Tulip," she said.

"She's Amy's pet," Tina added.

Okay. "To each his own, I guess."

"It started last December, when Tulip wandered over from Kellan's ranch," Douglas said. "Rachel wanted to slaughter it for steaks, but Amy welcomed her with open arms like it was a member of the family. She took to dressing it up, just to drive Rachel bonkers."

Vaughn peered at Douglas from around the stack of pastry boxes in his arms. "Did it work?"

"Like a cactus needle in a cat's behind."

He grinned, imagining Rachel's righteous indignation.

"I think she's kinda cute," Lisa said.

Chris met them, his stride a funky waddle due to the baby pouch on his chest. Rowen stretched his arms out and babbled at the cow. Chris scratched Rowen's floppy blond hair, then slung an arm around his wife. "I don't know, honey. I'm with Rachel. I think it looks like dinner."

Vaughn had met Chris and Lisa through Kellan many years ago. They were, hands down, the kindest, most even-keeled people Vaughn knew, if not the squarest. They'd settled into the roles of mom and dad so naturally and contentedly, it was like they'd been born parents-in-waiting—early to bed, no vices, and vocabularies free of curse words for as long as anyone remembered.

Early on, Vaughn had embraced a plan to live out his life as the fun uncle to his sister's kids, mostly because the idea of having his own scared the snot out of him. But if he could make things right with Rachel, and she wanted to start a family, he'd agree in a heartbeat, even if he didn't have it in him to drive a minivan or wear a baby pouch. Then again, he was going to do something today he never thought he would, so who's to say what the future held?

Jenna skipped out the kitchen door and down the steps. "Oh, good. You're here. Inside, quick. Plan's right on schedule."

She took the top two pies and raced toward the house.

Lisa fell in line with Vaughn, tugging Daisy with her. "What plan?"

Vaughn mustered a casual shrug. "Cake tasting, I think."

"I'm still confused. How did you get roped into bringing pies to a cake tasting?" she asked.

"Happy to help." He evaded her attempt to look him in the eye, knowing all too well about women's uncanny ability to read people's faces, especially moms. At the base of the stairs, he stepped aside and swept his arm out, motioning for her, Daisy, and Chris to precede him up inside.

Jenna stood in one corner of the sprawling kitchen, arranging cakes and pies on plates and platters, while Amy, Kellan, Ben, and another man Vaughn vaguely recognized as a local hovered around the television in the kitchen, debating an umpire's call. They turned from the TV to exchange hugs and handshakes with Lisa, Chris, and the kids, while Vaughn skirted the crowd to deliver the rest of the pies to Jenna.

"Is she here yet?" he whispered.

"No. She's been gone since before dawn, out on her horse, but I threatened to give her hell if she didn't show up for the cake tasting, so we'll see. I'll give her a few more minutes, then text her that we have an emergency. That ought to bring her home fast."

Vaughn nodded. Someone slapped him on the back and he turned to see Kellan.

His expression was jumpy, anxious even. "Hey. I didn't expect to see you today."

"Change of plans. I got a ride with Chris and Lisa." He cocked his head to the side. He was usually good about reading Kellan's moods, but this one had him stumped. Was he worried about Rachel's reaction to his surprise appearance? "Everything okay?"

"Sure, yeah. Beer's in a cooler in the dining room. I was about to get myself another one, so I'll show you where they are."

He had the odd feeling Kellan was hustling him out of the kitchen on purpose, and eyed the semifamiliar man before pushing through the swinging door to the dining room, wondering why Kellan hadn't introduced them. As opposed to Ben's lanky, youthful frame, the other man was pushing forty and wearing a heavy flannel plaid shirt and a mustache. He stared his way until the door swung closed.

The dining room was even larger than the kitchen and set up as a rustic country restaurant, with two long, weathered wood communal tables and bench seating. In one corner of the room, Matt Roenick sat playing Candyland with Jenna's boy, Tommy. Daisy hovered over them, her six-year-old motor mouth rattling on about her favorite candies.

"Hey, Vaughn," Matt said. Vaughn crossed the room and shook his hand. They'd known each other as acquaintances through Kellan for a lot of years, and it threw Vaughn off to see him sitting with kids playing a kid game.

Ten years ago, Sunday barbecues were all about football and steaks and a bunch of guys drinking beer. But now, Sundays were more about togetherness and family more than anything else. He liked the change. It felt right and good, like they were finally growing up and getting a clue as to what really mattered in life.

"What changed your mind about today?" Kellan asked under his breath when Vaughn returned to the beer cooler along the wall.

"I was promised cake." He selected an amber lager from a brewery near Santa Fe and sloughed the ice from the bottle. Kellan handed him an opener. "Would Amy really have turned into a bridezilla if I hadn't shown up today?"

With a snort, Kellan snagged a beer. "No. Who fed you that line? Wait—don't tell me. Only Jenna could make that sound believable."

"That she did." Vaughn passed him the opener. "Who was the guy in the kitchen?"

Kellan popped his beer open and took a swig. "That's Ben Torrey. He's a great guy. I think you've met him before. Used to work for me at Slipping Rock. Rachel getting shot and being out of commission was a wake-up call for Amy and Jenna. They got it straight in their heads how much Rachel does around here, so they surprised her by hiring a foreman. I hated to lose him, but his heart wasn't in cattle ranching. He's a farmer through and through, just like Rachel. He's going to help her reestablish the alfalfa crop."

Vaughn took a hit of beer, annoyed that he still felt a stab of envy every time Rachel's name was mentioned in conjunction with another man's. Since when was he the irrationally possessive type? To prove he could overcome his burgeoning caveman mentality, he asked, "He and Rachel getting along good?"

"Real well. He's a great fit here. He's moving into the main house this month until we can set him up in his own place on the property."

Well, goddamn. Now the guy was going to be living with her. He took another hit of beer, scowling. "Who's the other guy in the kitchen? I didn't recognize him. Does he work here now too?"

Kellan rubbed a hand on his neck, looking uncomfortable. "That's Howard Keibler. He works on Douglas's son's farm."

"What's he doing here?" Vaughn asked.

"Haven't you heard?" Lisa asked, sidling in to nab her own beer. "Amy's on a matchmaking warpath. It's her new mission in life to have everyone romantically attached in time for the wedding."

Yikes. "Poor Jenna."

Lisa leaned in toward Vaughn. "Howard's not here for Jenna. Amy thinks he'd be a great match for Rachel. And I agree."

Vaughn nearly choked. Why hadn't Kellan warned him that Amy was setting Rachel up with some dweeb local farmer right under his nose? He swallowed hard and looked to his friend, who was suddenly mesmerized by one of the photographs on the wall. One of Rachel's, no doubt. The fake-innocent look on his face made Vaughn want to punch him in the nose.

He chugged half his beer down before he was calm enough to speak. Then he schooled his features as best he could. "Rachel okay with that?" he asked Lisa stupidly, hoping no one caught the shrill edge in his voice.

Kellan finally dared to look at him. "Not sure. I didn't know about it until his truck pulled into the yard a half hour ago. But I bet you twenty bucks Rachel doesn't even show up today."

Was that his way of appeasing Vaughn? Nice try. "I'm not going to bet you that."

"I will," Jenna said, strong arming her way into the conversation. She stuck her hand out at Kellan. "Twenty bucks says Rachel's here by the time supper hits the table."

After a moment's hesitation, Kellan shook her hand. "You're on."

Vaughn had total faith that Jenna would make sure Rachel appeared, even though he had trouble believing they were still working together on the same plan, given that she hadn't seen fit to give him a heads-up about this Keibler guy. What the hell kind of name was Howard Keibler anyway?

"Get me in on this," Lisa said. "I'll double the bet that she not only shows up, but she agrees to a date with Howard before the night's through. Rachel is way over-due for some fun in her life."

"What do you think, Vaughn?" Jenna asked. "Do you think Howard and Rachel would make a great match?" She had a goading look in her eyes, and he had half a mind to believe she was daring him into challenging Keibler to a duel over Rachel.

And maybe he would, if Keibler lay a finger on her. His S&W was fully loaded in his shoulder holster. He rolled his shoulder blade and comforted himself with the feel of the heavy steel. "I'm not even going to touch that topic," he muttered, grabbing a second beer.

Too horrified to think straight, and still contemplating that duel, he plowed through the kitchen door to get a better look at the man all the women in the house seemed to think was a perfect match for the woman he loved.

For possibly the first time in her life, Rachel had no appetite for barbecued ribs, even though the smell drifting over the stable yard was divine. She stood in the stable, giving Growly Bear a final rubdown, grimacing in memory of the trucks and cars parked in their driveway that indicated her house was full to the brim with people. After dropping the grooming supplies in the bucket, she led Growly to his stall, knowing there was nothing she could do to weasel out of attending the party.

Amy, in her hapless quest to fix Rachel up on a date, had burst into her room the night before with new outfits from the Fashion Diva Outpost, Nancy Tobarro's shop. Two wispy, flowery dresses and a belted red sweater with leggings ensemble she swore looked great with boots. Rachel had tried explaining that she didn't want any man who wouldn't accept her as she was, but what a fiasco that turned into because Amy's response had been, "So, then you *do* want a man. I knew it!"

Amy's eureka moment had led to one of their typical shouting matches, which ended with Rachel vowing to stay far away from the house until the barbecue was over and Amy shrieking about Rachel being unreasonable, like Amy hadn't already won the lifetime achievement award for that particular personality trait.

As she'd expected, the next morning while Rachel was on the trail, Jenna called her to run damage control. Vaughn wasn't coming to the barbecue, she'd assured her, and then she'd threatened bodily harm if Rachel missed the cake tasting. So Rachel thought, what the heck. It'd be nice to enjoy a hot midday meal.

Besides, she was grateful to Jenna for taking over as Amy's wedding planner. All Rachel had to do for the various wedding-related activities was show up, so it would behoove her to do so, even if it meant making small talk with Amy's and Kellan's friends, and fielding any potential suitors Amy had rounded up.

She freshened up at the wash bin, then gave Growly one last look. "Well, Growly. Wish me luck."

She popped an antacid and plastered a brittle smile on her face, then walked to the house.

Amy was the only person in the kitchen. She smiled from where she was mixing ingredients in a huge green bowl. "Hi there. You're right on time to eat. Food's laid out buffet-style in the dining room, except for my signature pasta salad which I'm bringing out right now."

She hefted the bowl into her arms. It was overloaded with slimy-looking pasta.

"Yum," Rachel faked.

She held the dining room door open for Amy and followed her in.

Both tables were full of people, and the second Rachel walked in, all eyes snapped to her. Ducking her head to shield herself from their stares, she fought the urge to run back the way she'd come.

"Woo-hoo," Lisa Binderman called from somewhere to her right. "Twenty bucks to Jenna, Kellan. Pay up."

Rachel looked up, searching for Kellan. Her heart stopped beating.

Vaughn.

Dressed in a short-sleeve, button-down red shirt that brought out the darkness of his hair, he sat with his back to the wall in the left corner table, along with Kellan and Jenna. He kept his eyes on the television across the room, watching the baseball game and chowing down on ribs. Like he hadn't noticed her. Or like Lisa hadn't just hollered at the top of her lungs.

The only indication that he hadn't gone into a trance-like state of sports-viewing was when Kellan slid a twenty across the table to Jenna and he shifted his focus away from the TV to follow the movement of the money with his eyes.

Amy reappeared at her side. "Rachel, I'm sure you remember Howard Keibler. I invited him to join us for supper."

Huh? She tore her gaze from Vaughn and scanned the room. Sure enough, Howard Keibler sat near the window, grinning at her like a salesman. Did Amy honestly think she'd be interested in a guy like Howard Keibler? Not only no, but hell, no.

Then again, she couldn't fault Amy for not knowing that Howard had a penchant for getting overly friendly with his hands when he'd had a bit too much to drink, and had copped a feel on Rachel more times than she cared to recall after cornering her at livestock auctions and the county fair. He'd also asked her out at least a half dozen times already, but seemed to be having a problem understanding the word *no*.

Amy shoved a plateful of food into her hands. Good thing she did, because Rachel had been contemplating a plan to strangle her. Jenna too. What a little liar, telling her Vaughn wasn't attending. And why was he here in the first place? She'd told him to stay away from her. Since when had he stopped respecting her wishes?

Feeling the stares of the people in the room still on her, she looked at the plate of food and deliberated whether to ask to speak to her sisters in private to get her questions answered or make a break for it.

Make a break for it. Definitely.

She pivoted and had a hand on the door when Amy took hold of her shoulders. "Oh, no, you don't. I saved you a seat next to Howard."

Sure enough, a single, empty seat waited for her between Howard and Mr. Dixon. She barely caught the groan before it escaped her throat as she contemplated the many unsavory things Howard might do with his hands under the table if she sat next to him.

Harsh whispers and a tussle of movement near Jenna and Vaughn caught her eye. Kellan stood, clearing his throat. "Uh, actually, Amy, I was hoping Rachel could sit over here. I have some farm business I've been meaning to discuss with her and Ben." He gestured to the seat directly across from Vaughn.

Amy clucked in protest and shot Kellan a warning glare, but released her.

Not too late to run, she reasoned. Then Jenna was behind her. She took a firm grip on Rachel's elbow and whispered close to her ear. "It's time for you to cowboy up and put on your big-girl panties."

Rachel scoffed and whispered, "I'm pretty sure cowboys don't wear big-girl panties."

"Oh, hush. You know what I mean." And she strong-armed Rachel all the way to the table and sat her down, like she was no bigger than Tommy. "Besides, don't judge. Maybe some cowboys do."

"Do what?" Kellan asked.

Rachel looked across the table at him, at a total loss for words.

"Hi," Vaughn said.

She looked his way. He wore a kind, if cautious smile, and the only thought in her brain was, had she remembered to reapply deodorant when she freshened up in the stable? As her panic mounted, she remembered that she had, but she wished she'd had the chance to shower or change clothes. "Hi," she managed to croak out.

"So, Kellan," Vaughn said. "What's the plan for you and Amy moving in together?"

Kellan finished cleaning the rib he was working on. "Next week, she's moving into my place. Our place, that is."

"Three months before your wedding? That's awfully scandalous," Vaughn said. His arm darted out and he pulled Rachel's plate in his direction.

Too stunned to protest, she watched it go, holding her fork.

"You know me and Amy, we love to whip up a good scandal," Kellan said, his eyes on Rachel's plate too.

Vaughn scraped her pasta onto his plate. "Good timing, with the inn closed for the summer and the restaurant only open on weekends." He slid Rachel's plate back in her direction.

She couldn't decide if she was spellbound that he'd saved her from the pasta or horrified that he'd done something as intimate as take food off her plate in front of everybody they knew.

"That was the idea," Kellan said.

He looked like he maybe wanted to ask about the pasta, but Rachel was saved from explaining by Ben Torrey, who was sitting to her left. "Have you chosen a best man, yet?"

Kellan nodded. "Vaughn and Chris and I already talked about it. They know I asked my brother, Jake, to be my best man."

Vaughn rolled his beer along the table. "But I get to plan your bachelor party, right?"

"Not sure. Things are strained enough between me and Jake. I'm not going to step in it by making assumptions."

Amy, who'd been running around filling people's plates with seconds, plopped onto the bench next to Kellan. "On the other hand, if you had multiple best men, then it won't look as lopsided since I have both my sisters as maids of honor."

Rachel waved her hands. "You know I'd be just as happy watching from the audience, right?"

"Don't be ridiculous," Amy said.

"When am I ever ridiculous? I mean, honestly."

Amy released a deep, beleaguered sigh. "Well, Rach, you and I have another month or so to argue about it before you give in to my wishes. I want you and Jenna right up next to me when I say I do."

"What about me?" Kellan asked, nudging her with his elbow. "Sounds like it's going to be crowded up there. Will there be room enough for me to stand next to you too?"

Grinning like the fool in love that she was, Amy dobbed a smear of barbecue sauce on his nose.

"When I get married," Jenna said, "I want a big church wedding and a white dress, the whole bit. My bridesmaids in sky blue, white roses all over the church and in my bouquet. I can hardly wait."

Amy gave her a teasing smile. "All you need is the groom." Her eyes flickered to Matt, who was deep in conversation with Tommy and Daisy across the room.

Jenna's gaze traveled to him too. "That's proving to be

the tricky part. What about you, Rachel? What kind of wedding would you want?"

Rachel drilled her with her best warning look. Jenna's eyes got as huge as lemons.

Amy tapped a finger on her chin. "You'd elope, right? That's my guess. You hate being the center of attention. Heck, you don't want to be near the altar for my wedding."

Rachel pushed a rib bone around on the plate. "You both know good and well I've never once lazed around, daydreaming about my wedding day."

Jenna tapped her fingers on the table. "Oh, come on. We're just having fun. What kind of wedding would you have if you found that special someone? Would you elope, like Amy thinks?"

Rachel took a slow drink of iced tea and cleared her throat. *Do not look at Vaughn. Answer the question so they'll stop harassing you, and don't look at Vaughn.* Staring at her plate, she said, "Amy's wrong. I wouldn't elope. I'd get married right in the living room. By the fireplace. That's where our parents got married. I'd want to carry on the tradition. Only close family and friends, not a big fuss. I might not even wear white, but just a simple country dress."

Everyone at the table had gone quiet, listening. She looked at Amy, who was gazing at her with a dreamy smile. "Sounds wonderful. I hope you get to do that someday."

Don't look at him.

But she glanced in his direction anyway. He was watching her, his lips a flat line, his shoulders so tense they nearly touched his earlobes. He gave her a barely perceptible nod. Like he approved of her plan.

She grabbed her iced tea but couldn't lift it for the trembling in her hand. She held on tight to the cold glass, so lightheaded that she felt like her spirit was floating away from her body.

Maybe it did because the next thing she knew, Jenna sprang from the bench with such force the table rattled. "Okay, everyone. Stay in your seats. It's time for cake tasting. Lisa, come on and give me a hand, would you?"

With that, the two women dashed to the kitchen, returning with large platters before the door stopped swinging.

Jenna dealt the paper plates of desserts out as fast as a poker dealer might. "There are two bakers in Quay County who handle weddings. That's not a lot. We need to get one locked down for the wedding, so I have three cakes from each for you to taste and one bonus dessert option. First wave of samples is from Heavenly Confections. You've got a lemon drop layer cake, strawberry with an amaretto cream filling, and dark chocolate with a milk chocolate mousse ribbon. Keep track of what you like. I'll come around and ask you each about it in a minute."

Jenna was all business, going around to each table with her clipboard. All the cakes were pretty good. Rachel preferred the lemon best, but Amy was all about the chocolate. Kellan didn't seem to care, and neither did the rest of the men, all of whom scraped their plates clean.

Lisa and Jenna scurried to the kitchen for round two.

"Okay," Jenna said, coming through the door with a fresh tray. "This round is from Marla Ray of the Mesa Verde Inn, who runs a pastry business on the side. You've got your mocha almond cake, chocolate cherry, and vanilla bean with a custard ribbon. And, as a bonus, we're also tasting triple berry cream pie."

Rachel stared hungrily at the pie slice that was set in front of her. It looked as delectable as always, with whole, plump raspberries, strawberries, and blueberries shimmering in a glossy sauce, piled high above a cream cheese filling and topped with huge dollops of fresh whipped cream. Forget a wedding cake. If Rachel ever got married, she wanted triple berry cream pie at the reception. Whoever decided to offer it as an option at Amy's wedding was a genius.

"This from Catcher Creek Café?" Chris asked.

Jenna smiled serenely at Chris. "Yes. It's a nice addition to the options, don't you think?"

"I like the idea, but you never mentioned we were considering pie," Amy said.

Jenna's smile grew even wider. "It was Vaughn's suggestion. He brought the pies."

Rachel's throat threatened to close. She looked Vaughn's way, her eyes wide and questioning, but he wasn't paying her the least bit of mind. He sliced into his piece of pie with the side of his fork and ate a heaping bite.

Kellan, Chris, Amy, and almost everybody else in the room watched with openmouthed shock.

"Uh, Vaughn. That's a fruit pie," Kellan stammered.

"I know. It's fantastic," he said with his mouth full. He really did seem to be enjoying it.

"But you don't eat fruit," Amy said.

Vaughn nodded and finished chewing. "I realized this week that I was missing out on some of the best things in life because I was too afraid to try." He shoveled a second huge forkful into his mouth.

"You hate produce," Lisa said. "You've always hated produce."

He shrugged. "People can change. I've changed. Aspects of my life I thought were important, it turned out they were holding me back and blinding me to what I was missing. This pie is really damn good. You were right, Rachel."

She stared, dumbfounded.

"But . . ." Kellan said.

Vaughn speared his fork at him. "No, I'm serious about this, K. I dedicated my life to challenging Wallace Meyer's power, and what did it get me? I mean, sure, I've got a great job that I love, and without the motivation of sticking it to Meyer, I may never have gone into law enforcement. But, other than that, my obsession with Meyer has done nothing but harm to me and the people in my life. My parents were arrested, for Pete's sake.

"The real tragedy, and the part I'm going to have to work the hardest to make right, is that time and again, I allowed the woman I love to take a backseat to my hatred of Meyer and my fear of taking chances, when she should've been the first priority in my life all along. That will never happen again, and that's a promise you can take to the bank."

Woman he loved? What, in God's name, was he trying to accomplish today? He was either talking about her or some other woman, and she really didn't take him as the kind of man to go flaunting his feelings for another woman around her.

With a flourish, he scraped the rest of the pie from his plate and popped it into his mouth.

"Woman you love?" Chris asked, looking more baffled by the second.

Chin in hand, Amy leaned in. "This sounds intriguing. Who is she?"

Rachel swallowed.

A Cheshire cat smile spread over his face. "Jenna, may I have another slice of pie please?"

"Sure thing." Jenna hustled through the swinging door to the kitchen.

Vaughn dabbed a napkin to his lips. "Hey, Rachel?"

Her heart plummeted to her knees. "How's Growly Bear's shoe that I put back on? Holding up okay?"

What? She nodded mechanically.

"Did Chuck come around to reset the shoes for trail riding?" he asked, seemingly oblivious to her discomfort.

She cleared her throat. "Yes."

"Good."

Jenna arrived with the pie tin and refilled his plate. "Thanks."

Jenna grinned at Vaughn, a sly, knowing look. Whatever was going on with Vaughn, Jenna was in on it. That's why she'd lied about him not being there. They'd worked together to trap her. They'd set her up for this, whatever it was.

"Excuse me, Ben. Would you mind switching seats with me?" It was Howard Keibler, plate in hand, standing behind Rachel. "I was hoping Rachel and I could get to know each other better today."

"I don't think so," Vaughn said. He motioned with his fork to Ben, who was halfway to standing. "You stay where you're at. We haven't finished our conversation yet."

"We haven't?" Ben asked, lowering to the bench again, looking confused.

Howard pulled his face in surprise. "Help a guy out here, man. I'm trying to . . . you know . . ." He gestured to Rachel, wide-eyed like he was trying to pass a secret man-to-man message to Vaughn.

Subtle. Real subtle.

Vaughn cracked his knuckles. "What exactly did you come here to do, Keibler?"

Oh, my God. Didn't anyone else hear the menace in Vaughn's voice? Rachel glanced around the room. No one except Kellan and Jenna looked as worried as she was that Vaughn was going to drag Howard Keibler out by the shirt collar and beat the shit out of him.

Howard rolled his eyes. "Well, now you've forced my hand. Thanks a lot." Then he pinned Rachel with an oily gaze. "Rachel . . ."

Time to run damage control. She rose to block Howard from Vaughn's view, but she sensed that, behind her, he stood too. "Howard, I think there's been some kind of mix-up. How about you and I go chat outside?"

"No, I think right here would be fine."

All right. "I'm so sorry your time was wasted here today, Howard, but I'm not—"

"Come on now. Hear me out before you turn me down."

Vaughn folded his arms over his chest. "Actually, I think you'd better listen to what the lady's trying to tell you."

"No offense, Sheriff, but this doesn't concern you."

Rachel's stomach bottomed out. Wrong thing to say, Howard. Over his shoulder, she met Jenna's panicked gaze. "Help me," she whispered maniacally.

Jenna, a whole pie in her hands, shook her head, seemingly paralyzed by the unexpected turn of events.

Amy rushed around the table and draped her arm across Howard's shoulders, a proud mama expression on her face. "Give this a chance, Rach. Please? Howard has been growing alfalfa on Dixon Farm for ten years. The two of you would make a wonderful match. What's the harm in one date?"

Rachel opened her mouth to respond, but Howard beat her to it.

"Amy's right, Rachel. I've always told you we'd be great together. You really ought to give me a chance." And true to form, he walked two fingers up her arm.

She squirmed away.

"Howard?" Vaughn said, coming around the table, his hands in tight fists. "It's time for you to leave."

Rachel glared at Vaughn, trying to make her eyes say *Stand down, I've got this* but Vaughn's narrowed stare never wavered from Howard.

"I'm afraid Vaughn's right," she said. "You're a very nice man"—skeevy as all get-out, but relatively harmless—"nonetheless, my answer's still no." She grabbed the pie from Jenna and shoved it into Howard's hands. "Here, take a pie for your trouble."

Without missing a beat, he set the pie on the table and groped for her hand.

Rachel jerked it out of range and tried to scoot backward, but Howard wasn't so easily deterred. Lunging, he grabbed a firm hold of her hips.

Vaughn sprang into action. In a clatter of movement and noise, he wrenched Howard away from her, torquing his arm into a deadlock as he pressed Howard's face onto the table. "You touch her again and I'm going to kick your ass all the way to Texas."

The storm in Vaughn's eyes made Rachel's heart stop.

The collective gasps from the room seemed to suck all the air from the space. Rachel felt every bewildered stare like a heavy weight, pressing on her. Like that day in John Justin's while the world fell apart around her, she wanted to run as fast and as far as her legs would take her. She stared at the kitchen door, willing her legs to move.

Still holding Howard's face to the table, Vaughn met Rachel's eyes from over Howard's bent back. The murderous rage in his expression was fading, replaced by regret. He looked at Howard, blinking as though suddenly realizing what he'd done, and let go of him. "Rachel, I see you eying the exit, but please don't leave."

She cast him an incredulous look. He could ask that of her all he wanted, but the minute she figured out how to unfreeze herself, she was out of there.

Howard made a big show of brushing himself off and muttering about police being above the law.

Ignoring the rant, Vaughn looked around until his eyes landed on Kellan. "K, would you mind helping Howard to his car?"

His spine stiff with indignity, Howard looked down his nose at Rachel. "No need. I think I'm done here." Then he seized up the pie and marched in the direction of the kitchen. Kellan held the door and followed him out.

With Howard gone, Rachel stood face-to-face with Vaughn. He kept his eyes on her as he slid his fingers from her upper arm to her hand. She thought about pulling away, so foreign was the idea of him touching her in front of others, but she could barely breathe, much less move. He covered her hand with his and squeezed. "I'm sorry I lost my head. I really, really don't like that guy."

"Me, neither," she managed to push out of her lungs.

"I'm ready for one of you to tell me what's going on," Amy said. Rachel turned her way. She was motioning to Rachel and Vaughn's joined hands.

Lisa stood next to Amy. "That makes two of us."

For the millionth time that afternoon, Rachel was at a loss for words.

Vaughn's grip on her hand tightened. He turned his face to Amy and Lisa. "I'll explain."

A chill wracked Rachel's body. She squeezed her free hand around her middle. "Don't. Please."

He returned his gaze to her and cupped her cheek, stroking her skin with his thumb. "This is the only way I can see to wipe the slate clean and start over. The secrecy wasn't working. We've both told too many lies to ourselves and to our friends and family to move forward. It's time we stop beatin' the devil around the bush and tell the truth."

Determination was set like stone on his face. He was going to announce their secrets to everyone and there was nothing she could do to stop him. Her eyes slid to the door again. She watched Kellan walk across the room to stand by Amy, his arm around her waist.

Vaughn adjusted his hand on Rachel's chin and urged her focus back to him. He spoke while looking into her eyes. "Amy, the truth is, a year and a half ago, when Rachel was fresh with grief over losing your dad, I took advantage of her. It was the second worst mistake I've ever made." He lifted her hand and pressed it to his heart. "I am so sorry I took advantage of you when you were vulnerable like that."

The only thing worse than him spilling the intimate details of their time together was the way he was giving everyone a gross misrepresentation of what happened. The least he could do was paint an accurate picture. "You didn't take advantage of me. That makes it sound like I didn't meet you halfway."

His features relaxed a shade, but beneath her palm, his heart was racing. "It was still my fault. I set the tone of secrecy and lies. All I had to do was wait until the investigation concluded, but I didn't. And I know now that I sabotaged what we had on purpose because I was scared of the connection we had. I was scared of not measuring up to be the man you deserved. You were absolutely right to break things off with me after your mom overdosed, and I'm grateful you had the strength of will to do the right thing for both of us. But, like I said, that was my second worst mistake. I made my biggest mistake after the investigation closed the next week. I should've told you what you meant to me. I should have fought for you—for us—but I didn't."

"What's he talking about, Rach?" Amy asked. "You two were seeing each other in secret after Dad died?"

Rachel looked at Amy. "Yes."

"Tell them where you were the night your mom overdosed," Vaughn said. "Get it out in the open, Rachel. No more lies."

Even though it was the hardest thing in the world, she knew he was right. Coming clean about their relationship had already made her feel lighter. Scared, but healed. "The night Mom overdosed, I wasn't home, like I led you to believe. I was at Vaughn's house. I left her unsupervised, and for the longest time, I blamed myself for what she did.

"But this week, I realized that even if I'd been here, I still wouldn't have been able to stop her. None of us could've prevented what she had her mind set on doing. I'm finally finding my peace with it, but there's no excuse for the lies I told you. I already apologized to Jenna, and I planned to sit down with you tonight and talk it out. I'm so sorry I wasn't honest with you, Amy."

Amy blinked and looked at the ground. Kellan kissed the top of her head, and Jenna slid her arm around Amy's waist.

"It's okay. I'm not mad, just sad that you didn't think you could talk to us," Amy said. "You're right, you know. There wasn't anything any of us could do—about Mom's or Dad's choices. I wish you would've let us know what you were going through so we could've been there for you."

Rachel nodded. "I was ashamed that I'd been . . . weak, with Vaughn. All I ever wanted to do was protect you two from the world. I worked so hard at it, and then I went and caused this terrible thing to happen."

"You have nothing to be ashamed of. You've done a great job taking care of us," Jenna said. "The best. But I think Amy will agree with me that it's time for you to take care of yourself."

Amy nodded. "Jenna's right. We want you to be happy. That's why we hired Ben. And why I was trying to set you up on a date."

Jenna pinched the bridge of her nose. "Good Lord, what a disaster. That didn't turn out like I expected at all."

Vaughn scowled at Jenna. "Don't get me started." He released Rachel's hand and took her by the shoulders, turning her to face him. A hundred different emotions flashed over his face—repentance, hope—love. "All this time, you were right not to trust yourself to lean on me. I never came through for you when the going got tough. I never made you my first priority.

"But all I want, more than anything, is to have the chance to prove to you I've changed. That I can be a better man—for you. I'm going to do everything in my power, for as long as it takes, to prove that I love you and you have nothing to fear. Then, when you're ready, I'm going to court you properly. Like I should have done in the first place. Will you give me that chance? Can you forgive me?"

Rachel's head was spinning so fast that she pressed her palms to her temples to slow it down. She had to think clearly, had to find the right words, but he was waiting and everyone was listening, and all she could think to say was, "You ate berry pie for me."

He let out a nervous, dry laugh and pulled her into an embrace, resting his forehead against hers. "I'd eat broccoli for you, if that's what it took to prove I've changed."

She stroked his cheek. "I would never make you do that."

Heads touching, they breathed into each other, so close and intimate that the room beyond them disappeared. She held his cheeks in her hands as he worked his fingers through the hairs at the nape of her neck.

"Yesterday, I recused myself from all the different cases involving you. And Wallace Meyer and I have reached a new understanding, so there's no chance he'll give us trouble about the evidence I collected or bring up a civil suit against you for shooting Junior. You don't have anything to concern yourself with from here on out except your happiness, and that's all I'm going to focus on too. Tell me what you want—anything—and I'll make it happen for you."

Since Vaughn walked up her porch steps sixteen months earlier, her dreams for herself had shifted, but some fundamental parts would never change. "I want to plant alfalfa."

"I know you do. You're on your way with that, you and Ben. What else?"

Her eyes grew hazy with tears, but she didn't want to let go of him long enough to wipe them away. "I want my family to be safe and happy."

He rolled his forehead against hers, nodding. "We've got that covered. Keep going."

"I want to photograph the ocean. I've never seen the ocean before."

"I can make that happen, no problem. Whenever you're ready."

Then it hit her—none of the things she wanted mattered without Vaughn. What was the point of planting a field full of grass if she couldn't stand in the middle of it with him and share that fresh alfalfa smell? What was the point of seeing the ocean if he wasn't by her side to experience it with her? Her sisters were safe and happy and moving on with their own families. For the first time ever, it was Rachel's turn to grab hold of what she wanted.

"I want . . ." Her throat constricted. She swallowed and inhaled deeply.

"Whatever it is, I'll find a way to give it to you."

She realized now that the world wouldn't fall apart, and the universe wouldn't punish her for trying to find happiness. She'd had the rug yanked out from under her enough times by her dad to understand it was going to take some practice to relearn how to lean on someone else without bracing for a fall. But she didn't want to be the person who was too afraid to try. She wanted to be strong enough to trust, strong enough to face her fears and love out loud.

She felt it building up inside her like nothing she'd ever experienced, and it had to come out, all of it, right there in front of everybody they knew, like the words had a life of their own and the sheer power of them pried open the grip of fear around her heart and crumbled it into dust. "I don't want to see the ocean without you. And I don't care about alfalfa unless you're there to smell it with me. I want to whistle with you and ride horses with you—everything. I can't stand being without you. I love you like crazy. All I want is you. Only you. Forever."

He must have let out a breath he'd been holding, because with his ragged exhale, his body melted into her. His shoulders relaxed. "Forever's good. Forever is what I want too."

He slid his fingers from her neck and gathered her face in his hands.

Then he kissed her. Long and slow and sweet. She opened her mouth, letting him in. Letting him have all of her. She threaded her arms around his neck, pressed her palms to his back, and met his tongue with her own. And it didn't matter that her family and friends were watching, because nothing mattered except Vaughn.

Applause and cheers broke out, but Rachel couldn't find it in her to care. She was too filled up with love for

Vaughn, for the possibilities of their future together, and for the sense of peace that came with knowing she'd never be lost again.

He tore his lips away and held her tight against him. "I love you so much, Rachel. I'm going to give you everything you want and keep you in triple berry pies for the rest of your life—but I changed my mind about something. Forget proper courtship. Tell your farmhands they're on their own in the morning and pack a bag. You're coming home with me tonight."

Epilogue

Rachel stared at Vaughn across the top of his truck cab, feeling as jumpy as a fly on a light bulb. "I'm not the best at making small talk. What if I can't think of anything to say?"

Vaughn pinned her with a look of affectionate exasperation. "I've already told you, I'm not going to let you flounder. I'll be right there next to you, moving the conversation along. But if you get stuck, talk about horses. My parents could talk about horses until the cows come home."

"Ha-ha. Very funny." Sure enough, he'd coaxed a smile from her and eased her nerves like there was nothing to it. That was some skill he had. One more reason she loved him.

"Well, I'm a funny guy."

He came around her side of the cab and brushed a kiss across her lips. "You're going to be fine. And you might as well get used to having dinner with my folks because neither you or I can cook worth a damn. With Amy moved in to Kellan's place, leaving us to fend for ourselves, I'm pretty sure we're going to get tired of sandwiches and take-out eventually."

"Do you think your mom's going to hold it against me that I can't cook?"

Rolling his eyes, Vaughn filled her hands with a stack of boxes from the back of the cab. "Oh my God, woman. You need to relax. She's going to love you."

"I hope you're right. I've never had to meet a man's parents before." She straightened the ribbon holding the boxes together. "This is a whole lot of fruit. Wouldn't a basket have been enough?"

He fluffed the bow on top. "No, it needs the tower effect. Trust me on this. Is it too heavy? You want me to carry it?"

"No. I want to be the one to hand it to her."

They started up the driveway. Vaughn placed his hand on the small of her back. "I do have to warn you, she's going to ask about kids."

Rachel stopped moving. "What?"

"She's grandkid crazy, so she's probably going to mention you and me having kids. I thought you should be ready for that."

"Wait. *We* haven't even talked about kids. Hell, we haven't even talked about getting married."

Vaughn stuffed his hands in his pockets and rocked on his heels, like he didn't have a care in the world. "We could talk about it right now if you'd like."

"I'm five steps away from meeting your parents for the first time. Do you really think it's the best idea to discuss our future out here in front of their house?"

He shrugged. "That wasn't part of my plan, but you seem concerned."

Rachel strode toward the front door. "I don't know if *concerned* is the right word, but I do think we should have our story straight before we have a casual chat about marriage and kids with your parents."

"That's a great point."

When she reached the door, she whipped around to face him. "You're acting strange." The top box, filled with chocolate-covered strawberries, toppled off the tower. Vaughn dove for it.

Pushing up to his knees, he handed it to her.

"Nice catch." She tucked it back inside the ribbon and leveled a worried gaze at him. Now that he'd mentioned it, she realized she didn't know his take on marriage and kids. The past couple weeks, she'd been too wrapped up with being in love to think about the long-term details. "We are going to get married and have kids, right? I mean, you know, when you're ready?"

The front door opened to reveal a short woman with curly black hair and a welcoming smile. She shared Vaughn's nose and chin.

Rachel swallowed and her heart rate sped up. "Hello, Mrs. Cooper."

"Hey, Ma," Vaughn said, still kneeling. "We brought you a fruit tower. Would you take it from Rachel?"

Rachel made to move past him but Vaughn grabbed hold of her hand. "You stay right there. Ma, the fruit tower, please?"

"Oh." She shuffled around Vaughn and eased the boxes from Rachel's hands. "Goodness me. You remembered I wanted one of these. Thank you."

"Of course I remembered. That's why I'm your favorite son," he said, his eyes still on Rachel, his solid hands holding hers.

"You rascal. You're my only son."

Vaughn smiled up at Rachel. "Did my mother just call me a rascal?"

He was still on his knees and the way he was looking at her, his eyes warm and confident, his smile tender, set butterflies of anticipation fluttering to life in her belly.

"Yes, she did," she said breathlessly.

As if foggy glasses had suddenly been removed from her eyes, the colors and details of her surroundings popped out at her in stark relief. The hedges which had been trimmed flat along the house, the speckles of gray along the part in Vaughn's hair, the smell of a beef roast wafting through the door blending with the heady smell of a fire. His father's forge fire, no doubt.

"I hit my head on this front step when I was ten. Fifteen stitches," Vaughn said quietly. "And I have pictures taken of me standing on this step before my first communion, senior prom, high school and college graduations, and my graduation from the police academy. So I guess it's as fine a spot as any to ask you to be my wife."

Oh, wow. Her heart felt so full it was crowding her lungs, impeding her breath. Kneeling before her was the best man she knew, the man she loved and planned to keep on loving for the rest of her life. And he wanted to marry her.

He produced a small, black velvet box from his pocket at the same time his mom yelled, "Greg! Get over here now—and bring the camera!"

Vaughn angled his head around Rachel's leg to grin at his mom. "Nice touch, Ma. Really adds to the romance of the moment."

Rachel couldn't help but laugh, he made her so impossibly happy.

He opened the box. Inside was a gold band, inlaid with a row of sparkling diamonds. The most beautiful piece of jewelry she'd ever seen.

"I was going to wait until dessert, but I didn't want you going through the whole dinner worrying about my intentions. You wouldn't have enjoyed Mom's signature pot roast at all, and that would be a travesty." He glanced at the ring. "I didn't think a big diamond was your style, thought it might get in the way with your work. But we can exchange it if you don't—"

"No, I love it. And I love you." She pressed her lips together, fighting to contain her blossoming emotions.

"I love you too." He kissed her hand. "Rachel, will you marry me?"

Pretty sure her legs were about to turn to noodles and wanting to get closer to Vaughn, she dropped to her knees. He swiped her tears away with his thumb. She turned her face in and kissed his wrist.

"You know, I've always wanted to be a cowboy lawman's wife."

His grin broadened. "Is that so? It was the badge that did it for you, eh?"

She smiled back. "Among other things. I like the way you whistle."

He waved the box. "Are you going to give me an answer so I can put this ring on your finger, or would you like to continue going over all the ways you and I fit together so perfectly?"

She smoothed her fingertips along his jaw. "Of course I'll marry you, Vaughn. Nothing else in the whole world makes me as happy as you."

He slid the ring on her finger and admired her hand. "That's more like it." And then he gathered her close and kissed her. She could hear the squeals of joy from his parents, along with the clicking of a camera. She could hardly kiss Vaughn back, she was smiling so big. ·

For years, she'd fought what her heart was telling her to do. She'd let her mind convince her that happiness was out of her reach. And yet, she'd never stopped dreaming of a future with Vaughn, even when every other fiber of her being told her it was impossible. It turned out that her rebel heart knew what it was doing all along.

Keep reading for a special sneak preview of
Jenna's story in *How to Rope a Real Man*,
coming in May 2014!

Jenna Sorentino was nothing if not self-sufficient. That trait had served her well for twenty-four years, but it was a bitch of a problem tonight. Because Matt Roenick—hard-bodied, bright-smiling Matt—was only interested in people he could save. Try as she might, she couldn't figure out a palatable way to land herself in that position.

She sat two seats down from the head of the table at the rehearsal dinner for her older sister Amy's wedding, watching Matt cut up Tommy's chicken strips like he was the daddy she wanted him to be, all the while trying to dream up a problem Matt could solve for her that wouldn't make her feel helpless.

It wasn't that Jenna didn't have problems. Besides the problem of Matt never giving her more than the time of day in the eight months she'd known him, she had a category 5 hurricane brewing with her two sisters. But there wasn't another person on earth who could save her from that storm except herself. Not even the noble and dashing Matt Roenick.

That particular problem would have to wait until after Amy's wedding, though, because she hadn't damn near killed herself to put on the best wedding in Catcher Creek history only to ruin it with the truth.

A loud, banjo-heavy song exploded from the dance floor speakers. Jenna sipped her diet cola and tried not to wince outwardly. "It's too early for banjo," she called to Matt over Tommy's head.

He met her gaze and one corner of his lips curved into a smile, revealing the very same dimple that had made her go weak in the knees the first time she'd seen it so many months ago. "Is it ever the right time for banjo?"

She swirled the ice in her glass and gave him her best faux-scholarly expression. "There's a banjo window, but it's very narrow. Only nine to eleven at night."

His brows pushed together. "Not eight or seven, but nine?"

"Eight's too early. You have to get nice and relaxed before banjo sounds good."

He rewarded her joke with a laugh. "That makes perfect sense to me, even though I'd never heard the banjo rule before tonight."

She shook her hair away from her cheeks and smiled, trying to tell him without words how much she loved their easy camaraderie. "Yes, well, some things are so obvious, they don't need to be said."

His eyes glimmered, like he loved their conversations as much as she did. "I'll bear that in mind if I ever get the chance to take you to a bluegrass concert."

Her smile fell. To distract herself from the urge to point out that he had the chance any old time he wanted because Smithy's Bar had a standing event every Saturday night and all he had to do was ask, she picked a couple pieces of sawdust out of Tommy's hair that she'd apparently missed on his first brushing-off, then ruffled his dark blond locks.

Leave it to a five-year-old to get himself coated with sawdust in the scant minutes between the time they entered the Sarsaparilla Saloon and got seated at their table on the far side of the dance floor.

"Uh-oh, buddy," Matt said, nudging Tommy with his elbow. "I hate to break it to you, but it looks like your head's sprouting sawdust."

Tommy giggled. "If our floor ever got this dirty, Mama would pitch a tent."

Matt quirked an eyebrow at Jenna. "Translation please?"

Love for her earnest little boy roused a smile from her lips once more. "I think you meant pitch a fit, and you're exactly right. You know Mama loves clean floors, but this is a saloon, so it's supposed to be messy. It's part of the ambiance."

"Am-bee-ance," Tommy repeated, as though committing it to memory. Ever since it dawned on him that he'd be starting kindergarten in the fall, he'd been obsessed with rattling off big words, so Jenna made sure their conversations were dense with them.

It'd been her idea to hold the rehearsal dinner here. Kellan, her soon-to-be brother-in-law, had requested someplace casual, with dancing and beer. As small a town as Catcher Creek was, nothing in its blink-and-you'll-miss-it downtown district fit the bill. Good thing Jenna was intimately familiar with just about every bar with a dance floor in New Mexico between Albuquerque and the Texas state line.

A glance at Amy made her stomach drop. Amy's eye twitched and she was using the steak knife that'd come with her top sirloin to dice the side of steamed vegetables into tiny cubes. A sure sign her wedding nerves were getting intense.

Kellan was the only person in the world who could

talk Amy off the ledge when anxiety got the best of her, but he was deep in conversation about steer prices with Vaughn, Jenna's other soon-to-be brother-in-law. As much as Jenna wasn't going to let her own problems get in the way of Amy's perfect wedding, she wasn't about to stand by while Amy ruined it either.

"How's your meal, Ames?"

"Fine." Her voice was strained and she'd answered without meeting Jenna's eyes, focusing instead on slicing into a baby carrot.

Oh, crap.

Jenna pushed up from the table, smoothing the skirt of her swishy cotton dress as she stood. She met Matt's startled gaze. "Could you keep an eye on Tommy for a bit?"

"Of course."

"Amy, I need to talk to you outside. Could you spare a minute?"

Amy's knife and fork froze. She blinked at her plate for a couple beats before standing. "Okay, yes. Outside would be good."

Their movement must've caught Rachel's eye because she broke from her conversation with Kellan and Vaughn and stood. "Where're you going?"

As the oldest sister, Rachel had always been the mother figure and rock of the family that Jenna had needed growing up, supporting her through the toughest of times. As close as two sisters could be, they had an understanding of each other that ran deep and didn't need words. However . . . from Jenna's first recollection of her sisters, Amy and Rachel had gotten on like two tomcats locked in a barn. There wasn't a situation the good Lord could throw at one that the other couldn't make worse without even trying.

With Amy looking like she was going to blow a gasket

at any moment, the last thing she needed was Rachel getting involved before Jenna had a chance to run damage control.

Without relinquishing her hold on Amy's shoulders, she pressed close to Rachel. In as low a tone as she could muster, she hissed, "Bring us three shots of tequila, STAT."

"What? You don't drink."

But Jenna was already hustling Amy from the table. She twisted her neck and drilled Rachel with a *don't mess with me* glare. "Tequila. Now!"

The fenced-in patio out back of the saloon was bathed in a soft yellow glow from the strings of twinkle lights crisscrossing the tin roof. As they stepped out, a weathered, older man was snuffing a cigarette in an ashtray. He tipped the brim of his hat to them, then made his way back inside. The door bounced a few times before sealing shut, dulling the music to a muffled rhythm of vibrations.

Jenna spun Amy to face her. "Okay, what's wrong?"

Amy wrapped her arms around her middle. "Nothing. What makes you think something's wrong?"

Jenna pinched the bridge of her nose and silently recited the alphabet, a mom trick she'd learned as a way to maintain patience when under duress. And it worked near about all the time. Well, sort of. If she didn't count the fact she'd never once made it past *N*.

"Spill it, Amy."

Amy's tongue poked against the inside of her cheek and Jenna could tell she was fighting hard to keep her composure. "Jake texted Kellan on our way here. *Work emergency.* That's it. Two words. And Kellan can't get him on the phone."

From everything Amy had told her, Kellan made his only brother, Jake, his best man as a kind of olive-branch gesture, trying to mend their decades-old rift. And it had seemed to work, if they all ignored the fact that Jake hadn't attended Kellan's bachelor party, or shown up for the rehearsal at the church that afternoon. She'd figured intimate gatherings like this made him uncomfortable given the fragility of his and Kellan's reconciliation, but it'd never occurred to her he might blow off the actual wedding.

"Jake's a cop, and not a rural cop like we're used to dealing with. LAPD is a different beast by far," Jenna said. "I bet work emergencies are par for the course. There's nothing he can do about that. Besides, he still has time. The wedding's not until three."

"That's what Kellan said, but I looked up flights from L.A. to Albuquerque on my cell and the next one's not until tomorrow at nine-thirty, L.A. time. It's a two-hour flight, then a three-hour drive here, if everything goes perfectly. And that's not counting time spent in the airport or at a car rental place. With the time difference, it's impossible. But Kellan's acting like nothing's wrong, like he still believes Jake'll make it work. And I don't know what to do."

It wasn't like they could delay the ceremony, because every detail of the wedding and reception, from the caterer and DJ to the photographer, was hinging on a three o'clock start time, including the minister, who had a second wedding to perform later that evening. Still, a little fake optimism never hurt anything. "I bet everything will work out and he'll make it on time." *If he hooks up with Superman or bribes his way onto a private jet.*

Wide-eyed, Amy shook her hands, palms out, fingers stretched. "Don't patronize me. I'm freaking out here!" The shrillness of her voice made Jenna's teeth ache.

She grabbed hold of Amy's shoulders and rubbed,

praying that Rachel materialized with their shots in the next thirty seconds.

"Even if Jake doesn't make it, everything will be fine. Vaughn is Kellan's best friend. He'll stand in as best man at the wedding, and he's really good in front of crowds so he'll be able to pull off a last-minute toast at the reception, no sweat. I'll make sure he has a speech planned, okay? I'm not going to let anything ruin your special day, so calm down."

The doors burst open. "Don't tell her to calm down. Believe me, she hates it." It was Rachel, balancing three shots in her hand. "Here, take a glass before I drop one."

Jenna passed a shot to Amy, then took one for herself.

Amy frowned down at hers. "What are we doing with this stuff?"

Jenna clinked the lips of their glasses together. "What do you think? Shooting it."

"I get really silly when I drink, Jen. You know that," Amy said.

"That's what I'm counting on." And if one shot didn't turn her from stressed to silly, Jenna wasn't above buying round after round until Amy's buzz set in.

Rachel nudged Jenna. "How long's it been since you had a drink?"

"Well, Tommy's five, so . . . nearly six years. Wow. But I need it tonight. We all do."

"Isn't this what AA calls enabling?" Rachel asked. "Am I causing you to fall off a wagon, or something?"

"I'm not an alcoholic and you know it. It's just that I lost my appetite for the stuff when I got pregnant."

Rachel sniffed her shot, then screwed up her face. "This tequila is making me lose my appetite. Why can't we shoot whiskey instead?"

"Because whiskey's not ladylike. Now hush up. You're not weaseling out of this shot by whining. Do it for Amy."

"You don't have to do it, Rachel," Amy said.

Jenna pinned Rachel with her best scolding expression. "Don't listen to her. She's the bride; she doesn't know what she's talking about. As the wedding planner, my word trumps all."

Amy shook her head. "I don't think that's—"

"Fine. For Amy." Rachel raised her glass in a toast, then tossed the tequila back.

Jenna and Amy followed suit. The liquor flooded Jenna's throat with the warmth of an old friend—or maybe her worst enemy.

The taste and burn reminded her of high school, which was pretty pathetic, but there it was. It sent her right back to long nights of partying in the vacant desert with Carson Parrish and all the other misfits she'd wasted away her teenage years with. She might've been angrier at the memories or at herself, except that she was damn proud of how she'd turned her life around.

Back in the day, her tolerance was such that it took her at least three shots to work up a buzz. Tonight, the drink settled in her muscles and brain almost instantly.

Amy shuddered and handed her empty shot glass to Jenna.

"All right, why did we do that?" Rachel said, stacking her glass on Amy's.

Jenna draped a fortifying arm across Amy's shoulders. "We're not sure Kellan's brother is going to make it to the wedding."

Rachel didn't flinch. "That's because he's an asshole."

"Rachel, he's family now!" Amy scolded.

Jenna rolled her eyes. *Here they go . . .*

"Yeah, I get that," Rachel pressed, "but there's no rule in the books that says family members can't be assholes. In fact, I'd wager there's no more focused collection of assholes in the world than people have in their own families."

Amy made a sound like a snort that got Jenna's attention fast. The second she looked her way, Amy burst out in giggles.

God bless tequila.

A squeak warned of the patio door opening again. Kellan stepped out, ducking under a strand of low-hanging twinkle lights. Amy smushed her mouth together and tried to stop laughing.

"Okay, womenfolk, what's this pow-wow all about?"

Jenna rattled the stack of empty glasses. "We were getting some fresh air and enjoying a splash of New Mexico's finest tequila."

"Not really," Rachel said. "I only sprang for the cheap stuff."

Jenna patted her arm. "That was called sarcasm, sweetie."

Kellan's eyes twinkled as he gave Amy a once-over. "Are you getting my bride drunk on our wedding eve?"

Amy snorted through her nose, clearly fighting another bout of giggles. Kellan's smile broadened and he pulled Amy from Jenna's arms into his own.

This was a good man Amy was marrying. The kind of man who took care of things and people. Like Rachel's fiancé, Vaughn, did. That her sisters had found such fine matches eased some of Jenna's guilt about her plan to leave town.

Amy threaded her arms around Kellan's ribs. "Just a little bit drunk."

"Good. Makes it easier for me to take advantage of you."

"I'm always easy for you to take advantage of like that."

"True enough."

Rachel groaned and started for the door. "I don't care

that you're getting hitched tomorrow. I'm not going to stand around and listen to you talk dirty to each other. I'm going back in."

Jenna poked her arm as she passed. "Like you and Vaughn are any different."

Rachel kept moving, but flashed Jenna a coy smile that hinted at the love and happiness Vaughn had brought into her life. The kind of love Jenna wanted for herself. She stared blankly at the swinging door as it closed behind Rachel, almost afraid to look back at Kellan and Amy in the throes of their own love story for fear that jealousy would turn her insides ugly.

A fast song came on in the bar, along with the DJ calling out a line dance.

No more pity party. Not with a song calling for her to whisk Tommy to the dance floor and boogey down. And if a slow song came on and Matt Roenick asked her to dance, then so much the better.

She wound through the crowd pouring off the bar stools, then zigzagged through tables en route to the dance floor, searching out Tommy and Matt as she moved. Lo and behold, they were already dancing, along with Kellan's six-year-old goddaughter, Daisy. Matt didn't see her, busy as he was modeling the steps to the Watermelon Crawl for the kids.

In Jenna's experience, kids made lots of men nervous, especially those of the single, unattached variety, but not Matt. From the day he came into her family's life to negotiate an oil rights contract, he got down to the kids' level and played or talked with them like it was the most natural thing in the world.

Blame it on her hormones or Darwin's theory of evolution, but seeing a man interacting with kids or babies got her blood stirring and her imagination looking into the future. To top it off, clearly Matt could hold his own on the dance floor. He handled the kids and the steps like he did everything else in his life—with smooth, easygoing confidence and genuine enjoyment. It was the single-most endearing quality about him that had caught her attention all those months ago and dropped her deeper and deeper into longing every time they were together.

And, sweet sundae, did she long for him tonight.

She hung back, watching. Daisy didn't give two wits whether she did the steps right, but Tommy's tongue was poking out the side of his mouth in concentration as he watched Matt's boots.

During the butt shimmy part of the choreography, Tommy hammed it up, and Jenna couldn't stifle a laugh, he was so cute.

The laugh caught Tommy's attention. "Mommy, I'm dancing! Just like we practice at home."

She met Matt's amused expression with a wink, then smiled at her son. "I can see that. Great job." She scooted close to the kids and grabbed Tommy and Daisy's hands to help them into a turn.

Matt leaned her way during a kick and weight change. "He told me you two do a lot of line dancing and two-stepping in the living room before bedtime."

True enough. She could dance until her boots wore out and the band went home or the radio broke. It was her favorite way of letting off steam since she'd stopped raising hell in order to raise her son right.

"I can't think of a better way to end the day." Well, she could, but it'd been a while—too damn long, in fact—since she'd had the pleasure of indulging in that particular pastime.

They turned again. She helped Tommy line up in front of her, then got busy staring at Matt's behind as he kicked and moved with the music. It was such a fine view, she nearly hummed her appreciation out loud.

Maybe it was the tequila, or maybe the prolonged view of Matt's posterior, but she wasn't worried about tomorrow as she had been for months. She'd run herself into the ground organizing every detail of the wedding and reception, and felt great about what she'd accomplished. She deserved a little R&R tonight before the wedding day craziness was upon them.

On the far side of the bar, she caught a glimpse of Kellan, Amy, and Rachel laughing while Vaughn told them an animated story with lots of gesturing. Her sisters and Tommy, and now Kellan and Vaughn, were her only living family, and she'd do anything to make sure they were happy.

A stab of conscience cut through her gut. That wasn't entirely true.

She'd do anything for her sisters and brothers-in-law . . . except stay in Catcher Creek one day longer than was absolutely necessary.

She shoved the unpleasant awareness from her mind. Tonight wasn't the time to worry about that. Neither was tomorrow. After the wedding would be soon enough to deal with the coming storm.

The ending notes of "The Watermelon Crawl" blended with the beginning notes of a waltz. Jenna's favorite dance.

Even so, she refused to ask Matt or even look his way with hopeful anticipation, far too proud to beg for his interest if he wouldn't give it freely. Not that he'd notice her looking. His brown leather boots seemed glued to the ground and he cracked his knuckles, his dark eyes haunted as they followed Tommy and Daisy off the floor with Daisy's mom, Lisa.

She'd seen that shadowed look flash over his features before. Moments of unguardedness that hinted at a private fight being waged in his mind. She'd become aware of its presence two months ago, the day he'd joined their family to celebrate Tommy's birthday with cake and ice cream at the Catcher Creek Café. And now that she was aware of it, not a night with him went by since that she didn't notice that dark look of anguish cross his face at least once. As soon as it revealed itself, it was gone, and he was back to being easygoing, happy Matt.

Talk to me, she wanted to press. *What is it and does it have to do with why you won't let me into your life?*

But she never did ask because she couldn't get him alone no matter what she tried. She couldn't even get him to dance with her tonight. Irritation flared, but she tamped it down. There she went, making everything complicated. Maybe interest had nothing to do with it. Maybe he didn't know how to waltz. He'd nailed the Watermelon Crawl, but partner dancing was a whole different bale of hay.

Jenna swished her skirt with her hands as she debated the merits of a trip to the ladies' room to save her from standing there awkwardly for much longer. This was one of her least favorite parts of being single—never knowing if she'd have a partner for the next dance. Nothing brought her aloneness into starker focus than when she was prevented from doing the thing she loved most because she didn't have a man in her life.

Salvation came fast on the heels of those dark thoughts in the form of a cute, young cowboy flaunting a starched red Western shirt and shiny belt buckle. He was too good-ole-boy for her taste, complete with a wad of chew puffing his cheek, but she smiled invitingly anyway. Dancing a waltz didn't bind her to the guy for life.

"Care to dance, miss?"

Her answer was on the tip of her tongue when Matt appeared at her side, a proprietary hand sliding around her waist. Well, well, well. . . . Perhaps all he'd needed was a rival to remind him she wasn't going to wait forever while he made up his mind.

"Sorry, man. She's spoken for on this dance."

Jenna bit back a swoon. Lord have mercy. She never thought she would have much use for testosterone-fueled machismo, but the aggressive edge in his tone called to the feminine part of her psyche in a way she hadn't expected.

Doing her best to turn her smile apologetic, she mouthed a *sorry* to the young cowboy, but he was already wandering off, scanning the crowd for another potential partner, leaving her free to concentrate on the big, solid man at her side. She ran her gaze along her shoulder, then up Matt's body until it landed on his face. "I don't remember you asking me to dance."

He turned her in his arms and took her right hand in his, his eyes flashing down the length of her. "Some things don't need to be said."

It was the first time their fingers had touched outside of a handshake. His hand was strong, with calluses she hadn't expected to feel on a lawyer. With a motion so slow it seemed to stretch time, he dragged his thumb over the back of her fingers as though cradling her hand in his wasn't nearly enough friction to satisfy him.

She responded with a slow crawl of her other hand up the muscles of his arm to settle into closed hold position. His body was unyielding beneath her touch—deliciously hard and male. A fantasy flashed in her mind of the two of them in her bedroom, standing together like this but without a stitch of clothing. Without any of the barriers that presently stood between them.

A corner of his mouth kicked up into a wolfish grin. "I guess we'd better get to waltzing before the song ends."

Before she could answer, he stepped her back into the

swirl of dancers and let the lilting rhythm of the music carry them away.

The lights had been dimmed to blues and purples, hushing the party crowd, while a disco ball gave life to the dreamy lyrics about summer love under a blanket of stars in the big old Western sky.

When they reached the far end of the dance floor, the arm at her waist pulled her nearer. His mouth dipped close to her ear. "Are you ready for Amy's big day, Miss Wedding Planner?"

His breath lighted across her neck, igniting a tremor of sensation through her body. She filled her lungs with air and released it gradually, regrouping, before she could find her voice. "I'm ready, all right, but by the skin of my teeth. I thought six months was plenty of time to plan a wedding reception. What a joke. Now I understand why people plan these things a year or more out. There was no convincing Amy and Kellan to take their time, though."

"I've known Kellan going on ten years, since I was a T.A. in an oil law course he was taking, and he's always been the jump-in-with-both-feet type."

No wonder he and Amy were so perfect for each other. Amy gave new meaning to the term *full steam ahead*. She turned her face to meet his eyes. "But you're not like that. You're more of a wade-in-slowly kind of guy." If their relationship moved much slower, they'd be going backward.

He tipped his head, considering. "I guess I am. Wasn't always that way, but I suppose I've gotten more cautious with age."

"That makes you sound old, but you're only, what, thirty-one? Thirty-two?"

He guided them around a couple who looked brand-new to the world of country-western dance, staring at their feet's stiff, boxy moves and counting the steps aloud. "I'm thirty-three."

"Still too young to be cautious."

His expression turned teasing. "I know it's taboo to mention a lady's age, but pardon me if I have trouble taking aging advice from someone who hasn't even hit thirty yet."

"Then maybe I shouldn't let on that I only just turned twenty-four in June." He got quiet, probably doing what everybody else did when they realized how young she was. She beat him to the punch. "I had Tommy when I was nineteen."

He was gentlemanly enough to mask his shock, but not before his eyebrows flickered up.

"I know, so young." With a flippant wave of her hand, she smiled warmly to let him know it was okay for him to be shocked. She'd been pretty darn shocked when she first found out too. "I guess I'm way too fertile for my own good."

Matt's shoulders stiffened. "Most people are."

What an odd comeback. In all the times she'd made that same joke about her pregnancy, she'd never heard a response quite like that. She was in the process of formulating a question, when, without breaking his impeccable rhythm, Matt added pressure to the hand at her waist, her cue that they were about to get fancy with their dancing.

Bring it, she thought as he lifted the hand she held, then expertly partnered her through a triple spin into a reverse that flitted the questions from her mind. She nearly laughed with the giddiness brought on by the complicated steps and the deftness of his execution. Now *this* was how dancing was supposed to be.

Breathless, she met him in closed hold once more. His hand slipped to her back with the control of a man who'd spun a lot of women around the dance floor in his day.

She shoved the petty thought aside. After all, she'd been spun around the dance floor plenty of times by plenty of men. And she refused to hold anyone else to their pasts, when she hated that she couldn't escape her own.

"I didn't know you could dance like this," she asked.

His cocky, lopsided smile sent a flash of heat through her. "One of my many secrets."

Before she could respond to such a baiting remark, he spun her in a double turn that twisted into a side-by-side shadow hold. Swinging her chin over her shoulder, she met his warm, confident gaze. Hot damn, this man lit her fire.

With a wink that told her he knew exactly how good a dancer he was, he launched them into windmills and reverses. A bit flashy given the prying eyes surrounding them, but it satisfied her womanly sensibilities that he was showing off for her. It would be nice for a change to have the good folks of Catcher Creek spreading rumors about her for something other than her days as a wild youth or the identity of Tommy's missing father.

When they'd returned to closed hold, Jenna shook her hair back and pinned Matt with her most flirtatious eyes. "You can't lay down a challenge like that and expect me not to take it up."

"What challenge? Are you trying to say that you think you can best me in a dance-off?" He scoffed. "I'd like to see the day."

The dare had her *tsk*ing good-naturedly. "That's not what I meant, though I have no doubt that in a dance-off, I'd shine the floor with your ass."

Continuing with a basic 1-2-3 around the floor, he laughed through his nose, his eyes twinkling. "You talk a big game, darlin'. Makes me concerned about what other challenge you think I've laid down for you."

The song ended and they slowed to a stop on the outer edge of the floor. People moved around them as a new song, a faster song, picked up pace. She traced the edge of his chiseled shoulder muscle below his chambray shirt. This is how it would be between them if they were a couple—smooth and romantic, like the waltz.

She moved her fingertips from his shoulder to his jaw. "Matt Roenick, one of these days you're going to tell me all your secrets."

He swallowed and his gaze dipped to her lips, so she angled them up, parting them, closing her eyes. All he had to do was lower a few inches and she'd finally—*finally*—know what his mouth felt like on hers. Didn't matter that they were surrounded by people. She'd waited eight long months for this.

Come on, Matt. Kiss me already.

Thrilling Fiction from

GEORGINA GENTRY

My Heroes Have Always Been Cowboys	978-0-8217-7959-0	$6.99US/$8.99CAN
Rio: The Texans	978-1-4201-0851-4	$6.99US/$8.99CAN
Diablo: The Texans	978-1-4201-0850-7	$6.99US/$8.99CAN
To Seduce a Texan	978-0-8217-7992-7	$6.99US/$8.49CAN
To Wed a Texan	978-0-8217-7991-0	$6.99US/$8.49CAN

Available Wherever Books Are Sold!

Visit our website at www.kensingtonbooks.com